A Scoundrel's Guide to Heists and Hearts

THE HARP & THISTLE
BOOK 2

ARDEN CONROY

Dragonblade Publishing, Inc. is an imprint of Kathryn Le Veque Novels, Inc.
P.O. Box 23
Moreno Valley, CA 92556
ceo@dragonbladepublishing.com

Produced in the United States of America

First Edition June 2025
Trade Paperback Edition

ARE YOU SIGNED UP FOR DRAGONBLADE'S BLOG?

You'll get the latest news and information on exclusive giveaways, exclusive excerpts, coming releases, sales, free books, cover reveals and more.

Check out our complete list of authors, too!

No spam, no junk. That's a promise!

Sign Up Here

www.dragonbladepublishing.com

Dearest Reader;

Thank you for your support of a small press. At Dragonblade Publishing, we strive to bring you the highest quality Historical Romance from some of the best authors in the business. Without your support, there is no 'us', so we sincerely hope you adore these stories and find some new favorite authors along the way.

Happy Reading!

CEO, Dragonblade Publishing

For the adventurous hearts.

Chapter One

The National Gallery, London
November 1889

EVELYN SPARROW NEVER would have expected a potato to be the catalyst of her pre-wedding nervous breakdown. But then again, life sometimes delivered peculiar surprises. However, it would be a few more days until the accuracy of that statement would be fully realized.

Late returning from her luncheon hour, Evelyn hurried along the employees' corridor of the National Gallery, the skirt of her dark-gray wool dress swishing with the rapid movement. Upon her arrival to the conservation department's studio, two men lifted their heads from their furrowed concentration.

"You're late." James Burlington frowned as he set aside a pair of pliers. He was in the process of removing a painting from its frame. The painting featured a heavily pregnant woman in a green, wispy, fifteenth-century dress. The woman held her husband's hand before her, and a mirror behind them reflected the painter.

The Arnolfini Portrait by Jan van Eyck.

Evelyn disliked this painting. It had an unsettling air about it, though she couldn't pinpoint why, exactly. She swallowed and put her attention back upon Mr. Burlington. He had a long, thin face with a three-finger space between his upper lip and nose that Evelyn thought made him look extra snobbish, a perfect fit with his disdainful personality.

"My apologies." Evelyn began walking over to her desk while removing the hatpins from her green hat. Large feathers embellished one side of it. "I was accosted by a group of pigeons." As she reached her desk and set the hat down, she stopped dead in her tracks and the blood drained from her face.

A potato—rather, half of a potato—sat squarely in the middle of her neat desk.

"What is this?" she asked quite loudly, her voice cracking. Nervous, she reached out to the potato and lifted it to study. She spun around to Mr. Burlington, holding the potato in front of her with accusation. *"What is this?"*

Mr. Burlington stared back, his mouth slightly open.

Evelyn whipped around to her other male colleague. Unlike Mr. Burlington, who was roughly the same age as Evelyn, Mr. Currow was married with two adult children, and his favorite joke was to blame them for the ever-multiplying gray hairs upon his head. "Mr. Currow? Can you speak to this?"

David Currow had paused with his paintbrush lifted in mid-air. But he didn't respond, either. Instead, he exchanged a look with Mr. Burlington.

"Well?" Evelyn squeaked. Normally affable, today, she had absolutely no patience.

Mr. Currow scratched at his neck with the wooden tip of the brush. "I believe that is a Solanum tuberosum. Or rather, the tuber of a Solanum tuberosum. It's a starch root vegetable, otherwise known as a potato. Quite good smashed up with butter and salt and placed over minced lamb. My wife has an excellent recipe for—"

"I do not care about recipes, Mr. Currow. In any form." In fact, Evelyn did not know how to cook. Being the daughter of a baron, and tomorrow the wife of an earl, she'd never had a need to learn. Or a desire to.

Panic pumped hard through her veins, and she flitted about the room checking the rubbish bins for the other half of the potato while Mr. Burlington and Mr. Currow watched. There may have been a snicker or two, but she was far too focused to say for sure.

Resisting the urge to kick over Mr. Currow's rubbish bin, she gave him a pointed look and moved onto a bin set against the wall.

This was her last day of work for the remainder of her life—not that anyone outside of her family knew this—and she was as mad as a bull staring down a Toreador.

Evelyn Sparrow was a celebrated paintings conservator. The only woman art conservator in all of England. The only woman employee at the National Gallery. Tomorrow, it would all be gone. The ten years of freedom she'd negotiated in order to marry whomever her parents wished without a fight—they had chosen the Earl of Wellingham—was up. Ten years that included university in America, an apprenticeship at the Louvre, and now her dream career of paintings conservator.

She'd thought ten years would have given her time to conquer the world, if she wanted, before being forced into the life expected of all aristocratic women. But it was only in the past year that her male counterparts had begun to take her seriously and see her as an equal.

Sort of, Evelyn thought as she heard snickering again.

Rising up to her full, willowy height, Evelyn huffed her way back over to Mr. Burlington—from where the snickering originated—and sniffed the van Eyck while the woman in the green dress mocked her with a smirk that seemed to say *I have a husband and baby. I am better than you.*

The painting had no starchy scent, no hint of potato anywhere.

Evelyn shot a death glare to her colleague. "If anyone would be insipid enough to use a potato on a painting, it would be you, Mr. Burlington. Where is the rest of it?"

Mr. Burlington gave a mocking gasp and placed a hand over his heart. "Your words injure me, Miss Sparrow!"

Mr. Currow laughed from the other side of the room.

"This is not funny, Mr. Burlington." Evelyn shook the potato at him. "You know better than to use a potato on priceless artwork. You can't possibly be that idiotic!"

Humor glinted in Mr. Burlington's eye, which, somehow, made Evelyn even more furious. But just as her amused colleague opened his mouth to retort, the door to the studio creaked open, followed by a velvet, deep voice. "Am I interrupting something?"

Evelyn tampered the urge to react to that familiar voice. It was her client, someone she secretly hoped to see any given day. And he couldn't possibly have caught her at a worse moment.

Evelyn resisted the urge to flush, though if she was successful or not, she didn't want to know. She met her client's eye for the briefest moment before having to look away. He was so exceptionally handsome she often felt shy looking at him. "My apologies, Mr. McNab." Evelyn glared down at an amused Mr. Burlington as she rested one fist on her hip. "I was merely reprimanding my colleague for being foolish."

Oliver McNab—or as he'd informed her several months ago, *"Call me 'Ollie,'"* something she wouldn't dare do—crossed the room toward Evelyn. As usual, Mr. McNab looked exceptionally dashing in his three-piece suit. Clearing her throat as he stopped before her, the faintest whisper of expensive cologne tickling her nose, she reached up to her auburn hair to make sure it was still in place.

"Fascinating," Mr. Burlington said, evidently observing Evelyn's nervous tick.

She saw understanding cross the man's face and kicked him. He let out an exaggerated howl of pain.

"Should I come back later?" Mr. McNab looked between them, sounding unsure.

Evelyn allowed her eyes to sweep over his strong jaw, perfectly styled dark-brown hair, and those emerald-green eyes that haunted her. His face, his physique, were fit for a Renaissance painting. She had to look away. "No, that's not necessary,"

Evelyn reassured him.

"Why are you holding a potato?"

Evelyn tossed the tuber into Mr. Burlington's lap, and he hurriedly caught it just before it landed in an unfortunate spot.

Evelyn frowned at him. "I cannot tell if my colleagues are stupid or playing tricks on me."

Mr. Burlington smirked. "Oh, I assure you, Miss Sparrow, Mr. Currow and I would never dare toy with you. I would like to keep my bollocks, thank you."

Evelyn gasped at the utterly crude word.

Mr. Burlington laughed and stood from his chair, setting the potato aside while Mr. Currow followed. The men commented it was their luncheon hour now and departed.

Mr. McNab looked down into the rubbish bin. "I don't understand."

Evelyn cleared her throat. "There is a prevailing, very incorrect, belief that potatoes can clean paintings. It's a holdover from olden days, when conservation science was not as developed as it is today. I found that potato half on my desk when I returned from my luncheon hour, and I have been searching for the other half."

"Did one of your colleagues use it?" he asked.

"I would hope they would know better, but I am unsure." Evelyn swallowed and looked about the room. What would everyone do when she didn't show up for work tomorrow? What would happen to the paintings here—would they be well taken care of? Or would they be cleaned improperly and further damaged? What about the McNab family's artwork—would it be taken care of?

Her looming departure hit her hard again. Hot tears stung the backs of her eyes, but she forced them away. She had to finish out the day without getting upset, without letting anyone know what was going to happen.

"I suppose you're here to see your brother's artwork," Evelyn said, knowing full well that Mr. McNab's visit was purely business. He followed her over to the paintings in her corner of the studio. "As you know," she began as they both studied the collection, "the fire at your pub several months ago did a number on your brother's artwork. But, little by little, I've been able to work through much of it, with the help of my colleagues when they can."

Mr. McNab leaned forward to study the painting she had recently finished restoring. Art restoration was a different career path than art conservation, but they all knew well enough how to restore artwork that had been affected by smoke, soot, and water. Earlier in the year, Mr. McNab's affluent heiress sister-in-law—before she'd married his brother—had donated an enormous sum of money to the museum because she'd wanted "only the best" to restore her beloved's artwork.

And Mr. Ollie McNab was the family representative for the project. Mr. McNab came in almost daily, at his brother and sister-in-law's request, to see how the art restoration was coming along.

"This is the one you were working on yesterday?" Mr. McNab asked while observing the completely cleaned and now freshly varnished painting on the easel before them. "I know you've finished a few of these now, but each time I'm in utter awe of what you do."

There was no holding back the severe flush that overtook Evelyn's entire body at Mr. McNab's praise. Of course, this kind of praise from anyone would have induced a blush. But that it came from, in her opinion, the most handsome gentleman in England made it a tad more flattering.

"Thank you, Mr. McNab. I appreciate the compliment."

Mr. McNab looked over at her and gave her his bright smile. He always looked so friendly. Even when he wasn't smiling, his eyes looked happy. Evelyn reached up to touch her hair again before forcing her hand over to her magnifying glasses. As she secured them over her ears and eyes, she blinked up at Mr. McNab through the magnifying glass and found a funny look on his face. He seemed slightly drunk, which was silly. Anything in these glasses viewed at a distance was warped and skewed. He probably wasn't even looking at her.

Evelyn leaned forward to look at a particular spot of the newly restored painting. "This one is by Gustave Courbet, a French artist. See his signature here?" She pointed to the lower corner. "I believe you said your brother briefly communicated with the artist at the end of his life?"

"That's right."

"It's always fascinating to me when there's an extra bit of personal history to a painting." She then pointed to a spot on the artwork. "This one, as you know, was thick with soot damage. I was able to use a vulcanized rubber sponge to remove it, inpainted any parts where the paint had flaked off, and repainted over it to make it seamless, as if nothing had happened to it."

She pointed to another area on which she had done extensive work and Mr. McNab lowered his face beside hers to look. His scent swept over her again and her heart galloped at his closeness. "Dantes is especially excited to get this one back," Mr. McNab said. What would he say if he knew how fast Evelyn's heart raced in the moment?

"You're welcome to take it to him today, if you'd like." Evelyn removed the magnifying glasses. She set them to the side.

Mr. McNab stood up to his full height and scratched at his jaw. "Unfortunately, he does not want me to do that." He then shifted on his feet.

Evelyn noticed the reaction. "Why not?"

"He prefers to get them himself. I think because I'm the one who comes here every day, he likes the opportunity to check in every once in a while."

Evelyn sensed this wasn't the full truth but didn't say anything, as McNab family dynamics were none of her business.

As Mr. McNab returned to observing the Courbet painting, Evelyn studied him. He always dressed in bespoke suits when he visited the museum, looking far more refined than her colleagues and most of the other museum staff. She knew he owned a working-class pub called The Harp & Thistle with his older brothers, though she had never been to it and wouldn't dare impede on a client's personal life. But Mr. McNab's sister-in-law, Lady Vivian, was the daughter of the Duke of Chalworth. Maybe that was how he'd gotten the money for his clothing. Like Lady Vivian, Evelyn was an aristocrat, though Evelyn was on a lower rung of their social class. Evelyn knew many of the women in their class could be quite focused on appearances. Surely, the daughter of a duke insisted on sprucing up the McNab brothers to keep up appearances.

Evelyn began fussing with the items at her desk. Mr. Ollie McNab was engrossed in looking over his brother's painting to report back, most likely. Mr. McNab had been coming here for these paintings for months now, and in that time Evelyn and he had, sort of, grown to become friends.

But, tomorrow, that would all end.

If only she could stop thinking about tomorrow, tomorrow, tomorrow! The blasted day would not stop popping into her mind.

For the hundredth time, hot tears threatened to rise again, but she was able to force them back once more. While Mr. McNab moved on to another of his brother's paintings, one in the middle of restoration, she allowed herself to secretly study him from a woman's lens one final time. Unlike many men, he was taller than her. Built well, as if he did heavy lifting often, which he probably did at a pub. There was also an air about him that was simply magnetic. She was drawn to him, but this wasn't unique to her by any means. Mr. McNab, being a frequent visitor to the museum, had somehow befriended every person of the museum's staff. If he had the time, he would make a point to visit different departments and somehow could get even the biggest curmudgeon laughing.

How he did it, she had no idea. But he was so charming, and everyone else thought so too.

Handsome. Charming. And working class.

Evelyn tried to envision what Papa would do if she brought Mr. McNab home with her tonight.

Mr. McNab's older brother had married Lady Vivian, but as a rare independently wealthy woman and one of the highest-ranking women in the aristocracy, the duke's daughter had far more freedom in that regard. Though she didn't know what the Duke of Chalworth thought about their marriage, it wasn't as if there had been no consequences for Lady Vivian, either. After their marriage, people had been aghast by her decision. The Duke of Chalworth had apparently exchanged words with people at several social events. Mama and Papa had talked about it non-stop over the summer.

Evelyn decided if she brought Mr. McNab home, Papa would, quite literally, expire on the spot.

As Evelyn envisioned this, Mr. McNab removed his suit coat and draped it over a chair beside him. "Is it warm in here or is it me?" he asked, not turning around.

But Evelyn didn't hear him because he was in the process of rolling up his sleeves to his elbows. His hands were large, rough and masculine, and she found herself mesmerized by them, watching the minute movements of his fingers and wrist. Immediately, she thought of Michelangelo's statue of David, the large, veiny hand attached to a muscular forearm.

She closed her eyes to yank her mind back from the trail it was heading down.

"Are you all right?" Mr. McNab asked.

Evelyn's eyes flew open to find him facing her fully now, concern sitting upon his brow. "Yes!" she replied with haste.

"Will you be working on this one next, then?" He indicated something with his hand.

"Mm-hmm," she replied far too brightly, not looking at where he pointed. Because it didn't matter. Feeling another wave of emotion, she began rifling through her desk to distract her mind.

"Miss Sparrow, are you sure everything is all right?"

She paused as she came across an unopened box of paint brushes. A box she would never have the joy of opening and finding the brushes nestled inside in a perfect pattern.

"Everything is just fine, Mr. McNab," she said, but the crack in her voice belied the truth. She looked up and found him still watching her. "It's nothing, really. Just some silly things going on in my personal life."

He crossed his arms. "Anything I can help you with?"

She couldn't help but give a small, pitiful smile. "I wish you could. But you cannot, unfortunately."

"I find that things have a funny way of working themselves out, so please do not worry too much."

"I don't agree with that statement, Mr. McNab. Perhaps optimism for the future is a masculine trait. For I find women fear their futures, instead of embracing them."

"Why is that?"

Evelyn shrugged. "It may surprise you to hear this, but even as a woman as independent as myself, the direction of my life is completely controlled by men. I don't have the freedoms you may think I do." Her throat tightened alarmingly, and she immediately looked down at her feet, lest Mr. McNab see the emotion in her eyes.

He went to her and leaned against the desk, causing her to gulp. "Have I ever told you about where I came from?"

Still looking down, Evelyn shook her head.

"I started my life out as a street orphan. From Whitechapel."

Evelyn lifted her head at this surprising revelation. Never would she have expected Mr. McNab to be the product of one of the worst slums of London.

He continued. "My father was killed in a train accident before I was born, and my mother died of a laudanum overdose when I was still a baby. My brothers and I lived on the streets for much of our childhoods. Fortunately, for me at least, I don't remember much of those early days."

"What happened?"

"After many years, my grandparents tracked us down. I spent the rest of my childhood growing up with them, then when I was ready, I went on to Eton, and Oxford after that."

"You went to Eton and Oxford?" This was exceptionally surprising. Who were his grandparents? Evelyn knew she could be scatterbrained and often didn't listen to her parents' gossiping, a favorite pastime of theirs. But surely, Mama and Papa would have known about this. Though now that she was thinking about it, she recalled what they'd said when Lady Vivian had married her husband over the summer. Because of the stark difference between the two of then, it had put the McNabs in the newspapers. "Oh, but they have an *aristocrat* in the family!" Mama had said, and she and Papa had then burst out laughing.

At the time, Evelyn had thought they'd been making fun of the McNab brothers' low upbringing compared to Lady Vivian. However, if Ollie had gone to Eton and Oxford, it was quite likely they *did* have an aristocrat in their family. But who?

Mr. McNab bit his lip. "Well, yes, but I wasn't exactly the best student. My marks were horrific; they always were, no matter how many private tutors I had." He shuffled in his stance. "I'm not exactly the brightest."

"Don't be silly, Mr. McNab. One shouldn't speak of themselves like that."

"Even if it's the truth?" But his good humor returned. "Anyway, like I said, tough times tend to work out in the end. I love my life now. Despite everything being stacked against me, I now work in a successful pub with my brothers day in and day out. I've never been as happy as I've been these last several years."

Evelyn forced a smile. "I wish I had your confidence in the future, Mr. McNab."

He tilted his head, as if he genuinely cared. "If you change your mind and need the ear of a friend for what's bothering you," he continued, "you have mine."

Unable to help herself, she smiled up at him and nodded.

"Thank you, Mr. McNab, for the offer. I do appreciate it."

"Of course." As he said this, something behind her grabbed his attention. He moved past her and crossed the room to one of the studio's bookshelves, grabbed something, and hurried back. "Look what I found." He held out an object. "It's the rest of your potato!" He gleamed ear to ear at his discovery, as if he had done something magnificent for her.

Evelyn burst into tears and began wailing. The Earl of Wellingham would never be this kind to her. The earl would never proudly show her something he'd found for her. To the earl, Evelyn was the object to show off and use as he wished, not a person with her own needs and wants and emotions who would need comfort occasionally. The earl was far older than her, a widower with a round liquor belly and not an ounce of tenderness. And she was the lucky lady whom he'd decided would be his after his first wife had died. For whatever reason, he wanted no one else to be his second wife, and she knew this by the way his eyes followed her at social events, tracking her like prey. He touched, smelled, obsessed over her auburn hair as if he owned it.

But there was no room for complaint. She had consented to marrying him when he'd offered a large sum of money to Papa for her hand that would keep the family out of the poverty which threatened them. This was unheard of, as usually, brides came with a dowry for the groom. But if Evelyn had a dowry, which she doubted, it would have been funded by her sister, who'd had had to support the family financially a few times over the years.

Instead, the earl had paid *them* to take Evelyn off their hands.

How much money he'd given Papa, she'd never found out. But ever since then, the house's doors closed correctly, the peeling paint was no more, and the cracked, leaky ceilings were mended and unmarred. And Papa and Mama were much happier.

For that, she was glad.

But the thought of marrying terrified her. It was why she'd negotiated her ten years of freedom with her parents. She hadn't gotten much attention the first year of her debut, as she'd been known for having emotional outbursts, though as an adult, she managed them a bit better. But the attention she had received, she'd turned down immediately. Evelyn and her parents had had an explosive argument about it in the middle of a ball and she had stormed out. It had been quite embarrassing, but the next day, when her parents had still been recovering from the shame, the decade of freedom idea had sprung upon her. She'd framed it as ten years to grow up more, and had promised to agree to marry whomever they chose at the end of the ten years.

To her absolute surprise, they'd agreed to it in their moment of weakness.

Since then, Evelyn had become a "pioneer" for women in the arts, as the museum director had once referred to her at a fundraising gala.

All of these thoughts bounced around her mind like erratic rubber balls and her wailing only worsened. Why did she have to have a breakdown now? And why did it have to be in front of Mr. McNab? Oh, he must have thought her utterly mad.

Humiliated to be so exposed to a client, and desperate for a place to collect herself, Evelyn ran and shut herself in the small supplies closet. Tears streamed down her face and sobs reverberated through her ribs as she sat down and curled into herself.

For a while, she sat in the closet, and Mr. McNab had hopefully left, though she knew she'd been awfully rude to rush away without so much as a goodbye. Unfortunately, a moment later, someone knocked upon the closet door.

"Miss Sparrow?" Mr. McNab's voice was slightly muffled by the wooden door. "Are you all right?"

"No!" she cried back.

A long pause. "I had no idea you felt so strongly about potatoes."

"Oh, Mr. McNab," Evelyn mumbled to herself between her sobs. Then spoke loud enough for him to hear. "I am not crying about potatoes!"

"Why *are* you crying, then?"

"I don't know!"

"I'm opening the door, Miss Sparrow."

Evelyn buried her face in her arms, which rested atop her knees. There wasn't really anything she could do but let him in. She had quite literally backed herself into a corner.

The door cracked open, and a ribbon of light spilled into the closet.

"You may come in, but please close the door," Evelyn said. "I don't want you looking upon me at the moment."

Without arguing, Mr. McNab came in, shutting the door, and Evelyn sensed him sitting on the floor against it.

"What's the matter?" he asked in a gentle voice.

She swallowed. "I'm sorry, Mr. McNab, but I don't wish to tell you."

"Is it something I can help you with?"

Knowing it was dark and he wouldn't be able to see her, Evelyn lifted her head. "Unfortunately, it is not."

"All right. Perhaps distraction would be of help? Let's see. Something that would distract Miss Sparrow. Ah! This is an obvious one. I know my knowledge about art is practically zero despite your best efforts. But, seeing as we need a distraction right now, could you tell me about your favorite type of art?"

Evelyn sniffed. "Do you mean art style, technique, or period?"

Mr. McNab chuckled in the darkness. "Whichever you wish."

Despite herself, Evelyn smiled a bit and wiped away her tears, though more continued to trickle down. And she answered, for all three. She probably talked for twenty minutes straight, going deep into detail Mr. McNab would not care about, but one of her biggest faults was her inability to stop talking whenever the subject of art or art history came up. She had enough knowledge to talk through an entire day.

"Are you feeling even a little better?" he asked once he was able to sneak a word in.

Evelyn had been so focused on talking about art that she had forgotten all about the earl. And wouldn't you know it, she did feel better. Even her tears had dried up. "Actually, yes, I am," she said.

Mr. McNab clapped once, startling her. "Excellent! May I open the door, then?"

"I suppose. The others will be returning soon, though my red, swollen eyes will give away what I had been doing while they were gone."

The closet door creaked open, and Evelyn squinted against the sudden light. Mr. McNab was already standing, and he held a hand out to her. Evelyn, however, stood on her own without accepting help.

"I am very embarrassed you witnessed that." Evelyn forced a neutral tone. She needed to put space between her and her client.

He furrowed his brow at the change in her demeanor. "That's quite all right, Miss Sparrow. You don't need to be embarrassed. I can assure you I've made a bigger fool of myself in front of far more people, far more often." He gave her his gleaming smile, but it immediately fell away. "Not that you made a fool of yourself, I'm just, you know, trying to… Oh, I blundered that, didn't I?" He seemed to say that last bit more to himself.

Evelyn successfully managed to push away the feelings of despair and melancholy that had been eating her alive. Her heart now properly numbed, she felt more confident that she could get through the rest of the day. She excused herself to Mr. McNab, who seemed thrown off by her dismissal, and he walked out of the door and her life.

Evelyn steeled herself and lifted a paintbrush one final time.

Chapter Two

T HE MORNING AFTER Miss Sparrow had cried in the supply closet, Ollie McNab woke up early—normally, he rose at noon since his job required him to stay up until the early morning hours—and went back to the museum to check on her under the guise he was checking on the artwork again, as he so often did.

But she wasn't there. And no one knew where she was, either.

Mr. Burlington and Mr. Currow accused her of being irresponsible and had a few choice words about her unexplained absence. But to Ollie, nothing about her seemed irresponsible. This was all strange, and something about it didn't sit right with him.

If only he knew what she had been so upset about yesterday.

"Would you pay attention to what you're doing?" a dark, frustrated voice pulled Ollie from his thoughts. Ollie looked up to find a large man with irritatingly perfect black hair. Nothing was ever out of place on his oldest brother Victor's person. Not one hair, not a stain on his pub apron, not a dull spot on his shoes.

Ollie frowned and Victor's scowl deepened.

Realizing he must have done something wrong, Ollie looked down at what he had been doing before his mind had trailed off to Miss Sparrow. The beer cask he was carrying had fallen to the floor.

"If that breaks open, the money to replace it comes out of your wages." Victor set his jaw and lifted his own beer cask over one shoulder.

"It was an accident, Victor," Ollie retorted.

"Be more responsible."

Ollie let out a huff of annoyance but knew it was pointless to argue. Again, he threw the cask over one shoulder, just like Victor, and followed his brother out and behind the bar, where they secured the casks in place.

Victor headed over to a window and crossed his arms as he gazed out of The Harp & Thistle. Outside, the sky was gray and dark. "Prepare for a crowded afternoon," Victor said. "If people get rained out from work, then they'll be coming here."

Right as Victor said this, his prediction came true. The sky opened up and rain came down in sheets.

"Where's Dantes?" Ollie asked, putting away clean pint glasses that had drip-dried. If they had a rainstorm crowd this early in the day, and Dantes wasn't here, they would be in trouble.

Victor turned around. "He'll be here soon."

Annoyance hit Ollie at the way Victor was speaking to him this afternoon, short and snippy. "I didn't ask when he would be here, I asked where he was."

Victor scowled again before leaving the bar. "I have invoices to go through," he said before disappearing in the hallway leading to their office.

"Christ's sake," Ollie mumbled to himself, glad Victor was gone. Victor was ten years older than Ollie, and he often treated him like a child, though Ollie was rounding twenty-seven years.

The pub door opened suddenly, and the loud noise of rained-out workers echoed through the pub as they filled in the large, empty space. Lots of shouting and laughing, having a grand time leaving work early for beer and whiskey instead of toiling away on the docks or a construction site. Ollie swore to himself while he did his best to keep up with the incessant orders, manning the pub all on his own. Where were his brothers?

"Three pints over here, laddie!" A man, soaking wet, squeezed himself between two others seated at the bar. Ollie quickly filled and served the pint glasses, told the man what he owed, and hurried over to the large, brass register to ring up the order and record it in their register book. As other men shouted their orders, Ollie tried his best to count out the change, tripping over numbers a few times. The noise and energy were making it hard for him to think or concentrate.

He almost never handled the money. That was always Victor or Dantes.

After several minutes of fumbling about, including dropping and shattering one pint glass, Ollie found his momentum in solo serving the unexpectedly packed pub. He poured three whiskeys at a time, then poured pints in mere seconds, slid them across the bartop, and caught tossed coin. The rain outside worsened and was loud enough to hear over the rowdy workers.

Through it all, though, Ollie was rather irritated Victor or Dantes remained absent, but he didn't have enough brain capacity at the moment to dwell on it.

As he threw coin into the register and counted out change, he spotted Victor emerging from the hallway and growing still as he looked around the room, his mouth fallen open.

Ollie returned to his task, not able to keep his eye off of it for long. It was far too busy and hectic.

"You were doing this all on your own?" Victor was now at Ollie's side, and his voice was filled with surprise. Ollie should have felt annoyed by this, but in truth, he felt a bit proud.

See? He was just as capable as his brothers were.

Though admittedly, it was partially his fault his family didn't take him seriously. For the longest time, he'd hardly taken anything seriously himself. He'd worked as best as he could and had never been late, but that was the extent of it. He'd often partake with the customers—though they seemed to genuinely enjoy Ollie's company and Ollie thought it was important to get to know them all by name. Dantes had once joked the reason women came to their pub was to get a chance with Ollie. Dantes had said this in front of their whole family—the McNab brothers, but also Dantes's wife, Vivian, and Vivian's sister-in-law, Lady Litchfield—and no one had batted an eye.

It made Ollie feel cheap and ridiculous. He always thought he was having a grand time in life. After all, he only had the one. But Vivian had once called him a scoundrel, which at the time he'd thought had been nothing more than a joke. But she'd been serious.

And one thing he learned from Vivian was that women did not take scoundrels seriously.

And they absolutely did not respect them.

The realization had hit Ollie upside the head. And ever since, he'd been trying his best to grow up a bit. But they all had their ideas about him set in stone. If only he knew how to get his family to see he could have fun *and* be responsible.

"What happened here?" Victor's voice darkened once again. Ollie realized Victor had found the shattered glass.

"It was an accident," Ollie replied. "As you can see, it's a bit harried out here." Ollie resisted groaning when Victor began inspecting everything behind the bar.

"We're a little busy, if you haven't noticed!" Ollie slid more pints down the bartop, the gold liquid spilling over the sides. "Think you could help out instead of picking everything apart?"

But Victor ignored him and crouched down to the beer cask Ollie had dropped earlier. There was a puddle forming underneath it.

Ollie swore out loud.

Victor glared at him but didn't say a word just yet. Instead, he continued his inspection and watched Ollie hurry over to the register, count out change, and record the sale in the register book.

Victor plucked the book out from under him. And then he swore, too. "How much have you been charging for pints?"

A sick pit formed in Ollie's stomach. The pointed stare from

Victor actually pierced his body, he was sure of it. He continued working as quick as he could to avoid looking Victor in the eye. "The book's right there, Victor. You can see for yourself."

"Costs went up and we had to raise the price of a pint when we reopened last month. You're charging the old prices." Victor's eyes searched the page. "How many have you served today?" But he wasn't really asking Ollie. He was counting for himself.

Once Victor counted it up—what total he came to, Ollie did not want to know—he slammed the book down onto the bartop, causing everyone around them to look over for a moment before returning to their conversation.

Raw humiliation ate through Ollie, and it only worsened as Victor began counting the coin in the register, his face reddening with anger.

Ollie had ruined everything. The beer cask, the broken pint glass, miscounting change and charging incorrectly?

Victor turned back with murder in his face. "You cost us several pounds. *Pounds*! That's a lot of money, Ollie."

"Would you calm down?" Ollie clenched his jaw. "I made a mistake. It's not the end of the world."

"Not the end of the world?" Victor's whole body tensed, and Ollie resisted the urge to roll his eyes, knowing exactly what Victor was going to say next. He had heard it far too many times in his life.

"Do you have any idea what it's like to not have money?" Victor's voice was sharp, and he was dangerously close to Ollie now. "To sleep in putrid streets filled with rats and horse dung? To have to steal in order to feed your two-year-old baby brother? To be thirteen years old and teaching a toddler how to wee in an alley instead of his trousers?"

Ollie glanced around and was glad to see no one was paying attention to the scene any longer. Except for their regular, Billy, who seemed engrossed in the saga, sipping at his pint as his eyes darted back and forth between the brothers. Ollie ignored Billy and put his attention back on Victor, seething with anger himself now. As if he had any control over when he'd been born! As if he wouldn't have had to survive just like them if he'd been only a few years older. It wasn't his fault he had no memory of that life.

"No." Victor's voice lowered. "You had Grampy and Grammy and their fancy townhouse, a full stomach, servants, Eton, and Oxford. You're a spoiled brat and irresponsible to boot. Look at how badly you botched being alone for a short time!"

Ollie's mouth hung open. This was hardly the first time Victor had ripped into him like this, and it wouldn't be the last, but it was something Ollie would never get used to.

It was horrid.

Ollie shook his head to clear away the shock, but before he could respond, something strange happened.

Something, or someone, in the crowd caught Victor's full attention. Victor stared out at whatever it was, and Ollie tried to find his line of sight but only saw endless heads and hats.

Confused, Ollie looked at his brother again to find Victor had completely gone pale. And then, he looked immediately down to Ollie, horror written in his face.

"What—"

But Victor wouldn't let Ollie finish his sentence. "I'm taking today's losses out of your wages. I need to go take care of something."

"I can cover the day's losses with my savings, Victor."

"Absolutely not. That defeats the purpose of teaching you a lesson, doesn't it?" And Victor hurried off before Ollie could argue back.

Ollie watched his oldest brother hook around the end of the bar and weave through the crowd, coming to a stop to talk to someone. But Ollie couldn't see whom.

"Got yourself in a spot with your brother there, eh?" Billy's voice grabbed Ollie's attention. When Ollie looked back to Victor, Victor was gone.

Ollie let out a long breath and put his full attention on Billy. "You enjoyed that bit there, Billy? You seemed rather entertained by my brother ripping me to shreds."

"Aye!" Billy laughed. "That was more entertaining than vaudeville!"

"Thanks," Ollie replied darkly.

But Billy merely laughed again. "I have brothers too, you know. I find a fist to the face can be an excellent solution to problems."

"I'm not punching my brother in the face. Even if he does deserve it."

Billy lifted his pint glass, cheering it into the air, before taking a long gulp.

The pub door opened again, and Ollie was flooded with relief when Dantes walked through it, followed by Vivian and Lady Litchfield, who began shaking out their umbrellas. Dantes led the two women over to the bar and kicked two of their patrons out of their chairs for the women to sit. "Off," was all he said as his placed heavy hands on their shoulders. The two men looked back as if to argue but upon seeing the ugly scar that slashed across Dantes's face, thought better of it.

Vivian and Lady Litchfield sat in the vacated seats as Dantes went around the end of the bar to join Ollie.

"My, my," Vivian said, looking around. Always the picture of elegance, her dark hair was swept up with a mother-of-pearl comb. "I can't believe how crowded it is right now!" She put her attention back on Ollie. "Where's Victor? Why isn't he helping you?"

Ollie poured out two whiskeys for the women. "Don't know, don't much care."

"Trouble in paradise?" she said with a wry grin, now well-accustomed to the constant clashing between Ollie and Victor.

As Dantes appeared beside Ollie, Billy decided to join in and leaned over to Vivian. "I told him to get a swift fist to Victor's face. He said *no*."

"How noble of you, Ollie," Vivian replied with humor before taking a sip of her whiskey. Lady Litchfield giggled in response before taking a sip of her own drink as well.

"That would be ill-advised," Dantes added with a chuckle. "No offense, Ollie, but Victor would wipe the floor with you."

Ollie clenched his jaw.

"Where is he, though?" Dantes searched the crowd. "I'm surprised he's not up here breathing down your neck."

"He already was, believe me."

Billy laughed loudly and when Ollie shot him a death stare, briefly saluted the family before disappearing into the crowd.

As Ollie and Dantes got to work, Ollie mentioned Victor going pale after spotting something, or someone, in the crowd before disappearing.

Dantes, though, didn't seem to think anything of it. "Maybe he saw someone drop a coin," he joked.

But Ollie didn't laugh. Nothing seemed funny to him right now. He had never seen Victor react so severely before. Thus, he told Dantes he was taking a short break and decided to go investigate.

As Ollie made his way through the crowd, several people stopped him to chat briefly or say hello. They were all genuinely happy to see him, and it lifted Ollie's spirits.

Just ahead was a break in the crowd where he'd be able to slip down the hallway and likely find Victor in the office.

But as Ollie squeezed between two men on his way in that direction, another man doing his best to hurry through the crowd accidentally bumped hard into a group of women, who shouted after him with offense. The harried man, who wore a tweed flatcap, completely ignored them and continued on his way.

Annoyed, Ollie went after him and gripped his shoulder hard, forcing him to turn around, winning a loud, rude curse word in response.

Ollie opened his mouth to give a warning but instead froze in place.

Ollie was the shortest of the three brothers, though thanks to their giant, Scottish father, he still was rather tall. This man on whom Ollie had a death grip was a good head shorter than Ollie.

But his face? It was as if Ollie were looking in a mirror.

The two even held twin expressions of true shock. But the mystery fellow, after a moment, clenched his mouth shut.

"What the—?" Ollie began, but the man slipped out from his grip and pushed through the crowd again, shoving people out of his way, much harder this time. "Wait a minute!" Ollie called out. He was only seconds behind the stranger when the stranger slipped out the door. Ollie hurried outside, chased the man for half a block, but, despite having shorter legs than Ollie, he was also much quicker. Ollie could only watch helplessly underneath the awning of a neighboring bakery as the stranger disappeared into the rain.

Heaving heavy breaths, Ollie watched the spot where the man had disappeared. Someone who looked like him. No, he had to have been seeing things. He'd only seen the man's face for a flash of a moment.

Ollie hurried back into the pub and found Victor back behind the bar with Dantes. He rushed over to his brothers and began talking animatedly, telling them what had just happened, but it all came out jumbled and confusing.

"Whoa, whoa." Dantes set his hands on Ollie's shoulders. "What in the blazes are you talking about? You are making absolutely no sense."

Ollie looked around at the group—Victor, Dantes, Vivian, Lady Litchfield—and they were all looking at him as if he had sprouted horns.

He took a deep breath. "I just saw a man who could have been my twin."

Vivian pulled back her head. "What are you talking about?"

"He looked exactly like me," Ollie explained. "The only difference was he was a good head shorter. And maybe older. I'm not sure, though."

Dantes and Victor held each other's gaze.

"You know who he was, don't you?" Ollie concluded.

Dantes bit his bottom lip. But Victor had no problem replying. "Don't be ridiculous. You did not see a man who looks just like you." But his voice lacked the intensity it usually held.

"Do I have a twin?"

Victor frowned. "A twin?"

A more horrifying thought hit Ollie. "Was he my father?" He stepped toward Victor. "Have you been hiding this entire time that I have a different father?"

"Even you can't be that stupid, Ollie," Victor growled out. "Are you saying our mother went around with another man behind our father's back? Do you think that's the kind of woman she was?" His voice held a dangerous warning.

But Ollie didn't know *what* kind of woman she'd been, because unlike his brothers, he had no memory of their mother. Or their father.

Lady Litchfield's gentle voice cut through the tense air. "You have the same green eyes as Victor and Dantes. And the way Victor has explained it to me, your father had those same green eyes. And your grandfather has them as well. Isn't that correct?" She ended this with a small smile.

Ollie looked up at Victor and found his brother watching the marchioness. "So, that man wasn't my father," Ollie said, feeling idiotic.

Victor replied, "Don't be daft," in a quieter voice, without looking away from Lady Litchfield. But then he seemed to get a hold of himself. "I don't know what you saw, but I know for a fact you don't have a twin. I was there when you were born. God help us all if there were two of you."

"Victor, that's not very kind." The marchioness's gentle voice came through again.

Victor stiffened and Ollie knew he was itching to retort. Instead, the eldest McNab brother said, "Two pounds."

Ollie blinked. "What?"

"That's what I'm taking out of your wages for today's mistakes. Two pounds."

Ollie looked over to Dantes, hoping to find the ire he felt reflected in his other brother. But, not for the first time, Dantes was trying his best to distance himself from being in the middle of it, turning and backing away, even though Ollie knew Dantes would never agree with this.

"Two pounds?" Ollie shot back to Victor with offense.

Victor crossed his arms. "Maybe this will finally teach you a lesson on responsibility."

"You know I'm horrific at anything with numbers. I can't *grow* into understanding them." *And you should have been out here with me, anyway.* But of course, Ollie wasn't bold enough to say that.

"This is going to be how it goes from now on," Victor said without an ounce of understanding in his voice. "From here on out, every error you make will come straight out of your own pocket. I don't know what else to do with you. Perhaps this will be the thing to finally get you to grow up."

Ollie again looked at Dantes and found emotion battling in his brother's gaze. It almost seemed like sympathy, which didn't make sense. But Dantes looked away quickly. Perhaps he'd interpreted that wrong. "I don't have to agree to this," Ollie said to Victor, but his voice had weakened.

"You don't?" Humor reflected in Victor's eyes. He was mocking Ollie. "Why don't you focus on what you do best, then, if you don't think you can manage agreeing to it?"

Ollie clenched his teeth. "And what's that?"

"Faffing about. Leave business matters to Dantes and me. We know what we're doing. And we can handle it."

Ollie didn't know by whom he felt more betrayed. This behavior was not unexpected from Victor, even though it still stung. But Dantes always seemed to have Ollie's back.

Ollie swallowed and excused himself before he gave away the betrayal he felt, then disappeared in the pub's crowd. He wanted to get as far away from his brothers as he could, finally coming to stop at one of the front windows, where he watched the rain pour outside, matching exactly how he felt on the inside.

Chapter Three

EVELYN STARED DOWN at her white-gloved hands resting atop her lap of overly frothy, white, silk chiffon. As her family's carriage crawled along the street toward the church in which her life would be forever altered, Evelyn forced her mind and heart into numbness. She would not allow herself to be emotional in front of her family.

Her family, generally one which exuded lots of noise, was unusually quiet. She looked up to observe them—perhaps her parents had somehow changed their minds—but was startled to find her sister watching her intently. The sisters were similar in appearance. Both had auburn hair, and both had brown eyes. But Cordelia was a few years older, and dressed far more opulently. For every plain wool dress Evelyn owned, Cordelia had three dripping in sequins and beadwork.

Evelyn held Cordelia's gaze and wondered what was going on in her sister's mind.

Evelyn also wondered if Cordelia had felt the same sickening feeling on her way to her own wedding years ago.

She averted her gaze and looked at Papa seated beside Cordelia. His top hat sat prim upon his head, orange hair sticking out from beneath the brim. His mustache was waxed and curled downward at the ends, a parallel to the frown it crowned.

Papa was lost in his thoughts, his hands knit together over his stomach. Evelyn wondered what he and Mama had talked about that morning while Evelyn had dressed and readied for the ceremony.

"We should be there soon." Mama's voice cut through the silent cabin. Mama fanned her round face with a paper fan decorated with hand-painted posies. Evelyn had inherited redness from both parents. Her father's hair, and her mother's complexion. Mama's pale skin flushed at the smallest slight, hence the fan. "Just think, Evelyn, this time tomorrow, you will be a countess, just like your sister!"

"I'm a *contessa*, Mama," Cordelia said with her signature haughty air.

Mama waved her free hand. "In English, it's countess. You are home right now, my dear, not in Italy."

"This hasn't been home for nearly ten years. Nor has Italy. And thank goodness for that! In Paris, a dowager *contessa* like myself is free to do as she wishes." Cordelia ended this with a smirk Evelyn knew would send their mother's face cherry red.

It worked.

"Stop arguing!" Father interjected right as they stopped at the church. Evelyn thought she was going to throw up. "Please. Things are already tense as they are. Let's not heighten the feeling."

As if on cue, an endless waterfall of rain suddenly dropped down from the sky. The entire family jumped and gasped at the sudden onslaught.

"Oh, no!" Mama shouted with true distress as her hands flew up to her cheeks, her fan tumbling to the floor. "And just as we arrived at the church! What horrific timing!"

Evelyn slunk in her seat. As if the day couldn't become more wretched.

"Did you bring an umbrella?" Mama asked Papa.

He looked affronted. "Me! Did *you*?"

Mama harrumphed. "Well, maybe we could wait a minute or two and see if it lets up? The door to the church is a good ways back from the road. Look, puddles are already forming on the walking path! Evelyn is going to get soaked! Oh, your darling hair! Your dress!"

The buttons on the back of Evelyn's bodice were beginning to irritate her. Normally, Evelyn's dresses had buttons on the front so she could dress herself, as she didn't care much for being touched by other people. It was something she had been doing for as long as she could remember. She had not had a lady's maid for many years. It had been a battle fought for a long while. This was another time her parents had given up on yet another one of Evelyn's antics, but at least this one had saved them money. Thus, she was not used to the little buttons digging into her back. She squirmed.

After five minutes, however, the rain only seemed to worsen. And after a bit of back and forth, impatience mounting while waiting for the footman to appear, Father mumbled something about finding an umbrella in the church and dashed out of the carriage.

With only the women now, the air in the cabin seemed to lighten just a bit.

"How are you feeling?" Cordelia finally asked, looking Evelyn intently in the eye once again.

"Like I'm going to throw up," Evelyn responded.

"That's normal," Mama added with haste. "I doubt there's a single bride out there who doesn't have nerves beforehand."

"I despise these buttons," Evelyn said, shifting with discomfort again. "How do you live with it? I cannot stand how each tiny button is digging into my spine."

"You get used to it," Mama replied. "I know you prefer them on the front, but a wedding dress should always have them on the back."

"Why?"

Mama briefly looked at Cordelia as if asking for help. But her sister didn't offer any comment, so Mama gave an explanation herself. "Because husbands like to unfasten the buttons on the wedding night, silly!"

Evelyn could feel the blood drain from her face and had a vivid image of the Earl of Wellingham at her back, his stubby fingers hurriedly unbuttoning the bodice with greed.

"Now I'm really going to throw up." Evelyn groaned.

"Mama, don't scare her." Cordelia gave their mother a wide-eyed look.

"The girl needs to know what's going to happen tonight. Evelyn…" Mama now turned her body to face her daughter. "Do you know what happens on a wedding night? What a husband and wife…do together?"

Cordelia decided to be helpful. "A man and wife go to bed and f—"

"*Cordelia!*" Mama shrieked.

Cordelia only smiled.

Evelyn rubbed the bridge of her nose. "Yes, I know what happens." Her Vassar College friends back in New York had been a wealth of information regarding this subject. Sometimes, a bit too much information. "What I want to know is: How to prevent it from happening?"

Cordelia leaned forward and placed her hand on Evelyn's knee. "You cannot, I'm sorry to say. They're brutes. Filthy, smelly, hairy brutes. I pray every night, though, that you will have a husband like mine."

Evelyn furrowed her brow. She had only met Cordelia's husband a few times and didn't think there was anything worth remembering about him. "What do you mean?"

"I mean, a husband who dies not long after your wedding. And then, when his replacement is a perpetual bachelor who prefers men over women, you get to live as a wealthy, merry widow!"

Mama gasped quite loudly at this. "*Cordelia!*"

But Cordelia shrugged. "It's true. I hated the man you and Papa chose for me. And I hope Evelyn's earl croaks tonight."

Despite knowing better, Evelyn couldn't help but laugh.

Cordelia always knew how to make her feel better. As if her sister knew Evelyn's train of thought, she gave her a wink.

Mama huffed before looking over at Evelyn. "I suppose, then, I do not need to have that conversation with you?"

"Please don't," Evelyn begged.

"Very well." Mama lifted her chin. "I will, however, give you marriage advice. The first year, for even the most in-love couple, is hardest. You're two different people trying to learn how to live together and under the same roof. And your responsibilities will be different. You will now run a household, not play with paint."

Mama continued talking, but Evelyn's mind began trailing off. She wondered what her colleagues—well, former colleagues—were thinking right now. Regret hit her. She should have resigned, or at least told them what was going to happen.

But she'd been too afraid to. And she hadn't wanted to acknowledge what her future had held.

Cordelia interrupted her thoughts. "Are you all right?"

Evelyn could only look back at her sister, but only for a moment. For her eyes were beginning to sting.

"She's fine," Mama said. "Just typical bridal nerves, is all. Think about the home you'll be living in, Evelyn! The gowns, the jewelry—"

"You're thinking about that for *yourself*, aren't you?" Cordelia snapped back.

Both Evelyn and Mama stilled for a moment.

"You think I don't know why she's being forced into this? Have you ever stood near the earl, Mama? Smelled him? Heard him talk? The most insipid rubbish comes out of his mouth."

Mama gasped.

"I went through hell with my husband." Her voice was snippy. "But you didn't care about that, did you? You only cared for the money you knew you'd convince me to send with your sad stories about leaking roofs."

"Cordelia!" Mama's face was bright red again.

But Cordelia shook her head. "No. I wish all of this had been laid out to me before my wedding. I wish I knew that the anger and fear I felt was *not* normal. You reassured me that my husband was a good man, just rough around the edges. But he wasn't. I had him pinned from the moment I met him. He was a horrible man, and I'm glad he's dead."

Evelyn lifted her eyebrows sky high at this.

Mama picked up her paper fan and furiously began to fan herself. And promptly fainted.

Evelyn shouted out, but Cordelia rolled her eyes. Fainting on cue was Mama's favorite way of escaping uncomfortable moments.

"Is that true?" Evelyn asked, glad to have a moment alone with Cordelia. This was the first time she had ever heard any of this.

"Unfortunately, yes." Cordelia stared for a beat longer at their unconscious mother. "Now that we're finally alone, tell me the truth. How are you feeling?"

"Honestly?"

"Yes. Honestly."

Evelyn began to twist her fingers together. "I don't want this."

"I figured as much when I learned you negotiated ten years to yourself. Rather brilliant. Wish I had thought of that, but I don't think they would have given that to me. Back then, I was too much of a rule follower and it wouldn't have been a stubborn argument like I'm sure you put up. I also don't think Mama and Papa were as desperate financially when I married, either. Sure, they weren't in the best place, but it wasn't as bad as it was when the earl decided to set his sights on you. I couldn't believe my ears when they told me he paid for you and not the other way around. I wonder how much money the earl gave them?"

"A lot," Evelyn offered. "I could not say how much, but it had to have been an astronomical amount."

"I'm surprised they didn't come to me. They had already for many years."

"Maybe they didn't want you to know how dire it was at home."

"Or they knew once the new *conte* marries, if he ever does, I won't be able to send them money any longer. The well will dry up."

"That makes sense. I didn't even know how bad it had become for them until I moved back home after living in Paris. That was only a little over a year ago. And then the earl saw me." Queasiness rolled through Evelyn's stomach at the memory of that first evening with him following her around and sniffing her hair.

Cordelia nodded just as the door to the carriage opened. Papa appeared with the footman, and he sighed when he saw Mama had fainted. He tried shaking her shoulder to awaken her and was successful after a moment.

"Everyone is inside waiting." Papa was huddled under a black umbrella and had to shout over the sound of the rain. "Let us get inside. Quickly!"

Mama went out first and opened an extra umbrella the footman handed to her. Mama and Papa waited off to the side as the footman helped Cordelia disembark. Cordelia looked over her shoulder one last time at Evelyn as she prepared to step out.

"Wait," Evelyn said, causing her sister to pause. "Will I be all right? I mean, will everything end up being all right?" Mr. McNab's words from yesterday popped into her mind at the moment, his confidence in the idea that everything always somehow worked itself out. Oh, how she wished a man who looked and acted like him waited for her at the altar! Perhaps this wouldn't have been nearly as terrifying.

Cordelia's face took on a serious expression. "I don't know," she said and the footman reached out to take her hand.

The family was now waiting for Evelyn to emerge. Evelyn poked her head out and looked down the sidewalk. People were dashing into nearby stores to get out of the rain, holding soaking-wet newspapers over their head in desperation.

Where did that sidewalk lead? What kinds of lives did those people down the street have? Were they happy? They were likely happier than Evelyn in this exact moment, at least.

She wasn't familiar with this part of London. Bucking tradition a bit, this was the church in the earl's parish, not Evelyn's. So what those shops people were dashing into, she did not know. Confectionaries, flower shops, perhaps a millinery or two. Curiosity tugged at her.

"Evelyn, you must come out of there! We don't have time to dilly-dally. People are waiting!" Papa shouted over the loud rain again. Fog was rolling in. She couldn't even see halfway down the block any longer. It was like they were suddenly in a little bowl, just her, her family, the silent footman, and the church before them.

As the footman helped Evelyn step out, she did her best to ignore the twinge of discomfort from his hand touching hers. It was standard for a footman to help this way, whether she liked it or not. And as he covered her with an umbrella, she met Cordelia's eye. Her sister's pointed gaze was intense with meaning.

Evelyn gave her a wordless expression that said, *"What is it?"*

Cordelia nodded her head once. Probably realizing Evelyn didn't understand, Cordelia then mouthed something.

"What are you doing?" Mama asked from beneath an umbrella Papa held over her. "Why are you doing strange things with your mouth?"

But Cordelia ignored her and mouthed something again. *"Run."*

Evelyn's eyes widened and Cordelia gave her a small smile.

Evelyn looked out at the pouring rain. Then back at her family. Back out to the rain. She couldn't run away.

Right?

"Evelyn, we must get inside." Papa grabbed her arm and began pulling her toward the walking path that led to the church door, where figures stood awaiting them. Because of the fog, she could not tell if they were clergy, her husband-to-be, or someone else entirely.

Her heart beat faster.

Images of her desk, her easel, the paintings at the museum—both in the studio and where they were admired by the public—flashed in her mind.

Laughing with her old American university classmates.

Listening in on lectures, raising her hand to ask questions.

Mr. Ollie McNab, his near-daily visits to the museum. That kind and genuine smile of his.

Papa was now *dragging* Evelyn up the stone walking path, his hand gripped tightly on her arm like handcuffs.

As they reached the door, she could finally see who was standing there. It was the earl. Making sure she arrived? That she was walking toward him?

That she wasn't running away?

That sick feeling that had been haunting her all day twisted and morphed and became pure panic. Her body began to shake, sweat formed at her brow, and her heart was about to break through her ribs. She felt like a rabbit cowered upon the grass as a hawk descended upon her.

She met his eyes. There was no kindness there.

"I find that things have a funny way of working themselves out." Mr. McNab's voice echoed in her head.

Mama and Cordelia hurried up the two stone steps leading to the door, and the earl let them pass and followed them in while one of the earl's footmen took and shook out their umbrellas. Papa climbed the steps, too, but turned and watched Evelyn, waiting.

Evelyn didn't think, as her body did what the rabbit would have done.

She turned around and ran.

Ran for her life.

Papa shouted her name, but she ignored it. She ran down the walking path, down the sidewalk, and to the next block. She ran, and ran, and ran. She took turns down random streets. A right here, a left there. People shouted with surprise as she ran past them. "A runaway bride!" she heard several times.

Evelyn zig-zagged her way through London until she could run no more. She spotted a bench up ahead and collapsed into it, her chest heaving with exhaustion.

The rain poured down on her as she lay upon her back with her eyes closed. But she soaked in the moment. She felt…free!

And despite herself, she smiled and laughed up into the fog, into that thick, lead gray that hung overhead, as the water washed away the terror.

Once her breathing had leveled, Evelyn stood up, her shoes squelching and her legs nearly collapsing beneath her as she braced herself on the bench. Wherever she was, the street was all but abandoned by pedestrians and traffic.

"Now what?" she asked aloud to herself as she looked both directions down the street. Where in the blazes could she go? She couldn't go home, that was for certain.

She couldn't go to work in a soaking-wet wedding dress.

But she also wasn't too worried about it; the rush from the run was still fresh. Thus, she began meandering down the road.

"I must look utterly mad," she mumbled, passing a large, glass storefront window, reflecting a soaking-wet bride, her dress and veil limp, her hair stretched long into wet tendrils.

And yet she smiled.

When Evelyn came to the corner, she took a left turn and spotted stables up ahead. She quickened her pace, crossed the empty street, and went inside.

The scent of hay and horse assaulted her. A few men mulled about in tweed waistcoats and flat-caps, smoking pipes and cigars and talking amongst themselves.

One spotted her, hesitated, then nudged the man beside him.

They all began to stare.

"Hello," she said, lifting one hand in greeting.

"By Jove," one said, his pipe frozen halfway to his mouth.

"Are any of you cab drivers by chance?"

They continued to stare, but one came to his senses. A portly man with red cheeks. He stepped forward. "Aye," was all he offered. The rest of the group went back about their business.

Evelyn walked toward the man. "I was wondering if perhaps you could take me somewhere."

He took a puff from a pipe as he looked her over. "Not to a wedding, I presume?"

Her eye twitched. "No."

"Where to then, lass?"

She had no coin on her. She had nothing on her, and nowhere to go. But a wild idea came forth. It was mad, but it seemed to be her only option. "Do you know The Harp & Thistle?" she asked, a bit unsure.

The man's bushy eyebrows shot up to the sky. "You want to go to a pub?"

"Yes. Please."

The driver studied her. "You have coin?"

Her heart sunk to the floor. "I do not."

"Can't take you anywhere without coin, lass."

She bit her bottom lip in thought. What would Mr. McNab do if she showed up like this? If she showed up asking for help?

She wasn't sure he would help. A mad, soaked, runaway bride showing up at his place of work?

But what other choice did she have?

"I can get your payment upon arrival."

"How?" The driver eyed her skeptically.

"I know the owners of the establishment."

"You know the McNabs?"

She braced herself as hope finally reared its head. "I do. I am friends with the youngest one."

"Ollie?"

She started at this. He must have been a regular patron of their establishment.

"Yes, sir."

The cab driver threw his head back and laughed loudly, his entire body shaking from it. "All right, lass, hop in over there." He pointed toward his hansom cab, the horse patiently waiting for its next drive. As Evelyn climbed in, she heard the driver chuckle to himself again and say, "A bride leaving the altar for Ollie McNab. Wait until the boys hear *this* one!"

❧ ❧ ❧

Chapter Four

THE RAIN CONTINUED to slide down the windows of The Harp & Thistle while Ollie watched the squiggly patterns it made on the glass. It was hypnotizing in a way. Oddly calming.

Searching for a break in the crowd, Ollie got a brief glimpse of the group still at the bar. His brothers, Vivian, the marquess. They were all much older than Ollie. In a different season of life. Marriage, families… At least that was the case for all of them except Victor, but even he had found his place in life.

Then there was Ollie. An outcast. A joke.

Never would he admit this out loud, but he was incredibly hurt his brothers were treating him as their employee and not their equal. Ollie tore his attention away from them and back out the window. His jaw set tight. They didn't trust him. He knew they found his antics irritating at times, but he was so much younger than them. Victor and Dantes had led similar lives in their twenties, hadn't they? Hadn't they often attended parties and shuffled around women?

Surely, they had. Everyone *he* knew in their twenties did that. Surely, it had been the same when his brothers had been his age. But then, he wouldn't really know, would he? Dantes had been breaking out in his boxing career, while Victor had still been working on the docks. Ollie had been away at school and, he supposed, and didn't truly know what they'd done during that time.

Ollie's thoughts about this were cut off when a hansom stopped in front of the pub. Usually, their patrons walked here from work, so this was a bit unusual.

Someone dressed head-to-toe in white climbed out and talked to the driver momentarily. Ollie squinted. It was difficult to see through the sheet of rain on the window, but was that a bride?

The pub's door opened, but Ollie couldn't see the new arrival through the crowd.

And his curiosity piqued further when the entire pub went completely silent.

Ollie weaved his way through the crowd and finally was able to see that it was, in fact, a bride!

A soaked-to-the-bone and violently shivering bride, at that.

Trying not to panic, the bride seemed to be searching for someone in the pub crowd.

Had her husband-to-be abandoned her at the altar? Was he here hiding?

The woman turned her pinched face in Ollie's direction before looking the other way at the bar and began making her way over to it.

Ollie's eyes nearly popped out of his skull as he realized the bride was Miss Sparrow.

The pub crowd resumed their loud chatter, mostly about the soaking-wet bride who had appeared, but Ollie watched Miss Sparrow with intent curiosity. He stared as she walked through the crowd, people separating to allow her to pass, and she stopped to talk to Ollie's brothers, whom she reached first. Ollie wanted to go over there but was frozen in place. Miss Sparrow, the most straight-laced woman he had ever known, demanded attention in her white dress. Not because it was a bridal dress in a pub, but because she was the most stunning bride he was sure had ever existed, even with the rain's affect.

He couldn't hear anything said, but he could see the mix of surprise and concern on their faces. While Victor and Dantes watched with discomfort, Vivian and Lady Litchfield did their best to comfort Miss Sparrow.

Vivian searched for and found Ollie in the crowd and waved him over, her face grim.

Why would Miss Sparrow have been in a wedding dress? In the months they had known each other, she had never once mentioned an impending wedding. Or a betrothal. Or a fiancé.

A strange feeling of regret hit him, but he didn't understand why.

"Miss Sparrow," Ollie said, the surprise in his voice ringing clear. "What are you doing here?"

Evelyn whipped around. Strings of dark-red hair clung to her forehead and cheeks. A long veil and the hem of her white dress had turned gray with London street filth.

Her breathing was erratic. "I didn't know where else to go."

Ollie looked her over. "Were you at a costume ball?"

Victor groaned audibly, and Ollie immediately felt like an idiot.

But Miss Sparrow didn't seem to think anything of his question. "No. Quite unfortunately. I have just run off from my wedding." She added a nervous chuckle at the end of this.

Victor addressed the group. "Everyone, in back. Dantes, stay up here, if you don't mind."

Dantes agreed to this, as well as covering the fare for the hansom Miss Sparrow had evidently told him about, and everyone followed Victor into the office in back. Once everyone was inside, Victor shut the door while Ollie lit a fire. Miss Sparrow and Vivian sat in the chairs. Lady Litchfield and Victor exchanged a prolonged look while standing near the door.

But Miss Sparrow had all of her attention on Ollie.

Ollie cleared his throat. "Perhaps you could start from the beginning."

And so she did. Miss Sparrow told a wild tale of what she called "ten years of freedom." During that time, she'd studied at a college in America, interned at the Louvre, and ended up here in London with her job at the museum. Of course, he already knew about those travels. He had *not*, however, known about Miss Sparrow and the Earl of Wellingham's betrothal upon her return to London.

"That was why I was so upset yesterday." Miss Sparrow couldn't look Ollie in the eye. "The earl is not someone with whom I wish to spend my life and in fact, I was beginning to find the thought *horrific*. But it was part of the bargain, that I marry whomever my parents chose without a fight." She looked down at her dress, lifted her heavy skirts, then released them while letting out a singular laugh. "I suppose I refused to believe what was going to happen, perhaps hoping by some miracle the wedding wouldn't occur."

"But…it didn't occur, did it?" Ollie said.

Miss Sparrow looked up at him again, as if realizing for the first time she had escaped an unwanted marriage. "No, I suppose you're right. Not today, at any rate."

"What do you mean?"

She shrugged. "I can't imagine my family will relent on this marriage."

"But you're safe from it. For now, at least."

She gave him a small smile. "Yes, I suppose you're right."

Despite their argument from earlier, Ollie turned to his brother, exchanging a look with Victor.

Victor held his eye. "Do you know the earl she's talking about?"

"I've heard of the Earl of Wellingham, but I doubt he's some-one our grandparents associate with." The McNab brothers' grandparents were Scottish nobility—or "nobs," as Ollie privately referred to aristocrats—with lukewarm feelings about the English. They ran with a much wilder crowd than he suspected Miss Sparrow's family did.

That was another thing. In all this time, Miss Sparrow had never mentioned being the daughter of a baron, either. Not that he'd much thought about it, but he'd figured she'd been middle class, if anything.

Ollie watched Miss Sparrow put her attention on the fire. Her gloves had been removed at some point and her bare hands reached out to the warmth the fire provided.

She'd mentioned she hadn't known where else to go. But why would she have come here, of all places?

"You need a place to stay," Ollie concluded out loud.

She didn't turn toward him, and instead closed her eyes. "I can't go home tonight, of course. Nor can I go to a friend's—I know my family will be looking there for me. This was the only place I know of where I had the best chance of hiding safely. When I ran, I didn't have anything with me. No coin, no clothing, no food. But I can't go back." She gave him a pleading look. *Please don't send me home.*

Vivian and Lady Litchfield whispered together as Ollie went over to Victor. There was a cautious, guarded look in his brother's eye.

"What about the flat upstairs? Dantes's old place?" Ollie asked quietly. Dantes used to live in the flat just above the pub, until the building had caught on fire earlier in the year. It had since been redone and refitted with furnishings. Victor was planning on leasing it out to traveling businessmen because it would come fully furnished. And he could charge a higher rate for that.

"No," Victor replied darkly.

Ollie narrowed his eyes and lowered his voice further. "I wonder what Lady Litchfield would think if she knew you so easily refused to help a woman running a bad situation. Didn't she recently separate from a horrid husband?"

Ollie had noticed over the past few months that Victor and Lady Litchfield had become good friends. So much so, the marchioness hardly seemed to feel out of place at their pub these days, as she now drank whiskey alongside Vivian and talked quite easily with other patrons. Ollie decided to take advantage of this fact. Victor's face remained blank and gave nothing away. However, he did stop arguing about it. "Fine. She can stay for a few days if she wishes. But that's it."

"Thank you."

The two brothers studied each other for a long moment, and Ollie got the sense they were both trying to uncover the other's true motives. But he didn't arrive to a satisfactory conclusion.

Vivian and Lady Litchfield ended their whispering and Vivian sat up straight. "Miss Sparrow, you are also welcome to come stay with me or Anne. We have plenty of space. I think my home would be better than Lady Litchfield's, as she has young children in the house."

"Oh," Miss Sparrow replied, and she seemed to hesitate.

"We have a flat right upstairs, as well," Ollie added. "It isn't currently being used and you're welcome to stay there." He found he wanted to keep her close, but of course he would feel protective over any friend in need.

Miss Sparrow's face softened. "I would much prefer staying in the flat, if that's quite all right, Lady Vivian, Lady Litchfield. I'd feel like I'm putting you out."

Vivian smiled. "Of course you wouldn't be."

But Miss Sparrow didn't seem comforted by this. In fact, she started wringing her hands. "Forgive me." Miss Sparrow paused for a long moment. "I'm sure your servants are most excellent, but you must understand, I feel best staying somewhere without any ties to the aristocracy."

Vivian tried to suppress the surprise in her face, but Ollie caught it. "You are worried the servants would gossip is what you are saying. And that it would get back to your family."

Miss Sparrow swallowed and nodded.

"Well, mine have proven to me that they are trustworthy, but I understand that worry as I had it myself once." Vivian paused. "If you wish to stay here, that is fine by me as well. I would still like to help, though. Would it be all right with you if I sent some clothing over?"

Miss Sparrow released a huge breath. "Oh, that would possibly be the most helpful thing you could offer me." The women then briefly discussed what would be needed, and Vivian and

Lady Litchfield rushed out the door.

Moments later, Ollie led Miss Sparrow up the stairs that led the flat. In one hand, he had a key for the door and the other hand, a jug of water for the washstand. As he put the key into the lock, he said over his shoulder, "I'm not sure what you plan to do after this, but Victor agreed to let you stay for a few days." When he got a nod in response he added, "I'll just let you in and get the fire going, then I'll be out of your way."

Ollie pushed open the door and immediately disappeared behind a screen. The sound of pouring water told her that the washstand was over in that direction. As Ollie reappeared without the jug, Miss Sparrow found a knit blanket draped over a chair and wrapped it around her. She watched Ollie put a long match to the crumpled newspaper in the fireplace that would start the fire. Once lit, Ollie rose back up, feeling awkward. She would die of a chill if she stayed in soaking-wet clothes.

"I wouldn't mind it if you stayed for a few minutes, Mr. McNab. You don't have to rush out." Miss Sparrow pulled the blanket around her tighter.

Ollie felt torn on what to do. This wasn't some woman from the bar—this was Miss Sparrow. And apparently, the daughter of a baron. He really should not have been here. But he also didn't wish to leave her alone, either.

"What do you want to do in the meantime?" he finally asked.

"What do you mean?"

"You'll get sick if you stay in that." He indicated to the puddle that had formed around her feet.

Miss Sparrow looked down at the water-logged dress. "I suppose you're right. I do wish to remove it."

Ollie shifted; this was something for the ladies to help with. "Would you like me to see if perhaps Lady Vivian or Lady Litchfield are still waiting on their carriage? Or maybe, there's another woman downstairs that could be of help?"

"No!" Miss Sparrow shouted with a paled expression of horror. She immediately closed her eyes as if collecting herself.

"Please. I do not feel comfortable with practical strangers doing that." She swallowed and opened her eyes again. "I normally wear bodices that are fastened from the front so that I may dress myself. I don't ever have help with dressing."

"Do you not have a lady's maid?" This seemed unusual for the daughter of a baron.

Miss Sparrow shook her head. "I've gone through a few, though that was a long time ago. My parents were sure I was trying to be difficult, but I wasn't. I merely didn't want someone I didn't know helping with that, even if they were just doing their job."

Ollie could see the subject bothered her and couldn't help but wonder why. "Why did you refuse help?"

"I have a severe dislike of being touched by people. Unfortunately, my mother insisted my bridal dress have a million tiny buttons on the back of the bodice."

"Why?"

Miss Sparrow chewed her bottom lip, then smiled when his confusion continued. "Never mind, that, Mr. McNab." But then she began to fiddle her hands together. "I do feel quite cold and cannot stand another moment of this material sticking to me. I despise the way it feels. Would you be so kind as to help me?"

Ollie nearly choked. "You want *me* to help you? I really do think Vivian—"

"Please, Ollie. I do not wish to wait until she returns. I'm very cold, the dress is exceedingly uncomfortable, and I want everything related to the earl and the wedding as far from me as possible."

"But I'm a man."

"I know. But I suppose I also consider you a friend in these circumstances. I feel far more comfortable with your help than that of any of the others."

Miss Sparrow turned her back decidedly and Ollie suddenly felt quite shy, which was unusual. He was a scoundrel, and he very well knew it. He had unfastened many a bodice in his life.

Though, for someone who rarely went without a woman at his side, it had been many months since he had enjoyed feminine companionship. Though why that was, he couldn't say. Somehow, the attention of strange women had lost its luster. Perhaps, it was merely a consequence of getting older. A sign he was growing up.

"You're completely sure you want my help with this?" Ollie decided it best to give her one more chance to back out.

"Yes, Mr. McNab." She glanced over her shoulder and tried not to smile.

Ollie cleared his throat. "I will do my best not to touch you, then, but these are rather small buttons."

Miss Sparrow gave a single nod, and he began first by lifting the veil off of her head and laying it out over the arm of a nearby chair. He then went to work on the tiny buttons. It was rather unfortunate he did not have a button hook handy, as it took a bit to unfasten one.

"This is ridiculous," Ollie mumbled to himself with frustration after taking several minutes to only unfasten three buttons. "It would make more sense to cut these off."

But Miss Sparrow wouldn't have it. "I know it seems nonsensical, but I would like to return the dress to my family in the best shape possible, as they purchased it for me. I feel like I owe that to them, at the very least."

Ollie frowned to himself and didn't argue back. Five buttons had been unfastened. As a log popped in the fireplace, he fiddled with button six. The back of her bodice was now starting to yawn open, exposing a sliver of her bare back, causing Ollie to flush.

"I'm afraid, with the way that it is opening, that I may brush against you."

She didn't respond, so he continued.

Now three-quarters of the way through, the bodice completely exposed the top of her bare back and, also, white, lacy undergarments. This startled him, causing a knuckle to brush against her bare skin. It was warm, and soft, and goosebumps rose across its surface.

Miss Sparrow stiffened severely.

"Sorry." Ollie choked the word out. It then hit him hard. "Oh, I am an idiot," he mumbled.

"Why?"

"I figured out why the buttons had to be at the back of your bodice." A sick feeling roiled through him at the thought of a man Miss Sparrow detested undressing her with greed.

"Yes," she responded after a moment. "Now that I'm being undressed, I'm rather glad it is *you* behind me at the moment."

Ollie clenched his jaw severely at the comment she clearly didn't realize held innuendo, especially to a scoundrel like him.

Finally, the last button was released, and Ollie helped pull the bodice off one arm. Miss Sparrow turned toward him in order to pull it off the other arm.

The bodice now released, she reached back behind her and unfastened the skirt of her dress, letting it squelch to the floor.

Amused by the noise, she looked up at Ollie with a grin. Her bridal hairstyle, which probably had looked stunning hours earlier, was just starting to dry and the edges were frizzing. Little, red tufts stuck to her face, neck, and shoulders. And the wet, white chemise she wore was thin and clung to every inch of her body, revealing a small waist that flared out to wide, perfect, round hips normally hidden under a skirt. Nothing was concealed except the location of her freckles on pale skin.

Despite the wild state of her hair and clothes, she was absolutely breathtaking. And something about seeing her in such a raw state turned Ollie's blood hot. "That blanket looks soaked through. Let me find you another." His voice cracked as he hurried away. He had always enjoyed Miss Sparrow's company, finding the woman endlessly fascinating. But it was only now that her beauty ran him over like a stampede of horses. How had he never realized it before?

The image of her in a wet, clingy bridal chemise was going to haunt him for the rest of his life.

Ollie returned with a fresh wool blanket and turned to give her privacy to undress.

"You may turn around now, Mr. McNab," she said after a moment and she let out a chuckle as he did so. "You look quite embarrassed."

Shame radiated from his face. "I should probably tell you that your wet chemise didn't hide anything."

She merely raised one eyebrow and pulled the brown blanket tighter as she walked over to the sofa in front of the fire. As she sat, the blanket opened just enough to expose one bare, pale leg from the knee down. "Does nudity make you uncomfortable?"

Ollie was normally a very confident man, particularly around women. So why did he feel so ridiculous around her? "Not really, but you're...well...you know."

"An innocent?"

"You said you dislike being touched. I imagine, then, you must despise any sort of, erm, bodily exposure."

"While it is true I despise touch, nudity does not, in fact, bother me at all. Consider my career, Mr. McNab. For the better part of a decade, I've been surrounded by more human forms without clothing, than with. Think of the statues, the paintings, you see when you go to the National Gallery. I see more nude forms on a daily basis than clothed. Personally, I think nothing of it."

They stared at each other, him flustered, her smirking at his bashfulness. *Get a hold of yourself, man!*

Needing to do something, Ollie gathered up Miss Sparrow's wet garments and meticulously laid them out over furniture and across the floor to, hopefully, dry overnight.

As he completed the task, she said, "I suppose it doesn't make sense to continue using formal address now that you've seen me in my bridal chemise. At least when away from the ears of others."

Rather surprised by her bluntness, he looked back at her. "Perhaps. If you wish."

"I will be staying here for a short time, after all." The amusement of the moment melted from her face, however. She pulled the blanket around her even tighter and looked down at the floor. "Thank you for helping me, Ollie."

Hearing her say his name felt strange, but not in a bad way. He sat on the other end of the sofa. "I'm glad I can," he said, meaning it in every possible sense. "Evelyn." She was graceful, but he felt like a bumbling fool, as if he were a tot speaking a new word.

Thankfully, she didn't seem to realize that, but there was a quirk of her lips and a flush on her cheeks. "I apologize for not telling you about all of this yesterday."

"Why didn't you?" Ollie asked gently. "Surely, you know you could have."

She kept her eyes averted but gave a small smile. "I was doing my best to not think about it too much, I suppose. I felt that I was a bucket filled to the brim, and one more drop would send me over the edge." She paused. "Which did happen, anyway."

"I'm glad you ran."

She turned her head to him, surprise on her face. "You are?"

"Yes. I don't know anything about the man you were supposed to marry today, but it's quite clear to me that the idea of becoming his wife distressed you. I'm glad you got yourself away. What do you plan to do, though?"

She looked crestfallen. "I don't know. I don't know, Ollie."

He rubbed at his jaw in thought. "Well, let's worry about today. I work until the wee hours of the morning, so I have to return downstairs. But I can have food sent up here and then come back tomorrow after I get a few hours' sleep? How does that sound?"

Her wide eyes flew up to his. "I'll be alone in this building over night?"

His brow furrowed. "Yes, the pub closes and then we all head home."

"Could you come back up?" Evelyn stammered. "I don't want

to be alone."

"I think Vivian or Lady Litchfield could stay with you. Which one of them is returning?"

"I don't know. But both of them have family at home. Lady Litchfield has young children, and Lady Vivian has her husband. I really don't want to be an imposition on them."

Caution snaked through him, but he ignored it. It was one night, and he could easily keep separate. "I suppose I can sleep on the sofa for one night."

Evelyn's shoulders dropped. "Oh, thank you, Ollie. I owe you so much for this."

"You're already helping my family," he replied. But what would happen to Dantes's art collection now? Ollie was responsible for it, and he took that quite seriously. And after the way he'd botched everything so terribly today, the last thing he needed to do was also ruin Dantes's most prized possessions. He would figure it out tomorrow.

Chapter Five

AFTER OLLIE HAD left, and while Evelyn waited for the spare clothing, Evelyn decided to explore the flat. This was where Mr. Dantes McNab had lived when his artwork had been ruined by fire. Now he lived with his new wife elsewhere, and everything here had been replaced and was brand new. Though about the time the pub had reopened, Ollie had mentioned sometimes he or his oldest brother would stay in this flat overnight if they were too tired to make it home. She supposed that would be changing if it was going to be leased out.

As she did a loop around the room, she came to stop at the fireplace. Mantels were usually where important personal items were kept and here, she found the tintype of Ollie's parents that she had restored previously. It surprised her Mr. Dantes McNab had not taken it with him, but she supposed it belonged to all of the McNabs, so it made sense to leave it in a shared but private space.

Gently, Evelyn allowed one arm through the gap in wool blanket and lifted the photograph to study it closer. Ollie looked so much like his mother, while his older brothers took after their father. She wondered what they had been like, and she briefly considered asking Ollie before recalling he'd never known them.

A knock on the door took Evelyn's attention away from her thoughts and she set the tintype back onto the mantel. When she asked who was at the door, a woman's voice replied, "It's Anne Winthrop! And I've brought clothes!"

Relieved, Evelyn opened the door to find Lady Litchfield with a mish-mash of clothing draped over one arm. She bounded in. "I wanted to do my part and since Vivian has clothes that will fit you better than mine, I offered to bring them over. I do have to make it quick, though. A maid is outside waiting for me in the carriage, and I don't like leaving the children for too long at night." She paused, as if realizing how that sounded. "They're not alone, of course. Their governess is there, as well as the servants. But I prefer being there with them."

Evelyn recalled that, several months ago, Ollie had commented Lady Litchfield was married to Vivian's brother and that was how they knew each other. "What about your husband? Isn't he there with them?"

Lady Litchfield paled. "Oh! Well, he's away at the moment." She cleared her throat and looked away quickly before laying the garments out one by one over the sofa cushions. "I brought you a few day dresses, two nightgowns, chemises, bloomers, stockings. The undergarments have yet to be worn. Unfortunately, you're on your own with shoes, so you may want to make sure the ones you wore today dry out." Lady Litchfield then lifted a navy dress to Evelyn's front. "The hems and sleeves might be a bit short for you, and the bust a bit roomy. But it's better than nothing."

"Thank you for bringing these to me," Evelyn said. "I've never found a nightgown so appealing as these and cannot wait to pull it on after being caught in the rain."

Lady Litchfield laughed before resting her fists on her hips. She looked Evelyn over. "Now, I didn't want to ask earlier, but if you're betrothed to an earl, you must be from a family I may know?"

Evelyn gave a hesitant nod. "My father is the Baron Cheswick."

"Oh! I believe my husband and your father have played card games together at White's."

"Very likely."

"We've probably seen each other at balls and other events."

"Yes, probably." But Evelyn wasn't thinking about balls and other events. "Forgive me if this is too intrusive but, are you happy?"

The marchioness's fists fell. "Am I happy? Whatever do you mean?" She released a nervous chuckle.

"I've heard stories from Ollie—Mr. McNab."

Lady Litchfield's eyebrows lifted.

Evelyn shifted, uncomfortable. "I apologize. I shouldn't have asked."

The marchioness stepped forward. "No, it's quite all right. Am I happy being married to my husband? No, I'm not." She shrugged. "It doesn't do me any good lying about that to you. I am sorry to hear your parents put their sights on the Earl of Wellingham, of all people. I do not much like that man. He seems rather old for you, though, doesn't he? It would be one thing if he had a modicum of charm, but he is rather boorish. And he sneezes at the most obnoxious volume."

Evelyn had also made the same observation. "Yes, he does."

Both women looked at each other with amusement. Even though Lady Litchfield was older than Evelyn, and a mother with young children, she understood what it was like to be under the thumb of aristocratic men. Her separation afforded her some freedoms, but she would never be free entirely unless something were to happen to her husband. In the moment, it helped Evelyn's mood lift just a bit, knowing that someone out there kind of, sort of, understood.

"So, you and Mr. Ollie McNab are friends?" Lady Litchfield asked casually.

"Yes, I suppose we are. I'm sure you know about the paintings I am restoring for his brother?"

Lady Litchfield nodded.

"Mr. McNab is the one with whom I speak about it. The family contact, I suppose. He comes in to visit every day to see how it's coming along."

Lady Litchfield tilted her head and gave Evelyn a curious look over. "He goes in every single day?"

"Yes." Evelyn wondered why Lady Litchfield was questioning that. "Almost every single day. Not on weekends, of course."

"No. Of course not." The marchioness paused. "And you came here when you needed help."

Evelyn wasn't sure what Lady Litchfield was trying to understand. "My family would never think to look for me here."

"Right." For some strange reason, Lady Litchfield did not seem to believe this reasoning, though for the life of Evelyn, she could not figure out why.

A concerning thought crossed Evelyn's mind, though. "You're not going to tell people I'm here?"

The marchioness placed a hand over her heart. "Heavens, no! Please, do not worry about that. I will say, though, that you must realize this isn't going to simply go away. You may have bought yourself more time, but I would hazard a guess your parents will only be more determined to throw you down the aisle when they find you."

Evelyn pulled the loosening blanket tight again and sunk into a chair, defeated. "I'm trying not to think about it."

"Well, I think it's best to warn you. You will be talked about endlessly. People will say very unkind things about you, perhaps even to your face. But it won't last forever, either. Eventually, parlors and drawing rooms will tire of you and move onto the next scandal. And there will always be another scandal."

The use of the word *scandal* made Evelyn wince. Up till now, she had been focusing only on running away and finding safety. But now that the dust was settling, it was quite clear that there would be severe repercussions.

"What do you plan on doing?" Lady Litchfield asked in a gentle voice.

Evelyn studied the fire. She only had permission to be at the flat for a few days. But then what? "I suppose leave the country," she joked. "In truth, I have no idea what I can do. Mr. McNab was asking me the same question not too long ago. I hope I'll figure it out."

But when Evelyn looked back up to the marchioness, she noted the woman looked at her with a tight smile.

Not that Evelyn blamed the marchioness. She couldn't run forever. Eventually, she would have to go home. And she also knew Papa would not give up on her marrying the earl.

Lady Litchfield departed soon after, leaving Evelyn alone once more. And in this solitude, exhaustion from the relentless anxiety and emotion and all that running through London caught up to her. She changed into a nightgown that was three inches too short, but it was soft and warm, then went to the washstand behind a screen. Lady Litchfield had also provided a small cloth bag with lilac-scented soap, a toothbrush, and toothpaste. And while Evelyn changed, she overheard Ollie come in, call out that he had left food for her on the counter, and promptly left.

Too exhausted to peek in on the food, Evelyn collapsed into bed instead, hoping to rest for a short moment before eating. After turning on her side, she listened closely and could just barely hear the hum of the pub below. And soon, she was asleep.

WHEN THE PUB closed for the night, Ollie informed his brothers of Evelyn's fear of being alone and his plan to stay the first night. Dantes thought it a lark, telling Ollie, "She's afraid of the dark, but not the pub's biggest scoundrel?" Ollie knew Dantes was trying to lighten the mood after all the mistakes Ollie had made earlier, but it only made him feel worse. Ollie also won a scowl from Victor, and a few sighs, but, surprisingly, his brother made no argument about the "inappropriateness" of Ollie sleeping on the sofa. And as soon as he was able to, Ollie hurried upstairs and unlocked the door, shutting it behind him as quietly as he could.

The horrid day had taken its toll, and Victor was still furious with him over how much he'd blundered. Ollie would have to be extra careful and make sure he didn't fail elsewhere for a long while or he'd irrevocably damage his relationship with his brother.

Somehow, he needed to redeem himself.

The fire he had lit earlier in the flat was now hardly a faint, orange glow. Ollie tiptoed through the flat and peeked into the bedroom to ensure Evelyn was still there.

The woman, to his great relief, was out cold. He shut the door quietly.

After he readied for sleep and headed to the sofa, though, he noticed the food he had sent up for her earlier still sat untouched. She must have fallen asleep before she'd had a chance to eat.

Thus, the next morning, Ollie slipped out and went to the bakery down the block. He had no idea what she liked, so he bought several different muffins, scones, and anything else that looked appetizing.

When Ollie returned to the pub, he was surprised to find Victor there already.

"Do you ever go home?" Ollie asked, irritated.

Victor gave him a look of mild annoyance. "Of course I do. I couldn't fall back to sleep when I awoke this morning and decided to come in here and really dig into how much you lost us yesterday."

Ollie's face went hot.

Victor began scribbling a pencil across a sheet of paper. He was doing some complicated calculations that, to Ollie, may as well have been a foreign language. Then with a flourish, Victor finished and turned the paper to face Ollie, circling a large number at the bottom.

"What is that?" Ollie asked, uneasy.

"That's how much money we lost yesterday because of you. As you can see, it is not insignificant. Now, I know you think money flows endless like a river, as that's what our grandparents have led you to believe, but in the real world, money is *not* endless and if you lose too much of it, you lose your home and the food on your table. Then you end up living on the streets."

Ollie had to bite the inside of his cheek. The loss from yesterday had been far, far higher than they'd initially estimated.

"I'm hiring extra help for the next few weeks," Victor said.

"Why?"

"Because you cannot step foot in here until we've recovered financially."

Ollie squeezed the paper bakery bag in his hand when Victor shoved the piece of paper at Ollie's face. "I am not paying you to destroy my business and my livelihood because you're too daft to function!"

Ollie clenched his jaw tight. It was just as much Ollie's business as it was Victor's. But how could he speak up in this moment? Victor was right. Ollie was not smart, and it wasn't a big secret.

"Look, why don't I just pay you for what happened today? It is a lot, but I can cover it, too."

"No," Victor replied in a dark voice. "As I've already said, that defeats the purpose."

"But—"

"Also…" Victor pulled a newspaper out from under the bartop and slapped it down. "Miss Sparrow needs to leave the premises."

Raw anger flooded Ollie now. Who the blazes did Victor think he was? How could he cast off a woman in a desperate situation like that?

But then, Ollie looked down at the newspaper. And what he found made his heart stop.

In bold letters at the top was *Family of Runaway Bride Offers Reward for Her Return*

And below that was a picture of Evelyn. Ollie didn't bother reading the article—he couldn't stomach it—and slid the newspaper back to Victor. It wasn't so long ago that the newspapers had hounded his sister-in-law when she'd unexpectedly inherited a fortune. And then, the fire that had burned down The Harp & Thistle. Now they were harassing Evelyn, too? "Is this your plan to recover financially from my stupidity? Turning Miss Sparrow in for a reward?"

Victor crossed his arms. "No. But I also will not house a fugitive. She must leave today."

"She's not a *fugitive!*"

"She may as well be. All of London will be looking for her at that price. She needs to go back to her family, Ollie." Victor's face softened ever so slightly. "I am sorry for her predicament, but there is nothing we can do to help her. Surely, you understand that?"

Ollie shot Victor several choice words, grabbed the newspaper, and stormed up the stairs.

When he opened the door and headed in, he was surprised to find Evelyn appearing from the hallway. She wore a nightgown, and her hair was adorably messy, but she seemed to glow with rest. "There you are, Ollie. I just woke up and didn't know where you were."

He swallowed hard and tossed the paper bag and newspaper on the table before cleaning up the old food. The ire roused from Victor was replaced with the concern he had for Evelyn. "I saw you didn't eat last night, so I ran out to get breakfast."

Evelyn opened the bag and pulled out a muffin. "Thank you, Ollie. I meant to, after I'd gone to lie down for only a short while, but I fell asleep for the night instead. Apparently, sprinting about London in the rain makes one quite tired." She met his eye for a moment and concern pulled at her brow. "Are you cross with me? You look upset."

Ollie rubbed a palm over his jaw. "No. I had some words with Victor is all."

Evelyn took a thoughtful bite of her muffin, chewed, and swallowed. "Does he ever go home?"

Ollie chuckled, but the seriousness of the matter cut it short. "I, apparently, am not allowed to return to work for some time."

Evelyn took a seat at the table and motioned for Ollie to join. He did and grabbed a muffin for himself.

"Tell me what happened," she said before taking another bite.

And he did. How daft she must have thought he was! "I can't believe I bungled everything so badly," he said, feeling sick. "It's one thing to break a glass, or charge one order wrong, or miscount change one or two times. But how does someone make as many mistakes as I did?"

"I'm sorry, Ollie." Evelyn gave him a look of regret. "Wasn't it you, though, who said everything always has a way of working itself out?"

He shifted. "Yes. And it will work out eventually. But I've always gotten such little respect from Victor, and even Dantes sometimes. I really don't think they'll look at me the same again after this."

"Does that matter to you? What your brothers think of you?"

This question surprised him. "Of course it does. Doesn't it matter to you what your family thinks of you? At least, to some degree?"

Evelyn seemed to be contemplating this question as she took another thoughtful bite of her muffin and chewed slowly.

This seemed to be a good time to bring up the reward. Ollie pulled over the newspaper but didn't flip it to reveal the article about her just yet. "There's something else you should probably know."

She froze mid-chew and set the muffin down, then took a big swallow. "What is it, Ollie?"

As it would be better for her to read for herself than have him explain it to her he, hesitantly, turned the newspaper over so she could see the article.

Ollie watched as she read through it, her eyes darting quickly across the page. Her face paled, her lip quivered, then her shoulders tensed.

He had to give her credit, though. After the news had sunk in, she steeled herself, clasped her fingers together, and set her hands on the table. "It appears we both have our own predicaments."

Ollie rubbed at his jaw again. Now he had to make it all worse for her. "Yes, and unfortunately, because of that bit of news, Victor wants you out today."

Her face fell. "I see."

"I'm sorry." Losing his appetite, Ollie set his muffin to the side, suddenly disgusted by it.

"None of this is your fault. You don't need to apologize."

"That may well be true, but it doesn't make either one of us feel better about it, though, does it?"

"No, it doesn't." Evelyn sunk back in her chair and stared out the window in thought. He could see the inner workings of her mind whirring as she tried to calculate her next move. It was endlessly fascinating when her mind went to work like this. There had been many a time where, at the museum, she'd focus on a niche art history subject and talk to him about it for seemingly hours, with that same concentration that enveloped her now.

"I've been trying to think of what to do and I will admit I'm at a complete loss," Evelyn admitted, still staring out the window. "I was hoping I would be able to figure that out while staying here, but unfortunately, it appears my time is up."

"Out of curiosity," he hesitated, "what would happen if you returned home today?"

She began picking invisible crumbs up from the table surface. "Oh, there would be lots of shouting, and then I'd have to marry the earl regardless of my escape." She looked up. "Basically, the longer I stay away, the longer I delay the inevitable."

Ollie frowned. "What are you saying, that you're going to go home today?"

"What else could I do?"

"You don't have friends you could stay with?"

"None who would be able to keep me hidden from my family—they know who my friends are. And even if they did take me in, what am I supposed to do, hide there for the remainder of my life? Plus, I really can't hide anywhere else now. That reward they are offering is far too high. Few could resist something like that." She stared down at the newspaper. "My family is better off financially than many, but they don't have that kind of money readily available, either. I bet the earl is funding this." Her bottom lip began to quiver. "Oh, my parents must be so humiliated right now."

Ollie nearly reached out to put his hand over hers in comfort but stopped himself, remembering how much she disliked being touched.

"Do you want me to bring you home?" Ollie said it gently, hating the thought, but if that was what Evelyn wanted, what was he supposed to do?

Evelyn smiled, but it was more pitying than anything. "It appears I have no choice." And with that, she rose up. "I should go wash up and get dressed." She paused and turned back to face him. "You will bring me home, though? I think I may be able to get through the cab ride if you're with me. I understand if you don't wish to, though. It will cause an uproar if anyone discovered us together without a chaperone."

Ollie shrugged, not one to care much about lack of chaperones. "If that's what you want, it's the least I can do." Since he'd failed at giving her the help he had promised.

"You've done plenty already, Ollie. Thank you. Truly." And with that, Evelyn hurried off.

Ollie stared at the spot where she'd disappeared into the hallway. There was a feeling of despair left behind. Needing to distract himself from it, Ollie picked up the newspaper, ignoring the article about Evelyn, and began to read. One particular article caught his interest.

The Signature Swindler Strikes Again!

For the past few years, London has been hit by a rash of burglaries and last night was business as usual in that regard. The Signature Swindler, London's most famous thief, has struck again, shocking Scotland Yard with a new boldness: fine art theft.

An art heist! How fascinating. Ollie continued reading, eager to know the rest.

> *For some time, the Signature Swindler has stolen small but high-value items such as jewelry and pocket watches from their respective stores and wealthy owners. But with increased confidence, the thief appears to have moved on to bigger, more valuable objects.*
>
> *The museum director at the Bethnal Green Museum was making his morning rounds when he discovered three highly prized paintings had been stolen overnight: two Rembrandts and a Fragonard. This journalist was unable to hear between the museum director's sobs which specific artworks had been taken.*

Ollie lifted his head when he heard Evelyn return. "Look at this," he said with a bit of excitement. "There was a heist last night."

Evelyn's eyes went wide. "Where?"

"The Bethnal Green Museum."

Evelyn's shoulders fell with relief. "Oh, thank heavens it was not the National Gallery. May I see?"

Ollie handed the newspaper to her, and she read through it. "We've been worried about this," Evelyn said as her eyes darted back and forth on the page.

"About what, art theft?"

"About the Signature Swindler progressing to art theft. He's quite successful at what he does, unfortunately."

Ollie had never heard of this particular thief before. "You're familiar with him, then?"

Evelyn nodded vehemently. "Oh, yes, he's been the talk of the art community for a while now. We knew it was only a matter of time until he worked his way to robbing museums." She glanced down at the article and swallowed. "It appears now he has."

"Why do they call him that? 'The Signature Swindler'?"

Evelyn set the newspaper back on the table. "Rumor is he signs his name wherever he steals from."

"Signs his name?" How strange. "Then they should be able to find him easily, don't you think?"

Evelyn bit her lip in thought. "That's what I've been wondering, too. If he leaves his signature behind, why can't they find him? And, if he signs his name, why give him a moniker?"

"Maybe that's the newspapers' doing. They gave Vivian a moniker before, calling her *Britain's Richest Spinster* every time they talked about her in articles."

"I forgot about that! But yes, that is very true. Journalists do love outlandish monikers, don't they? But there must be a reason why they created it in the first place. However, the police have not released any information about that. I know people who have asked them about the roots of the moniker, and each time, the police refused to comment."

"What a mystery. There must be something they're hiding from the public."

"Oh, yes, I agree." Evelyn stared down at the newspaper but didn't seem to be focusing on it. Raw emotion radiated out from her, and Ollie wondered what she was thinking about. "Well, I suppose this isn't any of my concern any longer."

"What, the thief? Why not?"

She gave him a small smile. "Ollie, surely you understand I'll never set foot in the museum again once I'm married to the earl. It isn't a concern of mine that the Signature Swindler might target the National Gallery.

He frowned. "I *don't* understand, actually."

"I don't know when the wedding will take place now, but I won't be allowed to return to work. A countess doesn't work. In truth, no married women from the aristocracy work."

So, he would never see her ever again? Ollie was more distressed by this than he ever would have expected. But then he realized why: Dantes's artwork. Yes, that must have been it. "What about my brother's artwork?"

"I'm sure they'll find someone to replace me."

"But—"

Evelyn suddenly turned away, and her emotion seemed to dissipate, replaced by a hard wall. "I don't wish to dwell on this, Ollie. Your concerns are valid, but I assure you the museum will see that the artwork continues to be worked on. Now, I must get ready to return home."

Chapter Six

WHILE THE PREVIOUS day had been filled with rain and heavy, gray clouds, this day was starkly different. The sun was out and Londoners of all walks of life left their homes to enjoy the weather.

Evelyn was seated beside Ollie in the hansom cab he'd hired to bring her home. Also beside Evelyn was the clothing Lady Litchfield and Lady Vivian had kindly collected for her, which Ollie had promised to return after dropping Evelyn off at home along with the boxed-up wedding dress. At a later date, Evelyn would send back the clothing she currently wore.

The hansom rolled to a stop to make a turn and Evelyn watched the pedestrians cross. Her attention was captured by a man and woman holding on tightly to one another. She had no idea who they were, merely strangers with whom she'd happened to cross paths. Their clothing was plain, perhaps even a bit worn.

The woman said something, and the man laughed and leaned down to press a kiss to her cheek, causing his companion to wobble. The couple had wheels on their shoes—roller skates— and the man did his best to keep the woman from falling over. Both of them kept laughing at themselves. Evelyn had never experienced having a beau of her own, a man who walked—or in this case, skated—by her side, one she was glad to have there. Back when she'd lived in Paris, she had befriended several famous artists and caught the eye of a few. But as much as she admired them for their craft, they were not men whose attention she desired. They were all scoundrels, in the worst way.

Edgar Degas was the worst one, at least Evelyn thought. The only compliment she could give him was he was a talented artist. Nothing about him otherwise was admirable or likable. In the company of other artists, his tongue was sharp—cruel wit at the expense of others. He was the equivalent of a wet rag.

Evelyn's sister, a patron of the arts, had briefly had her eyes on Degas for some reason. Cordelia had called him "mysterious" and "an enigma." Evelyn had kept her mouth shut, as she'd known well enough that artists as a whole were impossible humans and Degas had, on numerous occasions, voiced his baseless belief that women artists could never be as good as their male counterparts. *"It is simply biology,"* he had explained over the rim of his absinthe. *"Go ahead and disagree with science. Men have bigger brains. We can't help it."*

Degas was also the only man who had ever laughed in Cordelia's face when she'd advanced upon him. *"I do not mix my personal life with art,"* he had said loud enough for the room to hear. *"You will never set foot in my life beyond the walking path outside my door, and you will never see anything beyond my paintings."* He'd then slammed his drink down to the table and stormed out of the room, leaving the party in a stunned silence.

"We should be at your house in about fifteen minutes." Ollie's voice grabbed Evelyn's attention. "Not that I'm counting down the minutes or anything. I just feel like I should be saying something."

Evelyn smiled despite herself. "Of course you're not, Ollie. I realize I am not much in a talkative mood at the moment, as my mind keeps finding itself elsewhere." *Probably to escape*, she thought.

Ollie held her gaze. "Where does your mind find itself?"

The hansom cab began moving again and Evelyn glanced over to see the couple she had been watching had disappeared from view. "Nowhere particular. Revisiting old memories, I suppose."

"Anything you'd be willing to share?"

Was he truly interested? Or was this part of Ollie's natural outgoing charm, and it only seemed as if he were interested in knowing? She swallowed and forced her focus on Ollie's question. "I was thinking about Edgar Degas," she replied.

"The artist?" Ollie asked, his voice pitched with surprise.

"Yes."

Ollie watched her, waiting for her to continue. "Do you know him? Are you friends?"

Evelyn shrugged. "I suppose, if that's what you want to call it."

A muscle ticked in his jaw. "You were friends with many artists in Paris, then?"

"Of course! I worked at the Louvre, and my sister is a patron of the arts. She often took me to parties in Montmartre. I knew all of them to some degree." Evelyn began counting on her fingers. "Degas, Cassatt, Monet, though he was not a sociable sort and kept to himself mostly. There were also Berthe Morisot—I did find Berthe to be a dear—Renoir, Gaugin. Oh! And Toulouse-Lautrec, of course! I did adore him most of all, and I wish our friendship hadn't been so brief. I moved back to London right after we became acquainted. Unlike the others, he was my age. Actually, he exhibited at the Salon for the first time this year, I heard!"

Ollie sunk into his seat. "I recognize most of those names."

"It was a brief but fun time in my life," Evelyn said wistfully.

"This Toulouse-Lautrec. You liked him much?"

"Oh, yes! I..." She giggled. "It seems silly now, but I became a blushing girl around him. He was very kind and very funny. I met him at cabaret, where he was showcasing his artwork."

"I see," Ollie said blandly.

"He told me I was too tall for his taste. And too thin." She felt heat crawl up her neck. "He fell in love with Suzanne, anyway."

Ollie ignored that last comment. "Too tall and too thin?"

Evelyn forced a casual shrug. "Everyone has different taste."

"That isn't a difference in taste. The man clearly was mad."

What was Ollie saying? Did he think she was attractive? Her? But that was silly and Evelyn immediately scolded herself for thinking that even a moment. Ollie was only saying that to make her feel better.

"I'm six feet tall," Evelyn explained while reaching up to feel her hair. "And Henri is only five feet tall. He broke his legs when he was a child and they stopped growing. He prefers women to be, well, shorter than me at least."

Ollie seemed to relax at that tidbit and didn't offer further comment.

"What are you going to do about work, Ollie?" Evelyn noted the homes around them were becoming grander. They were getting close.

Ollie let out a long sigh. "I don't know. Honestly, I'm more worried about Dantes's paintings at the moment."

"Why?"

"I don't know." He paused. "I hope they get the same care you gave them. With how much I blundered yesterday, I'm afraid I'll now ruin the whole paintings business and go make everything worse."

Evelyn frowned. "Ollie, I assure you, they remain in good hands. Mr. Currow and Mr. Burlington have assisted with several of the paintings already restored. They are more than capable." Annoyance crawled through her. She was on her way home where she would be met with wrath of the highest order, and Ollie wanted to add this guilt and worry? "Do you think I'm pleased to be leaving that behind? That I won't be able to work on them any longer? All I wish is to return there and I can't."

Thankfully, he dropped the subject. Because the next words out of his mouth were, "What in the blazes is happening up there?"

Evelyn's attention sharpened and she began looking around.

"Where?"

"Up ahead, on my side."

Evelyn scrambled over Ollie to see his view, as the horse blocked hers. She ignored how hard his torso and chest felt under her. Sure enough, up ahead, several policemen were standing on the sidewalk.

Evelyn's curiosity was piqued. "Why are there so many police officers crowded up there?"

"I don't know," Ollie replied in a strained voice.

Putting her attention back to Ollie, she realized his face was quite close. Her eyes immediately looked down to his lips. They were appealing, full and soft with a cupid's bow, and would be beautiful in a painting. A strange feeling swirled in her stomach as Ollie made another strained noise. She was crushing him and immediately crawled back to her side of the hansom. "I am so very sorry. I didn't mean to crush you like that. Curiosity got the best of me, and I wasn't paying attention to what I was doing."

He cleared his throat. "You were lying on top of me, Evelyn."

Concern twisted within her. "Did I hurt you? I do apologize for that."

"I… Oh, blast it," Ollie replied, running his hands through his hair.

"I wonder…" Evelyn tapped at her chin in thought, already distracted. "Do you think that crowd of police officers has anything to do with the Signature Swindler?"

"I have no idea."

She felt a slight, unpleasant pang of guilt. "You seem upset with me."

"Upset? No. Exasperated? Perhaps."

But before she could reply—exasperated by what?—the driver called back over his shoulder. "Your stop is just ahead!"

"Thank you, sir!" Evelyn called back right as the horror of realization struck her. She looked out at the street and the buildings—really studied her surroundings—and panicked as she recognized them. "Oh, no," she said to herself. Then she clambered over Ollie again, causing him to groan.

"Ollie…" The panic in her voice was loud and clear. "Those police aren't there for the Signature Swindler."

"They're not?" His voice pitched higher than normal.

Evelyn looked back over to him and found his face reddened and his hands clasped together atop his head, as if trying to keep them away from something.

"What are you doing?" Evelyn asked, looking up at them.

"You, a person who despises being touched, are on all fours, atop me. Again. And I am a man, a simple one at that, and remain a man at the most inopportune times."

Realizing how utterly inappropriate her behavior was, she hurried back to her side of the bench seat. "Sorry." Her hands rushed over her skirt to smooth out the fabric. "I guess in the excitement of the moment I wasn't thinking." But as Ollie opened his mouth to reply, she turned her body expectantly, distracted once again. "I know why those police are there."

Ollie shifted in his seat, tugging at the legs of his trousers. "Why?"

"Because that's my house."

"That's not good. You suppose they're there for you?"

The hansom rolled to a stop beside a police officer who was on his own, picking at his teeth. The officer looked over and made eye contact with Evelyn. Evelyn froze. Did he recognize her? She tried to imagine what would happen once she climbed out. There would surely be lots of clamoring and noise as they realized who she was.

But then, the officer turned away to continue picking at his teeth without an audience.

Evelyn let out a breath of relief. Maybe this would go better than expected.

"Welcome home, I suppose," Ollie said.

"Yes, lucky me," she replied blandly. "I can only imagine the storm awaiting me inside, especially with all of *them* here." Evelyn tried see if she could see anyone through the window but couldn't. Images of Mama, of Papa, their expressions as she waltzed in through the door formed in her mind. Would Mama faint? Would Papa shout at her?

Was the earl inside?

She resisted the urge to shudder.

Evelyn could only imagine the sneer the earl would produce upon seeing her. In fact, she wouldn't be surprised if he immediately dragged her to the nearest church.

They would surely do his bidding. He was an earl, after all.

Evelyn looked at Ollie as her heart began to race again. "I'm scared, Ollie."

Ollie's face and voice softened. "I know. I don't like this. Any of this."

"I don't have a choice." Her voice cracked. Ollie's concern for her was the only light in the harrowing moment. She wanted to delay her departure further. "Where are you going to go after this?"

"I'll drop off the clothes you're returning, and then I guess I'll go home and spend time with my cat for God knows how long. Weeks, months maybe, where I'll feel pity for myself. I'll spend too much time wondering what you're doing at any given moment. Hoping that you're happy, knowing that you're not, and feeling rubbish over it."

"You have a cat?"

Ollie gave her an amused look and there was a twinkle in his eye. "Yes, I do."

"Oh, I do adore cats. Please give them a little scratch under the chin for me."

You're sure you want to say goodbye? A little voice asked in Evelyn's mind. She had a brief flash of an image of her onboard a ship, waving at Ollie at the dock, sobbing as the ship sailed away.

That was odd. Where had that come from?

"Goodbye, Ollie." Evelyn pushed the funny image away. "Maybe we will pass each other on the street someday."

"I hope we do." Ollie climbed out of the hansom and extended a hand to help her down. Briefly, she hesitated at the potential touch but forced herself through it, as it was an automatic reaction on his part. She accepted his offer of help. As her feet met the pavement, she held Ollie's gaze. His hand felt warm and strong against hers. Emotion crackled, but all he offered was a small farewell nod. And then, he let her go.

She turned her back to him for the last time and forced herself forward, one foot in front of the other, until she approached her front door.

"Who are you?" One of the officers stepped into view, blocking the door. He studied her red hair. "Are you that runaway bride?"

Fear rendered Evelyn mute.

Another officer joined. "She sure looks like her, doesn't she?" He scratched at his head by pushing his hat up. "What was her name?"

"Ellen, I think?" the first officer replied. "Are you Ellen?"

"Ellen?" Evelyn blinked. "No, I've never heard of Ellen before."

"It's not her, then."

"Blimey."

Evelyn moved one step forward.

But the first officer laid a heavy hand on her shoulder to stop her. "Where do you think you're going?"

Her body screamed at the feeling of a strange man's hand on her shoulder. She shrugged her shoulder hard to fling it off.

A flash of anger crossed the officer's face.

"I'm going to the house." She indicated toward her home, affronted by the audacity of this man. It didn't matter that he was an officer of the law. Who did he think he was to put his hand on her, to stop her from going where she pleased?

"You're staying right here, miss, until we know your business here. The family up there is frantically searching for their missing daughter. You've surely seen the paper this morning? There's a large reward for her return!"

"How can they be searching for her if they're inside?" Evelyn asked wryly.

The two officers exchanged looks of bewilderment. "Have you come to collect the reward?" one asked.

"Do I get the reward if I turn myself in?"

"I—" The man stared at her totally befuddled. "Why, you impertinent—"

"Hush up now, will you?" The other officer elbowed him hard. "If this is the runaway bride, running your mouth will only get you in a load of trouble with the boss."

The officer scowled at Evelyn. "Stay here," he said authoritatively before he went into the house. One by one, the other officers in the crowd began to notice her. And one by one, the voices dropped from their conversations.

Evelyn felt as if every pair of eyes in the world now stared at her.

The front door flew open, loud in the sudden silence, and Papa's lanky form appeared in the doorway. He ducked under the awning to walk through it. "Evelyn!" He shouted so loud, it made her jump.

The earl followed him out.

Evelyn felt the blood drain from her face upon seeing the earl. Her heart began to pound hard with panic. Her nerves twitched all over her body. She should have been stepping forward to meet her father, she should have been going toward the house.

But she couldn't move.

Again.

"What the blazes do you think you're doing?" Papa now stood before her and hissed the words as low as he could. "Are you trying to drive us to madness?"

"No."

"Have you *gone* mad?"

"No!"

"Then explain where you've been and why you ran off yesterday! Did you know your mother and sister and I looked all over London until sunrise this morning?"

Evelyn looked at the ground.

"Do you care at all about our worry? For heaven's sake, Evelyn." Papa ran his hands through his orange hair. "Do you think about anyone but yourself?"

Hot tears welled up in her eyes. But what could she say? She'd been selfish for running away. It hadn't occurred to her how much her parents would worry. It hadn't occurred to her they would go looking for her until sunrise.

"All I wanted was to get away," she said, and she knew it made no sense the moment the words had left her mouth. And how horrifically selfish it sounded.

But before Papa could respond, the earl spoke. "Well," he said, his voice far calmer than Papa's. Too calm. Frighteningly calm. Despite the fear he instilled, she looked up to see him.

The pupils in his eyes were huge, and there was a wickedness to the mild smile he offered her. "Where is your pretty, white dress, Evelyn? You did look so beautiful in it yesterday."

She was too frightened to respond, to admit she had forgotten it in the hansom. Nervous, she glanced around and realized the police officers had surrounded them to watch the show.

But then something beyond the crowd caught her eye. Ollie was still here! He was about twenty feet away, though, watching the scene grimly from a distance.

When she turned back around, she met her father's eye. He, too, looked in the direction of Ollie, then back at her. She couldn't tell if he knew whom she was looking at.

Regardless, he didn't say a word.

"Well," the earl continued, "I suppose it doesn't matter. Quickly, though, we must depart. Now. Whatever it is that you are wearing…" He frowned at the too-short dress. "It will have to do."

Evelyn swallowed. "'Have to do'?"

"Come now, darling," the earl said. He reached up to her hair and twirled a strand around his finger, staring at it. "Our time awaits. You didn't really think you could get away from me, could you?" He leaned over to her ear. "You belong to me already, Miss Sparrow. I own you, and running cannot change that. Go to the ends of the Earth, and I promise I will come drag you back."

The earl grabbed her shoulders tightly, squeezing them in his hands with all his might. Evelyn yelped with pain, but this only seemed to flame the earl further and he shook her.

"You will do as promised to me. You will get in my carriage right now. We will be going back to the blasted church and then we will be going back to my home. You can thank your antics for this: You will never see your home or family again."

Papa stepped forward. "Now wait just a minute. That was not part of the deal."

The earl dug his fingers harder into her shoulders. Her body screamed in response. "It wasn't in the deal that she would run off like that, either, now was it?"

This rendered Papa silent.

While the crowd of officers and curiosity seekers watched, the earl spun Evelyn around to his carriage, its door yawned open, waiting to pull her into its depths of hell.

The earl pushed her toward it. And then, something quite unexpected happened.

"Get your blasted hands off of her!" A man's deep, velvet voice caused the earl to stop.

Evelyn was surprised to find Ollie staring down the earl with fury. His green eyes were wild, holding a look she had never seen on him before. He pushed the sleeves of his jacket and shirt up to his elbows, as if he were preparing for a fight.

Evelyn expected the earl to throw her into his carriage but, to her surprise, he let her go entirely and seemed to forget all about her. "Who are you to dare speak to me that way?" The earl sneered as he looked over Ollie. "London scum needs to learn its place."

Panic pounded in her ears, throbbed through her veins. Her

entire body felt as if it were on the verge of twitching erratically. Her legs begged to run, run, run again.

The noise, the activity, whirled in her mind. Everything seemed to slow.

The earl and Ollie continued their shouting. Her ears roared with her pounding heart. Her breathing quickened with it.

A man in street clothes waved the morning's newspaper at her.

Papa said her name.

She looked over to Papa. "Who is that?" he asked.

But Evelyn couldn't speak. If she did, all of the energy that boiled in her body would create a scream that would decimate the ears of everyone within a mile radius.

The earl made a stupid mistake, however, and shoved Ollie. Hard enough to make Ollie falter back.

Returning to the present, Evelyn gasped and stepped toward her friend. But he recovered quickly.

The fury that had clouded Ollie up until now exploded from him. As the earl made to lunge forward, Ollie had no choice but to pull a large fist back, then meet it with the earl's face.

The earl flew back into the wall of police officers, who scrambled to catch him. While being fussed over, the earl put a hand to his reddened cheek, his jaw dropped open, and he stared stupidly with enormous eyes, as if shocked to his very soul someone below his station had dared lay a hand on him.

And then he pointed a finger at Ollie and shouted, "Assault! Assault! That man tried to kill me!"

"*Kill* you!" Evelyn shouted back as the police officers scrambled, taking this accusation seriously despite witnessing the moment. The man in streetwear began to shove his way toward her. But she wasn't paying enough attention to notice. "You deserved every bit of that hit, and you know it," she shouted.

The earl lunged for her, but she jumped back.

Only to be accosted by a police officer.

"Unhand me!" Evelyn demanded.

"That's my daughter!" Papa bellowed from somewhere.

Someone shouted her name. Her head swiveled in that direction only to discover a man with a boxy, handheld camera pointed right at her.

Blast!

It was pandemonium. Police officers everywhere shouted to each other, fanned the earl, and ordered Evelyn to cooperate. She looked around frantically for Ollie but couldn't see him any longer.

"Evelyn!" Papa called out.

Evelyn tried to jerk away from the police officer who held her, but it was useless. "Keep it up," the officer said trying to keep her still, "and I'll have no choice but to cuff you!"

Instead, and without thinking too deeply, she kicked behind her—hard—and connected her shoe with his shin. The officer shouted out with pain, letting her go. She spotted the man with the camera again and really hoped he hadn't caught that moment.

Evelyn pushed through the crowd of scrambling police officers. Hands reached out to grab her, missing by mere centimeters. Over a man's head, she spotted Ollie again, now at the very edge of the crowd. Somehow, he had snuck through the wildness without notice from anyone, probably because her behavior was demanding everyone's attention.

Evelyn made her way out of the crowd and hurried over to Ollie.

And despite the madness, she smiled.

"Hello, Ollie," Evelyn said as she stopped before him.

"Some crowd you attract," Ollie replied before motioning her to follow him.

Evelyn glanced back. Fights had erupted everywhere, and the officers were trying to break them up, forgetting all about her.

But her father hadn't forgotten.

He watched her, a head taller than everyone else, helplessly. He was too deep into the crowd and would never make it out in time to grab her before she ran away. Again.

"Let's leave before they realize you've escaped," Ollie said.

Evelyn held her father's gaze for a beat longer before hurrying after Ollie, leaving the circus behind. "Where are we going?" she asked.

"My house," Ollie said. The hansom cab was still there, waiting. As he climbed in after her, he added, "And just so you know, you are never coming back here. As long as I can help it."

Chapter Seven

MRS. CHAPMAN, OLLIE'S housekeeper, greeted them in the entryway of his townhome. Though her perpetually heavy-lidded, dour expression remained in place, he knew she was likely surprised to see him home at this hour, as he never was. And then there was Evelyn beside him to boot.

"'Tis a bit early in the day, don't you think?" Mrs. Chapman said with a judgmental tone as she looked over Evelyn. Her light-brown hair was pulled back in its usual severe knot, which only made her sunken-cheeked face even more sinister-looking.

Ollie shot her a glare. "Could you please bring tea into the parlor for Miss Sparrow?"

"Oh, that does sound lovely after all of that," Evelyn said as she looked around. "This is your home?"

"Yes, it is." Ollie had been carrying Evelyn's pile of borrowed garments, topped by her wedding dress, and handed them to the housekeeper. While Evelyn was distracted by studying her surroundings, Ollie spoke directly to Mrs. Chapman. "Bring these up to one of the spare bedrooms."

"Not yours?" Mrs. Chapman asked with a cool expression.

"No." He paused as he considered what to say next. "She doesn't know it yet, but she's going to be here for a bit."

Mrs. Chapman's eyebrows lifted high. "Since when do you keep one of your women under your roof?"

Ollie gave Mrs. Chapman a meaningful look. "You know it's been a while since I've done any of that."

With dramatic flair, Mrs. Chapman cocked her head, as if searching her memory.

"Look, it isn't like that." Ollie had to make sure his housekeeper understood nothing was going on between him and Evelyn. He wouldn't hear the end of it otherwise. "She needed help. I'm able to offer it."

Mrs. Chapman gave Evelyn a long study before releasing a small chuckle. "Mr. McNab, do you truly expect me to believe that?" But she let out a sigh. "How long do you expect to keep her here?"

Ollie rubbed his hands over his face at her continued use of the word *keep*. "Could you please just make a room up for her?" Mrs. Chapman often struggled with the fact that Ollie wasn't her child to boss around, that he in fact was the owner of the house and she was his housekeeper. She had come to him on recommendation from Victor when she had filled in for Victor's housekeeper during a prolonged absence. It didn't occur to him that the age difference between him and his older brother would color Mrs. Chapman's view of him. "I'll explain everything later. All right?" Ollie said, making sure the frustration in his voice was apparent.

Mrs. Chapman gave him that cool expression again but turned away and left. Ollie led Evelyn into the parlor.

"You mentioned a cat earlier?" Evelyn asked, and even Ollie could tell she was trying not to sound too eager.

He couldn't help but grin. "Yes, but I have no idea where she is at the moment."

"Oh." Evelyn looked down to the ground.

"How are you feeling? Are you all right?" Ollie asked, sounding concerned. He took a few cautious steps toward Evelyn. This turn of events had been completely unexpected. What a disaster this whole situation was! But he couldn't leave her back there. And though it was rather uncouth to have her stay here, it didn't seem to be much of a choice, either.

He could only imagine what her family was going to do to track her down now.

Evelyn crossed her arms and forced a small smile. "I'm fine."

"Well, here, why don't you come rest." Ollie led her over to a sofa and directed her to put her feet up. Then he fluffed several pillows and placed them behind her. "How's that?"

"Actually, this is rather nice," she replied while running her hand over the sofa's brocade fabric.

He took a seat in a nearby chair. "I'm sorry for hitting your— I mean, the earl."

"That's quite all right, Ollie. You'll get no complaint from me."

"I'm not the type to do that, though."

"Not the type to, what, fight back?"

Ollie wanted to respond with a retort. But Evelyn was right, wasn't she? He never fought back. Whether it was a physical fight with a drunk or Victor kicking him out of their place of business, Ollie never fought back.

Even on the rare occasion there was a fight at The Harp & Thistle, it was always Dantes and Victor breaking the men up, not Ollie. The only time Ollie ever raised his fists was when he was forced to spar with Dantes for practice before his brother had a boxing match. Or like today with the earl.

That was it.

Eager to *not* respond to her question, Ollie clasped his hands together, feeling pitiful. "Again, you're not going back to your house. You do realize that."

Evelyn's throat moved on a swallow, and she nodded.

"Unless you have a better idea, you'll have to stay here until you figure out what you're going to do."

Evelyn pushed herself with her elbows. "Ollie, you know I can't do that!"

"Why not?"

"Because I would basically be living with you!"

"Not forever," he said, turning his palms up to the ceiling. "But as long as you need."

"But—"

"Who would find out?"

Evelyn frowned. "What about your housekeeper?"

"Mrs. Chapman? No, the most she would do is tut-tut at me. The cook, Mrs. Bradley, she could care less about anything as long as you compliment her cooking."

Evelyn seemed to relax a bit.

"You'll have your own room of course, plus free rein of the house. You can eat and drink whatever you wish. I know it's not as grand as your home, so I hope it suits."

"Ollie, your townhouse is lovely."

"You seem surprised by that," he said, teasing her a bit.

Evelyn's eyes briefly widened.

"Everyone looks rather comfortable here." Mrs. Chapman sidled in with tea and biscuits. "Is there anything else I can get you? Pajamas, perhaps?"

"Thank you, Mrs. Chapman." Ollie hastened the words out. "But we're fine."

She gave him a pointed expression before disappearing out into the hallway. A moment later, her voice echoed from down the hall. "Hammie! Din-din, Hammie!"

"Who is Hammie?" Evelyn sat up fully to take a sip of her tea.

"My cat."

"You named your cat Hammie?"

"Sort of." As he said this, a tiny, dainty mew came from the parlor door. Ollie found his fluffy, gray cat sitting there with big, round, gray eyes.

Evelyn gasped and placed a hand over her heart. "Oh, my goodness, what a precious little kitty!"

The cat mewed again and began walking toward them, evidently curious about the new face. She stopped a few feet away from Evelyn and stared up at her.

"Oh, and she has a precious little bow around her neck!"

Evelyn's eyes seemed to glitter with the cuteness. "Hammie, is that your name, little kitty?" Evelyn leaned forward and held her hand out, hoping to tempt the cat toward her.

But the cat suddenly arched her back and hissed at Evelyn before running out of the room.

Poor Evelyn looked crestfallen.

Ollie had to choke back a laugh to keep his face and voice serious. "She doesn't like being called 'Hammie' by anyone except Mrs. Chapman. She only ever tolerates it from me half the time."

Evelyn tilted her head. "Is that not her name? What is her name, then? She looks to me like a Duchess or a Princess."

Ollie shifted, feeling embarrassed. "It's, um, Hambone."

Evelyn blinked. "Hambone?"

Blast, she better not ask how he'd acquired the cat. "Yes, that's correct."

There was a very awkward pause.

"May I ask where the name came from?"

Perhaps he could lie. Tell her a cute story about seeing Hambone in the window of a pet store. Or that he had rescued her from the river. Something far more admirable than the true story. But only the true story could explain the cat's name. Plus, lying was never good. "I was drunk," he said.

"You were drunk when you bought her?" Evelyn pulled her head back slightly.

"No. I got her from a rubbish bin."

Evelyn bit her bottom lip. "I sense there's a story here you're not sharing for some reason."

Ollie let out a nervous laugh. Evelyn was the daughter of a baron. He was so used to her in an academic setting, surrounded by books and art, in her utilitarian gray dresses, that he had never seen her amongst her roots: the aristocracy. Discounting the soaking-wet wedding dress, he'd never seen her dressed like an aristocrat, but he could imagine her flaming hair and tall form in a lush, silk ballgown. She would be as regal as a queen.

He recalled her father, her would-be husband, and her family's home. Evelyn was far more elegant than he was. It didn't matter that his grandparents were noble Scots—he'd been born in the slums to a poor Irish mother and lived there for a time as an orphan. His roots would always follow him, just as Evelyn's roots would always follow her. She was proper. He was a ragged street orphan from Whitechapel. She worked during the day at a museum—he worked at night at a pub. It didn't matter what his house looked like, or how many commas his bank account had.

Evelyn clasped her hands together. "Oh, do tell me the story, Ollie!"

He pulled at his collar. "It's rather embarrassing."

"Don't be silly! Please, I beg you to tell me. I have a feeling it is great fun."

He sighed. There was no escaping it. "All right. But I did warn you."

She nodded eagerly.

"It was Christmas Eve a few years ago," Ollie began. "A work night for me."

She furrowed her brow. "You all work on Christmas Eve?"

"I do." As he said this, he realized he was always the only one working Christmas Eve, as only a few people would come in on that day. Even he could handle the lack of business on that day, so Victor and Dantes were never there. "Anyway, it was pretty empty in the pub, not much going on, and I accidentally got a bit drunk with the lads there. You know, as one does on Christmas Eve."

"Right, especially while working…" Evelyn replied, clearly unsure.

"It was snowing out and rather chilled. I went out to quickly dispose of some rubbish and when I lifted the lid, a pair of enormous, round eyes greeted me. I screamed."

Evelyn laughed.

Ollie couldn't help but grin and there was a strange but pleasant warmth that rushed over him. "After I recovered, I looked closer into the bin, expecting a rat or something, but instead, I found a cat. And it was the filthiest cat I'd ever seen. Despite this fact, and probably because I was drunk, I lifted her out and she swiped a claw at me and hissed. It took me a moment to realize I had interrupted her dinner. Inside the bin was an entire Christmas ham she had lifted from someone and had been trying to eat before I rudely interrupted."

Evelyn laughed again, quite heartily this time. "She stole an entire ham?"

Now, he grinned ear to ear. "Oh, yes. Anyway, like I said, I was in my cups and brought her and her prized ham back into the pub. It was the highlight of the evening, and we placed wagers on whether or not she'd eat the whole thing."

Evelyn's eyes were wide with interest. "And?"

"Well, no. It was nearly the size of her. But I did bring it home with me." Ollie thought back to that day. "Christmas morning, I awoke quite fishy about the gills and a bit sick to my stomach. There had been a terrified scream. Mrs. Chapman found the cat gnawing on the smelly, old ham in front of the tree." He chuckled to himself. "Anyway, with the help of the lads at the pub, we decided her name should be Hambone. I told Mrs. Chapman this, too, in the midst of my begging that she stop screaming because I was too ill to think of another name."

Evelyn gave him a wry look. "Is that all true, or are you jesting?"

Ollie placed a hand over his heart. "On my honor, despite her fancy look today, Hambone came into my life while eating a whole ham in my rubbish bin on Christmas Eve."

Evelyn was smiling as she glanced at the door the cat had moments ago exited, but as the moment ticked by, the grin melted away. "Thank you, Ollie, for letting me stay here. Taking in strays seems to be a weakness of yours."

The mood in the room shifted. "Of course."

Evelyn let out a long sigh. "I keep thinking about my job."

"At the museum?"

"Yes. I feel awful that I left them in the lurch like that, and I'm sure with it being nearly evening now, they've seen the morning paper. The evening edition will be out soon and I'm sure there'll be even more in there."

"You think so?"

"I know so. There was a journalist at my house earlier. Did you see him?"

Ollie had not and shook his head.

"He took at least one photograph I'm sure will be printed tonight. Or would that be out already now? I'm dreading that quite a bit." Evelyn fell back on the sofa. "I keep digging myself deeper and deeper. I can't run forever. I know that! But I can't make myself succumb to my fate, either."

"I know."

She sat up from her slouch to see him better. "The earl paid my father for me, and they signed a contract. An actual contract! That is not a normal occurrence. It's usually a verbal agreement, and usually, the father pays the groom. Not the other way around." She paused. "Papa was determined to get me into the earl's hands today. They will stop at nothing to get me back, I can assure you."

Ollie pressed his lips together and looked away.

There was a knock on the doorframe, and Mrs. Chapman appeared with an envelope in her hand. "I found this slipped under the front door. Did you hear anyone?"

Dread curled through Ollie's stomach as he quickly rose to his feet. A letter slipped under his door?

He looked at the face of the white envelope. Curiously, there was no name written there, but instead was a word written in the swirliest calligraphy he'd ever seen. But all it read was *Hello*.

It was quite unsettling.

"What is it?" Evelyn appeared at his side.

"I'm not sure." Ollie opened the envelope and inside was a single piece of folded paper that, in the same flourished calligraphy, read:

The National Gallery
       10:00 P.M.

Ollie turned it over, sure there had to be more information, but the back was blank. He thanked Mrs. Chapman and when she'd left the room, he handed everything over to Evelyn. "Do you recognize that handwriting?"

Evelyn furrowed her brow. "No, I don't. It's quite unique, though, isn't it? Whom do you suppose it's from?"

"I don't know. It didn't even occur to me it would be something like this. But if they want to meet us at the museum, surely, it's for you? Or might it be for me, as it is my house?"

"Or it's a trap." Evelyn frowned as she stuffed it back in the envelope. "Who knows I'm here, though?"

"Me. Mrs. Chapman. Mrs. Bradley, the cook. And the hansom cab driver."

"Do you think the driver wants the reward for me?"

"I don't know. Though he might not know about it. While we were driving to your house originally, he asked me to read a street sign for him. He can't read. He likely doesn't know about it. Yet, at least."

Evelyn held up the envelope. "I don't think this is the handwriting of an illiterate man."

"Good point."

"I'm going to go. See who it is."

Ollie didn't like this. It was quite obvious someone was trying to capture her, whether it be someone who wanted the reward, or her father or the earl. "That is a very bad idea, Evelyn."

But Ollie knew it would be a losing battle to keep her from that meeting. He could see her mind turning with thoughts and questions, the alertness in her eyes.

Ollie decided to let her mind take time to work through whatever it was she thought about and kept quiet until she was ready to respond.

Eventually, she looked back to him. "I was already thinking

about going, anyway. I want to leave a note for my colleagues apologizing for leaving my position abruptly. Ideally, I'd go in and tell them that in person, but it's too risky for me to leave during the daytime. It's far easier for me to conceal myself at night."

He nodded slowly. "That's true, but I still think it's a bad idea to leave at all. Even I can see it's a trap."

"But from whom? I think Papa saw you, but he had no idea who you were. And there's no way he could figure that out without a lengthy investigation, much less in a few hours. I can guarantee, too, that since I ran off again, his time's been spent placating the earl and dealing with my mother. Not looking for me."

Ollie weighed this over, and he still didn't like it. "Is this really what you want to do?"

"Yes," Evelyn replied with a decided nod, and he knew he wouldn't change her mind. "Of course, I would take care to examine the area first, check over my shoulder to ensure I'm not being followed. They didn't specify where to meet, either, so I'm assuming they would want to meet outside at the main entrance. I could get there early, write my note, and then meet our letter-sender after."

Ollie let out a long sigh. "I suppose I'll have to join you, then, and make sure you don't get yourself into any further trouble than you already have."

Evelyn gave him a sheepish, little smile before returning to sipping her tea. But because of that sheepish, little smile, with her large doe-eyes on nothing but him, Ollie's heart skipped a few beats.

Chapter Eight

"THIS IS HOW we get in, then?" Ollie's voice was hushed as they finished crossing Trafalgar Square. He angled his head back to study the building as the London fog coiled around him. Both he and Evelyn had worn clothing to conceal their identities as best they could. Ollie wore a gray frock coat with a turned-up collar, and a black top hat tilted just a bit forward to shadow his face from lamplight. Evelyn wore a hat borrowed from Mrs. Chapman, and a dark, wine-colored silk dress from the dresses Lady Vivian had lent her.

Ollie had had difficulty deciding how they should dress. As he was someone who dressed both as working class and upper class, Evelyn had let him choose. His argument was if they blended in with the working class, they would be less likely to have problems with hecklers or muggers. But if they dressed upper class, they were less likely to be bothered by the police.

Ollie had decided that being unbothered by the police was the more pressing option.

They were now at one of the museum's back entrances for employees. It was inset in a tall, stone wall with pillars atop rising like mountains to the roof.

"This is it," Evelyn replied, but her voice rang rather unsure. For she had realized something rather important: She did not have a key. She pulled the door handle, hoping someone had forgotten to lock it. However, it didn't budge.

"Is it not opening?" Ollie asked, moving closer to the door to observe for himself.

Evelyn stepped aside to give him room. "No, it's—"

But Ollie used all his might to pull the handle. Then he rammed hard into it with his shoulder in case it opened inward. He grimaced in pain and rubbed his shoulder. "It's stuck."

"Ollie, it's locked."

"Oh. Right." He paused. "And you…don't have a key?"

Evelyn resisted the urge to smile at Ollie's charm. "Unfortunately, it did not occur to me that I would have to have one. When I go to and leave work, the doors are open, so it's never been a thought." Evelyn took a few steps back to study their surroundings. There was a line of windows that went both right and left, but they were too high and out of reach thanks to the partial stone wall.

"If I can somehow get atop this wall, I can see if the windows are unlocked," Evelyn thought out loud.

"Let me try." Ollie studied the wall for himself, no doubt calculating how to climb up. There was a wrought-iron handrail bolted in the wall along the stairs that led to the door. He tried putting his foot up on the rail, but the angle was too sharp and he couldn't get a good footing.

"Why don't you give me a boost?" Evelyn suggested. "If someone catches us, it would be far better if I were the one caught sneaking about and not you. I could easily explain it away as me forgetting something important inside."

"Yes, but that wall is at least ten feet high. That's not safe."

"I'll be fine."

But instead of helping her as requested, he stood in place, his lips pursed and eyebrows pulled together.

Charmed again as she realized the issue, she then said, "I give you permission to touch me."

The tension in his face fell away. "All right. Here, then, put one foot in my hands." Ollie crouched down to one knee and knit his open palms together. Evelyn did as asked and placed her hands on his shoulders for balance. His shoulders were large and hard and caused a funny feeling inside of her.

"Ready?" Ollie asked, looking up at her, and she nodded back. "One, two, three!"

Ollie lifted her as if she were as light as a feather, causing her to yelp with surprise. But between his height and hers, she was able to easily pull herself atop the stone wall. Strangely flustered, Evelyn crawled over to the window. But it was locked, too.

"Blast!" she cried out. She looked over the wall edge down to Ollie. "What time is it?"

Ollie pulled out his pocket watch. "Ten minutes to ten."

Now quite anxious, Evelyn rubbed her face with her hands. Her fingertips bumped into the edge of Mrs. Chapman's hat. The housekeeper had been aghast at the thought of Evelyn parading around London hatless.

But at the feel of the hat, a funny thought crossed her mind. "Ollie, I'm coming back down!" She looked over the edge and realized how high up she was. "Oh, dear, how do I do that?"

"Slide," Ollie said. "Don't jump. I'll grab you."

"All right." Evelyn resisted the urge to whimper with fright. She lay flat on her front and began to creep backward. "You're sure about this?"

"Of course. Keep sliding."

Evelyn shuffled back until she was able to hang over the edge a bit. Ollie clasped his hands at her waist as she moved down further and lifted her gently.

Once she was back on her feet, she turned around to face him. He had only held on to her for five seconds at the most, but she could still feel the way his fingertips and palms had pressed into her.

Evelyn cleared her throat, realizing how close they stood to each other. He stared down at her in his top hat, the shadow over his eyes and his lifted collar making the moment feel even more private. Her heart raced. "Thank you, Ollie," she said. But she felt funny—lightheaded—and the words came out quiet.

The corners of his mouth lifted ever so slightly, and his green eyes shamelessly caressed her face and down to her mouth. "You are very welcome." His deep velvet voice seemed to curl around her like smoke.

Evelyn swallowed and moved quickly toward the door but tripped over Ollie's foot. She let out another yelp of surprise, but Ollie's arm shot out to grab her. However, Evelyn was so embarrassed by what she had done that at the same time he reached out, she rapidly overcorrected herself.

At first, she didn't realize what had happened and squeezed her eyes tightly in case she was about to hit the ground. But she wasn't falling. And her hands, lifted to brace against the fall, were pressed against something hard and warm. Not cold ground. And her nose detected a scent. Not of concrete or stone, but something quite masculine. Woodsy. Like cedar.

Evelyn opened her eyes and was startled to discover Ollie was now so close that if she leaned just slightly forward, her nose would touch his, and in the chilled, November night, their breaths swirled together in curling steam. Somehow, she wasn't laid out on the ground like a squashed bug but was pressed up against him, his arm solidly wrapped around her with protectiveness.

Evelyn had always thought Ollie was quite handsome, but until now never realized how much he resembled Eugène Delacroix. Eugène Delacroix had been a French romantic painter from earlier this century and younger portraits of him showed a dark-haired, broody, square-jawed man. The first time she had seen Thales Fielding's 1825 portrait of Delacroix, she was at one of the Impressionists' flats, though now she forgot whose. But she remembered how awed she was that a man could be so handsome. Cordelia had teased her relentlessly that night and for years had called him Evelyn's *Painted Beau*. But now Evelyn saw that same dark, mysterious broodiness in Ollie as he held her close. Desire, thick as honey, poured over her and once again, she found her blasted heart racing.

The slight grin Ollie had had a moment ago was now gone. Those hypnotic, green eyes had darkened, and his brow furrowed. A muscle in his jaw hitched. Did he know what she was thinking in the moment?

"Please let go of me," she said, breathless and disconcerted by her inner musings. Though she was far more affected by his nearness than she ever would have expected—she decided to blame it on the top hat—it was quite clear Ollie was *not* happy to be holding her in such an intimate way. He had become so tense, so rigid, she worried he might injure himself. She must put space between them.

Evelyn jerked away from his grasp, and he released her while muttering an apology. She shivered off the sensation of Ollie's touch and tried to ignore how he now refused to look in her direction.

"How much time do we have now?" she asked. A funny idea had crossed her mind while she'd been atop the wall, though she wasn't sure it would work. What she needed was a thin, slender object, but she wasn't sure where to acquire one. Quickly, she looked around before realizing she had something on her person. She reached up to her hat, pulled out a hatpin, and crouched to be eye level with the lock.

"Five minutes," Ollie replied from somewhere behind her.

Evelyn set to work at the lock. The sharp end up the pin slid into the mechanical parts easily. "I don't know how well this will work," she muttered. She poked and prodded every direction she could, but alas, it did not work.

"May I?" Ollie asked.

Frustrated by her failure, and while time continued to tick by, Evelyn stood back up and handed the hatpin over to Ollie with a huff.

Ollie grinned wide. "You can't be good at everything, Evelyn."

She could feel her face redden and didn't know how to reply

to that.

Fortunately, Ollie had far better luck. The second he crouched down and pushed the pin in, he made a funny circular movement, and the door made a clicking noise.

Evelyn gasped. It had taken him mere seconds to do that. "You did it! Brilliant, Ollie!"

Ollie stood back up and handed the pin over to her. "I'll teach you how to do that someday, perhaps. It's a little trick Victor taught me when I was very small."

Evelyn shoved the pin back in place. "Good thing, too. But we must get upstairs, post-haste."

They hurried inside and up the stairwell, their rapid footfalls echoing loud. As she followed Ollie, Evelyn thought she heard another set of footfalls running after them, but when she looked back over her shoulder, nothing was there. The echo must have been skewing the sound of their own movements.

Moments later, they were in the conservation studio. The familiar smell of paint and wood and canvas invited her in and comforted her. She hurried over to Mr. Burlington's desk and threw down the letter she had written earlier. It was a short apology and vague explanation for what had happened. But she still couldn't bring herself to say she would never be back.

It seemed Evelyn was bad at two things: breaking and entering, and finalizing decisions.

"In my letter, I asked Mr. Burlington to oversee the rest of your brother's art restoration," Evelyn said while walking over to her corner of the studio. "He'll complain but will do it and do it well." She lifted one of Mr. Dantes McNab's smaller paintings and laid it out atop her desk. It was one of the saucier paintings Ollie's brother owned. Evelyn wasn't bothered by the nudity, but this painting, of a woman bathing herself, had more sensuality to it than most nude paintings.

Ollie shifted and cleared his throat.

"Does this make you uncomfortable?" Evelyn looked up to Ollie, slightly amused a known scoundrel could be made bashful about this artwork.

"A bit," Ollie replied, unsure. "It's a little saucy, though, don't you think?"

Before she could share she'd had the same exact thought, Evelyn sensed movement out of the corner of her eye.

She spun in the direction of it and stared into the darkness, unblinking. But there was no noise, and no further movement. Perhaps she was seeing things.

"What's the matter?" Now whispering, Ollie stepped closer to her. "You look like you've seen a ghost."

"I saw someone. Or something," she whispered back. "Who's there?" she called out louder.

But nothing responded.

"Let's go," Evelyn said, the small hairs all over her body standing on end. "I don't much like being here at night."

"Nor I." Ollie followed her out.

One last glance into the dark corner sent chills up her spine and she hurried out into the hallway, pausing at the stairwell they had used earlier.

"When we came up these stairs did you hear footfalls following us?"

"No, I didn't, but I wasn't paying attention, either." He paused. "Why? You think we're being followed?"

"I don't know." She looked around to ensure they were still alone and lowered her voice. "Instead of going back to the door we came in through, I'm going to go through the museum itself to meet our letter-sender out front of the main entrance. If we're being followed, it's probably a police officer or maybe our one security guard. But if it is the police, I guarantee another officer is waiting outside the door we came through."

"Good idea."

Evelyn hurried until they reached the room of French paintings. Frothy pastels of the eighteenth century whirled by.

Evelyn swore she heard footfalls again. "Ollie!"

"I heard that, too. Let's go. Quickly." He held his hand out to her, and she hesitated but took it. Someone was definitely coming after them and they needed to stick together and escape.

They next found themselves in the Spanish paintings room. Everything around them was dark, dramatic, full of movement and severity. Eyes following her, Cardinal Carlo Cerri judged her from his chair. The flapping ravens in Guercino's *Elijah fed by Ravens* seemed ready to leave the painting and dive at her.

Without realizing it, Evelyn squeezed Ollie's hand. And he squeezed back.

On they ran, through different rooms. Down the stairs. Past the Dutch and Flemish room. The footfalls were louder, getting closer and closer.

But then Evelyn remembered—they *had* to go out the door they'd come in in order to meet the letter-sender at the main entrance. She had no way of unlocking the other doors and didn't have time to pick them. She quietly told Ollie this and began leading the way.

Finally, their exit was ahead. They ran through it and out into the cool, misty night. The door shut behind them. No police officers lay in wait, and Trafalgar Square was in sight. Evelyn heaved a breath of relief.

But the door opened again.

Evelyn spun around, fearful.

Ollie did too and swore at the sight before them. He pushed Evelyn behind him.

For before them stood a terrifying man, face fully concealed by a midnight-blue Venetian Volto mask with gold stars, a black tricorn hat, and a black cape that obscured everything else.

His only visible feature were his eyes in the eye holes—dark-brown eyes, Evelyn noted.

Was *this* the letter-sender? Or had they roused a ghost?

The man didn't say anything. He simply stood there watching them, his shoulders relaxed. But Evelyn noted something curious: The man's full attention was on Ollie. Evelyn did not seem to exist.

Then his eyes squinted in a way that, underneath the full mask, said he was *smiling*.

"Who are you? What do you want?" Evelyn was trying her best to sound unperturbed.

The man ripped his attention off of Ollie and pierced it into her. "Why are you breaking into the museum, wee lass? Don't have a key?" His voice held a thick, Irish accent. Another observation filed away for later. "Naughty business, that."

"What is it to you?" The words squeaked out.

The man's eyes squinted with a smile again. "I thought you two would be waiting outside shaking like little mousies, and I was prepared to convince you to let me inside."

Evelyn kept her mouth clamped shut. He'd wanted them to let him in the museum? Ridiculous. How would he think he could convince her, unless it had been under threat?

Blast it all—of course it would have been under threat. Immediately, her mind went to Jack the Ripper. This couldn't be the famed terrifying killer, though, or at least she hoped it wasn't. She swallowed. What was he hiding under his cape?

"Imagine my surprise to find you breaking in," the terrifying man continued. "I suppose I don't much care why you were. Thank you for answering my note, though. You made my job far easier than I ever expected."

He moved as if he were going to walk past them and, honestly, Evelyn was more than happy to let him.

But Ollie apparently had other ideas in mind. He stepped into the masked man's path and put a hand on his chest, preventing him from passing. The man was much shorter than Ollie, but even with a full disguise exuded an air of cocky confidence. Evelyn was sure he would fight back easily if it came to throwing fists. Or worse.

The masked man chuckled. "You think you can stop me, boyo?"

"You're the one who sent the letter." Ollie said this as if he had just figured it out. Maybe he had. "What do you want from us?" His voice was hard and dangerous. And when the man didn't respond, Ollie added, "Answer the blasted question."

"Me? Want something from you? Why, I was only out for a stroll when I saw you two break into the museum. 'Fancy that,' I said to myself and followed you in. See, I am very interested in the arts myself and wanted to ensure you two weren't up to any shenanigans."

Evelyn jumped in. "Nice try, but you said you were going to convince us to break you in, which would never happen, by the way. But you *did* sneak about in the shadows until we came back outside. You waited for us instead of leaving. Why?"

The masked man merely laughed, irritating Evelyn. "Now, if you will excuse me," he said, and the masked man had somehow got past Ollie like a slippery eel. He lifted his tricorn hat in a salute, revealing thick, black hair beneath. "I have a *saucy painting* to hang up in my sitting room." And with flair, he spun around quickly, kicking up his cape. Evelyn thought she saw something gold flash, but before she could see what it was, the man's back was to her and, somehow, he melted into the velvet darkness of night.

"What an absolute clown." Ollie huffed.

Evelyn rushed forward and looked all around Trafalgar Square, but the man had somehow disappeared completely. Her mind whirred at his comment about the saucy painting. Closing her eyes to concentrate further, she tried to focus on what that flash of gold under his cape had been. The man's arm had been holding something against his side. All she could see was a gold corner of something. She spun around, horrified. "Do you realize what he did?"

"What he did? He's gone and that's all I care about. What a buffoon."

She shook her head hard and took a few steps toward Ollie. "No. Ollie. The part about the saucy painting. Don't you realize what he was telling us by saying that?"

She didn't wait for him to respond. Now fully panicked, Evelyn raced back into the museum, up the stairs, and into the studio. She ran across the room to her desk, worry mounting. But her worst fear was realized, and she cried out with distress.

"What's the matter?" Ollie asked between labored breaths as he arrived at her side.

"Look." She pointed at her now-empty desk.

Ollie swore and rubbed his hands over his face.

The Gustave Courbet painting, of the woman bathing herself, had been taken. In its place was a signature in the magnificently flourished handwriting from the mysterious letter. And in that flourished hand the Signature Swindler's signature was revealed:

Bollocks.

Chapter Nine

HAMBONE WAS PLAYING with a little bell, batting it between her fluffy, gray paws before chasing it under the sofa. She didn't reemerge, but Ollie could still hear the tinkling of the little bell.

He couldn't believe they'd crossed paths with the Signature Swindler. The man was an absolute menace. But there were a few things Ollie still couldn't quite figure out. Had the note the cad sent been meant for Ollie, or Evelyn? Because when they'd first crossed paths with him, he'd stared at Ollie as if Evelyn hadn't been there. It'd been quite uncomfortable in the moment.

But it made the most sense to have been for Evelyn, as she could give him access to the museum, had she still carried her key. But how had he known she worked there? How had he known she was even staying with Ollie? The Signature Swindler had been breaking into places for years. Why trick Evelyn into helping him gain access, when he could do it on his own without anyone seeing him? Because as far as Ollie knew, he and Evelyn were the first people to actually see the Signature Swindler in the midst of his theft.

It didn't make *any* sense.

There was also something deeply unsettling about the Signature Swindler. Maybe it was because they could only see his eyes. Everything else of his face, including his nose and mouth, had been covered by the strange mask.

Ollie shuddered.

After the unfortunate meeting with the Signature Swindler, and realizing the painting had been stolen, Ollie and Evelyn had been quiet the entire walk back to the house, concentrating on staying in the shadows of night. They'd had to go unnoticed for Evelyn's sake, lest someone snag her for the reward. It had gotten close at one point, when a large group of people had unexpectedly come out of a fancy restaurant right as they'd been walking by. Evelyn had gasped, apparently recognizing them, and bolted down a dark alley without warning. Ollie had had to run after her but, for what felt like an eternity, couldn't find her. When he had caught up with her two blocks away, on a crowded street, at that, he'd grabbed her hand without thinking so they wouldn't get separated again. Instead of apologizing for running off and giving him a fright, she'd jerked her hand out of his. Hard. Ollie had immediately realized his error, felt immensely guilty, then *he* had apologized. But he couldn't stop thinking about it, either. He tried telling himself he knew she disliked being touched, so it wasn't personal, but he couldn't help but take it that way.

Did Evelyn really dislike touch that much, or was it worse because it was him?

Ollie had enough brains to see the stark difference between the two of them, and he knew firsthand people were the product of their upbringings. Despite who his grandparents were, Ollie had remained some lad from the Whitechapel slums. He would never be as polished as other nobs, never have all those manners and rules nailed down. He'd learned how to talk in Whitechapel and would never have the right accent. Nor would he ever be as educated, despite his grandparents' desperate attempt.

Ollie might have appeared polished, might have dressed well, might have had a nice home, might have a title in the family. But the second he opened his mouth, people knew what he really was. Just some street rat.

Evelyn probably thought that as well.

Really, he shouldn't have cared what Evelyn thought of him, and he couldn't figure out *why* he cared in the first place. That was, aside from the fact that she was a friend and he did care about what his friends thought of him. Right?

Actually, he wasn't sure that was true. To some degree it was maybe, but he *really* cared a lot about what Evelyn thought about him.

But as he tried to think too hard about why he cared what she thought, his head started to hurt.

Dantes was the one who cared what people thought, not Ollie. Ollie was the one who told Dantes not to give a fig what a bunch of idiots thought.

No, he didn't care at all what his friends thought about him. He was the one, after all, who'd invited his friends from Oxford to visit The Harp & Thistle when it had originally opened years ago. He was the entire reason their pub attracted both the lower class and the upper class. If he cared what his friends thought of him, he wouldn't have told them he had decided to join his working-class brothers in the family pub. Much less invite them.

Yet here he was, caring that Evelyn Sparrow might be repulsed by him and his working-class roots.

Back to being irritated, and now with a headache, Ollie stood up from the sofa and began pacing. He was alone in the parlor for the moment and had to shake off these negative thoughts before Evelyn came in.

Moments ago, they had returned from the museum and Evelyn had gone looking for Mrs. Chapman to return the hat she had borrowed, leaving Ollie alone with his idiotic brain.

"You're a fool," he mumbled to himself. "Get a hold of yourself, man!"

Someone cleared their throat from the doorway. Inwardly cursing at himself, Ollie turned to find Evelyn standing in the doorway watching him. "Is everything all right?" she asked, sounding unsure.

Ollie began pacing again. "Everything is just swell."

"Please, sit down." Evelyn's eyes followed him back and forth across the room. "There's nothing we can do about the painting right now. It's the middle of the night."

Ollie paused and turned to face Evelyn. She was trying her best to look relaxed, no doubt in a bid for him to mimic her, but it didn't work. His hands flexed closed, open, then closed again. He needed to redirect his ire away from Evelyn's dislike of him and onto the Signature Swindler. "That bloody Irishman!" was all he managed to sputter out before pacing again.

With a sigh, Evelyn began following Ollie in his pacing. Hambone poked her lion-like head out to see what they were doing but quickly lost interest and returned to batting at her bell.

"In the span of two days, I've completely destroyed everything people relied on me for and I feel like rubbish for it. It's one thing to let Victor down—he's never happy with me, no matter what I do—but Dantes has been on my side a number of times. When he finds out what happened to his prized possession, his painting, he is going to despise me for the rest of my life!"

"He won't despise you for the rest of your life."

Ollie glanced at Evelyn. "When the fire took Dantes's flat, he blamed Victor for losing his possessions and for the fire damage to the paintings. You know what he said to Victor about that?"

Evelyn waited, seemingly unsure.

"He said, 'I don't care about my things, but my paintings? I will *never* forgive you for losing them.' And he was completely serious." Ollie tried to imagine Dantes's reaction when he learned one of his paintings had been stolen under Ollie's care. Ollie envisioned a gargoyle rearing up to its hindlegs with a roar, its eyes glowing red, its teeth sharp and bloodthirsty. Ollie gulped.

"It wasn't your fault though, Ollie." Evelyn's voice pulled him from the vision. "A thief followed us in after we *broke into a museum.*" Now Evelyn began pacing while Ollie watched. As she passed the sofa, a fluffy paw reached out, trying to snag the hem of her skirt. "I could go to prison for that!"

"Pretty sure we both could," Ollie replied, feeling worse.

"Regardless of what you think, the paintings were under *my* care." Evelyn huffed. She reached the end of the room, turned, and walked back toward him. "My care, not yours. Please do not put that on yourself." She stopped moving once she'd passed him but spun around to face him once more. "If it ever gets out that I practically *invited* an art thief into the museum, my professional reputation will be completely destroyed! Do you know how hard I worked to gain respect? And that's assuming they don't find out about me running from the altar!" Her face reddened with emotion. "A man with my position starts out with basic respect by others. As time passes and he proves himself, his respect builds. When I began, I was at negative one hundred!" Her finger shot up into the air. "I have to do twice the work, earn twice the respect, to be considered equal to my male colleagues. All because I'm a woman!"

Ollie didn't know much about being a woman, of course, but he could see in Evelyn's passion and anger that she had genuinely struggled significantly to grow in her career. There was no doubt in his mind she was being truthful and, perhaps, even minimizing it.

"Well, I think you're…." He faltered, trying to think of the perfect word. What word embodied everything he thought about Evelyn? The glowing respect he had for her brilliant mind, her beauty that became more jaw-dropping to him each day, her determination and wit that he was envious of.

"Smart," was what he came up with.

Christ, he sounded like an idiot.

"Thank you, Ollie," Evelyn replied after a moment, her red eyebrows hitched. "I don't *feel* very smart right now, though."

"Nor do I. Not that that's any different from normal." Time to move on. "I've been wondering. Why did the Signature Swindler send that note? Why not simply break in without our help?"

"I don't know. I've been wondering that, too." Evelyn sank into a chair and leaned into the arm. She stared off into the fire in thought.

"Do we go to the police?" Ollie asked, referring to the stolen painting.

"No," Evelyn said. "Remember, we cleaned the signature off my desk. That would have been the only way for them to believe the Signature Swindler took the painting. If we told them the painting was stolen, we'd get into a lot of trouble. Breaking in, for one. The museum finding out it's gone would cast me out forever. It's a privately owned piece. If they even noticed its absence, they may simply think your brother came to retrieve it. That is, until he really *does* come around for it." She now looked directly at Ollie. "I don't know if I will ever be able to return to my position at the museum because of the runaway bride business, but I don't want to be remembered as the woman who practically invited an art thief into the museum. I do not want that to be my legacy."

"Of course not. What do you suppose we do, then?"

Evelyn's little slippered foot, peeking out from the hem of her skirt, began bobbing up and down. Ollie watched, mesmerized. "We need to find it before anyone realizes it's missing."

Ollie tilted his head. This was interesting. "How do you sup-posed we do that? We have no idea who the Signature Swindler is. All we know is he's an Irishman and he dresses strange."

"That was just a costume, Ollie. I doubt that was his normal, everyday attire."

"Oh." Once again, Ollie had shown what a dolt he was. Ob-viously, it had been a costume.

"Let's go back a bit," Evelyn said. "What do we know about the Signature Swindler so far? Aside from what you've already mentioned."

Ollie squinted his eyes in thought. "He likes to…steal stuff." Every time he opened his mouth, he sounded more daft.

Evelyn gave him a small grin. "Yes, that's correct. He's been doing this for a few years. Sticking with small items so far. But that changed recently." Suddenly, she clapped her hands together with excitement. "He stole art from the Bethnal Green Museum!

What caused him to go from jewelry stores and houses to that museum?"

"I have no idea," Ollie admitted. "It seems far riskier."

"It certainly is. But the items are of far, far higher value."

"More risk, more reward."

"Exactly!" She sounded positively gleeful.

"All right, so what are you thinking?" It was clear she was heading in some kind of direction.

Evelyn folded her hands neatly in her lap and began watching the fire again. "We need to revisit his previous crimes. Talk to witnesses. The police have been tight-lipped about the heists before this. For all we know, the witnesses may have some key information kept secret. That information would never be released to the public."

"That's true."

Evelyn frowned. "The only problem with that is the most logical next step would be going to the Bethnal Green Museum. But how do we approach them without looking suspicious? And that goes for the jewelry stores as well. We aren't any sort of authority. Why would they share anything with us? They would probably get suspicious and contact the police, too."

A concerning thought crossed Ollie's mind. "Plus, what if they recognized you?"

"Drat. I keep forgetting about that part."

Ollie rubbed his chin in thought. "Well, the most easily identifiable part of you is your hair, do you agree?"

Evelyn reached up to touch her hair. "I suppose so. The newspaper article did keep mentioning my red hair."

"All we really need to do is cover it up somehow. There must be hats that cover your hair fully." Mrs. Chapman's hat had only covered the very top of Evelyn's hair. "What about a bonnet?"

Evelyn laughed. She thought he was joking, and her laugh melted away when she seemed to realize he wasn't. "Bonnets are very old fashioned, Ollie. I would stand out more by wearing a bonnet than if I walked around hatless."

"Well, we can't take you to a hat store, either."

"No, I don't have any money since I cannot go to my bank. They will know me upon sight."

Ollie furrowed his brow. "Surely, you know you don't need to worry about that."

She was quiet for a beat. "I don't want your money."

"Don't be silly. If you need something, I will, of course, help you get it."

To his surprise, Evelyn's eyes were becoming misty. "Thank you. You are more concerned with my wellbeing than my own parents."

He wished more than anything that he could go crouch by her chair and take her hand in his. But he didn't dare. "Not living up to familial expectations is something I can definitely relate to."

She looked up at him and smiled gently despite the misty eyes. "Oh, Ollie, we are in shambles, aren't we?"

"A bit, yes."

She laughed. But then her face became serious. "Wait a minute. I just realized something. Mr. Burlington knows someone at the Bethnal Green Museum. How silly am I? That could be our in!"

"Do you not know them, too?"

"No." Her face fell. "And I would have to ask Mr. Burlington directly about his contact there. I'm not sure how we could do that without getting into trouble."

"Would he turn you in for the reward?"

Evelyn considered this for a moment but didn't decide one way or another.

The long, active day was beginning to weigh on Ollie. He was growing more tired, and he could feel his mind sputtering out. "Why don't we sleep on it and revisit it tomorrow? I don't think either of us is at our best right now."

Evelyn let out a long sigh. "Yes, I suppose that's best. It's not like we can do much leaving during the day. At least, I can't."

"No. I don't like keeping you holed up, but I don't want to put you at more risk than necessary, either." He wondered what was going through her mind at the moment. Her eyes were expressive, but the events of the last few days had made them more weary than anything.

Don't you wish you could hold her again? A little voice in his head cut in and Ollie became overwhelmed by the urge to wrap his arms around Evelyn, protecting her from the world, make her feel everything would be all right.

Of course, Evelyn would murder him in his sleep. Instead, he shook off the feeling. Once this business with Evelyn was over, he was going to have to return to his scoundrel ways and revisit his old flames. For reasons he couldn't understand, he had stopped that behavior some time ago and it clearly had addled his brain.

Ollie said *goodnight* to Evelyn, and each went to their respective bedrooms. Once he lay in bed, he found his mind wandering, that little voice in his head kept repeating her name, haunting him.

Evelyn, Evelyn, Evelyn.

He wondered if she was already asleep, what she was thinking about if she wasn't, if she felt safe in his home.

Looping his hands behind his head, he stared up at the dark canopy as he recalled catching Evelyn earlier. She'd fit so perfectly against him in his arm. Their faces had been close, breaths swirling together in the autumn night air. It had been a lover's embrace, though accidental.

And instead of being put off by her nearness, which was how he should have reacted by holding a mere friend in a lover's embrace, his body had instead hummed in a way he'd never felt before.

Alarmed, Ollie yanked his mind back. He tried to conjure up the identities of the women he'd been with before but for the life of him couldn't remember. A wave a shame hit him at this realization. And it only worsened when he thought about returning to those old habits.

In truth, it did not sound appealing. And he used to relish women's attention.

What was the matter with him?

Chapter Ten

"YOU'RE NOT GOING anywhere." Ollie glowered at Evelyn from across the dining room table, clearly irritated she had announced she would be going to the millinery herself. After some back and forth, she had finally agreed to let him cover her financially while she hid at his home, on the condition he allow her to pay him back in the future. But they remained in disagreement about her leaving the house.

Evelyn was exasperated. Maybe it wasn't the best idea for her to go to the millinery, even one in a part of town she quite likely wouldn't run into anyone she knew, but she was getting fidgety being stuck inside during the day. And after sleeping twelve hours straight, eating an enormous breakfast of sausage and eggs at the noon hour, and dawdling in a hot bath, she felt like an entirely new woman. One restless to her core, like she could conquer the world!

She was itching to go out and do that, ill-advised or not.

"Ollie, be serious," Evelyn replied. Though it was now three o'clock in the afternoon, they were having their second meal of the day. Ollie normally ate a late supper at the pub long after an enormous breakfast at home, with nothing in between. The cook was thrilled to be making multiple meals with Ollie and Evelyn now there.

Food was plentiful and that edge of hunger that had gnawed

at Evelyn for the last few days had subsided. The afternoon sun shone brightly through the large windows. The sky was sapphire blue, and a bird sang happily at the window.

"How many people are in London?" Evelyn turned up a hand before biting into a tiny éclair petit four. "I know red hair isn't the most common hair color, but I'm hardly the only one in the city with it. I won't stand out amongst all the people going about their business. Then, on my way back, I'll have my hat."

Ollie had been poking his fork at a tiny square cake that could easily fit in the palm of his hand with room for more. He set the fork down to rub the bridge of his nose. "You saw the evening edition of the paper when you had breakfast. I watched you study the photograph of the earl grabbing you. I was in the background of that photograph, Evelyn! They doubled—doubled!—the reward for your return to the earl. Not even to your father, straight to the earl now. They're not faffing about when it comes to finding you, they've an entire fleet of police officers whose full-time job is to find you. They're breaking down doors and flooding the streets, upturning everything in their path to locate *you.*"

"No one will recognize me. I won't be out flaunting myself and will do everything I can to blend in with the crowds. Life is full of risk, is it not? I cannot hide forever." She took a sip of her tea.

Ollie scoffed. "Do you have any idea how many people I know with the kind of money they are offering in the reward?"

Evelyn had the good sense to show some humility. "No."

"None," Ollie replied with pointed annunciation.

She lifted an eyebrow to show her skepticism. "What about your grandparents?"

He stammered. "Right, so I know two, then. Regardless. The coin they're offering for your return will make even the most saintly nan greedy to turn you in. That is the kind of money that changes not only one life, but generations of lives."

Evelyn waved her hand dismissively. "All I'm asking is to go to the millinery myself, not to run around Hyde Park. I won't even go to the shop I usually go to. I'll go to a brand new one. Of your choice."

"Absolutely not. Just give me your hat size, and I will go find you a hat that covers your hair."

She felt a sinking feeling at losing the one opportunity to get out in the sunlight. Maybe she was being a bit silly, but surely, heading out for a short time to a part of the city where no one knew her would be safer. "But—"

"If you insist on putting both of our hides at risk, I'll have no choice but to get you an outfit to match our favorite art thief."

Evelyn couldn't help it. She huffed.

Ollie, knowing he'd won this round with humor to boot, grinned in that easy way that always made her heart palpitate. Evelyn forced herself to look away from him. Staring at Ollie had become a bizarre habit as of late, and she didn't know why. Yes, his green eyes were captivating, his neatly styled dark hair begging her fingers to run through it, and now she knew how hard his body felt against her own.

Evelyn recalled the first time she'd laid eyes on Ollie. He'd come into the museum with Lady Vivian, who had not yet married Ollie's brother, to discuss the art restoration after the pub fire. Evelyn had been working on a nude painting at the time and had become flustered when Ollie had stood beside her to see it. He'd smelled so nice—the exact same way he did now, she realized, recognizing that faint scent of freshly scrubbed man and cedar—and he had quite literally been the most attractive man she had ever seen. England, America, France… Of all the places Evelyn had lived, she had never met or seen a gentleman who'd made her stomach flip flop the way Ollie had. Especially when he'd smiled at her.

Nowadays, Evelyn felt far more comfortable around him and no longer tripped over herself in his presence. And while she couldn't stand when anyone touched her, when Ollie did it, it was different. Like her skin had burst into flames. It was so strange, she still wasn't sure if that was a good or bad thing.

Ollie leaned to the side in order to check his pocket watch. "Speaking of which…" Ollie looked up and snapped the silver cover closed. "Shops close in a few hours and I'm sure traffic is horrific. Have you decided what you want to do about the Bethnal Green Museum?"

Evelyn cleared her throat and reached up to touch her hair, feeling nervous under his gaze. "No."

"You are far more intelligent than I am, so I'll leave that up to you. You have more at risk, anyway. I don't want to push you into something you don't want to do." Ollie strangely fidgeted after those words, as if embarrassed. He then jumped up from his chair quickly, nearly knocking it backward, and stood rigid beside the table, ignoring the chair. "Goodbye for now, then," he said, awkwardly tossing his napkin to the table.

Evelyn decided to blame his odd behavior on stress. "Please be mindful of what you buy, Ollie. I don't care to wear an entire peacock upon my head."

Ollie laughed, filling the room with his warmth and presence. A funny palpitation hit her heart as she watched him leave. The room immediately felt cold and empty the moment he left it, making her feel gloomy.

Deciding to take advantage of Ollie's absence, Evelyn explored the house. The townhome wasn't overly large—most weren't—but it was inviting and comfortable. Or at least, it looked like it should have felt that way. But that emptiness upon Ollie's departure permeated through the house. And there was something that felt lacking. Never would she say that out loud, but she couldn't quite put her finger on what the cause was. Most of the furniture was new, from at least within the last ten years or so, whereas in her social circle, furniture was used generation after generation. Everything of Ollie's was newer and didn't have that *worn but comfy* look to it. But the newness of the furniture wasn't the cause of her unease, either.

Evelyn set her hands on her hips as she looked around the

parlor, seeking out the cause, but only finding Hambone curled up on the sofa. Then she moved on to the library, where furniture gleamed, and so did the new books. She studied the long hallways of wood paneling, noting even in the hallway something felt off.

Upstairs, she poked her head into the room she was using. It had the same hollow feeling.

As she went back out into the hallway and shut her door behind her, her eyes fell upon Ollie's closed bedroom door. She tiptoed over to it, glancing around to ensure she was alone, and put her ear to the door in case Mrs. Chapman was in there. But there was no sound.

Which meant no one would know what she was about to do.

Gently, Evelyn turned the brass knob of Ollie's bedroom door and slid inside soundlessly, shutting the door behind her.

Her heart raced at being in his room. It was so unbelievably inappropriate for her to be sneaking about in here, but she was also far too curious to see the room for herself and it might have been her only opportunity to do so.

Besides, who would know? Unlike her familial home, where someone was always watching her every move, no one paid her much attention here.

Evelyn went to the fireplace to study the mantel, just like she had back in the flat above The Harp & Thistle. Back there, she'd found the tintype of the McNab brothers' parents. But here in Ollie's bedroom, all Evelyn found were random knickknacks to fill the space. A cut crystal cat she assumed represented Hambone was the most personal item she found.

Evelyn frowned but continued her tour about the room. That odd, empty feeling continued to linger.

Finally, she came to that which she'd put last. Ollie's bed. It had four posts and dark-blue, velvet curtains with satin, gold ties that held the curtains open. Feeling bold, Evelyn ran a finger over the bedding.

This is where Ollie sleeps every night, she thought to herself as her attention slid over to the pillows.

Unlike at her house, where decorative pillows were on every piece of furniture, Ollie's bed had two pillows for sleeping upon and only one decorative pillow in the middle. She suspected the decorative pillow existed because of Mrs. Chapman's insistence his bed look nice.

And Ollie had complied, adding one solitary frilly pillow, to tease his overbearing housekeeper. Technically, he'd complied with her request and she could no longer pester him about it.

Evelyn had to cover her mouth to resist a giggle.

She casually strolled her way around the end of the bed to slide up against the nightstand. Unable to help herself, she ran her palm over the surface of the pillow. It was soft and cool to the touch. Very different from her overly frilly bed back home.

With a swallow, Evelyn allowed her mind to wander over to what she was most curious about. How many other women had rested their heads upon the other pillow? How many had lain beside him, and how many had cried out into the night? How many days had it been since another woman had been here?

Her face flamed at the thought, and jealousy twisted her stomach into a knot.

Evelyn had never been intimate with a man before for obvious reasons. How could a woman who hated being touched have been intimate with a man? She couldn't.

But she found herself rather curious about it in the moment. What it would be like if her head lay upon the second pillow, in the dark beside Ollie, his arm over her waist, the front of his body against the back of hers as he pressed a slow, soft kiss to her neck?

Now practically feverish, Evelyn placed cool palms at her hot cheeks and swallowed the hard lump in her throat. She jerked her mind back from the strange fantasy. Because that was all it was, a fantasy. Yes, she had accepted Ollie's touch under situations when she'd needed his help, but otherwise, it had practically burned her. And even if that weren't an issue, she wasn't one to incite passion in a man—if one didn't count the earl, of course. Degas had been so kind as to inform her of that previously. That evening, the famed artist had told Evelyn in front of all their friends, *"I couldn't even paint you if I wanted to. You have the warmth and desire of the jagged edge of granite."* Degas had then knocked over his absinthe as he'd passed out on the floor.

Evelyn ran her hand over Ollie's pillow again. He was so different from her in that regard. Devilishly handsome, he oozed sexuality. He was a human magnet.

Evelyn didn't ooze anything except being a stuffy, old academic type.

The human equivalent of jagged granite.

As she studied his pillow, she made a funny observation. The pillow she assumed Ollie used was flatter than the other one, as if the other hadn't been used in some time, if ever. She then realized the nightstand on his side of the bed had a photograph. She hesitated. Surely, if she looked closer, she would see the face of the most beautiful woman in the world.

But perhaps, if Evelyn saw the woman Ollie lusted after, it would finally clear her head of him.

Evelyn leaned closer, her heart quickening. The silver frame housed a photograph behind glass. Briefly, her own reflection stared back until she focused on a very unamused black-and-white Hambone with a Christmas present bow atop her head.

Evelyn let out a gasp, realizing why this house felt so empty and odd.

One of the most important things to aristocrats were family lines, tracing back familial roots to the nobles of yore. Evelyn had been through hundreds of houses that belonged to such families, most of which had been in the same family for countless generations. And in every room and hallway of these houses, no matter what style the house was in, there was one aspect shared across every single aristocratic household.

Portrait after portrait of family members, some dead for hundreds of years, hung with pride in every room and hallway. Furniture used by generation after generation worn with love and time. Family lore and history was soaked into the bones of the structures and furniture. Family crests were displayed where all could see.

Meanwhile, there wasn't a single item in Ollie's entire house that was tied to his family. Aside from anything related to Hambone, of course.

Sadness washed over Evelyn. It never really hit her how isolating being an orphaned child would be, much less that it would follow into adulthood. Ollie rarely talked about it, but he had made a few frustrated comments in passing that his brothers had known their parents, but Ollie never had.

But why was there nothing here from Ollie's grandparents? She knew they were Scottish nobility. Surely, they had portraits or family heirlooms they would want to pass on to him?

A noise at the bedroom door caused Evelyn's heart to stop and the resulting jolt of fear that zapped her threw her to the floor. Someone was entering the bedroom.

From here, she could see under the bed and watched the bottom of the door swing open.

Please don't be Ollie. Please don't be Ollie, she repeated to herself.

The door opened to reveal a dark, woolen skirt.

Whoever the woman was took two slow steps into the room while leaving the door open. She stopped.

Maybe she would leave, thinking the room was empty. That would be quite fantastic.

"Do you plan on spending the entire day in here, Miss Sparrow?" Mrs. Chapman's voice was unamused.

Evelyn shut her eyes tightly against the mounting humiliation. Maybe if she didn't move, or didn't breathe, Mrs. Chapman would go away and they would never speak of this.

"Is there a reason you are in Mr. McNab's bedroom?" The housekeeper was not going to let Evelyn get away with this.

Drat. How would Evelyn get out of this one?

With no other choice, Evelyn stood up from the floor. She was on the other side of the large room from the housekeeper and felt very small. "I dropped something."

Mrs. Chapman lifted one eyebrow. "What did you drop?"

Evelyn paused before letting out a long sigh. "I didn't think that far ahead."

The housekeeper crossed the room. "What do you think you're doing, sneaking around in Mr. McNab's bedroom?"

"I was merely curious about the home Ollie—Mr. McNab keeps. He did tell me I could go wherever I pleased."

"Did your family not teach you manners? It is quite obvious he did not include his bedroom in that invitation."

Evelyn could feel her face turn red. As Mrs. Chapman herded her out of the room, Evelyn hung her head with shame.

The housekeeper followed Evelyn to make sure she was heading toward the stairs. "Just a moment, Miss Sparrow," the housekeeper said.

Though she wanted to run down the stairs and retreat into the parlor, Evelyn forced herself to face the woman.

"I can't quite figure you out," Mrs. Chapman said, her forehead wrinkled as she looked over Evelyn. "To be clear, I know *who* you are."

Evelyn tried to keep a level face. "Whatever do you mean?"

"I know you're the woman everyone is looking for. The runaway bride."

A long pause. Evelyn finally said, "And you're going to turn me in."

Mrs. Chapman's expression remained pinched. "No. Frankly, I have no desire to garner the attention that would put upon me. I don't much care to have my name and face plastered all over the newspapers because of your dramatics. And I know the cook feels similar. Believe it or not, money doesn't rule over everyone."

Evelyn shifted.

"Mr. McNab has also made it quite clear that if either of us turn you in, we will live to regret it. Of course, neither of us could imagine what, exactly, he could do and have concluded it was an empty threat. However, as we have no intention of leaving our positions, we will have no issue following our employer's request to keep you hidden. What I want to know is *why* he is protecting you."

"Protecting me?" Evelyn considered this. "I don't know if I would put it that way. He is allowing me stay here until I figure out what I'm to do next. I have nowhere else to go."

"I want to tell you something, and I'm only going to tell it to you once. What you do with it is your business."

Evelyn swallowed and nodded once.

"I have seen that man return home utterly defeated far too many times."

"I don't understand."

Mrs. Chapman huffed. "I shall be more plain, then. Far too many people take advantage of him. His brothers. His grandparents." She closed her eyes and shook her head with distaste. "Women. Who bloody knows who or what else. And I've, frankly, had enough of it." Her eyes opened again and her gaze was sharp. "Mr. McNab is a good man with a kind heart. He doesn't deserve to be treated the way he is. And it's clear this arrangement you two have is going to end in a disaster and he will not take it well."

What in the blazes was the woman on about? Evelyn took a patient breath. "Mrs. Chapman, forgive me, but I think you may be misreading something. Mr. McNab is a client of mine. He was willing to help me in a desperate situation, and if anything, I would consider him a dear friend. I'm not sure what you think is going on, but if you wish us to speak plainly, that is as plain as I can be. The only reason I am here is because I quite literally had nowhere else to go. No one would expect to find me here, and Mr. McNab was kind enough to offer a spare room, as his brother kicked me out of the flat above their pub, where I had planned to stay originally."

Mrs. Chapman mumbled to herself, and Evelyn swore she'd said, *Of course he did.*

"I do not plan on being here a moment longer than I need

to," Evelyn said, completing the thought.

"You say all that, insist you are dear friends, yet I found you sneaking around his bedroom."

Evelyn forced down her embarrassment. "I wasn't sneaking."

"What would you call it, then?"

"I...was mildly curious and it got the best of me. And I had nothing else to do. I was exploring the house and happened to end up in there by accident."

Mrs. Chapman narrowed her eyes. "You contradict yourself."

Evelyn thought it best to keep her mouth shut.

"No matter. I see you will not admit to it." And the house-keeper began to descend down the stairs.

Evelyn huffed and began following the woman, her footsteps rapid in order to keep up. "Excuse me, but what are you insinuating? Not admit to what?"

The housekeeper continued her descent without turning around. "You have designs on him, Miss Sparrow, which is quite the shock for a woman already betrothed to another."

"I do *not* have designs on him!" Evelyn retorted. "And he most certainly does not have designs on me!"

But Mrs. Chapman didn't say another word, instead disappearing into the depths of the home.

Chapter Eleven

A S SOON AS Ollie had found a hat for Evelyn, he hurried home as fast as he could.

It felt a bit silly, but he thought it was quite literally the most perfect hat he could buy for her. It was dove gray felt and would cover the entire top of her head while the wide brim dipped low, hiding the back. From the front, the brim curled up and rose at a jaunty angle, accented by a spray of pink, silk flowers and gray feathers, kept together by a large, blue, velvet bow.

Even though the hat itself wouldn't be a surprise, perhaps it would lift her spirits. Evelyn had seemed morose lately. Not that he blamed her, of course.

As Ollie waited on the crowded tram for his stop, he clutched the hat box tightly while biting the inside of his cheek to keep from grinning like an idiot. Buying a gift for Evelyn had been an exhilarating experience. He had never bought a gift for a woman before, and even though Evelyn was only a friend, he still found himself strangely excited by it. Ollie couldn't wait to see her eyes light up when she saw it.

He was in good spirits as he walked through the front door. Mrs. Chapman hurried to meet him upon hearing his return. Rapidly, he told the housekeeper about the outing and how brilliant the hat was.

"Mr. McNab, please!" Mrs. Chapman interrupted in a low but

anxious voice.

"What's the matter?" Ollie was heading farther into the house to find Evelyn, but Mrs. Chapman stepped in front of him to stop him. "Am I not allowed to enter my home?" he jested.

Mrs. Chapman gave him an unamused look. "I've been trying to tell you, through your incessant talking, that you have dinner guests."

Ollie frowned deeply. "I don't have a dinner planned."

"I know that."

Unexpected guests? Who could that be? Cold fear snaked through Ollie. "Blast, is it the earl and the baron?" The thought of Evelyn being stuck with them while Ollie had been away made him sick to his stomach.

The housekeeper shook her head. Relief flooded him, but only briefly. No one knew she was here, so it shouldn't be someone for her, then. Maybe it was Victor and Dantes, with more lost sums to shove in Ollie's face. He swallowed. "Who's here, then?"

Mrs. Chapman's face twisted with regret. "His Grace and Her Grace. The Duke and Duchess of Invermark."

Ollie slapped a palm to his face. He would have paid good money for it to have been his brothers and not his grandparents. "What are they doing here?" Ollie groaned.

Mrs. Chapman fidgeted. "When I opened the door they came barreling in, with no regard to manners. I informed them you were out and instead of leaving like everyone else in the world would, they insisted they wait for you. And ordered me to tell Cook to have dinner ready at a 'normal time,' with extra annunciation on those last words." There was a long pause. "When was the last time you talked to them, Mr. McNab?"

With a grimace, Ollie admitted it had been almost six months now. Granted, there had been numerous invites for him to visit them during that time, but Ollie had always had some excuse. Apparently, he'd avoided them for too long and was now going to pay for it. At the worst possible time.

Fergus and Marjory, as Ollie generally referred to them instead of "Grandfather" and "Grandmother," had taken the McNab brothers in when Ollie had been four. Dantes and Victor had been sent to boarding school, though Victor had run away and left permanently two years later, and had raised Ollie as a nob. However, despite only living in Whitechapel for four years, it had been some of the most formative years of his life. It was where Ollie had learned to talk and walk, where he'd made his first friends, where he'd had his first so-called family: the gang of street boys Dantes and Victor had taken up with to survive the streets without parents or a roof over their heads.

It was also where Ollie had learned to eat on his own—with his hands, not with five different forks—where he learned how to pick locks, and where he'd learned how adults acted, though largely the tattered, drunk men and the street women they'd spent time with, not polished gentlemen and ladies prudishly dancing at a ball.

And when the first years of one's life were rooted in the slums, there was no way to ever fully escape it.

Not to say Fergus and Marjory hadn't tried.

Too many times, Ollie had been caught breaking into girls' bedrooms late at night, after being invited by said girls. The first time he'd been caught, they had both been sixteen. At eighteen and after two years of his shenanigans, his grandparents had been so put out by his behavior, he'd been sent to Oxford year-round. The intention had been to surround him with young men of his own age and station, to emulate the behavior of his peers. And while his peers may have spoken better, eaten better, and acted better, they had not been much better behaved at all. There had just been more rules to work around.

Unfortunately for Fergus and Marjory, Ollie's first years of life had been wild and lawless. By the time he'd been with them, he'd known well enough life would go on without following stifling rules.

Additionally, being in Oxford without Fergus and Marjory

breathing down his neck had allowed him more time and freedom to see his brothers. When he'd been in London or Scotland with his grandparents, or at boarding school in Eton, seeing his brothers had been impossible, even if they hadn't been far away. Oxford had provided the freedom to visit them almost whenever he'd pleased. They'd been only a train ride away, and over his Oxford years, he'd become close with them once more.

And during this time, Victor and Dantes had begun tossing around the idea of opening a pub.

They'd just needed a bit more money first.

Unbeknownst to their grandparents, the McNab brothers had pooled together their share of their inheritance from their father's railroad company, and The Harp & Thistle had come to be, the name a nod to their long-dead parents: their Irish mother as the harp, their Scottish father the thistle.

Ollie had begun working there in addition to attending classes.

And then Ollie's scoundrel Oxford mates had gone, too. Turned out, nobs enjoyed letting loose just as much as the working class.

Ollie had graduated from Oxford at the bottom of his class and had promptly broken the news of the pub to Fergus and Marjory, who'd been aghast. Marjory had cried for an entire day straight while Fergus had hidden in his library. Their reactions had seemed rather dramatic to Ollie, even for them. When he'd confided in friend from university, that friend had said, *"Well, yes, you're not supposed to work. You're the spare, Ollie, didn't you know that?"*

He had not, in fact, known that, and soon discovered he'd been the only one who'd been unaware of that crucial fact. Victor wanted nothing to do with the title, and at the time Dantes was a famed pugilist with a rough reputation. It did make sense Ollie would be considered the spare heir, as he had been raised in the aristocratic world.

Fergus and Marjory had tried their very best to train him

well. They had hired the best etiquette tutors in the United Kingdom. Sent Ollie to the best schools. All of it a desperate attempt to salvage their own scoundrel son's even wilder offspring. But despite their stifling dedication to improving Oliver McNab, his roots had remained in Whitechapel, and there had been nothing they would ever be able to do about it.

Ollie would always be a chimera of the wealthy and the poor.

As he thought about all of this, he stared down the hallway at the closed door that led to his parlor. Behind it was an awaiting storm—he could already feel it crackling in the air.

His entire family was now cross with him at the same time. Even though they often clashed, it was still a wretched feeling.

"Where are they?" Ollie asked with a sigh, though he already knew. He was trying to delay facing them. That euphoria he had felt earlier was now completely gone.

"In the parlor," Mrs. Chapman replied.

"And Evelyn is with them, I assume?" What an absolute nightmare this was turning out to be. Evelyn and his grandparents would have been like oil and water. Plus, there was also the fact she was even here in the first place. She was unmarried, and so was he. Even though she was here to escape a bad situation, it would still be quite the scandal for her stay to be discovered.

At Ollie's request, Mrs. Chapman took the hatbox to put in a safe place for him to fetch later. "Miss Sparrow is upstairs napping," the housekeeper explained. She then looked down at the hat box in her hands. A funny look crossed the woman's face. "Buying her pressies now," she replied in a wry tone.

Ollie resisted the urge to sigh at yet another conundrum under his roof. "What is it now?"

Mrs. Chapman glanced up the stairway. "I don't mean to add more to your shoulders, but you should know I found your lady guest in your bedroom earlier."

Admittedly, that was strange, and yet the thought of it sent a thrill up his spine. "Really? Why was she in there?"

Mrs. Chapman shrugged. "She claimed you told her she had

free rein of the house."

"I did."

"And she claimed she ended up in there by dropping something."

Ollie laughed. "She was curious, that's all."

"It doesn't bother you?"

Ollie tried to imagine Evelyn sneaking around his bedroom like she had at the museum. He grinned like an idiot.

Mrs. Chapman raised her eyebrows at this reaction, causing Ollie to force the grin away and clear his throat. "When I confronted her," Mrs. Chapman continued, "she was at your bedside."

Evelyn had been at his bedside. "Doing what?"

"I don't know. When I found her she was trying to hide by lying on the floor."

He waved it off. "I'm not bothered by it. I doubt she'll do it again, not since you scared the daylights out of her."

Ollie expected the conversation to be over, but Mrs. Chapman lingered with the hatbox. Obviously, there was something else. "You may as well tell me what's on your mind before Fergus comes out here," Ollie said.

Mrs. Chapman paled at the mention of *Fergus*. "Forgive my intrusion." She closed her eyes as she spoke. "But is there something going on between you and Miss Sparrow?"

Ollie was suddenly quite aware of his face and how badly the muscles wanted to twitch. "No," was all he replied with. What exactly did she expect him to say?

"A woman doesn't go tip-toeing about a gentleman's bedroom for no reason," Mrs. Chapman replied.

"Her reasoning was boredom."

"Mr. McNab—"

"No, Mrs. Chapman. I assure you nothing untoward is occurring and I have no idea why you would think that in the first place." This was the truth, too. His scoundrel ways were not unknown to Mrs. Chapman, but surely, she could see for herself there was no attraction between Evelyn and himself. Well, all right, there was no attraction from Evelyn, at least. Ollie wasn't so daft to believe he could ignore his ever-growing attraction to her. He'd thought she was beautiful from the moment he'd first laid eyes on her! But at least he was able to hide it.

Or he hoped so, anyway.

But he knew how she was. He may have been a scoundrel, but women were always willing participants in whatever happened between him and them. And, perhaps most importantly, Evelyn was as attracted to Ollie as she would be to a brick wall. His admiration of her beauty, of her mind, would never be reciprocated.

So, despite the fact that he desperately wanted to explore the willowy redhead and see that auburn hair spilled over his dark bedding—and knowing she had been at his bedside only made it worse—he would keep his admiration to himself.

Mrs. Chapman said Ollie's name, bringing him back down to Earth. Her arms were crossed, eyes halfway closed and mouth in a tight line as she waited for him to refocus.

However, before she could pester him further about his attraction to Evelyn, Fergus began bellowing for her.

He had to go deal with them now. "Let Evelyn continue to sleep so she doesn't come downstairs," he said to Mrs. Chapman as he began walking toward the parlor. "I will get them out posthaste."

Mrs. Chapman bowed. "Yes, Mr. McNab."

While the housekeeper disappeared, Ollie put a hand on the parlor's doorknob, closed his eyes for a moment, and steeled himself. If his grandparents discovered Evelyn was here, that would be disastrous. The sooner he could get them out, the better.

Ollie went into the parlor and found Fergus pacing while Marjory sat upright in a wingback chair, her head rested against the back, eyes closed and jaw slack. Hambone was nearly a mirrored kitty version of Marjory. The cat was asleep at the duchess's feet, on her furry back, paws up in the air, kitty tongue hanging out of an open, sharp-toothed mouth.

A staccatoed snore from Marjory cut through the room.

"Oliver, there you are!" Fergus said with a deep, jovial chuckle upon his grandson's appearance in the room. The man's familiar Scottish accent remained thick as frozen butter. Fergus, unlike Ollie, was as towering and wide shouldered as Victor and Dantes, and as hairy as a wolf.

Fergus ambled over and shook Ollie's hand with crushing strength. Ollie's eyes watered as he resisted the urge to yelp.

"Does your housekeeper understand me when I speak?" Fergus asked, one eye squinting more than the other.

"Of course she does," he wheezed. "Why?"

Fergus thrust an open palm in the direction of the sideboard, where several liquor bottles and their respective glasses sat.

"She isn't a footman, Fergus. You are welcome to pour a drink for yourself, you know."

Fergus grumbled. "If you had proper staff instead of only a housekeeper and cook, then there wouldn't be any need for me to pour a blasted drink for myself."

"What would I need a full staff for? It's only me here."

"Yes, what about a wife? Since we're on that subject." Fergus patted Ollie hard on his upper back, then gripped his shoulder to direct him over to the sideboard.

Irritated, Ollie poured his grandfather a drink and handed it over.

"What about your grandmother?" Fergus indicated his glass before taking a sip.

Ollie frowned and poured his sleeping grandmother a drink. Why had she come here just to pass out in his chair? Without thinking, he mumbled to himself, "What is it, lady's napping hour?"

"What was that?" Fergus crossed his arms and leaned toward his grandson.

Ollie realized his error and decided to pour himself a drink, too. "Nothing."

"Who else is napping for you to call it 'lady's napping hour'?"

"The cook." Ollie took a hasty sip. It was too big of a sip and it burned his mouth. His eyes began to water.

Fergus narrowed his gaze at Ollie but let the subject drop. "Back to the conversation about a wife."

"Ah, Christ."

Fergus gave him a pointed look. "We're having Duncan Campbell and his wife and daughter over for dinner in a week. You will be joining us."

"Thanks, but no."

"It wasn't a request, Oliver. It was a command."

Ollie's neck was beginning to feel stiff. How many times had he heard that line? "I thought you hated the Campbells."

"I never said that."

"You rant about the Campbells every time you're in your cups, going on and on about how they terrorized our clan for thousands of years and are the devil's spawn, or something like that."

Fergus eyed Ollie. "Perhaps that's what you need, laddie. A Scottish devil woman."

Marjory interrupted with another loud snore.

"I'm perfectly fine on my own," Ollie replied. "Not looking for a wife. But thanks."

"One week, my house, at this time." Fergus threw back the drink and held his empty glass out for a refill. "They're expecting you there, including Isla."

Ollie grudgingly refilled it. "Who the blazes is Isla?"

"The daughter! She's a bonny lass, which is all you care about, anyway."

"That's not all I care about."

"Och," Fergus replied dismissively, clearly not believing Ollie for a moment.

What *did* he look for in a woman? It wasn't something he had ever really thought about. The women he had history with had little in common, except for being attractive. It was all he'd cared about at the time. One day he would want a wife and family, but that day was not now. He was twenty-six, far too young for such a thing.

In thinking about it, though, he would want a kind, patient woman. One who was smart enough to make up for his lack of brains, but despite her intelligence didn't realize how brainless he was. Wasn't hypersensitive to cats. And, of course, beautiful, too. He did enjoy the touch of a beautiful woman. He was, after all, only a man. *Evelyn ticks those boxes*, a voice in his head said.

A rustling noise captured his attention and then, "Oh, Oliver! You've finally decided to join us," Marjory said sleepily from her chair. With a yawn, she stood up and crossed the room to her husband and grandson. Hambone, startled out of her deep sleep, mewed loudly at the duchess, as if offended, and trotted out of the room. Fergus handed the portly, graying woman her drink.

For a while, conversation went away from Ollie, and they caught up on the happenings in Fergus and Marjory's social circle, the nobs whom Ollie had grown up around after leaving Whitechapel. Mostly, they discussed whose grandchildren were getting married or having babies. But they kept bringing up Miss Isla Campbell. Miss Campbell volunteers for the poor. Miss Campbell helped plan a garden that won awards. Miss Campbell this, Miss Campbell that. That was all good for Miss Campbell, but Ollie really could not care about some woman he hadn't known existed until a few minutes ago.

It wasn't lost on him how much they seemed to be focusing on the subject of marriage and babies, though. However, if Ollie allowed them to talk about it now and get it out of their system, let some of that excitement out, when he bailed on the dinner next week they wouldn't be nearly as mad.

He checked a nearby wall clock and realized they had already been here for half an hour. Ollie started to fidget with a button on the sleeve of his jacket. The longer they stayed, the more nervous he became at them somehow discovering Evelyn's presence in his house. "It was great for you to drop by completely unexpectedly, but—"

"No 'buts,' laddie." Fergus chuckled. "We know you avoid us as much as you can. Now tonight, we are having dinner together like proper family. Whether you like it or not."

Hambone, as if sensing her human's inner distress, came over and began to weave between his legs. She then sat and stared up at him, a toy felt mouse hanging from her mouth.

It must be nice to be a cat.

At this, Mrs. Chapman came into the parlor to inform them dinner was ready to be served. As Fergus and Marjory left the parlor, the housekeeper pulled Ollie to the side.

"Miss Sparrow is awake," she whispered to Ollie in a sharp voice.

Ollie felt a sense of dread. "What do you mean, she's awake? Did you tell her not to come down?"

"I haven't seen her. As I was coming into this room, I could hear her moving around upstairs. Footfalls and other generic sounds. Drawers opening, perhaps."

They both stepped out into the hallway and stilled to listen to the sounds of the house. There was nothing but empty, quiet air. Even Fergus and Marjory were silent in a rare moment.

"Are you sure?" Ollie asked, his shoulders easing at the lack of noise.

But now Mrs. Chapman was frowning to herself as she extended an ear, as if questioning herself. "Whatever you heard, it wasn't her. It's quiet," Ollie said in a low voice. Then, he straightened, feeling more confident. "Let's make sure we only have one or two courses for the dinner. I need them out of here."

Mrs. Chapman's eyes went round. "One or two? Why, they will be quite offended by that, Mr. McNab. And I'll never hear the end of it for the rest of my days."

Ollie began walking toward the dining room, Mrs. Chapman following. He glanced back at her. "I promise I'll fix everything with them after tonight. But right now, I need to get them out before Miss Sparrow awakens."

Mrs. Chapman nodded with pursed lips and went in the direction of the kitchen, while he went to the dining room.

Ollie felt bad about excluding Evelyn and hiding this dinner from her, but if Fergus and Marjory discovered an unmarried woman was staying in his house, especially with this unexpected Miss Campbell business, they would spontaneously combust.

Even more so once they realized Evelyn was the runaway bride.

Dinner started off without a hitch, to Ollie's great surprise. Soup was served first, and as was customary, discussion about the weather was the forefront of conversation for a time.

"This soup is very good," Marjory said after finishing hers. "What is it?"

"I have no idea," Ollie replied, poking his spoon around the soup bowl. "I see beef…and vegetables?"

"You don't know what your cook serves?" Marjory lifted her eyebrows high.

Ollie set his spoon down and took a calming breath before responding. "Isn't that why I have a cook? So I don't have to think about it?"

Marjory decided not to push the subject, and the issue was thankfully forgotten when Mrs. Chapman reappeared to take the soup bowls away. But just as she grabbed the last bowl—Ollie's—they heard footsteps coming down the hall.

Ollie's heart stopped.

Mrs. Chapman lifted her head to look him in the eye, and the blood drained from her face.

"Is someone here?" Marjory asked with a quizzical voice. But before Ollie or Mrs. Chapman could run out of the room to stop Evelyn, she appeared in the doorway.

Ollie's eyes anchored onto Evelyn's. It felt as if, for a moment, time stopped. But that moment ended when she realized the duke and duchess were present. He had to give her credit—she didn't react upon seeing them other than a curtsy, then she slid across the room with liquid elegance. She had done her auburn hair in intricate braids that circled the crown of her head while the violet chiffon dress she wore hugged her slender form. The shoulder sleeves were a tad big, and the slightly too-low neckline exposed her pale décolletage. But despite the bad fit, it remained regal with sequins and crystals that winked at Ollie in the dim candlelight. Evelyn commanded the attention of the room, and Ollie was sure if the room had held thirty people, every single one would have stopped to watch her.

Mrs. Chapman nudged Ollie hard and gave him a severe look. He realized his mouth was hanging open and promptly slammed it shut.

The housekeeper pulled out a chair for Evelyn as Ollie was still too stunned to do it himself. She then rushed out with the soup bowls and to gather another place setting.

Evelyn's nearness made his heart race. So used to her in plain, woolen dresses with a simple knot in her hair, it was shocking to see her transformation from academic to aristocrat. Once he'd gotten a hold of himself, however, he realized his grandparents were staring at him with utter horror.

"I'm sorry," Marjory forced a tight, unblinking smile. "I didn't realize you were expecting a guest, Oliver."

Ollie opened his mouth to speak, but Fergus interrupted with bluster. "Who in the devil are *you*?"

Ollie swore under his breath. "Fergus, Marjory, this is Miss—"

Evelyn interrupted him quickly. "Annabelle Smith."

There was a heavy pause. Ollie cleared his throat. "Right. Miss Annabelle Smith, these are my grandparents, the Duke and Duchess of Invermark."

As she met the elder McNabs' scrutinization, Evelyn's discomfort was only given away by a slight paling of her face.

Ollie studied his grandparents. Did they realize she was the runaway bride?

Fergus continued his scrutinization. "Where did you come from? We've been here for over an hour and had no idea there was anyone else in the house." Fergus then shot a pointed look to Ollie.

"My apologies, I only arrived a minute ago," Evelyn said helpfully.

"A minute ago? A minute ago, Mrs. Chapman was in here and we never heard anyone ring at the door."

"Oh, really?" was all she replied with.

Ollie resisted the urge to groan.

"Forgive me, and call me old fashioned." Marjory forced a laugh before putting a pointed stare on Ollie. "But why is an unmarried, unchaperoned woman at your home, Oliver?"

Ollie rubbed a hand over his jaw. He could feel the anger radiating off of them. Soon, steam would be bursting out of their ears. He had seen it before.

As the silence stretched and Ollie didn't respond, Fergus threw back his drink. Ollie knew the man well enough to know that, if he wasn't drunk yet, he would be in mere minutes. Ollie braced himself.

"Well I...I had arrived with my...brother, who is a friend of Mr. McNab here." She paused and looked at him, her eyes widening, as if asking for help.

"Right." Ollie stammered as his mind tried to catch up with his mouth. "My friend Mr. Robert Smith." Another pause. "From...the pub." He looked away from Evelyn and over to Fergus and Marjory, who both had level faces, clearly unconvinced. He smiled at them.

"Yes! And poor Robert." Evelyn cleared her throat. "As we arrived, he felt unwell and returned home immediately. I came in to inform Ol—I mean, Mr. McNab what had happened. Since he was expecting us. For dinner."

Fergus and Marjory exchanged a long glance.

Fergus cleared his throat and knit his hands together on the tabletop. "What are you after, lass, his money? His name? His family legacy?"

Evelyn laughed—did she think Fergus was joking?—and

raised her eyebrows sky high at this. But Ollie felt the smallest modicum of relief. His grandfather's comment confirmed Fergus had no idea he was talking to a baron's daughter, much less the runaway bride.

"Do you really expect us to believe that hastily concocted story? You're one of his pub whores, aren't you?!" Marjory spit the word out with disdain. "My grandson has many of them and you look like one, with that horrid, fake red hair and second-hand clothing." Marjory stared at Evelyn's too-low neckline, and Evelyn stiffened. "You can't fool us, though, lass! We can see through you as if you were the thinnest glass."

Evelyn's lips parted with surprise and Ollie was sure she would never look at him the same again.

"Marjory, please." Ollie had to placate them before the situation got worse. And he knew well enough how easily it could. Once they were set off—which they were in danger of right now—there was no calming them.

"No, Oliver," Marjory replied, not taking her eyes off of Evelyn. "Miss Smith, I want to be quite clear so there is no confusion between any of us. I don't know who you are or why you are here. Perhaps you are nothing at all to Oliver, and that is my hope. But in case you are, know this: One week from today, my grandson will be meeting a woman of whom we are confident he will grow very fond, and both of our families are expecting a wedding in the near future."

Ollie glared hard at her but knew if he began talking, he would say something he couldn't take back.

"If you have any designs on him whatsoever…" Marjory continued. What was with everyone saying that tonight? "Rid yourself of the ridiculous notion. We know Oliver has been flippant about life so far, but that changes now. It's why we are here tonight. He will be marrying a woman with class, not someone who tries too hard—and unconvincingly."

His grandmother could have slapped him across the face and it would have had less impact. He couldn't bring himself to look over at Evelyn, to see what his family had done to her. Perhaps that was cowardly, but in the moment, he was a coward. He clenched his teeth with anger but couldn't bring himself to stand up to them. Just like he couldn't stand up to Victor.

Ollie had a death grip on the arm of his chair, the tension from his jaw now radiating throughout his body. But then, something strange happened. Beneath the table and out of view from Fergus and Marjory, Evelyn placed her hand over his.

His heart seemed to stop. It was a calming gesture, a way to say, "Let it go, Ollie."

And it worked.

At Evelyn's touch, at this small gesture, somehow, the anger in Ollie seemed to subside. It didn't go away, but the intensity eased. Maybe it was simply the shock that Evelyn, who was not one he would call *touchy*, had her hand over his.

Either way, he was grateful she was there.

Mrs. Chapman appeared again with the new place setting, and she arranged it before Evelyn. The room remained silent, and once the housekeeper had finished her task, she hurried out again without a glance back.

Marjory stood up hastily. "Thank you for the soup, Oliver," she said, though obviously, she wasn't really thankful for it. Marjory stared down Fergus, as he was still seated. Fergus, evidently realizing his wife was watching him with daggers in her eyes, hastily wiped a napkin at his mouth and stood up. While Marjory stormed out without another word and her nose up in the air, Fergus lingered.

"Remember, next week." Fergus paused in consideration, glancing at the door his wife had disappeared through. "Your grandmother, she worries about you. That's all."

Ollie thought the way they exploded at him was a strange way to show concern, but he didn't share that.

Fergus glanced at Evelyn and turned to leave but then paused. He spun back around and tilted his head. "You…" Fergus trailed off.

Ollie's stomach hitched, waiting for Fergus to recognize Evelyn and take her back to the earl.

But Fergus just rubbed his chin and watched Ollie for a prolonged moment.

"Och, never mind." Fergus waved himself off. And without another word, he left.

Ollie and Evelyn reeled. Finally, Ollie gathered up his nerve and pushed aside his humiliation. "Evelyn, I don't know what to say. I am so very sorry about that." He dared a glance in her direction finally, afraid he would find silent tears.

But Evelyn stared straight ahead as if she were made of stone. Her face was perhaps a bit paler, but nothing else gave away how she felt in the moment. No tears, no quivering lip. Nothing.

"But why did you come in here?" Now that everything had shockingly worked out for the best, his irritation with her mounted. "If you heard people here, why would you risk everything and come in?"

Evelyn jerked her hand away from his, as if she'd just realized it were there, and stood up. "I have to go," she said without meeting his eye. And she sprinted out of the room.

Chapter Twelve

EVELYN RAN AS fast as she could in the blasted, ill-fitting dress. After escaping the dining room, she hurried down the hallway, up the million stairs without a mind to how loud her steps were—*so unladylike*, Mama would have said—and slammed her bedroom door shut. After turning the brass key to lock the door, she flung herself into the bed and curled up under the blankets.

Squeezing her eyes shut, Evelyn focused on the heaving of her ribs. The tightness of the blankets that cocooned her was a small comfort and leveled off the turbulent emotions.

What awful people Ollie's grandparents were!

When Evelyn had awoken from her nap, she had realized people had been visiting and worried at first about who they were. Thus, she had listened in from the top of the stairs. When she'd overheard them refer to Ollie as their grandson, though, she'd been eager to meet them. Everyone in Ollie's family thus far had been so lovely and had gone out of their way to help her in a time of need. Even his oldest brother had been willing to help, despite the fact that he and Ollie were at odds with each other right now.

It hadn't even occurred to her that his grandparents would be the exact opposite. Ollie was the one raised the longest under his grandparents' roof, and he was also the most chipper of the three brothers. Thinking about it now, she realized she had figured his grandparents were that way, too.

Oh, how utterly stupid that was.

It made sense the duke and duchess had not believed her reason for being at Ollie's home. But they *had* made incorrect assumptions about Evelyn's relationship with their grandson. Even though it was strictly friendship between them, and his grandparents didn't know the true reason why she had been present, it *was* utterly scandalous for an unmarried woman to be staying at an unmarried man's home with no other guests around.

And she knew better!

Evelyn buried her face further into the mess of blankets. The duchess's humiliating scorn kept repeating in her mind. The expression of disdain, the voice of disgust, the harsh words, repeat, repeat, repeat. They'd thought Evelyn was some pub girl and had unleashed wrath upon her merely because they thought her of low birth, not a peer who could eventually be a countess.

Evelyn paused. At this point, would she even be a countess? While she didn't know what was happening outside of Ollie's house, she could make a well-educated guess that her home was wild with drama and her reputation at best was now questionable. Would the earl still want anything to do with her? The newspapers did say that once she was found, she would be sent directly to him and not her father. She had to assume, at least for now, that the earl still wished for her to be his bride.

She shuddered.

After a few minutes of burrowing in the blankets, Evelyn realized her breathing had leveled. She poked her head out of her cocoon to rest it upon her pillow and turned to her side to stare at the door. While the anger and humiliation had subsided, a dark melancholy had blanketed her in place.

What was all that about Ollie marrying someone? Where had that come from? He knew she was running from a similar fate, so why wouldn't he tell her about it? Unless their friendship was one-sided.

There was a knock at the door, followed by Ollie's muffled voice. "Evelyn?"

Evelyn didn't respond.

Another knock, louder this time. "Evelyn, are you all right?"

Evelyn let out a long sigh and climbed out of the covers to sit on the edge of the bed. She patted at her hair and felt it had become quite messy from the blankets, but the thought of taking it out and doing it all over again felt impossible. The sick melancholy the duke and duchess had left behind seemed to be nestling into her stomach, heavy as a boulder, as if it were planning on sticking around awhile.

It was her fault Ollie's grandparents had blown up at him tonight. If she hadn't been here, they would have had a perfectly pleasant dinner. Maybe they would have talked more about Ollie getting married. Maybe he would have been happy about it.

Evelyn swallowed the lump in her throat. It was silly for her to care. Why did it bother her imagining Ollie married to someone else? Yes, she thought him the most handsome gentleman in three countries but never had she cared before about an attractive gentleman being married to or betrothed to another lady. Why care in this instance, then?

It made no sense.

And yet, Evelyn found herself still stuck on the subject, wondering what this woman looked like. Evelyn imagined a beautiful woman with a big chest and large, soft hips and thighs hanging on to him. Bile started to rise in her throat.

There was a rattling sound at the door just before it burst open. Evelyn yelped as Ollie rushed through the door holding a butter knife. His green eyes were round with panic.

"Why didn't you respond?" Ollie seemed to be trying not to shout. "Didn't you hear me calling you through the door?"

"I'm sorry. I didn't," Evelyn lied. She just wasn't ready to face him yet.

Ollie hurried forward and set the butter knife down on the nightstand. He rushed a hand through his hair and had a wild look he was trying to tame by tightening his face. "I shouted through the door. Numerous times. What do you mean, you didn't hear me?"

All she could do was shrug. Ollie let out an irritated laugh.

"I don't need *you* cross with me now, too!" Evelyn said sharply. "I would like to be alone now, please leave."

"Not happening."

She scoffed.

"You scared me halfway to death, Evelyn." Ollie's tone held a seriousness she had never heard from him before. Immediately, she wanted to curl into herself. She looked down at her lap as he continued. "You said you had to go and then you ran off? I thought you'd left! I went outside looking for you and couldn't find you. I ran up and down my street until I realized you might be up in here. And then you wouldn't respond to me! I couldn't help but…" Ollie let out a loud sigh and ran his hands through his hair again before taking a deep breath and crouching on the ground beside her. "I'm sorry about my grandparents."

She didn't respond.

"But *why* did you come down? You must have heard them— they're so blasted loud. And you know no one should see you right now."

Evelyn considered the question. "I was curious."

"Curious?" Ollie asked, a bit confused.

Evelyn lifted her head enough to see his face. "Yes. You've never talked much about your family, and I've noticed you don't have portraits of them anywhere in your home. I suppose I kind of wondered what the people who raised you looked like. It didn't occur to me they would be…like that. Everyone in your family has been so lovely. I just assumed they would be too. I didn't give it any thought." She paused, feeling totally idiotic. "I'm sorry."

Ollie let out another sigh but then said, "It's fine. It's done, they'll get over it—they always do—but the most important part is they didn't know who you were. And that's really all I care about."

Evelyn swallowed and gave him a small nod.

Ollie stared off, thinking. "Wait. You said something about me not having portraits anywhere in my home. Is that why you were in my bedroom earlier?"

Evelyn jerked her head up to look him in the eye, her face flushed with heat.

Ollie grinned. "You must have known Mrs. Chapman would tell me."

"I was kind of hoping she wouldn't…"

"*Is* that why you were in there?"

Why else would she have been in there? She fidgeted, embarrassed. "Yes. I apologize, Ollie. It won't happen again."

"Your curiosity often gets you into trouble, doesn't it?"

Evelyn smiled slightly. "Yes, it does."

"You're welcome in there, anytime."

Evelyn furrowed her brow. What was he talking about? "Where, your bedroom?"

Ollie nodded.

Evelyn was now very confused. Surely, Ollie meant she was welcome in his bedroom if she ever needed something or to talk to him. Right? "Oh. Thank you? You as well."

"Me as well?"

"You may enter my room, too, if you ever wish to speak to me." She glanced over at the door. "Not that you need my permission."

Ollie chuckled with a crooked grin, one hand resting on the edge of her bed. "Right. To talk, of course." He pulled his hand away, briefly tensing before his usual ease settled over him again. He stood up.

Something about the moment felt odd to Evelyn, but she dismissed it. "Your grandparents are very good at knowing how to dig into someone's weaknesses."

"What do you mean?"

Evelyn didn't want to talk about her appearance to Ollie, so she stood up, too, and angled over to the dark-blue dress with the light-blue bow she had laid out earlier, draped over the back of a chair. Tonight, they were going to try to hunt down the Signature Swindler, but she couldn't do that in sequins. The blue dress was acceptable, she supposed, but she missed her gray, woolen dresses that fit her properly. "I really need to get my own clothing back," she said, mostly to herself.

"No, don't change the subject." Ollie appeared at her side. "What did you mean just now?"

"Ollie, please, this is embarrassing."

"Tell me," he replied in a serious tone.

It was quite irritating how good he was at getting her to talk. She ran a finger over a seam on the dress. "It's no secret women can be rather conscious of their appearance. And I'm no different."

Ollie frowned. "What are you talking about?"

"I don't meet beauty expectations. I don't have…" She looked down at the bust of her bodice, filled with air. "Well, what I mean is…" She grasped her hips then looked up at Ollie, who studied her, his brows pulled tight together. "And my hair!" She patted at the mess atop her head.

"Honestly, you've lost me. Come here." He beckoned her to follow him to a standing mirror and turned, expectant.

Evelyn scoffed but complied, knowing there would be no way of getting out of this. She went over to him, making sure the irritation was clear in her frown.

Ollie moved to stand behind her and she glared at him in the reflection. "This is what I see, Evelyn," he said. "No, don't look at me—look at you."

Determined to prove she was right, she complied without arguing. Ollie took a step closer to her. He was so near now that she could feel the heat radiating off of his body. He leaned down slightly so his face was beside hers.

"I see a woman with an ill-fitting dress and a mess of red hair, which is *not* fake. This is my real hair color, thank you very much, and it is not a gaudy color. I do know that's why they said that, and they wouldn't be the first to erroneously believe it." Evelyn turned to look at him directly.

"You're right. It's quite a nice color, in my opinion," Ollie replied with a glint of humor in his eye.

"Please don't patronize me." She glared at him again before turning back to the mirror.

Ollie chuckled. "Look, forget all of that. I'm going to tell you something I normally would keep to myself."

Evelyn eyed his reflection cautiously. "All right."

"Ignoring the trouble from earlier, when you walked into the dining room tonight, I was hypnotized."

Evelyn waited, hoping he would explain further. But sometimes Ollie was not very good at explaining things, so she would have to dig out his meaning. "What does that mean, you were hypnotized?"

"I, um…" He spoke in a low, deep voice that tickled her ear and caused her heart to race. "You walked into the room and slid across the floor, your back as straight as a rod, chin lifted ever so slightly, and you twinkled from head to toe. I couldn't help but watch. You thought Hambone should have been named Princess, but I think that would fit you better."

Evelyn raised an eyebrow. "I don't resemble any of Queen Victoria's daughters."

"I don't mean literally, Evelyn. Just that your presence was commanding. Like I said, I was hypnotized watching you look like this"—he indicated her current appearance—"while crossing the room toward us. Toward me."

Evelyn's gaze met Ollie's in the mirror as he let out a low, breathy laugh that swept over her neck. Her heart raced in response. If she leaned back, she would be against him. Maybe he would even wrap his arms around her waist. Would she like that, or would it make her want to run?

Get your mind out the clouds, Evelyn scolded herself. That's *not* happening.

"So, you thought I looked nice tonight?" She still wasn't following.

"No." Ollie was playing with her hair, and she was surprised to find she didn't mind. In fact, dare she admit she might even like it? "I thought—think—you look absolutely beautiful."

Evelyn's eyebrows lifted high.

"And…" Ollie still held her gaze as he looped a strand back around her ear. "My grandparents knew the effect you had on me. And they were threatened by it."

Her voice lowered. "Because you're supposed to marry someone else?"

That seemed to break the spell cast between them. Ollie took a few steps back and shoved his hands into his trouser pockets. His face took on that disarming ease yet again. "Someone else? Why, were you interested?"

"Be serious, Ollie."

"I know, I know. The mere mention of marriage sends you over the edge." Ollie grinned again. Lord, give her patience.

"Why didn't you tell me about that? I thought we were, you know. Friends?"

"There's nothing to tell you. It's not going to happen."

"Because you don't want to get married, either?"

"No, I do."

Evelyn blinked. "Really?"

"I love the idea of it. Together, for the rest of our lives? Facing all of life's ups and downs with that one special person? Yes, I want that. Just not yet."

Evelyn wanted to ask more questions. Like, did he think his grandparents were going to drop it that easily? They'd seemed pretty serious about it. But it wasn't any of her business, either.

"Can I ask you something?" Ollie said. And when Evelyn nodded, he continued. "Why did you hold my hand at dinner?"

Evelyn felt flushed and looked away. "I didn't realize I had."

Ollie laughed. "Come now, Evelyn. You and I both know that isn't true."

"Well, I didn't realize it at first. I'm not sure why I did it. I was so taken aback by His and Her Grace, and I guess I did it to keep you grounded. In a way." And maybe, for herself, too.

Ollie rubbed a palm over his jaw. "That's what I figured happened. I didn't think you would ever be that intimate with me."

"Heavens, no!" Evelyn immediately regretted how effusively she'd said that because there was a brief flash in Ollie's eyes. She hurried over to the dress she had laid out earlier. This whole conversation was strange and far too personal and edging on something that shouldn't be edged. "Ollie, tonight I would like to try to find our missing painting."

Ollie shoulders dropped at the change of subject. "Excellent. What are you thinking we should do?"

"I want to focus on the Bethnal Green heist. That one was a major change for him, where he went from jewelry to artwork. I want to figure out why he made that change. Perhaps it will help us locate the missing painting."

"Do you have any ideas on that? Why he made the change, I mean."

Evelyn shook her head before returning to the mirror and began letting out her hair to fix. "It's impossible to say right now. Maybe he was bored with jewelry. Maybe he was feeling more confident. Who knows?" As locks of red hair tumbled from the crown of braids she'd unraveled, Evelyn realized Ollie was watching her complete her task with very focused interest.

Something inside of her leapt. Her nerves, perhaps. Feeling rather strange at being the focus of his attention, she released the last braid. "Ollie, are you paying attention?"

Ollie seemed to snap back to reality and blinked several times before remembering what they were talking about. "Right. What do you plan to do, break into the museum?"

"No. I don't think that will be necessary. Remember, the theft was discovered by the museum director the following morning. I would like to talk to him and find out if there were any clues left behind the public doesn't know about, or if there is anything else he can tell us that may be helpful."

"But you said you don't know anyone who works there."

Evelyn bent at the waist to flip her hair over, where she combed and fluffed it with her fingers. "Correct. But if you recall, Mr. Burlington does. The director's name is Mr. Albert Martin. I don't know him, but I do know of him." She flipped back up and found Ollie staring at her again with a drunk-like expression. "Are you ill?" Evelyn asked with a frown.

Ollie blinked several times again but seemed at a loss for words.

Evelyn placed a hand on her hip. "I need to change, Ollie, and then we can leave."

Ollie swept his gaze over her in a way that didn't feel wholly innocent. She opened her mouth to ask him what he thought he was doing when he interrupted.

"Wait, I almost forgot." He hurried out of the room.

He was acting so odd. Between his admission of being hypnotized by her—which surely he'd only said to help her mood—but also the way he kept staring at her!

There had to be a reasonable explanation. But then, she recalled his grandmother had said Ollie had had many women from the pub. Evelyn was no fool. She knew that type. Ollie would be attracted to any halfway decent woman who responded positively to his attention. Maybe there'd been times where Ollie had said or done something that had made it seem he was attracted to her. But it was purely lust, and nothing more. She had seen the earl lust after her enough times to recognize it.

Ollie returned grinning widely and carrying a round hatbox. "For tonight," he said, holding the box out to her.

Evelyn took the hatbox from him and lifted the lid with anticipation.

The hat was wrapped in tissue paper. She set the box down on the foot of the bed and peeled apart the paper, revealing the hat. It was gray felt with a blue bow; pink, silk flowers; and gray feathers.

It was stunning.

Ollie had gone far and above what she'd expected. She would have thought he would get something from a department store, where hundreds of the same exact hat were sold to make it more affordable for the masses. It would have been a lot easier and cheaper for him to do that. And even though they had agreed she would pay him back once she was able to, deep down, she suspected he had only said that to placate her. He would never accept a shilling from her.

Once again, he had charmed her by doing something that made her feel special. But she knew that wasn't the case.

Ollie moved to her side. "You hate it."

Still, it was a kindness that reached her heart, despite her logical mind. Emotion began to bubble up inside her, and all Evelyn could do was shake her head hard.

Ollie swore. "I'm sorry, Evelyn. I didn't know what I was doing. I'm not really one to keep up with women's fashion. I liked the brim and thought the colors would look nice with your hair, completely forgetting the whole point of it was to *cover up* your hair."

Evelyn's lip started to quiver, and she let out an unexpected sob before her hand flew to her mouth to cover it up.

"Look, I'll take it back tomorrow."

"No." It was all she could manage to get out.

"No?"

Tears pooled in her eyes, and it made her mad. Why was she getting emotional over a hat? She was so happy right now, though. She thought back to all the times he'd sat with her in the museum, listening to her prattle on for hours about art history. Anyone else stopped listening after five minutes. And he hadn't given a second thought, despite the risk, to giving her a place to stay while she sorted out the disaster she'd made of her life. He was always kind to her. And to think his family treated him like the heel of a shoe!

The emotion broke through the dam and Evelyn became

overwhelmed by a very confusing feeling that made her heart shine and her stomach flip. A magnet seemed to be pulling her toward Ollie.

Before she realized what she was doing, Evelyn turned to face him, and the last thing she saw was his eyes widen before she leaned in.

And kissed him.

It wasn't a heated kiss. Her mouth stayed closed, and so did his. But his lips were as soft as she had always imagined.

The kiss lingered.

He didn't pull away.

Instead, he placed a large, warm hand on her lower back as the other slid into her hair to cup the back of her head. He moved with familiarity, as if they kissed all the time. As if the way he held her was the first step of more to come. Realizing this could become more knocked her back into reality. She pulled her face away just a millimeter and for a moment, their rapid breaths mingled, his green eyes as bright as emeralds, as if he couldn't believe what had just happened.

Kiss him again, a little voice in her head said.

Instead, Evelyn took several steps back to get out of his reach.

Ollie took a sharp inhale through his nose, and he lifted his palms in a defensive motion, as if she were about to come for his life. "Evelyn, I didn't mean to do that."

She shook her head. "Ollie, *I* kissed *you!*"

His brow furrowed, as if this were impossible news. "Are you sure?"

"Yes!"

"But I held you. I'm so sorry. I wasn't thinking and that caught me by surprise." Ollie began to pace as if he were filled with shame, which was not comforting at all. He stopped and rubbed his hands over his face. "You're completely sure you kissed me? Not the other way around?"

As she was just as confused as he was, she didn't have a retort.

"Evelyn kissed me." Ollie pinched his chin, deep in thought. "Interesting," he added on.

Evelyn huffed. "It won't happen again. I was just emotional! I think." All right, so she didn't really have an explanation of why that had happened. It had seemed to happen on its own, as if Ollie's handsomeness had pulled her to him. She could still feel that magnetic pull, in fact.

"You were emotional because of a hat?"

Evelyn wasn't going to respond to that. It would sound absolutely absurd. "I love the hat, Ollie. Thank you."

"I can get you another one tomorrow, if that wins me one more kiss."

She narrowed her eyes at him. He laughed.

Chapter Thirteen

THE BRASS DOOR knocker echoed down the dark, foggy cobblestone street. Ollie found himself at a small townhouse in a middle-class area of London with which he was unfamiliar.

He waited, eyes anchored to the glossy, black Georgian door, hands shoved into his trouser pockets, his head down just enough for the brim of his top hat to conceal his eyes should anyone walk by. But he wasn't feeling casual; he was quite on edge. Somewhere nearby, Evelyn was hiding in the shadows, and even though she was out of sight, he couldn't stop thinking about her.

It had been a few hours since they'd kissed, and he still felt her lips against his. His fingers still felt the thick, wiry strands of her hair, the curve of her back against his palm. It was as if the moment had somehow burned into him.

Ollie still wasn't convinced Evelyn had initiated the kiss. It didn't make sense. She hated touch, so wouldn't that include kissing? She'd recoiled from him any time he'd touched her unexpectedly. And the kiss had been an unexpected one full of hesitation, further evidence he'd been the one who'd leaned in first and she hadn't known what to do. It had only lasted a moment, a slight brush before lips had met, a closed-mouth kiss, then nothing more.

No, he didn't believe for a second she'd initiated that kiss.

He was the one losing his mind over her. Whenever Evelyn

was around, his stomach did nauseating flips. At first, he'd thought he was getting ill. Maybe he was, but the illness wasn't one remedied by a physician's visit.

No, it was far direr.

It had started to dawn on him when she'd walked into his dining room, hypnotizing him. Something had practically hit him upside the head. Evelyn Sparrow was gorgeous—and he didn't have a bloody chance with her.

And then there was the gut punch that had followed. He'd thought he'd lost her when she'd run away. It had been the most horrific feeling when he couldn't find her. He hadn't known what to think, and he'd nearly fallen apart because of it.

Ollie couldn't deny it any longer. Evelyn was not just some woman from the pub, or walking down the street, or a lady nob from some insipid ball. She wasn't even a simple friend.

No, Evelyn was something else entirely.

But how had it all managed to change in one day?

Not long ago, she'd been the woman fixing his brother's art collection. Mere hours later, all he wanted to do was take her in his arms and protect her from the wrath of Fergus and Marjory, from her family, from the earl, from the world. Comfort her, soothe her. With words, with his mouth, with his body. With every minute movement she made, he wanted her more. With every swish of her skirt, every lock of tumbling hair, the craving to feel her against him one more time got worse. Not better.

Ollie cleared his throat. He was utterly depraved.

And he desperately needed to get a hold of himself. Evelyn Sparrow was not an option. His family would absolutely flip. Victor, Dantes, and Vivian had all made it quite clear that of all the women in the world, Evelyn was the only one off limits.

To Dantes and Vivian, Evelyn was the woman restoring their prized artwork. They wouldn't want to sour that professional relationship—and had said so previously. They knew Ollie's reputation in chasing pretty women. He couldn't resist them, and he never stuck with the same woman for long. But he'd never taken any of those relationships, if they could even be called that, seriously, either.

To Victor, Evelyn was too far up the social ladder. Victor despised the aristocracy and everything it stood for. And also, he thought Ollie had the maturity of a child. He would never support Ollie being responsible for another person.

And to Fergus and Marjory, she wasn't Miss Elsa Campbell. Or was it Miss Isla Campbell? And Evelyn was English. The *English* runaway bride, which they didn't know about yet, but they would find out eventually.

If somehow they were able to rise above their families, they couldn't rise above their job responsibilities. Ollie partially owned The Harp & Thistle, so he had to be there nearly every day for most of the day. And he would never dream of asking Evelyn to leave her own career. She had made it clear it was what she wanted most.

Not that he was considering marriage and a family right now, of course, that was silly. This was all just a strange train of thought as he waited for someone to answer the blasted door!

Irritated, he knocked again.

Though he was in a tough spot with his family, family was still important to him, and it still mattered that his family would love the woman he ended up spending his life with. Years down the road, of course. But it *mattered*. He loved his brothers. His grandparents, well, they'd taken him in and he was grateful for that. Even though they hardly got along, they were the only family he had.

Ollie often wished he knew his mother's family. Perhaps they would have been more agreeable than the McNabs. But, alas, that side would always remain unknown. She'd had no family left in London, according to Dantes and Victor.

Ollie knocked on the door, harder this time. If no one answered, he would leave. But then what would they do? They had no other leads for the Signature Swindler.

Somewhere in the dark, Evelyn cleared her throat, growing

impatient now, too.

He wanted to kiss her again. Properly. He would pull her onto his lap, run his lips gently along her neck, leave her sighing, breathless.

He swore aloud.

"Is everything all right?" Evelyn whispered from somewhere nearby. The thick London fog concealed her exact whereabouts.

"Yes, I'm just frustrated no one is answering this door." No, he was thinking about bedding her because he was a depraved scoundrel.

"I think someone's coming," she replied and sure enough, the door opened, spilling a ribbon of yellow light into the night. Somewhere inside the home, numerous voices overlapped rapidly, indicating a small party of sort.

"Yes?" a man stood in the doorway, frowning up at Ollie. Recognition hit the man after a moment. "Mr. McNab?"

"Hello, Mr. Burlington," Ollie replied with barely masked disdain. Outside of the museum, James Burlington didn't seem nearly as intimidating.

"What are you doing here? How do you know where I live?"

Ollie faltered. How would he shift this conversation? "I need your help."

"Does this have anything to do with Miss Sparrow?" Burlington asked.

Ollie hesitated. He wasn't sure how much to share with Evelyn's colleague. He decided to be as vague as possible. "Sort of."

Burlington looked up and down the street as if searching for her, but the fog was too thick. "Have you talked with her? Do you know where she is? Is she all right?"

Ollie ignored Burlington's questions. "I need your help getting in touch with Mr. Albert Martin."

Burlington blinked. "Why do you want to talk to Mr. Martin?"

Ollie didn't respond.

Burlington looked back over his shoulder into his home then

stepped outside, shutting the door behind him. Silence and darkness surrounded them. "I'll tell you how to get in touch with Mr. Martin if you tell me what's going on with Miss Sparrow."

Ollie took a sharp inhale. "I'm not telling you anything."

"Then I can't help you."

This was a conundrum. But Evelyn had assured him they could trust Burlington. "You saw the newspapers. She's being forced into a marriage she doesn't want and ran away from it."

Burlington nodded. "I also saw the letter she left on my desk, apologizing for her sudden departure, leaving us to unexpectedly manage our department with one less person. Curious, how she did that *during* the time of her disappearance. And now here you are seeking me out for information that somehow helps her, though I cannot figure out for the life of me how."

Ollie stilled. The museum didn't realize Dantes's Gustave Courbet painting was missing yet. Even though it wasn't from their collection, it had still been under their care and it would create significant negative attention for the museum if its theft were discovered.

"Why should I help you and her with anything when she left us in the lurch?"

Ollie kept quiet.

"Is she staying with you?" Burlington tilted his head slightly in a study of Ollie. Then he grinned widely. "She is, isn't she? How fascinating. She left the altar for you."

He swallowed. "That is not true."

"Of course it is. The woman is obsessed with you. Surely, you know that."

Hope flickered inside him, but Ollie resisted the urge to argue against such a blatantly ridiculous statement. Evelyn was the most intelligent person he had ever met. Meanwhile, he couldn't even correctly count change for a cash register. "Can you help me get in touch with Mr. Martin or not?"

Burlington scratched at his jaw as he again eyed the area surrounding them. "Give me a minute." He then disappeared into the house.

Ollie let out a long breath. That had gone better than expected.

A moment later, the door opened again. Ollie had expected Burlington to emerge with a scrap of paper containing an address, but to Ollie's surprise, it was a new person. Mr. Burlington stepped out from behind the man, made the introductions between Ollie and Mr. Martin, then retreated into the house when Ollie refused to say anything in his presence.

This new, blond fellow was taller than Mr. Burlington, and he looked hardly a day out of university. "Yes?" the man asked while looking at Ollie with confusion. "You're looking for me?"

What luck he was already here! "Yes. You're the museum director for the Bethnal Green Museum, correct?"

"That's right. Paintings curator as well. What's this about?" Mr. Martin crossed his arms, concern pulling at his brow.

"I wanted to ask about your encounter with the Signature Swindler."

"Are you with the police?"

Ollie shook his head. "You don't know me, but I ask that what I'm about to tell you remains confidential."

"Now I'm intrigued."

The tension in Ollie softened a bit. This gentleman was far more agreeable than Burlington. "Something of mine was stolen by the thief who stole from you."

"And you know this how?"

"Because he signed his work."

Mr. Martin scratched his brow. "Oh, really? What did he write?"

"Bollocks."

Mr. Martin pulled his head back and dropped his hands to his side. "That's correct. That's what I found, too. What did he steal from you?"

Ollie hesitated. "I'd rather not say."

"Have you gone to the police?"

"No." Ollie shook his head. "And I'm trying to avoid them at all costs."

Mr. Martin shifted as he considered all of this. "What do you want to know?"

"Why did the Signature Swindler go from jewelry to paintings?"

"I have no idea. In fact, the police didn't even believe me at first." Mr. Martin stared off into the distance as he probably recalled that day. "I had just clocked in for the day when I noticed one of our paintings were missing, the Fragonard. I made sure that it hadn't been brought to conservation, and then we took inventory of the museum to discover the other missing paintings. I was sure it was because of a seasoned art thief, as there was nothing indicating hesitation. He hadn't taken down a painting and then decided to leave it for something smaller, for example. He'd known exactly what he'd wanted. Like you said, the Signature Swindler had never gone after paintings before, so even though I did think of him, it didn't make sense. But I still had to report the theft to police, who, after questioning me extensively, confirmed it was the first art heist for the Signature Swindler."

"How big were the paintings?"

"Oh, about…" Mr. Martin separated his hands about four feet apart. That was significantly larger than Dantes's missing painting.

"And there were three of them that size?" Ollie was struggling to believe this.

Mr. Martin shrugged. "About that same size, yes."

This was quite surprising to Ollie. It must have been incredibly difficult to get a painting that size out without notice, much less three of them. "Any idea how he got in or out?"

"He got in through a window," Mr. Martin explained. "Smashed the pane, reached in, and unlocked it that way."

"And that's how he got out, too?"

"That's what everyone assumes."

"And the police have no idea who he is?"

Mr. Martin shook his head. "The investigator was furious when he came to the scene. Said the Signature Swindler is slick. There's never been any trace of anything left behind, no clue to his identity. No sightings, no hair, not a misplaced glove or popped button. Nothing except his calligraphed *Bollocks* signature, that is. I do have to say, the man must have quite a sense of humor. I'll give him that at least."

"If I told you the Signature Swindler is an Irishman, would that make anyone stand out to you?"

Mr. Martin's eyebrows pulled together severely. "How do you know he's an Irishman?"

Ollie didn't reply.

The other man let out a long sigh. "No, that doesn't narrow it down, unfortunately."

"No one working at the museum fits that description?"

Mr. Martin shook his head.

Ollie asked a few more basic questions but didn't learn anything else that would be helpful. Once Mr. Martin had gone back into Burlington's house, Ollie left. As soon as they were out of view from Burlington's windows, Evelyn appeared at his side.

"No luck for us." Evelyn looked up at him, a pretty, curious face framed by the hat he had bought her.

He nearly told her how beautiful she looked, but Victor and his grandparents came to mind, squashing it.

"Unfortunately, no," Ollie replied, adjusting the brim of his top hat to lower it again. He made sure his frock collar still stood. "Did you hear everything he said?" He took a right turn at the corner with a destination in mind.

"I did." Evelyn followed. "I was hoping we would learn something helpful from him. But we didn't."

"Unfortunately, no, we did not. Though I thought it was curious the thief stole three large paintings. How could he have done that without catching attention? He seemed to be a loner, but maybe he's working with someone else, or he manipulated people to inadvertently help him like he did with us. Dantes's painting fit under his cape, but the three from the Bethnal Green Museum wouldn't have."

"That stuck out to me, too." Evelyn followed as he made another turn. They were now in an area busier than Burlington's neighborhood. "It seems pretty clear, though, that he tried going after something big and well known, perhaps expecting to get more out of it."

"Or to cause an uproar?"

"Perhaps. It must have been difficult to get multiple large paintings to his destination without notice and thus with my museum, he chose something smaller to transport easier."

An idea crossed Ollie's mind. "You think he's doing shady business selling the paintings?"

Evelyn glanced up as they walked by a doorway with a man passed out in it. "What else would he do with them? It's why he stole jewelry for those first few years, isn't it? Why would the motive change, just because he decided to change his target?"

"I don't know," Ollie admitted. He found the tram stop he was looking for and waited. Not a moment later, it arrived. He climbed in, and Evelyn followed.

The tram was desolate except for a few night-shift workers and one man asleep in the back. Because their voices would be overheard here, neither spoke for the duration of the ride. Finally, they reached the stop Ollie watched for.

They emerged in a very busy part of London and Evelyn continued the conversation where they had left off. "Do you have any theories about the thief's motives, Ollie?"

He stopped walking. "You're asking for my theory?"

"Yes, of course."

This took him aback. He wasn't a smart man, and he didn't understand why Evelyn would want to know his thoughts. He looked around. They should have only been a block away now. "I'm not sure. Isn't money always the motive of a thief to some degree?"

"Wait, where are we?" Evelyn was looking around, too. "This

isn't your neighborhood."

"No, it's Bethnal Green."

Evelyn gave him a questioning look.

Ollie started walking again. He wasn't quite sure yet what he wanted to accomplish here. He didn't have a destination, not really, other than the museum. It wasn't open, so they couldn't go in, but he hoped that being in the area of the first museum theft would lead to a clue.

Bethnal Green was a very poor area of London, and most of the residents who had jobs were weavers or had some tie to that industry. The people they passed were ragged, their faces weary and tired after years, sometimes decades, of wearing their bodies out for meager wages.

Evelyn seemed to be taking in the area with interest. Though she was in an ill-fitting blue dress, people still took a vague interest in them as they walked by. Ollie expected her to be timid with fear, but she was, in actuality, absorbed by her surroundings.

"Mr. Martin wasn't much help," Ollie said as they crossed a street with several others. "I figured since we were already out, we may as well come here."

"This time of night?" Evelyn asked.

They waited until a mule with a rickety, old cart ambled by. "It's as good a time as any."

"What are you looking for?"

"I'm not sure."

As he and Evelyn made it to the other side of the street, a filthy, shoeless child popped out from an alleyway. "Oi! Mister, you got any coin?"

"Not a good time, lad," Ollie replied. He wouldn't have minded tossing the child some coin, but at this time of night, it risked attracting attention. Dangerous attention.

The child kept following them. "You look like you can afford it."

Evelyn kept quiet, watching the scene unfold. Ollie took another turn. Just ahead was the Bethnal Green Museum. "Can't, lad. Got to be somewhere."

"Where, the whore house?"

Evelyn made a choking sound. The child laughed.

Ollie dismissed the boy and, apparently giving up on them, the boy ran on ahead.

"I'm surprised by you," Evelyn said once the child was out of earshot.

Ollie glanced down to her. "Why?"

"I would not have expected you to turn the boy down."

Ollie quickly looked around to make sure no one listened in. "Flashing coin at this hour would not be wise. Best we keep our heads down, get where we're going, and leave."

"Still surprises me you thought coming here late at night was a good idea."

"As long as you keep your head on straight and mind your own business, no one will bother you."

"All right," Evelyn conceded. But not a moment later, they heard a child crying out for help. Evelyn grasped Ollie's upper arm with worry. "Oh, Ollie, it's that boy again!" She pointed about twenty feet in front of them. The boy who had been asking for coin had his hand stuck under a door handle at a building up ahead. He was writhing and kept crying out, "Help me! Help!"

Evelyn rushed over to the child. "Oh my goodness! Are you hurt?" She began to fuss.

Ollie, however, knew better and instead of helping the child began looking around their surroundings. Sensing movement, his eyes stopped at a spot across the street. Behind grungy, dented rubbish bins, the head of another boy popped up, as if he were about to sneak out of his hiding place.

Ollie shot a withering look to the child, who seemed surprised to be discovered and promptly sprinted away.

Ollie turned back around to find Evelyn still fussing over the crying boy. "You are quite the little actor." Ollie crossed his arms and gave the boy a bemused look.

The boy immediately stopped the act and looked back over

his shoulder with a frown.

"His hand isn't stuck." Ollie easily pulled the child's arm away from the door. The child scowled up at him. "See? He knows throwing a hysterical fit and wailing loudly will distract your mind from reason. Look at the size of his hand, look at the size of the handle. How could he possibly get stuck? *My* hand couldn't even get stuck in there."

Evelyn, of course, didn't have a response for that and looked back and forth between the child and the door.

"What's your name?" Ollie asked the child.

The child, still scowling at being caught, replied, "Frankie."

"No, it's not."

Frankie crossed his arms. "I ain't telling you my real name."

"Fair enough."

"How'd you know my trick, mister?"

Ollie gave the boy a small smile. "I did the same trick, when I was even smaller than you."

"You did?" Evelyn asked, her voice pitched with surprise.

Ollie nodded. "Worked about half the time, believe it or not."

"Not fair!" Frankie said. "I did ask nicely, first!"

Ollie laughed. "I know. All right, all right, but don't go making trouble for me." Ollie reached into his pocket and pulled out the first coin he felt and handed it to the boy. The child's face lit up. "Hey, thanks, mister!" and Frankie skipped away looking quite happy with himself.

Ollie watched after the child for a moment with fondness. A few snippets of memories popped up, of him running around Whitechapel picking pockets. That must have been when he'd been four. He smiled wistfully. When he turned back around, Evelyn was watching him with a softness in her eyes. He didn't know why, but it made his heart skip a beat. "What?" he asked.

"You were very kind to that child."

Feeling a bit sheepish, he made a dismissive sound. "It was nothing," Ollie said. "He reminded me of being a boy myself, and I have the means to give him a little something."

"Most people wouldn't, you know," Evelyn replied. "Even those that could afford to several times over you."

But Ollie just shrugged. What could he say? But at the soft smile Evelyn offered him, he cleared his throat. All he wanted to do was change the subject. "Museum's right up there."

They passed a worn-down pub, in front of which several men were outside smoking and talking, next door to the museum. As they passed by—or, as Evelyn passed by—all conversation ceased. The men's attention on Evelyn rankled Ollie and he shot them a murderous glare behind Evelyn's back. The men smartly turned away.

"Do you ever hope to be a father, Ollie?" Evelyn, unaware, asked as they finally reached the museum.

Ollie rubbed the back of his neck. "Sure. Eventually."

Evelyn stared off with a funny smile that looked more sad than anything.

"What is it?" Ollie asked.

But she ignored the question. "What are we doing here?" Evelyn asked.

Ollie admitted he didn't have a plan, and they began to discuss how the Signature Swindler had gotten in. It took a good fifteen minutes, but they walked around the building hoping to identify the window he'd probably used, staying in the shadows, lest people think they had a nefarious purpose. But it must have been fixed, as they couldn't find it.

"I'm surprised by how desolate it is here," Evelyn said. The street was relatively empty, aside from the pub next door and a block of tenements across the street.

"I wonder if anyone over there saw anything." Ollie indicated the tenements across the street.

Evelyn lifted a shoulder. "Perhaps. Though most people would have been sleeping. The thief is very good at being invisible, too. I would be more surprised if someone *had* seen him."

Soft footfalls echoed through the air, coming their way. Ollie exchanged a worried look with Evelyn. Was it a police officer coming to ask what they were doing? Had the Signature Swindler followed them? That was a terrifying thought.

The footfalls were getting closer, and as they approached from around the corner of the museum, Ollie realized it was probably an opportunist, someone who had seen him give Frankie the coin. "Get behind me," Ollie told Evelyn in a low, warning voice.

Evelyn did not argue.

Only concerned with protecting her, Ollie put his arm back to keep her behind. His arm and hand found contact with her side. He was about to apologize when he realized she wasn't moving away. In fact, she was holding on to him.

Electricity rushed over his skin.

But the thrill was short-lived.

The footfalls were closer, louder.

And then, someone appeared around the corner.

It was Frankie tossing an apple into the air. He then crunched into it.

Ollie's tension was quickly replaced with annoyance. "Frankie, you gave us a fright!"

Frankie took another loud crunch of the apple and chewed with his mouth open before swallowing it. "What are you doing? You looking to break in?" Frankie asked with another mouthful.

"Frankie," Evelyn said. "Did you know someone stole from this museum?"

Ollie clenched his jaw. What was she doing? The last thing they needed was for this far-too-curious child to be getting involved in their business.

Frankie took another bite of apple and seemed to be considering the question as his mouth made smacking noises. "Everyone knows about that."

Evelyn looked at Ollie and held his gaze, trying to communicate something to him. But he couldn't figure out what.

"You know about the Signature Swindler, then?" Evelyn asked.

"Yeah, I know about him. Why?" Frankie chucked his apple core into a nearby bush.

"Do you know who he is?"

Frankie narrowed his eyes at them. "I ain't saying nothin'."

Ollie was not surprised. It was entirely possible Frankie was trying to look tough by appearing to be in-the-know about this. But even if he were in the know, why would the boy tell complete strangers anything that pertained to his neighborhood? Ollie also knew Evelyn would keep trying to push the question. So he quickly asked his own to redirect. In the unlikely chance this child knew who the Signature Swindler was, he would never give up the man's identity.

"You know, we're really fascinated by the Signature Swindler," Ollie said.

The boy crossed his arms and frowned. "Why?"

"Who doesn't like a good art heist? It's fascinating, too, how he was able to escape with three paintings without anyone seeing anything."

"Who said no one saw anything?"

Ollie held his breath, afraid it would send the child running. "People saw?" he asked as casually as he could manage.

"Yeah, lots of people! They just know to keep their mouth shut to the police. What would that get us? Nothing!" Frankie pointed to the main entrance. "He came out there carrying the paintings and lots of people watched! I watched from right there." Frankie pointed to a low, stone wall at the sidewalk.

"Was anyone helping him?" Ollie had to tamper down the rising excitement. Finally, they might get some useful information!

"Nope," Frankie replied, and he didn't offer anything else.

"So, he carried them? All on his own?"

Frankie's little shoulders shrugged right as a beetle flew by and dropped down to the ground. Frankie crouched down and began gently poking it with a stick.

They were going to lose the boy's attention, and fast.

"Frankie..." Ollie hoped to grasp the last thread of the child's focus.

Frankie looked up at him for a second before returning to the beetle. "What is it, mister?"

"How was the man able to carry three paintings on his own? Was a cab waiting for him?"

Frankie didn't respond and Evelyn gave Ollie a tight-lipped look that said, *At least you tried*.

But then the beetle flew away. Frankie watched it disappear before standing back up. "He didn't have to carry them far, that's how! All he had to do was carry them across the street."

Chapter Fourteen

E VELYN REELED AT the revelation the Signature Swindler had ties to Bethnal Green. And right across the street, of all places! Frankie looked up at her with the innocence of a child, clearly not realizing how important this news was. The boy had seen a hard life—she could tell by the tattered edges of his clothing and the guardedness in his eyes—but that innocence still remained. She thought about Ollie as a small, bright-eyed boy filled with wonder, with hope, despite sleeping in alleyways at night.

"Frankie…" Evelyn was trying to keep her voice level. "Why did he go across the street? What's there?" As far as she could guess, either the thief lived there or stored his stolen goods there. Or maybe a buyer lived there, though that seemed the least likely to her. Or perhaps someone tied to art buyers?

But Frankie only shrugged.

She wouldn't get that answer, and he may not even know. "Do you know him? The Signature Swindler?"

The boy bobbed on his feet. "Yep!"

She shot a wide-eyed look at Ollie. "Could you by chance tell us where he lives?"

Frankie considered that. "Nope."

That didn't surprise her, but it was worth a try. "Then could you please tell him we would like to meet with him?"

"I can't do that, either."

Disappointment hit her. "Why not?"

Frankie shrugged. "He's already waiting for you."

Evelyn met Ollie's eye again. He was not pleased by this news. Admittedly, Evelyn was not exactly thrilled, either. They were now at a severe disadvantage. They didn't know how the man knew they were here, or if the thief was dangerous. They still didn't even know what he wanted from them, though now she supposed he wanted the reward for returning her to the earl.

"Wait!" Frankie yelled suddenly. "That's why I came here. I was supposed to give you this and then I forgot." Frankie shoved his grubby hand into a pocket and then pulled out a wrinkled piece of paper. He held it out for Evelyn to grab.

It had the same overly ornate handwriting they had seen in the Signature Swindler's previous note.

At the top, it read, *Hello* again.

And then Evelyn read out loud:

Curiosity killed the cat—isn't that how the saying goes? But then, cats have nine lives. So how many lives do you curious kittens have?

Find me at the scene of the crime.

Evelyn furrowed her brow as Ollie made a strangled noise of irritation. "Why must everything be secretive with this idiot?" Ollie asked. "And what's the deal with the cat? Is he threatening us?"

Evelyn looked at both sides of the paper as if hoping to find the answer that way. "I'm not sure," she admitted.

"What do you want to do?" Ollie asked.

They only had two choices. They could leave and go back to Ollie's, with no questions answered. The artwork would still be missing. Ollie would still let down his brother Dantes. And it was not a mark she wanted in her career, even if she never went back to work. Her career was a source of pride for her, but there was more to it. If it was discovered she had lost a painting in a heist by inadvertently *helping* the thief, it would create an even bigger barrier for any future women who worked their way into academics or the arts. It was already hard enough for women. If Evelyn was remembered as this much of a failure, that would put a bad taste in the mouths of the men who ruled everything.

Their other choice was to go inside, confront the thief, and get the artwork back.

It seemed pretty obvious what they had to do.

"I want to end this," Evelyn said with determination. "I don't want this hanging over me."

"Nor I." Ollie looked down to Frankie. "So, the thief. You said you know who he is."

Frankie nodded.

"Anything worth telling us? Like, is he dangerous?"

"I'm eight. How should I know?"

Ollie grumbled to himself. "Fine. How do we get in, then?"

Frankie frowned. "Through a door?"

With a long sigh, Ollie motioned for Evelyn to follow. They left Frankie behind—he wasn't allowed inside, according to him—to search for a way in. As they had done previously, they checked for unlocked doors and windows.

"Have you ever been to this museum before?" Ollie asked as he tried pushing up a window sash. It didn't budge.

Evelyn peered through the window to see inside. "No, I haven't."

"It's a strange place to have an art museum," Ollie added, peering in the window beside Evelyn. Whatever room they were looking into, it was too dark for her to identify any artwork on the walls. "Amongst the squalor and poverty sits this fine art museum. It's strange to me."

"The Prince of Wales built it in 1872. I'm sure he intended it to be something positive for the local community."

"It's practically begging to be robbed, to be honest. Hence, why the thief likely chose it, pretty convenient for whatever he has going on across the street there."

Evelyn led Ollie a bit farther down the long, outside wall and paused at another window. She cupped her hands around her face to block out any light and see into this room as well. "Art museums are for everyone, Ollie, not just the wealthy."

"Do you honestly think the people who live here can afford the entrance fee? They can hardly clothe and feed themselves, Evelyn."

Evelyn pulled away from the window to find Ollie's usual easy demeanor was absent. "I'm sorry, Ollie. I didn't mean to upset you."

Ollie made a dismissive noise and went down along the wall on his own. Evelyn followed but kept a distance. Clearly, she had touched a nerve, though unintended.

Up ahead was a side door. Ollie stopped before it but didn't look back at her.

"Ollie, if I said something wrong, I didn't mean any offense by it."

Ollie scratched at an eyebrow. "You didn't say anything wrong. But I do find this museum insulting. To me, it's another way for nobs to thumb their noses at everyone else. But to you, it's an opportunity for all. Sometimes I forget how different you and I really are."

Evelyn tilted her head. "You really think we're that different?"

"Maybe there are some similarities between how we were raised, but we have had different life experiences, too. And our views of this museum is evidence of that."

"Would you rather it not exist at all?"

Ollie shoved his hands into his pockets. "I don't know," he admitted. But it was clear he was irritated with her, and it didn't feel good. "I'm not here to debate the existence of this museum. I'm here to see the cad inside, get my brother's painting back, and go home."

Sensing a tension mounting between them, Evelyn decided to put her focus on getting through the door and off her own negative emotions. She removed one of the hatpins Ollie had bought her and stared down at the lock.

Ollie held out his hand, expecting her to hand over the hatpin.

"No," Evelyn replied stubbornly. She crouched down to do it herself. He didn't argue. She set to work, sliding the sharp, metal point into the keyhole and began to poke and prod. She recalled how last time Ollie had rotated it around a bit, too. She mimicked that movement, determined.

So she didn't know what it was like to worry about having enough food. And she didn't know what it was like to not have shoes because her feet kept growing and her parents couldn't afford to replace another pair. She would never understand what the less fortunate experienced. But while her life had been safer and easier, it hadn't been carefree, or risk-free, either. She still was under the thumb of those more powerful than her. She still was a pawn to her family.

"No one likes me much, anyway," she mumbled as she pressed the hatpin into something inside the lock. She pressed too hard, though, and the pin slipped. She wanted to scream but forced it back, lest it make everything worse.

"What was that?" Ollie replied.

Evelyn gritted her teeth as she tried pushing the hatpin against the same spot that had slipped a moment ago. "I said, no one likes me, anyway. You seem to think I'm some toff darling, but I'm not. Most people find me intolerable." Another slip, and Evelyn let out a frustrated groan.

"Evelyn, let me—"

"No!" She bit out the word harsher than intended, realizing she was trying to prove something to herself, to Ollie. He thought she was a spoiled princess? Watch her pick a lock, then! No one knew any toff darlings who could pick locks with their hatpins!

The hatpin slipped for the third time. Evelyn growled and threw the instrument to the ground.

As she'd aged, she could more easily identify when her emotions were mounting too quick and too fast. This was one of those moments, and she would have a fit if she didn't calm herself down. Evelyn took a deep breath and closed her eyes for a moment, willing the rising steam back down.

Once she felt more in control, she opened her eyes to find Ollie watching her.

Ollie picked up the hatpin. "If you can resist kicking me in the shin, I can show you how to do it."

Evelyn let out a sigh. "I'm not kicking you in the shin."

"Good. Come here, then," he said. Evelyn hesitated but eventually complied. "Rule number one: No stabbing Ollie with hatpins."

Evelyn glared at him. He laughed but conceded the hatpin to her. He then held his hand over hers for a moment, meeting her eye, and when she didn't protest wrapped his hand around her own, light at first, but then fully embracing it.

His hand over hers caused that strange but pleasant warm, honey feeling to spread through her body. But right behind that would be the nerve-screaming sensation where she would desperately shake someone off.

But strangely, she didn't want to shake Ollie off. Yes, she was annoyed with him and with the hatpin and this whole moment in general. But she sort of liked Ollie's hand over hers in the moment.

Actually, she liked when Ollie touched her. *That* was why she sometimes jerked away from him. It wasn't because she was repulsed by it—it was because she liked it, but it was so unusual for her, she misunderstood what that meant.

Evelyn let out a little gasp of surprise upon this realization.

"What's wrong?" Ollie pulled his hand away.

"Touch me again," she said hastily. She wanted to test her theory.

Ollie scratched the side of his nose. "Ah, not entirely sure what you mean by that."

"The way you just did," Evelyn replied blandly.

An amused twinkle of mischief in Ollie's eye sent goosebumps all over her body. But he complied with her request.

She still held the hatpin in her hand, and now Ollie's hand

wrapped around hers once more. She waited, aware of every breath she took and released, but there was no feeling of disgust. Only pleasure.

"Evelyn, what's going on?"

"I like this," she said, looking up to meet him directly in the eye.

"You like me holding your hand?"

"Yes! Isn't that amazing?"

But Ollie responded by rubbing his chin, as if mulling this over. "And what does that mean, exactly?"

"I don't know. Quite curious, though, isn't it? Rarely, I can tolerate touch, like if my sister gives me a hug. I thought I disliked your touch because of the way it makes me feel, but I'm now realizing it isn't a *bad* feeling, just a *strong* feeling." But then she remembered what they were doing. Her smile fell away. What a silly conversation this was. "Never mind. Will you show me how to do this now?"

Ollie was frowning, as if trying to wrap his mind around what she had revealed, before returning his attention to the lock. "Right. So, when you put the hatpin in, you need to find the lock pins and push them each in. There're usually two or three." He found one, pushed the hatpin against it, and she felt it move.

"I felt that!" A rush of excitement hit her.

Ollie gave her a small grin. "This is why I had to show you. Since you can't see what it's doing, you have to feel it through your hand. Let's try the other one." He did a small circle with the hatpin and found the other pin. It moved, too, with gentle pressure.

"Brilliant," Evelyn said.

"Now you do the last one." He let go of her.

"Me? You're sure?" She didn't like the empty feeling his hand had left behind, but there wasn't any time to dwell on that.

Ollie nodded.

With focused concentration, Evelyn found the final lock pin. Her tongue stuck out of the corner of her mouth as she tried to gently, but firmly, press in the last pin.

Not only did the hatpin not slip, but the lock pin moved.

Evelyn gasped. "I did it, Ollie!"

Ollie gave a crooked smiled at her pride and excitement. "Good girl," he said in that low, velvet voice before taking her hand and lifting it to his lips.

He let it linger for a beat while holding her gaze. Evelyn could feel her face go hot as her heart began to pound.

For a short moment, it was pleasant. Tingles radiated from the spot his lips touched her and spread up her arm and all over her body. But it became too strong. Without thinking, she yanked her hand away from him. Hard.

Ollie stared at her for a long beat, a pained expression on his face. But before she could say anything, he stood up to his full height, placed his hand on the door handle, and said, "It's best if I go in first."

"Ollie." She took a step toward him.

"Like you, I want this over with," was all he said before opening the door and walking through. Evelyn held back, looking into the dark doorway. She couldn't help but feel Ollie hadn't been strictly talking about the stolen artwork just now. He'd been talking about her, too. He wanted *her* over with.

Of course, she should've known better. She had intruded on his life, his home. And though he kept assuring her he was happy to help her, she was beginning to wonder how true that was. Maybe he was fine with helping her for a few days. But not longer, most assuredly.

Tonight, once they returned, Evelyn would put a final plan in place of what she was going to do. Even if she had to stay up all night to figure it out. The last thing she wanted was to be a burden to a friend.

Decision made, Evelyn stepped through the door, which promptly shut behind her, startling her.

It was incredibly dark in the museum and the only reason she could see anything was because of the windows. Evelyn went farther in and looked around. This room did not have any paintings. Instead, there were glass cases all along the walls. There was also an odd, dusty smell.

The room, even though the museum itself wasn't very old, felt ancient.

"Where are we?" Ollie spoke in a hushed voice.

Evelyn peered into one of the glass cases. This particular case acted as a protective surround for a large slab of stone. On the stone was a carving of a man wearing some sort of very tall crown. Around the man were curious symbols carved in neat columns. Amongst them were eyes, birds, and other animals Evelyn didn't immediately recognize.

"We appear to be in ancient Egypt," Evelyn concluded, turning back to Ollie.

Ollie's eyes darted around the room. "Have you ever known old museum objects to be haunted?"

"No, I don't believe in ghosts. But I do think humans can imprint upon objects. Once, thousands of years ago, teams of people created everything in this room. And I do believe people leave a piece of themselves when they create. You can sense the humans who interacted with these objects."

Ollie glanced around again with a clenched jaw. "All right. Time to leave this room."

Evelyn gave a small laugh and followed him out of the room into a darkened hallway.

Neither spoke, as the stillness and silence of the building was too unnerving. Evelyn could hardly see an inch in front of her face, and the only reason they were able to see anything at all was because of open doorways that led into moonlit rooms.

Evelyn peeked into one of the rooms, finding ancient Greek statues and busts. The white, marble objects dotted the room like spirits in suspension.

"If he asked us to find him at the scene of the crime," Evelyn began, "I think we should track down where he took the Fragonard, as he only took one of those."

Ollie made grunt of agreement.

They passed another room and out of the corner of Evelyn's eye, she spotted paintings. She quietly nudged Ollie and he followed her inside.

Immediately, Evelyn knew they were in the wrong room. But it was a room that felt familiar to her, offering a short respite from the creepiness of the dark and desolate museum.

"Italian Renaissance," she said mostly to herself as she meandered along the wall. A painting caught her eye and she stopped to observe it. A blonde woman wearing a thin, white, Renaissance-style dress watched as a man, nude aside from white fabric draped over his lap, slept soundly. Both were relaxed and lounging in a forest while mischievous satyrs played around them.

"*Venus and Mars* by Sandro Botticelli," Evelyn explained without looking away from it. "It's on loan here from the National Gallery." The woman in the painting was soft and voluptuous. "The god of war and the goddess of love. Painted around 1485, possibly a wedding gift with the bride and groom as the models." Rarely did art make Evelyn uncomfortable, but when it did it was hard to identify why, exactly. Calling out the goddess of love made her want to fidget, for example, but if anyone asked why, she wouldn't have been able to explain it.

Ollie appeared at her side and his closeness made her heart race. It seemed as if she were suddenly more aware of everything around her. "Lounging about with the goddess of love and he takes a nap? What a fool."

"Perhaps Venus spent the morning tiring him out."

Ollie's eyebrows flew up to the ceiling. Evelyn gave him a coy smile before returning to the hallway, amused at being able to shock Ollie.

Ollie hurried to catch up to her. "Or maybe, it's more that love conquers all? Even war?"

"Very perceptive, Ollie." Evelyn smiled as she continued walking. "I was teasing you. You are correct."

"Really?" Ollie beamed. "Usually, I'm the biggest idiot when it comes to art history."

"Nonsense."

"It's true. Whenever you tell me about it, I have no idea what you're talking about. And I don't absorb any of it, or very little at least. My brain gets all jumbled by history and facts, especially when you go into the science part of conservation."

Evelyn paused and turned to him. "Regardless, you always seem so interested in what I'm telling you. In fact, you're the only person I've known who listens to me for more than a minute."

Ollie frowned slightly as he considered this. "That's because I *like* listening to you talk."

Evelyn blinked. "You do?"

He nodded. "You could talk to me about numbers and maths, the most mind-numbing subject in the world, and I would hang on to every word you utter. I wouldn't understand any of it, but I'd hang on to your every word regardless."

Feeling flushed, Evelyn thought back to the times she had prattled on and on about art history. It hadn't occurred to her that Ollie had truly listened. She'd thought he'd been being polite because no one listened, yet she talked endlessly regardless. If she started on about a subject that fascinated her and the listener was clearly bored, instead of stopping, she would go on about it more in a desperate, almost stubborn, attempt to get their attention.

But he was telling the truth, now that he mentioned it. She could envision it now, the way he would sit there at her desk, his chin in his hand, that funny sort of drunk look on his face as he watched her talk. It wasn't boredom—it was interest.

But before they could continue their conversation, Evelyn saw the flash of a shadow in the hallway.

The air around them shifted. Evelyn grabbed Ollie's forearm. "Did you see that?" she whispered, fearful. For she wasn't quite sure if she had genuinely seen something. She didn't believe in ghosts, but this museum was beginning to make her wonder.

Ollie lowered his voice. "No. What was it?"

"I don't know." Evelyn hesitated before taking a step toward the door and peeking out into the hall. The darkness seemed to take over like the London fog often did outside. It slid through the air, weightless, impenetrable.

"Stay here," Ollie directed. "I'll go see what it is."

"Are you mad? I'm coming with you."

His jaw clenched tightly. "I think it would be best if you stayed in here."

"Absolutely not." She punctuated this by crossing her arms in defiance.

"I swear I get into more trouble with you around than without."

"And yet you don't seem to mind the least bit."

"I don't, now that you mention it."

Evelyn grinned, but before she could respond, received the fright of her life instead.

"You know…" a disembodied voice rang out from somewhere. "You two make me sick."

Evelyn nearly jumped out of her skin and let out a yelp. Ollie leapt in front of her in the doorway. "Who's there?" His voice growled with warning.

No one stepped forward, but a terrifying cackle echoed down the dark hallway. Evelyn stood on her tiptoes to look over Ollie's shoulder and held on to him for balance. They waited for a long beat, but the man—most assuredly the Signature Swindler—said nothing further.

"You there!" Ollie shouted down the hall. Footfalls quickly receded. "Stay here," Ollie said. "I'm going to drag this fool back."

"I'm coming with you."

Ollie swore, but there was no point in arguing. Together, they hurried down the hallway, the doorways to different rooms zooming by. Up ahead, a door opened and then slammed shut.

They stopped to catch their breath. It occurred to Evelyn how utterly foolish it was to be chasing a thief through a museum. They still didn't know how dangerous he was. "We're mad, aren't we?" she said through heaving breaths.

Ollie laughed in agreement. "Better this with you than getting mud slung at me by Victor any day."

Admittedly, this was kind of fun, in a slightly terrifying way.

They began running again through the darkness. Evelyn was several feet behind Ollie now, but running as fast as she could to keep up with him was the most invigorating feeling. It gave her an intense rush as their feet hit the ground hard and echoed through the building.

At a sudden sense of dread, Evelyn glanced back over her shoulder.

There was a brief flash of the midnight Volto mask. And then, nothing at all.

Chapter Fifteen

OLLIE REALIZED HIS footfalls were the only ones echoing. And he didn't know how long Evelyn had been missing.

They had been running through the halls of the Bethnal Green Museum looking for the blasted thief, and Ollie had insisted on being in front of her to keep her safe.

It had been foolish to not keep her in his view.

Now she was gone, and he didn't know where she had disappeared, or how, or when. Had they simply lost each other? Or had something more sinister happened?

Ollie braced his palms against his knees to catch his breath and keep his mind from becoming too erratic.

"Evelyn?" Ollie called out between labored breaths. But all he could see was doorway after doorway disappearing into an inky-black horizon.

Most likely, she had become distracted by something and run off without remembering it would be prudent to tell him. It wouldn't be the first time she had done that.

But they had also heard the Signature Swindler only moments ago.

Ollie thought the man was nothing more than a clown. But maybe he *was* dangerous.

Panic mounting, he hurriedly retraced his steps, checking every room he'd passed. They had been on their way to find whatever room from which the Fragonard had disappeared. But what in the blazes was a Fragonard? Was it Renaissance? Pre-Raphaelite? Romanticism? These were all terms he recalled Evelyn using before, but in his panic, he couldn't remember what they meant.

"Evelyn!" Ollie cupped his hands around his mouth and shouted as loudly as he could, ghosts or not, as he was sure he was going to wake the dead with the racket he'd made.

He continued down the hall, turning a corner. Then he peeked into a room, but like the ancient Egypt room, this room had no paintings in it, just displays. It was not a room that would help him.

Door after door, Ollie flung them all open. In rooms with paintings, he looked for gaps on the walls. Others, he passed by quickly.

Where was Evelyn? He called out to her again, his voice pitched with worry.

She should have responded by now if she had wandered off. But why wasn't there any noise from her at all? She could have called back, even stomped her feet or kicked something to give him a clue to her location in this blasted building.

But she didn't make any noise. Which meant she was incapacitated.

He checked another room, finding yet another filled with paintings. He almost backed out when his eye caught something. A large, out-of-place blank spot on the wall.

Ollie hurried over to the blank spot. Was this one of the rooms from which the thief had stolen? It seemed like a painting should have been hanging here. But the thief's signature should have been in its place.

Remembering they had cleaned off the signature on Evelyn's desk, Ollie leaned in close and narrowed his eyes with concentration, hoping to pick up any faint ink that hadn't been completely cleared away.

His heart skipped upon spotting a small, very faint *s*.

This must be the room, he thought as he walked a quick circle around the perimeter, looking for any further clues. At first, he didn't find anything.

But as he returned to the door, something on the floor beside a center display case caught his eye.

It was small and pink.

He crouched down to pick it up, twisting it between his thumb and forefinger. It was one of the pink, silk flowers from Evelyn's hat.

Full-blown panic took over. Ollie shoved the flower into a pocket as his mind began to jumble thoughts together. Fear, questions, anger, curse words. He rubbed the heels of his hands over his temples, as if this could separate the jumbled thoughts into perceivable order.

What should he do? He could go to the police. This seemed like something to bring the experts in for.

And then he'd have to admit to breaking into the Bethnal Green Museum. And after that, he would also have to admit to breaking into the National Gallery because of course the police would ask how they'd crossed paths with the Signature Swindler in the first place. He *could* tell them about the note the thief had sent them and claim they'd met him outside the National Gallery only, but on second thought, that would make the police even more suspicious. The thief had evaded everyone so far, so why would he contact Ollie directly? It was still a question to which he had no answer, but he knew the police would raise their eyebrows at that.

Regardless, all of it would lead to admitting Dantes's painting had been stolen out from under Ollie's care.

His family would *never* respect him again after that.

And that didn't even take into account that the police would surely give Evelyn to the earl the moment they found her.

Ollie didn't want that. Selfishly, he liked having her around. Liked that he was the one watching out for her, taking care of her, when she had no one else to whom to turn. Granted, trouble seemed to find them at every turn now that she was around, but, as he'd told her earlier, he didn't really mind it much. And that was the truth. Maybe she attracted trouble, but she sure made life interesting.

But now he couldn't find her. His heart felt empty with her missing, as if someone had taken part of him.

Once again, someone he cared about was utterly let down by him. Worse, this time, she was in mortal danger. Was she hurt? Was the thief hurting her right now while Ollie scratched his head like an idiot?

Determined, Ollie rushed back out into the hallway labyrinth. He looked right, then left. Which way should he go? His breathing became hard and labored as visions of her being tortured by a masked thief pummeled his mind.

Stop. A little voice of reason pushed its way through the jumble in his head. *Take a few breaths and calm yourself until you can think straight. You can't help anyone until you do that.*

Ollie responded quietly back to his own mind, *But what if something happens?*

Then you will fix it.

I'm terrified he's hurting her.

I know you are.

She needs to be back with me. And I'm never letting her out of my sight again. I'm keeping her wrapped up safe.

I don't think she would enjoy that much, but all right.

After tonight, I'll do whatever it takes to keep idiots from hurting her. I don't care who it is. I'll take out the thief if I have to. And I'll tell the bloody earl off myself, too.

Sounds grand.

How could I forgive myself if anyone hurt her?

You wouldn't. But what happens after she leaves? You can't keep her forever.

Ollie thought about this. *But what if I could?*

You're starting to figure it out.

Figure out what?

But the voice didn't respond. Ollie was now even more confused, especially by the strange feeling in his heart. It was like an invisible hand were squeezing it. He placed his hand over his sternum. But the sensation quickly melted. Maybe it was a museum ghost toying with him.

That was a frightening thought.

"All right." Ollie was now talking to himself out loud. "If I were the blasted Signature Swindler, where would I take a pretty redhead?" He listened to the air, hoping someone would whisper the answer.

Of course, no one did. He had to figure this out himself. There was no Victor or Dantes to fall back on, no Vivian to look to for supportive words.

He already knew he was going to bungle this. But the stakes here were far higher than art or work. A woman's life was in his hands. A woman he… Ollie stopped that thought to refocus on current matters.

There was only one clue: the flower. The Signature Swindler had definitely taken Evelyn, evidenced by the flower torn from her hat. He knew her well enough to know she'd probably put up a fight, though the thief had also been able silence her.

One thing didn't make sense. Why hadn't the thief had a nice chat with them as planned? Why had he taken Evelyn and run off with her instead?

Maybe it was the reward for Evelyn. But that wasn't a new development, either. Something had made him change his mind between the time he'd written the note and the moment he'd taken her.

But on the other hand, the man was a thief. Honesty wasn't a part of him, and it was possible he'd written that note specifically to find an opportune moment to grab her, likely knowing she would not answer a note asking for her only.

And he obviously wanted money—he was a thief, after all. Perhaps he had realized it was an easy enough fortune for him to nab.

Frustrated and scared, Ollie shouted out a loud, very rude

curse word.

She was long gone now. Halfway to the earl's. He would never see her again.

But that would mean she was unhurt, at least.

Being gone, though? The thought was more distressing that he would have expected.

Ollie didn't know which way was which. Where was the exit? The front? The back? Where in the blazes did the earl even live? Maybe he could sneak into the house and pull Evelyn out.

As he turned the corner to find an exit and sprint the six miles to Mayfair, something metallic caught Ollie's eye. He doubled back.

There was a brass plaque on the wall. Embossed arrows pointed in different directions, but the one that held his attention pointed to his left and read:

Conservation Center

Ollie didn't even think. He ran. Somehow, he found himself at double doors with a large sign above indicating he'd found exactly what he'd been looking for.

Hesitating, he pressed his ear to the doors and thought he heard murmuring voices, but he couldn't tell for sure. Nor could he tell if they were male or female.

With a gentle twist, he turned the brass doorknob and grit his teeth with anticipation of something creaking.

He was able to open the door half an inch. An inch. Half a foot, without any noise.

Finally, he was able to look in.

At first, he was taken aback with awe. The room was enormous! At the far end was a two-story wall of windows, like one would see in a hothouse. Framed art hung over every inch of the plaster walls. Heavy, wooden tables were adorned with busts and statues and more framed art. A few dimmed electric lamps gave an eerie glow to everything and threw long, severe shadows.

Somehow, Ollie slipped inside noiselessly. Then another

memory unexpectedly flashed, of him tiptoeing through a dark hallway. *It was very late. He turned into a room and set his eyes on a mahogany wood box. Small, chubby hands lifted the lid. Inside the box, lined in red satin, were the most beautiful jewels he had ever seen in his life. He stuffed his pockets with them,* and the memory ended.

Ollie held his breath, surprised. He'd never recalled being a jewelry thief.

A man's voice brought Ollie back to the present and he pushed the memory away for now.

Sliding soundlessly through the room, Ollie took care to stay in the shadows. When he heard a man speak again, he went in that direction.

Ollie's fear was realized when he found the idiot thief in his even more idiotic costume. And in front of the thief, with her back to Ollie, was Evelyn. In a chair. Her wrists tied behind her.

Calm down. That little voice spoke again. *She's alive and isn't in mortal danger. You have a moment to determine how to act.*

But Ollie wasn't patient enough and ignored his own advice.

A wooden shipping box was up ahead, containing something quite tall. It was the perfect spot for Ollie to hide close enough to Evelyn where he could hear their conversation. He slid over to it and listened.

IN THE MIDST of running behind Ollie, Evelyn was unexpectedly yanked into a room and gagged one second before a blindfold was secured over her eyes. She made muffled sounds of protests and squirmed with all her might while flailing her legs and arms, hoping to make contact with the Signature Swindler, who had, apparently, decided to kidnap her.

And she promised to make him regret it.

The thief mumbled curses to himself as he tried to secure her limbs. There was a brief scuffle in which something knocked into her hat, pushing it askew. Moments later, the thief managed to twist her arms behind her back. Both of them heaved for a moment, trying to catch their breaths.

He began tying rope around her wrists and didn't keep it loose for comfort.

She swore at him.

"'Tis not very ladylike of you, Miss Sparrow," the man replied gruffly in his heavy Irish accent.

Evelyn could hear the amusement in his voice, which only made her madder. As she had done before to the police officer, she kicked behind, making contact with his shins.

The thief hissed a curse. "Do that again, and you'll be hog-tied."

She asked, "What do you want?" but the gag made it impossible to speak clearly.

"You want the answer to that question? Then you're going to come with me, as quiet as a wee mousie."

Evelyn had to decide quickly what to do. She could try fighting back, running away, screaming, or complying.

If she tried fighting back, she would lose. The Signature Swindler was slighter in height than Ollie, but she couldn't recall who was taller between her or the thief. Even if he was shorter, he was still likely significantly stronger than her due to the unfortunate fact that he was a man. Also, she was at a disadvantage with her arms tied behind her back and her eyes covered.

Fighting back wasn't an option.

And if she ran, she would run into something and knock herself out. Not a helpful option, either.

If she made lots of noise, there was no telling how he would react. He wouldn't run away—she could judge that already—but she wasn't sure how far he would go to stop her.

Nor was she eager to find out.

Unfortunately, it seemed as if complying was her only choice. "Fine, I'll go with you." Her voice was muffled against the gag.

For a moment, nothing happened and Evelyn wondered if he'd changed his mind.

But then he removed her eye covering. Blinking to adjust her eyes, she was startled to find, right in front of her, the terrifying man dressed head to toe in black, the Volto star mask and tricorn hat covering everything but his dark eyes.

Still gagged, she glared back.

The dark eyes smiled through the eye holes. "Now you can see so you don't go walking into anything. If you cooperate, I'll remove the gag. And then after that, the rope around your wrists. But only if you do as I say."

She nodded, as there was nothing else she could do.

"Excellent." The thief peeked out into the hallway and Evelyn noted she couldn't hear anything. Had Ollie realized yet she was missing? Would he come looking for her?

Of course he would.

But there was a little nagging feeling she couldn't shake off. What if he didn't? He wasn't a fighter, and he'd seemed rather disturbed by the museum at night. What if he was too scared and left? Would he leave her behind?

The Signature Swindler gripped her upper arm and started leading her down the hallway. Evelyn opened her ears as much as she could but didn't hear Ollie anywhere nearby.

She was crestfallen.

Not a moment later, they came upon double doors and the thief led her through them.

Evelyn gasped when she saw the room. It was enormous, with one entire wall nothing but floor-to-ceiling windows, as well as hundreds of glass panes that looked out over a tree-filled garden. The lighting in here must have been absolutely superb during the day!

As the thief led her farther in, Evelyn studied her surroundings. What was this incredible room? It seemed to be a storage room, with different types of art stored together in nonsensical groupings, but off to the side, she recognized a small conservation area. Wistfully, she stared after it.

"What is this room?" she asked, forgetting about the gag, so it came out almost impossible to understand.

"Did you not see the sign? That's right, you were blindfolded. It's the conservation center."

It was incredibly unorganized for a conservation center. Yet she was still filled with wonder at it.

The thief led her over to a chair and motioned for her to sit in it. She did. It was rather uncomfortable, but she made no complaint. Not that he would care, anyway.

The Signature Swindler stepped forward and crossed his arms as he studied her. What did he want? Why had he separated Evelyn from Ollie when he had already planned to meet the both of them?

Evelyn reviewed the meager clues she had.

He was an Irishman with dark eyes, not blue, as one would generally expect. He had ties to the tenement across the street from the Bethnal Green Museum, though what those ties were, she didn't yet know. This information didn't help her in the moment.

He knew where Ollie lived. But she still wasn't sure if his initial objective was to get to Ollie or to Evelyn.

And he knew her name. That meant he knew about the reward to turn her into the earl. This pushed her toward the idea she was what he wanted. Not her, specifically, but the reward for her.

The good thing about that, though, was he wouldn't lay a hand on her. He wouldn't hurt her. The earl wouldn't give the reward if anything happened to her, of that she was confident.

This provided some relief, at least.

"I'm going to remove the gag," the thief said. "If you scream, I promise you'll regret it."

The threat sounded weak. She was sure he wouldn't follow through with it. But she also wasn't about to tempt fate, either.

The thief took a hesitant step forward and—finally—she could talk again!

"Is this all really necessary?" she immediately asked, ensuring her voice was sharp. Her neck was tense and she turned her head to stretch it.

The thief considered her question. "Yes."

She huffed. "What do you want? You knew we were here—you gave us that silly little note. Obviously, you had planned to meet with us, but you took me instead."

Unfortunately, because of the mask, she couldn't read his face at all while he didn't reply.

"What. Do you want," she reiterated.

"The man you're running about with. Ollie McNab, is it?"

She kept her mouth shut. They still weren't sure whom the thief had originally been after: Ollie or Evelyn. "I'm not telling you anything," she replied in a haughty tone.

"And he has two brothers, right? They own a pub."

Again, she kept her mouth shut on this. Why was he asking questions about Ollie when it was she with a reward over her head?

"You know who I am." She decided to redirect the conversation.

"Yes."

"Is all of this to get the reward? Turn me in to my jailer to make some money with no regard to why I ran?"

The thief stared at her behind that unsettling mask. "Why *did* you run?"

She scoffed. As if he really cared.

"A question for a question."

She narrowed her eyes at him. "What does that mean?"

"I ask you a question and if you answer, then you can ask me a question."

Evelyn gave some thought to this. "Very well."

The thief began to slowly pace. "So. Why did you run?"

"Because I don't want to get married."

"In general, or to the earl?"

"Both."

"So—"

"Ah!" Evelyn interrupted. "You asked a question. That means I get two now."

The thief stilled for a moment. "All right. Ask two."

"What do you want from me?" Finally, he would have to answer.

"I had some questions to ask you."

Evelyn let out a grunt of frustration. "What kind of questions? This is ridiculous. Why did you have to kidnap me to ask?"

The thief paused and his eyes grinned through the mask. "That was three questions."

She rolled her eyes.

"I will tell you my questions in a moment. I had to *kidnap* you"—his feet shuffled as he paused to turn his pacing around—"because it would be the only way to get answers. No chance I would get them with your friend around."

"It's incredible how your answers to my questions don't help me in the least or provide any answers to anything," she said dryly. It felt as if she were running in place.

The thief laughed quite loudly. "As I said, if your friend were around, nothing would be discussed or answered."

She stayed quiet this time, hoping this silly conversation would move forward.

"It's admittedly quite tempting to turn you in—don't think I haven't strongly considered it." He began his slow meander again. "But I haven't yet because I want to know the nature of your relationship with your friend Ollie McNab."

"Why?"

The thief held up one gloved finger. "Not your turn."

Evelyn let out an annoyed sigh.

"I find it curious of all the places in the world, you're hiding with him. A secret relationship, perhaps?"

"No," she replied. And then, "Are you turning me in?"

"No," the thief said, surprising her. Wouldn't he want to get rid of them quickly and get his reward? "I have something else entirely in mind."

Unease snaked through her. "What's that?"

He shook his finger. "Not yet. As you said, there is no secret rendezvous between you and your friend Ollie. And yet, I find that incredibly hard to believe."

Evelyn began to wonder if the thief was someone known to Ollie. It could explain why he always wore a mask. "Because of his reputation." This was a guess based upon with the duke and duchess had said during the explosive dinner. She also made sure to state this, not ask as a question.

The thief paused. "Excellent point, but no."

She waited and fought the urge to ask anything further. He seemed to know something she didn't. Maybe, if she stayed quiet, he would expand on it.

It worked. "The simplest way I can explain it is, I am a man. I am not young, nor am I old, but I have seen plenty in my lifetime. And I'm an observer. I prefer to watch people than interact with them."

"Get to the point."

"I've been observing Ollie for some time now. He is interesting to watch. Ollie lives a life I'm envious of. He plays all day at a pub owned by his family. Goes to fancy balls with his insipid grandparents. Beautiful women, rich and poor, throw themselves at him. Life for him is easy and carefree."

A hot flame ignited in her chest. "You follow him? Is that what you're saying?"

The Signature Swindler looked at her through the mask with those disturbing, smiling eyes. "He is merely a curiosity. Something fascinating to observe."

"That is…incredibly creepy."

"I mean no one any harm."

"Yet look at me tied up."

"You're a runner, lass. And I have only this one chance to talk to you. You gave me no choice."

She resisted the urge to roll her eyes at him again before realizing he had forgotten about their questions game. The thief was more interested in hearing himself talk, it seemed, and she was going to take advantage of this. "What did you want to talk to me about?"

The thief turned his head and looked toward the door. Evelyn looked, too. Had he heard something? Or was he determining how to escape with her?

"I never intended to make myself known," the thief said. "I was quite content with watching Ollie from afar. But then you came along."

"You're mad."

The man laughed. "Indeed." He paused. "I have a curious theory, but I must test it first."

"Lovely."

"I need you to imagine something for me. Ollie is at the pub working. There's a beautiful woman there."

"I don't care."

He ignored her and continued. "She has her eyes set on Ollie. She whispers to her friends that she's finally mustered up the courage to go talk to him herself."

Evelyn squirmed. Unfortunately, she had a vivid imagination and could see this scenario as if it were real. And she didn't like it one bit.

"The woman taps Ollie on the shoulder. Ollie turns and sets his eyes upon her. She says something insipid and then giggles and covers her lips with her fingertips."

Evelyn started pulling at the rope around her wrists, getting angry when she couldn't free herself.

"Ollie is overcome by desire, by the woman's beauty, and he puts a hand on her waist."

"I get it," Evelyn blurted out, wishing he would stop.

But the thief wasn't done. "Ollie knows what he wants. He pulls her into an empty hallway and presses her against the wall. His blood is hot, and his c—"

"Stop it!" Evelyn shouted louder than she'd meant. She jumped to her feet, her wrists still secured behind her back. "I swear, if you say one more word—"

"Ah, lass, not another word." The thief put up both hands in surrender. "You have proved my theory correct, and that's all I wanted."

Evelyn was seething now. She clenched her teeth and took several hard steps over to him. She got into his face, met by those infuriating smiling eyes. "What theory is that?"

But the man was hardly perturbed. Evelyn decided he was truly, utterly mad in the most literal sense.

"Did that upset you? My little story? It wasn't made up. I watched that exact scenario unfold a few summers ago, though I didn't stick around to see how it ended."

"Go to hell," she seethed back.

"You know he's a scoundrel, Miss Sparrow, don't you?"

She wouldn't give him the satisfaction of a response.

"There is something rather curious, though, that may soothe the fire in your veins."

"Is it me bashing your face in?"

The thief laughed. "No. Curiously, one day Ollie stopped his women-chasing ways. No weaning period, no easing into it. One day, he was a scoundrel, the next, he was as chaste as a saint."

"I don't care," she growled back.

"Ah, but you do. You're white hot with anger. And it's because you are mad for the man, aren't you?"

"No." Evelyn tried to make her denial hard. But even she could hear how weak it was. "Like you said, he's a scoundrel."

"But he's also told you he has curiously stopped chasing skirts. Didn't he?"

Again, she didn't say anything.

The thief suddenly glanced in the direction of a tall shipping box nearby and his eyes smiled again. He looked back at her and lowered her voice to a whisper. "Like I said, I've been a curious and amused observer of your friend. And I can confirm he has in fact, stopped his scoundrel ways. He wasn't lying to you, lass. And I can pinpoint the exact moment he stopped."

Evelyn couldn't help herself. "When?"

The thief leaned into her ear. "The moment he set eyes on you."

Evelyn took a sharp inhale. "You're lying." The thief was a master of deceit. He was toying with her for his own amusement. He was entertained by cruelty.

"No," the thief replied, still quiet. "And to take it one step further, you're madly in love with him, aren't you?"

Chapter Sixteen

THAT HOT FLAME in her chest roared into an inferno and the following moment seemed to happen at a sluggish speed. She shouted something—though what, she couldn't remember—and lunged at the thief.

To her utmost glee, this seemed to surprise the man, and he floundered back.

At the same time, Ollie appeared from out of nowhere and tackled the thief to the ground. Shouting enveloped the trio as the two men scuffled. Evelyn watched with bated breath.

Amidst the scuffle, Ollie knocked the man's tricorn hat off, exposing the dark hair beneath, and then reached for the mask.

Evelyn stilled, eager to finally see who the cruel thief was.

But the thief was too slippery. Somehow, he managed to evade Ollie's reach, rolled away, and jumped up to his feet.

"What did you do to her?" Ollie shouted through his heaving breaths. He, too, climbed back up to stand. "If you pulled a single hair on her head—"

"Ollie, I'm fine." Evelyn could see how worried he was, and it pulled at her. "Honest. He didn't hurt me."

Ollie turned to look at her, and it was as if he were just now noticing her. For a prolonged moment, he stared. Then he looked down to where her arms wrapped behind her. "Did he tie your hands?"

"Oh. Well, aside from that, he didn't do anything to me. He just talked, incessantly. A rather irritating fellow, I may add." Though she couldn't see the thief's expression, she gave him a pointed look, anyway.

"Quite an interesting conversation we had, though, wasn't it?" the thief gloated.

Ollie began untying the rope around her. "What was so interesting about it?"

Evelyn hesitated. She absolutely could not tell him what the thief had just revealed. Incorrectly. She was absolutely *not* in love with Ollie. If he had accused her of lusting after Ollie, perhaps she would eventually agree. But love was an *entirely* different story. "I don't know."

The rope fell away, and Ollie moved to stand in front of her. "What do you mean, you don't know?"

Heat crept up her neck as she scrambled for what to say. "He watches you."

Ollie frowned deeply. "Sorry?"

"He watches you. Thinks you are amusing to watch, and he's been doing it for a while now, though he didn't say how long." But he had apparently been doing it longer than Evelyn had known Ollie. How many years had the thief been watching Ollie? It was unsettling and strange. Why Ollie, though? The thief had not revealed the reason, other than blaming it on a general curiosity. But there had to be more to it than that. Right?

Concern knit over Ollie's face. As he mulled over this tidbit, he lifted one of her wrists to observe closely. Her skin was red where the rope had been. Ollie lightly swept a thumb over the raw spot and the intensity of the gentle touch against the tender skin rankled her. She jerked her hand away and clutched her wrist against her chest.

A muscle in Ollie's jaw ticked, the only hint her reaction bothered him.

The Signature Swindler, apparently losing interest in them, was meandering around the room as if he were shopping. He lifted a painting, bobbed his head as if considering it, then secured it under his cloak.

"What in the blazes are you doing?" Ollie said to the thief, turning his back to Evelyn.

The thief didn't look up. "What does it look like?"

"Where is the painting that you stole from us?"

"Now why would I tell you that?"

"I want it back."

"Do you, now?"

"Yes." Ollie's voice was hard. "Enough of this madness. I'm not chasing you around London for it. If it doesn't appear on my doorstep by noon tomorrow, I'm going to the police."

The thief chuckled. "No, you won't. Even she knows that."

Ollie looked over his shoulder at Evelyn and all she could do was shrug one shoulder.

Ollie returned his attention to the thief. "I think you've done enough. We'll leave you alone if you return it by tomorrow."

The thief had pulled a fountain pen from somewhere and, with a comical flourish, signed his name atop the rough, wooden table from which he had taken the painting. "How about we strike a bargain?" he asked while securing the cap back on the pen.

"A bargain?" Ollie replied, frustrated by the man's antics. "I already gave you my offer!"

"Tomorrow by noon, I'll send you a note with instruction on where to meet me to retrieve the painting."

Evelyn bit her lip. Was it really as easy as that? "Just like that, you're going to give it back?"

"He did ask nicely," the thief replied.

Evelyn narrowed her eyes.

"And, to retrieve it, you must also go to a location of my choosing."

"How about the tenements across the street?" Evelyn asked with a smirk.

The thief stilled. Finally, after a long moment, he said, "No."

She had hit a nerve. "What are your ties there?"

"Who tattled?" He had recovered from that odd moment and his eyes were back to smiling. "Nah. Not there. I'd like something with a bit more…flair."

Evelyn and Ollie exchanged a look. What option did they have?

"Fine," Ollie said after Evelyn gave a small nod. "Note by tomorrow noon and we'll meet you at whatever place you decide fits your ridiculous game."

The thief bent over, flipped the tricorn hat up from the floor, lifted it in a cheer, then spun around to disappear into the shadows.

OLLIE WATCHED THE blasted thief disappear like a ghost. It was unsettling and he was glad that, this time tomorrow, they might be rid of the idiot for good. Assuming he came through, which was questionable.

Ollie turned back to Evelyn, who was putting pointed focus on her skirt.

He wasn't sure what to do or say, what his place was in all of this.

Earlier, she'd admitted she liked him touching her. If anyone but her had said that, it would have sounded like innuendo. But he could see in her surprise that she'd meant it. And, strangely, he found himself pleased by her discovery. It made him feel oddly special to her, even though he wasn't. But it also didn't make sense. Evelyn had recoiled from him several times over. He couldn't forget those moments. And her claim she liked his touch had been during a moment he'd been teaching her something. It wasn't one in which he'd held her hand to keep her close, or when he'd kissed her. Or she'd kissed him. Whatever it was that had happened.

"You're sure he didn't hurt you?" Ollie asked, trying to shut his mind up. Unfortunately, they still didn't know who the thief was, but now Ollie's curiosity was piqued even more. It was rather strange the man had been watching Ollie. That, admittedly, was incredibly weird and a bit sinister. But it made no sense, either. Ollie was just another Londoner. Why had the thief focused on him, of all people?

Furthermore, why would the thief have even admitted that to Evelyn? It must have been a part of the game he seemed to be playing with them. But what the purpose of that game was, Ollie still couldn't understand.

"Why did he take you instead of meeting with the both of us like we were expecting?" Ollie asked.

Evelyn stopped fussing over her skirt. "I don't know." When she looked up, he was startled to see how forlorn she looked. Her eyes were dull, and the delicate skin around those eyes was darkening.

"All of this should be over tomorrow, Evelyn," Ollie reassured her. He wanted to fix everything for her and make her feel better, but this was all he could offer. And he wasn't even sure it would ever end.

She gave him a small smile. "Except you're still barred from work, and I'm still hiding from my family."

True. "It's better than nothing, at least." Her weariness apparent, he needed to get her home post-haste and began walking through the large, cluttered room while she followed. "Do you think we'll really get the painting back tomorrow?"

"Maybe," she replied. "I do trust he'll send a note. He seems to enjoy toying with us, and he will follow through with that part at least."

As they reached the double door, Ollie stopped. "Did he tell you why he follows me? I have to admit that…was an unexpected discovery. That I don't like one bit."

Evelyn looked up at him with wide eyes. "No, but you want to know the strangest part of it? He said you never would have known about him if it weren't for me."

Ollie furrowed his brow. "What does that mean?"

"The only reason he made himself known to you is because I showed up. Otherwise, he would have watched you, for who knows how long, and you never would have known."

"He made his presence known because of the reward money."

"Maybe." Evelyn's mind seemed to be wandering and that lingering discomfort still had not dissipated.

"You're sure he didn't hurt you?"

Her attention went back to him. "Yes."

"Something's bothering you, though. What is it?"

"Nothing."

"Did he say something you're not telling me?"

Her mouth opened slightly as if surprised he had asked. "Don't be silly, Ollie. The man was being a pest is all." But the words came out too quickly, too high-pitched, to convince him.

However, before he could press the issue further, Evelyn adjusted her hat and opened the door. "No more of this. I'm quite tired and would like to leave. Perhaps we go to the tenements across the street and see if anyone is up and about? We could ask them if—"

"No. No one will tell us—total outsiders—anything useful. And anyway, you look ready to collapse."

She let out a long sigh but didn't argue.

Minutes later, they found their way back outside, tracked down a hansom, and swiftly returned home.

As Ollie's house came into view, the driver slowly pulled the horse over to the side to stop. They were two houses over, but Ollie wasn't about to correct that. He paid the man, who tipped his hat in thanks, and the horse trotted off.

As they began walking, Ollie readjusted his top hat and collar and Evelyn surprised him by taking his arm. He resisted the urge to flex his hand upon her touch.

"I apologize for earlier," she said. "For pulling away from you like that."

Ollie looked down to her with a frown. "You don't need to apologize for that."

She gazed up at him from beneath the brim of her hat and gave him a small smile. His heart hitched. "I feel badly. I wish I knew why I have such severe reactions to touch sometimes."

"There's no deep explanation needed, Evelyn. You simply don't like it. While it may be unusual, it's how you are. It takes some getting used to for me, that's all."

"But I had told you earlier that I enjoyed you touching me. It wasn't a lie. And then I went and did that."

His heart skipped again at hearing those words and he cleared his throat. "You had just been tied up by the Signature Swindler. I don't think anyone would blame you for wanting to be left alone after that. And anyway, look at you right now, walking with me arm in arm. See? No harm done." He gave her a crooked grin to mask the confusion he truly felt.

He paused in front of a neighbor's home, as in a strange way, he didn't want this moment with her on his arm to end. She looked up at him, long lashes framing her round, doe eyes. Around them, the street was dark, quiet. It felt like they were the only two people in the whole world.

I want to kiss you again, he wanted to say. But he wouldn't dare. His pride would never recover from *that* recoil.

Instead, he lifted his hand to her face and cupped her cheek, eliciting a small, sharp inhale from her.

No words were exchanged between them, and the moment was nothing in the grand scheme of things, but it was one he would hold secret to his heart forever. One he would look back upon wistfully some day when he was in his forties, fifties, slinging pints down the bartop, perpetually unmarried, probably back to his scoundrel ways.

Those days are over and you know it, that little voice of reason cut in. *They will never come back. Do you even want them to?*

Evelyn stared up at him with a softened gaze, her eyelids

lowered as she searched his face. When she put him under her spell like this, he couldn't think straight enough to answer his own question.

Kiss her, you bloody fool.

No, not yet.

What are you waiting for?

The perfect moment.

What if this is it?

But Ollie didn't respond to himself. This was not the time. He didn't know when the time would be, if it ever would be, but this wasn't it. Too much had happened tonight, and she wasn't ready. Not yet.

Though he did greatly regret that fact.

Dropping his hand to end the moment, he began walking with her again and, despite possibly losing the only moment he would have in his life to kiss Evelyn Sparrow a second time, Ollie felt like he floated above the clouds with her hanging on his arm. But his head was pulled out of those clouds when he realized someone was standing in front of the house.

Warning snaked through him.

"Keep your head down and keep walking," Ollie cautioned low enough so the unknown man couldn't hear. Evelyn didn't respond, and he didn't know if she'd heard him, either.

Evelyn did, however, lower her head to conceal her face with the brim. Ollie wasn't sure if that meant she'd heard or not, but at least she had her wits about her.

As they got closer to his home, he noticed someone else was leaning against the wall of his home, sleeping.

There was no chance he would be able to enter his home safely right now. Something about these men didn't sit right with him.

As they walked by, he could feel the watchfulness of the standing man. Was he looking for Ollie, and would he recognize Ollie on sight?

Both men were dressed in plain, woolen jackets and flat caps.

This, unfortunately, told Ollie nothing, other than they weren't nobs. But Ollie had a strong suspicion they were somehow tied to the earl.

The standing man continued staring at Ollie and Evelyn as they walked by, his hands coolly shoved into his trouser pockets. Evelyn tightened her hold on Ollie's arm. Ollie nodded at the stranger, hoping it would alleviate the tension.

And they passed the man by without incident. Ollie released a breath he hadn't realized he'd held.

"Out for a stroll this late?" the man called after them once their backs were to him.

Ollie felt his body tense again. They stopped walking.

While his heart raced, Ollie looked back over his shoulder, trying to think of a response. "The wife has trouble sleeping. Sometimes a late stroll helps."

"I give mine a shot of whiskey and she sleeps like the dead."

Ollie forced a laugh and then turned back around, continuing to walk, trying not to pace too fast. Moments later, they turned the corner and were out of sight.

Evelyn immediately stopped and turned to face him. "Please tell me you know why those men were there."

But Ollie could only shake his head. "No, but I don't have a good feeling about it."

Evelyn looked as if she were about to cry from exhaustion. "What do we do now? We can't meander around London until they leave!"

It might not work, and it might be a bit mad, but Ollie came up with an idea.

"Follow me," he said, looking around to ensure they were alone. She didn't argue.

Ollie snaked his way through the yards of his back neighbors—thankfully, only one dog barked—until he came to the stone wall of his property. With little effort, he boosted Evelyn up high enough for her to climb up on it. And then he followed. Thanks to a large tree, he was able to scramble up.

Both leapt down from the high wall and rushed through the darkness of his garden.

They entered the house through the back entrance, unnoticed.

Everyone would have been asleep at this hour so he put a finger to his lips, indicating they were to remain quiet. They hurried up to the second floor as soundlessly as they could.

The house was dark, and they peered out a front window through a gap in the curtains.

"Who do you suppose they are?" Evelyn looked over his shoulder. But all they could see were the tops of the men's hats.

"I don't know, but they're clearly waiting for us."

"You think they're tied to the earl?" Evelyn asked, the concern apparent in her voice.

"Unfortunately, I do. But not to worry—they don't know we've arrived home. Nor can they stay out there forever."

A noise made them turn around, and Ollie felt Evelyn jump when Mrs. Chapman appeared in her nightgown with a lit candle.

Her face pinched. "Those two men kept banging on the door not long after you left for the evening. I told them to bugger off, but they wouldn't."

"Who are they?" Ollie asked.

"They said they're journalists." Mrs. Chapman hesitated. "They also said someone told the earl she's staying here." She jutted her chin to Evelyn.

Evelyn didn't say anything, but she gripped the back of his arm. That she sought him out for comfort and support again gave him a little leap of happiness despite the seriousness of the matter.

"Go get some sleep," he said to Evelyn. He suspected Mrs. Chapman knew more than she was sharing but didn't want Evelyn to know the seriousness of the matter.

"Are you sure?" Evelyn asked before biting her lip.

But Ollie insisted again, and this time, she didn't argue. Evelyn disappeared into her bedroom and the door clicked shut behind her.

Ollie turned back to Mrs. Chapman. "All right, tell me everything."

Mrs. Chapman nodded. "They arrived pounding on the door ten minutes after you left, which was very lucky for you. I answered and they asked for you."

"Did they say anything about Evelyn?"

"I told them you weren't home, but they remained. Several times I asked them to leave when, finally, they said they weren't going to go anywhere because they heard Miss Sparrow was here and they were waiting for the police to show up, too. I, of course, denied knowing anything, and Cook wants nothing to do with all the commotion, so she's been keeping to herself."

"Wait. They said Evelyn had been found?"

"Yes." Mrs. Chapman pursed her lips. "I pressed more because that didn't make sense. Apparently, someone had advised the police that she was here. And the journalists wanted to be here to get photographs of the police carting her off."

A wave of fear washed over Ollie. "Did they say who told the police?"

But Mrs. Chapman shook her head. "Who knows she's here?"

Ollie tried recalling. His grandparents had seen her but hadn't seemed to realize who she was. Maybe they'd finally figured it out. He wouldn't put it past them to turn her in, especially with the way their dinner had ended.

Then there was Mr. James Burlington. He had suspected Evelyn was staying with Ollie, but that hadn't been confirmed to him, either. Burlington hadn't set his eyes on her. And he'd willingly helped Ollie get information on the Signature Swindler.

Of course, the blasted thief knew about Evelyn. This seemed the most obvious answer, and the simplest answer was almost always correct. The thief would get a large reward for turning her in, and he clearly liked money.

But that wasn't all. His own family, plus Lady Litchfield, knew she was here. Mrs. Chapman and the cook knew, too.

Ollie didn't think any of them would turn Evelyn in. But, like he had said to Evelyn before, that reward would tempt the most saintly nan. It was just too large a sum.

If anyone in his family, or his house, had turned Evelyn in, it would have been Victor.

The thought made him sick. Victor, as far as Ollie was concerned, was just as obsessed with money as the Signature Swindler. Couple that with the fact that Ollie had made all those big mistakes that had hit them financially.

Everyone had their limit. Was this Victor's?

Ollie concluded either Victor or the Signature Swindler had turned in Evelyn's location. Though he really hoped it wasn't his own brother.

"Too many people know she's here," Ollie said in answer to Mrs. Chapman's question. "And I have no idea whom amongst them it would be."

"What are you going to do, Mr. McNab?" Mrs. Chapman asked in a soft, concerned voice.

"I don't know. But for now, no one knows we've returned. This will have to be figured out in the morning."

Chapter Seventeen

THE POLICE, AND resulting crowd, began arriving after breakfast. Evelyn had just left the dining room when she heard the commotion outside. She almost went to go look out the window when Ollie had spotted her from the parlor.

"Don't!" he shouted as he hurried out of the room. "Stay away from windows. They still think we're gone."

Panic mounted. The walls were finally starting to close in. She should have realized she wouldn't be able to be on the run for long but had hoped it would have been more than a few days. "What do I do?" she cried out, not expecting an answer.

"What do you want to do, Evelyn?" Ollie asked.

She knew she couldn't run forever. She had to marry the earl, whether or not she wanted to.

But she could also run away, head north, stay in a hotel for some time.

Though, because it wasn't safe for her to go to her bank, she didn't have the money to do so. And there was no way she could ever ask Ollie for that. He had already done so much for her.

As desperate as she was, there wasn't much of a choice.

No longer could she run. No longer could she avoid her fate.

But she did have to take care of one thing first before returning to her family.

"We're supposed to get a note from the Signature Swindler

by noon," she said. "That's only half an hour from now. Though with that crowd, I doubt it will get to us. But still, I want to get the painting back before I go home."

Ollie's face fell. "What are you saying?"

"I can't do this anymore, Ollie. Look at what chaos this is causing you!" She threw a hand toward the window. "I have been far too much of an imposition. I have to end this madness; it's out of hand. It's obvious the Signature Swindler turned me in. We can get the painting back, he gets his money, everyone's happy."

"*I'm* not going to be happy when you leave, Evelyn," Ollie said, making her feel worse.

His words gutted her. The memory of their kiss began to swirl around her, sending sparks throughout her body. It was torture. In some other life, perhaps she could have seen if something more could happen with Ollie, perhaps she could have kissed him one more time, but that was an impossibility. She would never know if he could have fallen in love with her if everything had been just a bit different.

Evelyn swallowed. Her legs were restless again. "As soon as noon hits, I need to leave the house. I may go mad if I stay any longer. I can't be here with that out there." She paused. "That's it, then, I suppose. We get the painting back today, and I'll go home after that."

"Is that truly what you want?"

Vague images of her and Ollie dancing together rose up in her imagination. Riding through Hyde Park together. Dinners together, walks together. All mundane things to which she'd given hardly a thought before this, but that seemed exceptional if he were with her. But it would never be. "Yes. It's what I want." And then she hurried up to her bedroom.

She didn't emerge until the clock struck noon, and they left. "Did the note arrive?" she asked Ollie as they made their way to the servants' entrance.

"No, but I'm not surprised, either. I don't know if you heard, but the police began knocking on the door. Mrs. Chapman was able to convince them we weren't here, but I don't think she can hold them off much longer."

It would all be over today, which should have been a relief. No more hiding, no more running, no more of the imposition she was. Yet it wasn't comforting.

As soon as they stepped out of the servants' entrance and into the sunshine, Evelyn spotted something on the ground. "Ollie, look." She pointed at an envelope kept in place with a round stone.

Ollie let out a sigh and picked it up. As usual, *Hello* was written on the face of the envelope in dramatic script.

Ollie pulled out the piece of paper and read it.

And his face completely drained of all color.

"What is it?" Evelyn spit the words out. The dramatic change in Ollie's demeanor scared her. Something truly bad was written on the note.

Ollie continued to stare down at the paper, wordless. Evelyn went to his side to see what it said for herself. She didn't know what she was expecting, but she definitely wasn't expecting what she found. All it was was an address on Whitechapel Road. They needed to be there two hours past noon. And not a minute late.

"He wants us to meet him in Whitechapel?" Evelyn frowned. "Does this address have any significance to you?"

But Ollie didn't respond. Instead, he mumbled a string of curse words and ripped up the letter into little pieces, before letting it blow away in the wind.

"*Ollie!*" Evelyn hurried after the bits of paper as they lifted into the sky, but it was no use. The note, the address, were gone. "Why did you do that?!"

"Because I refuse to go to that address," Ollie responded with evident strain.

She needed to push down the rising anger because something significant had happened and she needed to uncover what it was. "Please tell me what it is."

"It's where my mother is buried." He shook his head, a vacant look on his face. "The blasted idiot wants us to meet him at my mother's godforsaken grave!" His face twisted with pain. "What kind of game is he playing now? What is the blasted point of all of this?"

The revelation hung in the air, putrid and heavy.

Ollie walked past her and toward the stone wall, and she decided to keep quiet. They climbed back over, and she followed him in silence through the neighboring gardens. They had two hours until they had to meet the Signature Swindler, but she hesitated to ask what they were going to do to pass the time.

In the end they walked aimlessly around London. Evelyn kept glancing at the uncharacteristically quiet Ollie. His normally bright-green eyes were dark. His jaw was tense, his back rigid.

She had tried a few times to offer words of comfort, but they hadn't worked. Because there *were* no words that could offer comfort. She had to give him the space he needed for the time being.

They went to the Thames and walked along its foreshore to keep away from the crowd. The only people around were more interested in finding historical objects left behind by the past than Evelyn and Ollie.

Evelyn tried showing him old buttons and coins she'd found, but Ollie mostly grunted in response.

Sometime after that, they found themselves walking along the streets of London again and Evelyn realized they were in a familiar area.

"I think we're close to my house," Evelyn said with surprise as she looked around. It was a residential street, so there weren't many people, and it wasn't an area she had found herself in very often. But still, she recognized it. Back before she married, Cordelia used to go for walks up and down this exact street after the luncheon hour. Cordelia said she liked the street because of the large trees that lined the road. "Ollie, what time is it?"

Ollie checked his pocket watch and spoke for the first time in an hour. "Just a few minutes before one. Why?"

A jolt of excitement hit Evelyn and without thinking, she grabbed Ollie's hand and began running down the street with him dragging behind. He did manage to keep up the pace, despite being caught off guard.

Three blocks down, Evelyn thought she saw a familiar form and paused. A woman up the street was walking at a slow pace.

Evelyn went to hurry toward her, but Ollie pulled her back.

"What in the blazes are you doing?" Ollie asked. "You're racing down the street for God-knows-what-reason, and now you've targeted that woman like a border collie itching to get to its sheep."

Evelyn pulled her hand away from him. "Did you just compare me to a dog?"

Ollie let out a long sigh. "Evelyn. What are you doing?"

Evelyn glanced back over her shoulder. The woman was getting farther away. "I think that's my sister."

"And you're running after her? That seems extremely foolish."

Evelyn shook her head. "Cordelia isn't like my father or mother. She's one of the only people I wholly trust in this world."

Ollie tilted his head and paused for a moment. "Any chance she could be the one who turned you in to the earl?"

"No. There's no chance of that. She's the one who encouraged me to run away from him. And as far as I know, she doesn't know where I've been."

Ollie rubbed his jaw and stared down the street. "You really want to go talk to her? Despite how risky it is?"

Was it really that risky, though? Evelyn trusted Cordelia. Cordelia was not on board with the marriage. Could she have changed her mind?

"You're hesitating," Ollie pointed out.

Evelyn lifted her chin in defiance. "Don't be silly. I have no reason to hesitate. Now, I'm going to go talk to her before we head to Whitechapel. Are you coming with me or not?"

Grudgingly, Ollie followed, making sure to reiterate he

thought this was a bad idea.

As they hurried to catch up to Cordelia, Cordelia unexpectedly turned and stepped up to the front door of a house.

Cordelia knocked on the door, the door opened, and she stepped inside.

Evelyn made a sound of disappointment and stopped at the path that led up to the door. The property had square-trimmed hedges in front of the house and along the path.

"Who lives here?" Ollie asked as they both angled their heads back to look up at the townhome. It was modest but well kept.

"I'm not sure," Evelyn admitted. "I can't even think of anyone she still speaks to in England who would live here."

"What do you want to do, then?"

Evelyn looked over to Ollie. "What do you mean?"

"She could be in there for a few minutes, or a few hours. We can't wait, or we risk being seen."

"True," Evelyn conceded. "Let's at least give her a few minutes."

"Why do you even want to talk to her?"

There was a fluttering movement at the corner of her eye and Evelyn glanced over to find a small bird had landed in the hedge. It looked at her with little jerky movements of its head, round, black eyes watching her with interest.

"My sister can tell me what's going on in my family right now, if my parents are willing to give up on the whole earl business or not."

"Do you think they are?"

"Probably not. But I must speak to her." She pulled her attention away from the little bird and directly to Ollie. "Maybe she can help me figure out how to get out of this quandary."

Ollie studied her with his mouth pressed in a tight line. He then looked up at the door. "Five minutes," he said. "If she's not out in that time, we have to keep moving. It's unwise to be hanging around a neighborhood you're familiar with, even if only slightly."

The minutes slowly ticked by and anticipation at seeing her sister again grew.

And then, the door opened again, sending a rush of excitement through her.

Ollie grabbed Evelyn and pulled them both down into a space between two hedges.

Cordelia stepped out of the house—though Evelyn could only see her from mid-thigh down—and then turned back around to someone standing in the doorway. Unfortunately, Evelyn couldn't get a good look at who they were, but she was able to see the woman's raspberry-pink dress was bedecked in sequins, crystals, and metallic embroidery. Rather flashy for the afternoon.

"Thank you for seeing me at a moment's notice," the unknown woman said to Cordelia, her vowels elongated to sound aristocratic, but it was more comical than anything. "I know time isn't on your side."

"Of course," Cordelia responded, tapping the tip of a closed parasol against her foot. Evelyn knew this as a nervous tic of her sister's. "I appreciate your help in this matter. And your utmost secrecy. I'm sure you understand the sensitivity of the matter at hand for my family."

"Yes," the woman responded after a bit of a hesitation. "I'm just glad you have finally located your sister."

"I'm sure you are," Cordelia responded a bit dryly.

"This makes for many happy people, does it not?"

"Quite."

"I wonder how the earl will react," the woman added with a wistful tone.

Evelyn and Ollie exchanged a look. They were talking about Evelyn and she did not like the sinking feeling it created. Especially as Ollie's gaze reflected her own sickening suspicion.

When Cordelia didn't add anything further, the woman said, "Now, you've assured me the rest of the funds would be made available when, again?"

"The rest of the payment will be yours tomorrow."

Nausea took hold of Evelyn, hardly believing what she'd heard. Somehow, with the help of this unknown woman, her own sister seemed to have turned her in to the earl.

How could she have? How could Cordelia, the person she'd trusted most, have done this to her?

Ollie's words echoed in her mind. *That amount of money will tempt even the most saintly nan.*

Cordelia was the one who'd encouraged her to leave.

However.

Evelyn also knew the new *conte* controlled Cordelia's allowance. While he had been generous thus far, that could change at any time. It could change when he married, or someday he could simply decide to reduce it for no reason at all. Perhaps Cordelia had thought about this when the reward for Evelyn had doubled. It would give Cordelia safety, security. Money of her own no one could take away from her.

Without any warning to poor Ollie, Evelyn crawled out of the hedge and jumped other her feet. "You!" She pointed to her sister, and her throat became tight. "You're the one who turned me in! You betrayed me!" Evelyn's voice cracked.

Cordelia made a squeaking noise as her hand flew to her heart. Finally, Evelyn was able to get a look at the woman in the doorway. To her surprise, she had no idea who the woman was. She was quite beautiful, and the jewelry she wore matched the flashiness of the dress. Whoever she was, she wasn't blue blooded. But between the location of her home, and the dress and clothing that demanded to be seen, Evelyn postured the woman desperately tried to appear upper class.

"Ollie?" the flashy woman then said, surprise written all over her face. She looked at Evelyn. "Oh." She paused. "Oh!"

"Penelope," Ollie replied with a tight nod and a strangled voice. "I mean, Miss Findlay."

"Silly Ollie." Miss Findlay tapped his shoulder. "You know we are *friendly* enough for me to be Penelope to you. What do you think of my new house?" She indicated behind her. "Perhaps I could give you a personal tour." A lilt in her voice hinted at her true intentions.

A million questions filled Evelyn's mind. Who was Miss Findlay and how did she know Ollie? Why was she so informal with him? Why was Cordelia making a deal with her?

The pieces came together quite easily, though. None of this was any grand mystery.

Cordelia and Miss Findlay were splitting the award for Evelyn's return. Miss Findlay was clearly one of Ollie's old flames—the tension in the air between them was unmistakable—and she'd mistaken Evelyn's stay at Ollie's as something more than what it had been. Maybe she hadn't liked this and had intervened, going to Cordelia to strike a deal. Keep things private, split the money.

Or perhaps, Ollie and Miss Findlay had been in touch all this time. Not an old flame, but a flame. Present tense.

Maybe Miss Findlay had come by the house for a visit, and Ollie had kept it from Evelyn.

Evelyn's heart pounded as jealousy singed her veins. But the sense of betrayal from her sister weighed heavily as well.

Unable to stand with these people another moment, Evelyn suddenly turned around and began running.

"Evelyn, wait!" Cordelia's voice called after her. But Evelyn wouldn't wait.

Hot tears threatened to spill from her eyes, but she was too furious to let them. On and on she ran block after block until finally she could run no more.

There was an empty park bench in a small park she didn't know. As she collapsed into it and gasped for breath, she listened to the birds sing happily, cursing them for it.

And she cursed at herself. How stupid could a woman be! She knew Ollie had been a scoundrel. She knew he had a past. She thought she didn't care, especially as both Ollie and the Signature Swindler had confirmed that had all been part of a past life of his.

But that appeared to not be true.

Yet the thief had had no reason to lie about that. In fact, she wasn't even sure why he would tell her that in the first place. But for some foolish reason, she'd believed him. She'd believed the thief. She'd believed Ollie.

The thief, a master of deceit, had included one little detail that had made his claim feel so real: Ollie's scoundrel behavior had stopped the day he'd met Evelyn.

Evelyn couldn't decide if the thief had been lying or not. Or if Ollie had pulled the wool over everyone's eyes.

An especially happy bird, who looked suspiciously like the one faffing about at Penelope's home moments ago, fluttered down to the ground and began to sing. Evelyn stuck her tongue out at it.

A noise caused her to turn around. Ollie was approaching with a deep wheeze. He slid down onto the bench.

"You have got…" He stopped to catch his breath. "To stop doing that."

Evelyn waited a beat, but no one else appeared. "Where's my sister?"

Ollie leaned his head back against a tree trunk behind them, his breaths still heavy. "I have no idea."

"I'm surprised to see you. I figured you would be indulging in a tour about now." Evelyn was studying a button on one of her gloves.

Ollie took several deep breaths. Considering his next move, perhaps? Not that she cared, of course. If Ollie wished to visit Miss Findlay's living quarters, who was she to get in the way?

"Erm…" Ollie scratched the side of his nose. "That woman back there, Miss Findlay—"

"Ollie, please. I don't care." Truly, the less she knew, the better.

His breathing leveling out, he moved to lean forward, resting his elbows on his knees. He tilted his head to the side and gave her a roguish grin. "If you don't care, then you won't mind me telling you I haven't seen her since before I even knew you."

She narrowed her eyes at him, trying to find any hint he was lying to her. But he seemed truthful. And he didn't have a reason to lie about it, either. It wasn't like *they* were anything he would want to preserve.

Fine. It did make her feel better, not that she would tell him that. She brushed her hands over her lap. "I don't care, Ollie. You may go reacquaint yourself with her, then, if you like."

Ollie laughed, which annoyed her. "Do I sense a hint of jealousy?"

Yes. "Of course not." The stubborn side of her made a point to look directly at him when she said this.

His green eyes glinted back at her with mischief.

"I have no reason to be jealous at all," she said smugly.

"No, you don't."

Evelyn swallowed and decided it would be best not to dissect if there was a deeper meaning to that comment.

Either way, her worry about Ollie and this Miss Findlay was based purely on jealousy that wasn't rooted in anything other than her imagination and their shared past, which she'd of course had no part in.

"I'm sorry," she said to change the subject. With the silly Miss Findlay issue settled—honestly, she'd thought she was better than that—guilt reared its ugly head.

"Sorry for what?"

"For running off again. I know it worries you. I had to get away, and I wasn't thinking."

"You're right. It does worry me. Thank you for your apology. I accept."

Unable to help herself, she gave him a brief smile, but it didn't last. "So, it appears my sister was the one who turned me in. The very last person I would expect."

There was a long pause before he replied gently, "I'm sorry."

She shook her head. "No need to be sorry. You had nothing to do with it. I still wonder how she and Miss Findlay got themselves twisted together and how they found me, but I suppose it doesn't really matter, either. It doesn't change my fate."

Ollie was quiet a moment. "What are you going to do?"

Evelyn stared out over the desolate park. There was a large fountain turned off for the cold seasons. "Nothing. Except look at my sister in a different light, I suppose. Feel the betrayal for the remainder of my life."

Ollie sighed. "Sometimes, I wish we could pick our family. They can be far too excellent at making us feel horrific."

"Mmm."

"Evelyn."

Evelyn turned to Ollie and found him watching her with his mouth partially open, as if he wished to say something but couldn't quite get it out. Then he glanced down at her lips before leaning toward her. Evelyn's heart galloped from the sudden change in his demeanor. Her body felt a magnetic pull toward him, and chills went up her spine as he got closer and closer.

But all he did was lean into her ear. And in a low, deep voice, his breath caressing the skin just below her ear, he said, "You should never be jealous of anyone else, Evelyn."

And he pulled away, mischief once again dancing in those bright-green eyes of his.

"I'm not responding to that," was all she managed to get out. She desperately wanted to seem unaffected by his words, by his closeness, by him. She would be gone in a few hours.

Chapter Eighteen

T HE CLOCK JUTTING out from the side of St. Mary's spire
showed they'd made it right on time.

Unfortunately.

For whatever reason, the Signature Swindler wanted to return the Gustave Courbet painting here at a church of all places.
Ollie had been dreading this moment ever since receiving the
note. Yes, he'd been a bit theatrical after reading the note, but he
also knew he had to come to this blasted place, no matter how
much he didn't want to. The thief had made a comment that he
would return the painting at the location of his choosing, and this
was his choosing.

He wondered, though, if the Signature Swindler knew about
Ollie's tie to this place or if it were a bizarre coincidence.

"Do you know where to go?" Evelyn asked.

"Not really," he replied. "I haven't been here since I was very
young." Guilt began to creep inside him. "I only remember my
mother was buried somewhere toward the back."

"Do you want to go say *hello*?"

The shame worsened from her innocent question. He was a
coward, and Evelyn probably thought so herself.

Resolving to get this over with, Ollie pushed through a
creaky, iron gate and walked through the graveyard, reading the
gravestones as he passed.

Sullivan.

Baxter.

Glover.

Sheen.

None of them were his mother's.

"I can help if you like." Evelyn appeared at his side. "What was her name?"

Ollie's mouth went dry. When was the last time he had said his mother's name out loud? She'd existed. He hadn't known her, but she had existed. Yet he could never talk about her. Anytime he did, his brothers would tell him to stop.

"Honora McNab. Lydon before that," he finally replied.

"Honora," Evelyn whispered the word as if it were something precious.

And it was.

"All right." She gave him an encouraging grin, a small beacon of light in the glumness that surrounded them. "Let's find Honora."

Ollie swallowed and gave her a tight nod and together, they walked the rows of gravestones, looking for his mother.

What would he say to her once he found her?

Would he even say anything? It felt silly to do so. She was long dead, wouldn't know what he was saying, and wouldn't care, either.

A priest came out of the church. He was tall and thin, with round glasses and a receding hairline. He waved his hand above his head with a grin. "Ollie McNab?" the priest said loud enough for them to hear.

Ollie and Evelyn exchanged a glance. Was the thief a *priest*?

Ollie cleared his throat and headed in the man's direction, Evelyn following close behind.

The man stuck his hand out to shake Ollie's hand, then Evelyn's. "Bartley Reilly. Or Father Reilly." He chuckled and pointed at his collar.

"I don't understand," Ollie said after a moment.

"Don't understand what?" Father Reilly replied.

"We were asked to meet someone here," Evelyn jumped in, to his relief. Ollie was feeling rather thrown off and not like himself. "You aren't him, are you?"

The priest blinked a few times before throwing his head back in laughter, causing Ollie and Evelyn to jump. "No! No, that's not me. I was asked to watch out for you." He let out a long sigh. "Ollie, you don't remember me, do you?"

"I'm afraid not."

"I knew your brothers. You know. Way back when. We all used to run about together, you included. You were a wee one, though. I'm not surprised you don't remember."

"Wait." Ollie squinted. "You were one of the street rats?" And then he remembered whom he was talking to. His eyes widened. "Sorry, I mean—"

But Father Reilly waved him off. "Yes, I was one of them."

"And you stayed here? In Whitechapel?" Ollie really kept putting his foot in his mouth. Could he shut his blasted mouth from saying something idiotic just once? If he weren't careful, he'd ruin their only chance at getting the painting back.

Father Reilly didn't seem perturbed by it, though. "I've been all over the world, but I felt called to return. You know that madman terrorizing everyone?"

"Jack the Ripper?" The unknown man had terrorized Whitechapel by murdering several women last year. However, no one was sure if he had stopped or if he were still in the area.

"That's the one. I felt, if there were anywhere I should be right now, it's here."

"But you know who the Signature Swindler is, don't you?"

Father Reilly didn't respond, but he studied Ollie over the rim of his glasses.

He wasn't going to answer that. "There's a reason he wants me here right now, isn't there?"

The priest hesitated. "Yes. However, we do have a minute, if you wish to visit."

Ollie understood that meant his mother's grave. He looked over his shoulder at the expanse of weathered gravestones, names slowly wearing away as time continued on. "We've been looking for her, but I can't remember where she is."

"I can show you." Just as Ollie remembered, Father Reilly headed toward the back of the graveyard, stopping at an expanse of brown grass void of any gravestones.

Ollie furrowed his brow as he studied the empty lawn. "But there's no one here."

A gentle hand touched Ollie's arm. Evelyn. "It's a common grave, Ollie."

His eyes flew to hers, desperate to discover she was jesting, but all he found was worry and, worse, pity. He tried not to look as horrified as he felt. "What do you mean?" But he knew.

"It's where someone is buried if there's no money to put them in their own grave."

Horrified, he looked back at the blank lawn. All this time, his mother had been in a common grave? Thrown into an open pit with strangers? Why couldn't Fergus and Marjory—but then, Ollie remembered they hadn't known. It would be years before they'd track down the boys and learn they had been orphaned.

They hadn't liked his mother, he knew that, but surely, they would have been able to look beyond that and use their wealth to give her a proper burial beside her husband.

"Should we visit your father, too?" Evelyn asked, trying to distract him.

She didn't mean it to, of course, but the question made him feel worse. "He's not here. He's up in Scotland at the McNab family plot."

"Would you like a moment with her?" the priest asked.

"I don't even know her," Ollie replied.

"That's all right. She knew you."

Ollie stared at the brown grass as Evelyn and Father Reilly left him on his own. What kind of conversation would he have with a mother if he'd had one?

I'm sorry I haven't been here, he thought to himself.

Why haven't you? that internal voice he sometimes had responded. Though he knew it was only himself, he was glad there was a response, even if he was creating it.

I didn't feel right. I didn't know you.

I knew you would come eventually. I had an eternity to wait, anyway.

Why did he feel amusement at his own joke? *Right.*

Are you happy, Ollie?

Am I happy? No, not really.

Why not? You seem like a happy person.

He considered his own question to himself. *For as long as I can remember, it feels like something is missing.*

Is it tied to your pub?

Maybe. Though the feeling had preceded the pub.

Are you sure?

He didn't respond.

Who is that pretty woman with you?

Ollie looked back over his shoulder and found Evelyn meandering about. She leaned down to look at something. *That's Evelyn.*

Is she the woman you're in love with?

He whipped his head back around and frowned at the ground. *Is she what?*

The woman you're in love with. I can tell you're in love with someone; I can feel it. Don't you feel it?

There was a very strange burning sensation in his insides, now that he thought about it. *I thought that was heartburn.*

He felt that vague, amused feeling again. And shifted his stance, uncomfortable by this bizarre conversation.

Is she one of them wealthy lasses? You boys seem to have a thing for them, don't you?

Ollie blinked. *"You boys"?* He had never once referred to himself and his brother as *boys.* Ever. Though, surely, in having a mental conversation with himself, such a normal word could be used.

Yes, that was it. Because he was assuredly not speaking to his dead mother.

Erm, yes, I suppose she is, he thought back to himself. *But I'm not in love with her—that's ridiculous. I do think she's beautiful. But love? Absolutely not.*

No response.

Seriously.

If you insist.

Thank you. Though he wasn't sure why he was thanking himself.

It's almost time, Ollie.

Time for what?

You're a good lad. You'll be happy soon, but you have to let it in, too.

Sorry?

Follow her, always, as she is guiding you to her heart.

Ollie waited for more—what in the blazes did that mean? But there was no further thought.

A flood of emotion filled Ollie suddenly at the absence of the voice, as if years of pent-up anguish had been released by his visit. Tears welled up in his eyes and he wanted to feel embarrassed by it, but he didn't. He sniffed and rubbed the heels of his hands over his eyes to wipe away the moisture.

"Ollie?" a hesitant voice called from behind him. Evelyn.

He cleared his throat and straightened his back. "Yes?"

"Father Reilly wishes to speak to us inside the church." Evelyn appeared at his side again, looking sheepish. "I hope you don't mind, but I gathered up some flowers for you to leave. If you want. They're mostly autumn weeds I found around here. You know, nothing special."

"You made her a bouquet?"

Evelyn met his eye but quickly looked away. "I'm sorry. Did I offend you?"

"No," he replied immediately, and he clasped his hands around the small fist that held the bouquet of weeds. They were flowers one found growing along the walls of decrepit buildings or in the cracks between cobblestones, yet it was the most beautiful arrangement of flowers he'd ever seen. A surge of warmth pushed away the despair that had flooded him only moments ago. "No, you didn't offend me. This is very thoughtful, Evelyn. Thank you." In truth, it was the kindest thing anyone had ever done for him, though he couldn't very well tell her that.

He took the bouquet and gently placed it on the ground. Somewhere deep within, where that internal voice came from, he felt warmth.

The priest appeared again in the doorway as they approached.

"Ollie, before you come in, I thought I should mention you two"—Father Reilly nodded over to Evelyn—"were in the afternoon edition of the newspaper. Were you aware of that?"

Ollie stilled. "No."

"Apparently, the gentleman to whom this young lady is betrothed is camped out at your house waiting for her. He is accompanied by her father, the priest who was supposed to officiate their wedding a few days ago, and the Commissioner of Police. There are dozens of officers, some from outside jurisdictions, doing a block by block search for the two of you."

"That's a lot more than I thought," Evelyn said weakly.

"I think they're desperate now. You're quite good at running," Father Reilly said with a grin.

Evelyn looked down. "I'm going home after this, Ollie. After we get the painting back."

Ollie had known this was coming, but it didn't lessen the negative feelings it dredged up. He was oddly distraught their time together was ending, more than he would have expected to be. Up until now, her departure had always been a vague, future problem. Now that it was here, it felt like he was falling, flailing about to find any surface at all to grasp on to. "I don't want you to leave." The words came out slowly as he admitted this to himself and her at the same time.

She lifted his gaze for a moment, her eyes searching his, but then she looked away again.

"Well…" The priest brightly clapped his hands in a jarring way. "How about we wrap up here, then?" He disappeared inside.

That was odd. How could the man be so cheery after what he had just told them?

Inside, the church was empty. But as Ollie's eyes adjusted to the darkness, he found Father Reilly walking through the pews. At the front, a few people were seated.

Making his way that direction, Ollie studied the backs of their heads, wondering which of them was the Signature Swindler.

The four men looked up at Ollie when he and Evelyn stopped before them, and then he looked back and forth at each other. Ollie didn't recognize any of them, but they seemed to be expecting him.

Ollie looked them over, trying to understand the situation. "Wait." Ollie stilled as his eyes landed on the last man. He had bushy eyebrows and a round stomach. "Tommy Malone?"

Ollie had met Tommy Malone as an adult when Tommy had mugged Ollie and Dantes a few months ago. Tommy had also run around with their street gang back when they'd been children. Dantes and Tommy had been happy to run into each other again, but Tommy had still taken their belongings.

And now, he occasionally came into The Harp & Thistle with his wife.

"Ah, wee baby Oliver!" Tommy laughed, his shoulders shaking with the sound.

"Once again…" Ollie grit his teeth. Why did everyone compare him to a baby? "I'm bigger than you."

Tommy laughed with glee again and nudged the wiry man beside him, who let out an audible oof. "What did I tell you, eh? Grew up to be a big fella!"

"Aye. Just like your big brothers," the other man replied in an Irish accent so heavy, Ollie had trouble understanding him. His face had lines that didn't make sense for age, which Ollie would place at about forty.

Briefly, Ollie thought perhaps this stranger was the thief, until he realized the man had a wooden leg.

"I'm nothing like Dantes and Victor," Ollie retorted. "I don't look like them, either."

All four men, plus the priest, focused on him with narrowed eyes.

"You know," the man with the wooden leg said, "you're the spitting image of—"

"Shut *up*, Colm." Tommy then said something in a language Ollie had only heard a few times. At The Harp & Thistle, numerous different languages were spoken by their patrons. The Germans, he could sometimes figure out what they were saying. And there was similarity between Italian, Spanish, and French. But this language was unlike anything else, and he always wondered what it was when he'd heard it.

Colm responded to Tommy in that language, and then others jumped in. Several of them began arguing and talking over each other, their volume becoming unbearable. Father Reilly, who was in on the conversation as well, made a motion with his hands that indicated he was telling them to calm down.

"What are they saying?" Ollie asked Peter Doyle, the only one who wasn't involved in conversation.

The man shrugged. "Couldn't tell you. Never learned Irish myself."

Evelyn loudly cleared her throat like a schoolteacher did to settle down an entire classroom. A sound that apparently was universal because every single one of the men stilled and became silent.

"Thank you, gentlemen," she said. "Now, we're here because we were asked by someone to meet them here. Are any of you that man?"

No one responded.

"A painting is to be returned," Evelyn continued while looking at each face. "Well?"

"Yes, about that." Father Reilly stuck a hand in one of his

black trouser pockets, revealing a piece of paper. "I was asked to give you this."

Ollie let out a noise of annoyance and ripped it out of the man's hand. "Of course that idiot isn't going to make this easy," he said to Evelyn. Someone chuckled at this but was told to hush.

Again, *Hello* was on the front in obnoxious, curly script.

I promised to return the painting to you, and I will.
    As a wedding present.
    Best wishes, and all that rubbish.

"What is he on about now?" Ollie was thoroughly confused.

"I don't understand," Evelyn studied the note. "He's not going to give it back until I marry the earl?" She stomped her foot. "Oh, I could wring that man's neck!"

"Maybe he *was* the one who turned you in," Ollie replied.

"Double the wringing his neck!" she declared, punching a finger up into the air.

"Which of you cads wrote this? Which of you is that idiot thief?" Ollie demanded, looking around at the men.

"None of us," Tommy responded. "He's not here."

"Then who in the blazes are you?"

Tommy slapped his hands to his knees before standing up and extending a hand to Ollie. "I'm Tommy Malone."

"I know who you are." Ollie rubbed the bridge of his nose. Tommy then turned to Evelyn and, before she could react, took her hand and shook it so hard, she stumbled. She frowned at him as she ripped her hand back.

"This is Colm O'Malley." Tommy pointed down the line of men. "Daniel Nee, Martin Halloran, and Peter Doyle. We were all close with your brothers way back when."

"But why are we all here? You, me?"

Tommy scratched the side of his head. "Seriously? He explained it in the note. You don't get it?"

"Get what?" Evelyn snapped back.

"You two have to get married to get the painting back. It's

the only way. We're your witnesses." Tommy indicated to himself and the line of men.

"Aye," the others added in unison.

Married.

To each other?

Rendered mute, Ollie could only react by his mouth falling open. This was the most preposterous thing Ollie had ever heard in his life. Why in the blazes would the thief want this? This was absurd!

Ollie tried to catch Evelyn's eye to see her reaction. She was scarlet-faced furious and refused to look at him. "What did you just say?" She took a step toward Tommy with murder in her eyes.

"You're here to get married," Father Reilly said with that irritatingly bright voice. Evelyn's head swung in his direction. "Ready?" the priest asked helpfully.

"No, I'm not ready!" Evelyn shouted back. "This is madness! And an impossibility! There are only two ways we could marry. We could run off to Gretna Green." She made a dramatic show of looking at her surroundings. "Doesn't look like we're there. Or we get a license and I don't recall ever apply for or picking one up, do you, Ollie? Plus, that takes about two weeks for it to filed and that's with *no objections* from anyone. He couldn't have waltzed in there yesterday after being struck by this brilliant idea and have a license ready today. Nor could he have pretended to be us, even if he had enough money to beg the archbishop for help."

The men stared at her, silent for a long moment.

Father Reilly cleared his throat. "Well, I don't know what to tell you, Miss Sparrow, but…" He then handed her a piece of paper. The paper had green ivy printed on it for decorative purposes.

But it was a marriage license. It had their names on it. And today's date.

Her mouth fell open.

She shoved it back to the priest and, with a huff, stormed back down the aisle. Ollie expected her to start running. But then she paced back.

She wasn't leaving.

"I have to agree with her." Ollie finally found his voice. "You can't make two random people marry."

"Well, no," Colm said. "But you aren't two random people, if what we've been told is correct. And you've got to if you want your pretty picture back. He won't budge on this, believe me. Stubbornest man alive."

"Why does he want us to get married, of all things?" Ollie asked. He almost wished he were back at the pub getting torn apart by Victor, instead of being here.

Colm just shrugged. What a helpful lot.

"I don't want to get married," Evelyn said, though Ollie noted the strength in her voice had weakened. "And how is marrying Ollie supposed to help that? Hmm?" She crossed her arms and directed that question to all men present.

"Fair," Daniel Nee said. "But if you're already married, then you can't marry someone else." He raised his ginger eyebrows up high to indicate they all knew whom she was supposed to marry, and it wasn't Ollie.

"Frankly, I think being married is grand." Tommy shrugged, and the other men replied "Aye" in unison again. Except for Father Reilly, of course.

A flush rose in Evelyn's cheeks as she met Ollie's eye. They held each other's gaze and the noise, the activity, around them began to fall away. All he could focus on was her doe eyes, as they considered him, as he considered her.

He adored her, though he'd never planned to tell her this, but could he be married to her? Admittedly, it would help ease the public flogging they'd received after it had been announced to all of London she had been hiding at his house. That would help the both of them, and get the journalists off their back a lot easier. And it would even help get his grandparents to back off him marrying the Campbell woman, or anyone else.

The question hung between them, and her cheeks pinked.

Maybe because she was a redhead, but she flushed more than anyone he knew. He knew her well enough to know it probably drove her mad, but he found it endearing. Ollie had to bite his cheek to keep from grinning as the flush in her cheek spread over her face and, he suspected, behind her high collar. He wondered if her whole body flushed, if it spread to her chest beneath her clothes. He recalled unbuttoning her wedding dress and the soft, bare skin beneath, the outline of her body under the chemise that had clung to her skin when the dress had slid off, as she'd stood there, white silk and lace clinging to her, as a hot fire had burned nearby.

Her wearing exactly that as he gently pulled her to the floor, stretched out alongside her, that pink flush rising over every inch of her body, fire spreading all over the both of them.

Someone laughed loudly about something, kicking Ollie back to Earth. Evelyn, still holding his gaze, swallowed, as if she knew what a scoundrel he was being. Then she reached up to fiddle with her hair. He cleared his throat and looked away.

Father Reilly clapped his hands together once. "Shall we begin?"

"No, we shall *not* begin!" Evelyn protested and then, with a huff, grabbed Ollie's arm, and dragged him to the back of the church and out of earshot from the others. "We need to discuss this. Can you believe we've been tricked into such nonsense? We should leave at once."

Ollie had to admit if any other woman in the entire world were in Evelyn's place right now, he would have already left.

Admittedly, the idea of marrying Evelyn didn't sound that bad. A bit unexpected, and the situation was rather unorthodox, but he didn't hate it. It didn't send fear through him like it did with the Campbell woman, or any other woman who had tried to casually mention it in the past. And he knew he wanted it eventually.

"I don't know. I really don't think it's that big of a deal." He shrugged.

"Not a big deal?" she scoffed. "Ollie, this is marriage. We would be together for the rest of our lives!"

Ollie shrugged again, surprising even himself.

"You can't be serious! You wouldn't be able to marry..." Evelyn trailed off, puffing her cheeks out when she couldn't think of anything to say. "Miss Findlay!"

He frowned. "Why would I want to do that?"

"Why would you want to do *this*? Surely, there's someone else out there far more fitting. And..." Evelyn paused. "Wouldn't you want your family present? Look at this, Ollie. You don't even know those people. A group of strangers at your wedding. Is that what you want?"

"I suppose not."

"Then it's settled then. No wedding."

A strange, very unpleasant sensation twisted at his stomach. "But if we do this..." He paused as the thought began to form. "There's no chance of you being forced into marrying the earl. Or anyone else, for that matter. Plus, it would be the best chance of repairing our reputations now that the whole city, perhaps even the country, knows you've been hiding at my place." Maybe that was why the thief had forced this, to help them. But why would he have cared?

To his surprise, Evelyn seemed to consider this. "True. But it also gives me a different problem. My father and the earl have a contract. The earl paid my father a lot of money to marry me. And he won't let that go. He would sue my family into oblivion. And win."

"How much did he pay?"

"I don't know. But you saw how high the reward is. It's probably exorbitant. Wait—" Evelyn stilled, but Ollie could see her brilliant mind at work. She looked him square in the eye. "Lady Litchfield."

"Sorry?"

"Lady Litchfield and her husband separated. What if we do this and then once the business with the earl is over, we separate?"

Ollie did not experience the same relief this seemed to provide Evelyn. Maybe because he remembered how much trouble the separation had created for Lady Litchfield. He briefly mentioned this.

"True, but at this point, could my reputation be ruined any further? I'm a runaway bride, Ollie, who hid at an unmarried man's house. The entire city is looking for me. I can't imagine people will ever look at me as anything other than an embarrassing disgrace. And, yes, us marrying will help that significantly, but not wholly."

"What about telling our families? That's the key part to all of this." Ollie tensed at the idea of his family finding out. What would Dantes say? What would *Victor* say? He wasn't sure what they would take worse. Ollie marrying Evelyn without them knowing, or Ollie marrying Evelyn and then separating from her?

Evelyn looked down at the ground. "This marriage has so far been the only way to solve my earl problem, but I'm asking far too much of you. Well, I'm not asking, really, we're being forced into this in a way. But how could I have you do something like this for me?"

"I'm happy to do it, Evelyn. It will be uncomfortable informing family, yes, but I think after a bit of time mine will understand. And like you said, it wouldn't be for long. Eventually, we will go our separate ways and return to our former lives." Something he should have felt more happy about. And though he had always wanted to marry and have a family, doing this for her would prevent that from happening. Once they married, that was it, even when they did separate. He wouldn't be able to marry anyone else. Then again, had he not been proven to be incredibly irresponsible? He didn't even know how to count coin correctly. He had no business being a father or a husband. A real husband, at least.

"We should discuss rules, then, just to make things clear," Evelyn added.

"Rules?"

"Yes." She hesitated then leaned closer to him and whispered. "This won't be a real marriage. There will be no...you know...intimacy."

Ollie cleared his throat. "Right."

She shifted on her feet and reached up to her hair. "I know lots of people have...needs. And if you find yourself in a position to...satisfy those needs with someone—"

"Evelyn, no." Ollie was horrified by the idea.

She blinked, surprised.

"I'm not going to do that to you," he said as seriously as he could.

"But we won't—"

"I don't care. I would never step out on the marriage. Even if we aren't intimate. Christ, I'm not that horrific."

"You're not horrific. I'm just saying, if you need—"

"And I'm telling you there is no one out there who could tempt me away from you."

Evelyn's eyebrows shot up to the sky and in truth, Ollie was stunned those words had come out of his mouth. "Hypothetically," he added.

She flushed and reached up to her hair again. "Very well, then, Ollie. You're sure you want to do this?"

He nodded. "I'm sure."

She then surprised him and gave him a hug. Oh, how wonderful she felt in his arms. "Thank you," she whispered into his ear and when she pulled away her eyes were misty. She knuckled at them.

Everything after this became a blur. They returned to the others and confirmed they would marry, keeping the separation to themselves.

Once they were in place, Father Reilly began, but Ollie hardly heard anything. He watched Evelyn, her pretty face almost angelic as she hung on to the priest's words. She glanced up at him with a sheepish grin. She thought the whole thing was silly, and it was. But still, he was getting *married*. And he could hardly believe it.

It was monumental. That awful heartburn returned with a vengeance as he kept his eyes on his stunning bride. She had no white wedding dress like the queen had made popular, and instead wore an ill-fitting one. He wore his sneak-about coat and hat, nothing fit for a groom. They were surrounded by the gang of boys who'd kept him safe was he'd been a baby. In a way, he supposed, he *was* surrounded by family. A family he never had a chance to know, at least.

That was touching, in a way.

If only his brothers could be here.

If only he could tell them about this. It probably would be best not to.

As Father Reilly continued in his monotone voice, in a room that had witnessed thousands of weddings over five hundred years, Ollie found himself suddenly overcome by emotion. He took Evelyn's hands in his and stared down at her with admiration. She didn't pull away. He knew it was probably because she was frightened. But the truth for him was he was going to embrace the moment. For a short time in his life, Evelyn would be his wife and he promised to be the best husband he could be.

They exchanged their vows, Ollie said "I will." Evelyn did, too.

A ring appeared from somewhere, but Ollie was too caught up in the moment to think about where it had come from. All he could focus on was sliding the ring onto Evelyn's long, dainty finger. He swallowed as he did it.

His life was changing.

But not really. This was not real. This would not last.

Then they reached that key moment both Ollie and Evelyn had somehow forgotten about.

Father Reilly said, "You may now kiss the bride."

Ollie tensed. "I do what?"

"You kiss your wife. Haven't you been to a wedding before?" Colm said from the pew.

Panicked, Ollie looked down at Evelyn and his heart raced faster and faster. Nothing in her face gave away her thoughts. She looked up at him with round, innocent eyes, her lips just slightly parted. What should he do? He'd promised no intimacy. Did this count as intimacy?

He had been waiting for the perfect moment to kiss her properly, where he could pull her close and kiss her, soft and slow, until her mind and body melted into his.

But this wasn't the perfect moment, either. They had an audience. And he didn't want to break his promise to her.

Evelyn Sparrow, his new bride, closed her eyes, long lashes sweeping over her cheeks, and waited.

Chapter Nineteen

EVELYN STRUGGLED TO settle her nerves. They agreed their marriage would be a temporary arrangement with a separation to soon follow. So why did she have the jitters as if it were the real thing?

Admittedly, these jitters felt different than the jitters from before, the ones that made her run from the earl. Those jitters were filled with a consuming fear and dread. Evelyn didn't feel fear or dread right now, just shaky nerves. And she didn't know what to make of it.

Uncomfortable with what that might mean, Evelyn put all of her attention on Father Reilly, though she didn't hear what he was saying, not really. It was all going in one ear and out the other. It was too difficult to hear anything beyond her heart roaring in her ears.

Funny how just days ago, she'd thought about Ollie on her first "wedding day." How it wouldn't have been so bad if his handsome face waited for her at the altar and not the earl.

Now here she was, living out that silly vision, at her second wedding about to promise her life to him.

But not really.

As the ceremony progressed, she snuck a glance up at Ollie. She expected to find him not listening, bored, perhaps antsy to leave.

To her surprise, he was watching her instead, his green eyes intense in the low light. There was a flicker when her eyes met his, but he immediately shuttered whatever emotion was there.

But goodness, he was breathtaking in the moment. Even though they were hardly dressed for the occasion, she was sure a more handsome groom had never existed. A tuft of dark hair had fallen out of place over his forehead, giving him a roguish appeal. Evelyn found herself wishing she could sweep it back, run her fingers through his hair, feel the embrace of his solid arms.

She gave him a tiny flash of a smile. It was more of a nervous tic, really. And without looking away, Ollie took her hands in his, startling her.

Oddly, the touch was comforting in the moment. The roaring in her ears began to dissipate.

Touch would bother her for life. It was as much a part of her as the color of her hair and the freckles on her skin. And Ollie was a man who thrived on touch. For that reason alone, they would never be able to work. Even though she found that sometimes, she found his touch pleasant, she would also never be a very physically affectionate person. But she suspected he would be.

Curious, she looked down at their embraced hands. She had been to many weddings and had never seen the groom take his bride's hands and hold them throughout the ceremony. They had always stood stoic, unmoving, probably trying not to throw up from nerves, good or bad.

Admittedly, their hands did look nice together. Her fingers long and slender, his large and rough. She almost wished she could be the beautiful bride in a white wedding dress for him, see how he would react to her as she walked down the aisle. And she almost wished she could see him dressed up as a groom, as her groom.

Swallowing, she returned her eyes to his, and she had the sense he had not once looked away from her the time. He was a good man, and this farce of a marriage was just another example of how kind Ollie was. She didn't deserve his kindness, yet he never questioned giving it to her.

Father Reilly said, "Oliver McNab, wilt thou have this woman to thy wedded wife, to live together after God's ordinance in the holy estate of matrimony? Wilt thou love her, comfort her, honor, and keep her, in sickness and in health; and, forsaking all others, keep thee only unto her, so long as ye both shall live?"

"I will," Ollie said, though of course he would not really agreeing to that last part. Or the love part.

Father Reilly continued. "Evelyn Sparrow, wilt thou have this man to thy wedded husband, to live together after God's ordinance in the holy estate of matrimony? Wilt thou obey him, and serve him, love, honor, and keep him, in sickness and in health; and, forsaking all others, keep thee only unto him, so long as ye both shall live?"

"I will," Evelyn responded, not really agreeing to the obey part. Or serve. Love? She couldn't think about that. Or the part where it was for life, because it wasn't.

One of the men witnessing the ceremony brought forth her wedding ring. To her surprise, it was quite intricate, gold with sapphires. Where had it come from?

But, of course, it had likely been supplied by the thief who had forced them into this position.

Oddly, as she thought about the thief, she swore she saw movement at the far end of the church. Something in the shadows. She looked over in that direction but decided her imagination had played a trick on her.

When Ollie placed the ring upon her finger, she stared at the blue sparkles. The moment was surreal, as if she were floating in nothingness. Never in a million years would she have woken up this morning expecting to be married by the end of the day. To Ollie, of all people.

When Father Reilly emphasized the part about "in the eyes of God" to the couple, he gave them each a pointed look. Evelyn swallowed in response.

Finally, the priest announced they were now man and wife

and directed Ollie to kiss his bride.

Both Evelyn and Ollie looked at each other, startled. How had they forgotten about this part!

Was he going to kiss her?

In front of people?

He was hesitating.

But she recalled when she'd kissed him. How wonderful it had felt. Magical, almost. Fear was quickly replaced with anticipation. They had both agreed there would be no intimacy. But surely, she could allow herself to enjoy the kiss that would seal their marriage? The only wedding kiss she would receive in her life?

Secretly eager for Ollie's lips to meet hers, Evelyn closed her eyes. She had to steady her breath. Her heart galloped. And as she leaned just slightly forward, her lips tingling with anticipation…

Ollie gave her a quick peck on the cheek.

Evelyn pulled back and her eyes flew open as her mouth dropped slightly. They'd gotten married and he'd *pecked her on the cheek*?

Evelyn tore an unsure look to Father Reilly, whose stunned face mirrored her own. "That's a new one," was all he said.

Colm laughed loudly.

Tommy added, "They really have it all wrong about you, Ollie, don't they?" And he joined in on the laughter.

But Ollie didn't respond. In fact, he didn't seem phased at all. He simply stared at her with a funny drunk-like expression.

Evelyn stepped back and began twisting the ring on her finger. It felt strange having it there. Again, she glanced at the shadows in the back but decided there was definitely nothing there.

The group surrounded the couple and congratulated them heartily. She responded in kind as she was now legally protected from being forced into another marriage. But she still had to inform her family, and face the repercussions from that.

There was a beacon of light through it all, though.

With this marriage salvaging her reputation, she might be able return to her position at the museum, and almost smelled the museum now, the paints and the canvases and her reference books. The boxes of fresh paintbrushes.

"Congratulations, lass." Tommy Malone shook her hand hard. "I predict many years of happiness ahead of you."

She forced a smile. "Thank you."

Ollie placed a hand on her upper back and minutely ran his thumb up and down as they became surrounded.

These men from Ollie's old street gang were loud and boisterous, talking rapidly over each other, jabbing Ollie and doling out marriage advice.

It was very loud, and Evelyn was starting to feel crowded.

Her nerves began to twitch, and her legs began to itch. Her breathing became erratic while Ollie's thumb continued its gentle caress, but with a bit more pressure, as if he knew what was going on. Which couldn't have been possible.

"Excuse me," she choked out and she hurried away before anyone could respond. Once she'd pushed through the door and made contact with the outside again, however, the coiling tension began to ease. Accepting this, she sat on the steps and took a few deep breaths.

A moment later, the door opened again. Ollie burst through, his chest heaving with short, shallow breaths. Once he saw her there, though, he faltered a bit, rubbed a hand over his jaw, and sat beside her.

"Are you all right?" Ollie had been holding his head in his hands but resumed a normal but tense sitting position.

Evelyn swallowed. "Yes. I was feeling a bit crowded in there." She knew what had caused him to panic. He'd thought she'd run away again. In truth, she *had* wanted to run but, this one time, she'd managed to force herself to stay.

Ollie looked her over, as if reassuring himself she was truly there, and then grinned. "So, what do you think?"

"About what?"

"About being married?"

Evelyn stared out over the graveyard and wondered about the people buried there. Their lives, their own weddings and marriages. "We should talk about that, actually."

Ollie's grin melted away and he cleared his throat. "Right. Of course."

"I would like to return to work. In order to do that, I need to inform my family of what has occurred as soon as possible. And for me to return to work, we need to get the painting back, which we still need to do." The thief had promised it, after all.

"Where are you going to go? After you decide it's time to separate, I mean." Ollie was still tense, which didn't make sense. This whole situation would be over soon. He should have been happy.

"My family will be explosively upset for a time once they learn what I have done. But once we separate, I could probably return to them then if necessary. They can't hate me forever."

"Are you sure they'd let you back home?"

Evelyn thought about it. She was confident she had made the right decision marrying Ollie with a planned separation, but the repercussions it would create would be difficult. Her family would never, ever accept Evelyn being married to a working-class man. Even though Ollie was halfway into the aristocracy, he wasn't really an aristocrat with his background, his brothers, and his pub. And aristocrats would never view him as one, either, even if he was the third grandson of a duke and duchess. He was too different.

"I suppose I could find my own flat, though I haven't the faintest idea how to live on my own." She looked in his direction with a hopeful smile, but he didn't meet it. Making a pure guess as to why, she then said, "Thank you for doing this. I wish there was something I could do to repay you for everything you have done for me."

But the way his jaw clenched, it appeared he was grappling with something. But whatever was on his mind, he decided to keep to himself. "You're welcome," he finally said. "When will you tell your family?"

"Oh, well—"

"We could go there right now and then hunt down a flat for you. I bet we would break the record for England's quickest separation."

"You're upset with me."

"Of course not. Why do you say that?" He stood up. "Upset. No, that's not what I think I'd call it." But before expanding on what he meant, Ollie went back inside the church.

⤜⤜⤜◆⤛⤛⤛

THEY ENDED UP deciding to head back to Ollie's house after the ceremony, still having to sneak in from the back entrance. Though the crowd was now mostly journalists and nosy citizens. There were a few police officers present, but it seemed more for crowd control than looking for her. It appeared Scotland Yard had concluded they weren't returning to Ollie's and moved their men to find her elsewhere.

Mrs. Chapman had quite the shock when they told her they'd gotten married. In fact, Ollie had to lead her over to a chair, where she proceeded to faint.

"If she reacts this way, imagine what my mother will do," Evelyn said while crouched beside the housekeeper, gently patting her hand. Ollie was fanning Mrs. Chapman with a newspaper. There were more articles about the earl and Evelyn on the front page, but neither of them cared enough any longer to read them. It all remained the same.

"I wonder at what point my grandparents will break down the door?" Ollie asked out loud. The noise from the crowd outside ensured that there wasn't a wink of silence inside. "To be honest, I'm surprised they aren't here already." He frowned as he continued to fan his housekeeper.

It seemed, until Evelyn met with her family, that Ollie wouldn't know anything but harassment. She had to put an end to it.

"I'll write them a letter today," she decided.

"You're going to tell them in a letter?" Ollie asked. "Is that wise?"

It would make telling her family a lot easier. But it would also leave room for them to deny it. To disbelieve her. For the letter to get lost before reaching them. "I suppose I'll have to tell them in person."

"Have them over," Ollie said. "Have them call off the blasted idiots camped out front of my house, and if they do that, then they can come by for dinner and you can tell them everything. Leave it vague so they're curious enough to comply."

Evelyn blinked. "That's brilliant, Ollie."

He gave her a tight-lipped smile that didn't reach his eyes. "I suppose even I can do something intelligent every once in a while."

"That's not what I meant." Evelyn frowned. Ollie had been acting so strange ever since their surprise wedding. "You're cross with me."

"I already said I wasn't."

Evelyn sniffed. "You're normally a very amicable person, but you've been snippy with me ever since we got married."

Ollie let out a long breath, as if he were trying to keep himself calm. "We were, in a way, forced into a marriage."

"But—"

"Yes, I know, it's temporary." His deep voice ground with frustration. "Forgive me, Evelyn, but you're not the only one being affected by it. Did that ever occur to you? Did it ever occur to you that perhaps I have my own feelings about our situation separate from yours?"

Evelyn jumped up to her feet and placed her fists on her hips, preparing to argue, but having to force her voice to a whisper, lest anyone hear them. "You said you were fine with it! You consented to doing this—you knew what it entailed. I don't understand. What is the problem with it, now that it's done? You can't be that miserable about it. I'll be gone soon enough!"

Ollie also stood and clenched his teeth hard. He also whispered angrily. "Yes, I know all of that, Evelyn, but I do possess the ability to have multiple feelings about something at once!"

What did *that* mean? How could he feel multiple ways about what they had done? What could he even possibly feel about it, anyway?

However, she didn't get a chance to ask because Mrs. Chapman had decided to rouse. Ollie ensured she was all right, and then left the room without a further glance at Evelyn when the housekeeper told him to stop fussing.

Mrs. Chapman rubbed at her eyes. "Did I truly faint?"

"Yes, you did," Evelyn said as she made her way to a table with a water pitcher on it. She poured a glass for the woman and brought it back to her.

Mrs. Chapman thanked her and took a long gulp. "That was quite the unexpected news."

"Indeed."

"You two really get married?" Mrs. Chapman asked over the rim of her glass before handing it over. But, Evelyn noted, she didn't ask why they had.

Evelyn took the glass and set it to the side. "Yes. You fainted before we could finish telling you it's only to protect me legally from marrying the earl. Obviously, I can't marry two people, no matter what kind of contract he and my father drew up together. I won't be around here much longer, though, don't you fret." Evelyn briefly explained their plan to the woman and expected to get a sigh of relief in return that everything would go back to normal soon enough.

Instead, Evelyn got, "This seems like a terrible idea. There is no way it will go as smoothly as you two think it will."

Evelyn shifted. "You may be right because Ollie has already begun acting strange."

Mrs. Chapman, still seated in the chair, tilted her head. "How so?"

"He's been on edge ever since. Moody. Which is unlike him."

The housekeeper waved it off. "Even if you plan on separating, it still happened. He probably feels a sense of responsibility for you he didn't before."

"I suppose that makes sense." Guilt gripped Evelyn's stomach. This hadn't occurred to her, but it should have. It seemed just the kind of thing with which Ollie would grapple.

"He's an honorable man," Mrs. Chapman continued, then she grinned. "Any chance you'll change your mind about the separation part of it?"

Evelyn laughed. "No. And even if I did, he would never agree to that."

"I suppose you're right. Mr. McNab isn't much the marrying type, is he?"

"No, he's not."

Mrs. Chapman carefully stood up from her seat, accepting Evelyn's hand for balance. "While you were gone, something arrived for you."

This piqued her interest.

Evelyn followed Mrs. Chapman up to her bedroom. On the way, she noted the door to Ollie's room was closed. She wished she could go in there and talk to him, but it was clear he needed a moment to himself.

This thought quickly dropped away from her mind, though, when she walked into her room and saw something familiar at the foot of her bed.

It was her traveling trunk.

With a gasp, Evelyn rushed over to it and threw open the lid. Inside the trunk were her dresses, nightgowns, and underthings. Hers! Clothing that would fit her! She rifled through it with glee, so happy to be reunited with these important belongings. "Where did this come from?" Evelyn finally asked, barely glancing over at the housekeeper.

"I'm not sure, actually." Mrs. Chapman stepped forward. "Two footmen knocked on the front door with it but didn't answer any questions, from me *or* the journalists. There's an envelope with your name attached, but I did not open it."

Evelyn felt a sense of dread as she closed the lid and found an envelope attached the top. With a deep gulp, she ripped it open, expecting the final clue from the Signature Swindler.

However, Evelyn received a great surprise to discover it wasn't from the thief.

The letter was from her sister.

Evelyn began to read with apprehension.

Dearest Evelyn,

I must say your wild, red head popping out of that hedge in front of Miss Findlay's home gave me quite the shock. You obviously came to the most incorrect conclusion about my visit to her, however, which is the purpose of this letter. I've sent it along with some of your belongings because the dress you had on looked utterly ridiculous. Please destroy it post-haste. Your hat was very nice, however, and I should wonder why you had a lovely hat and a horrendous dress.

Anyway, Miss Findlay is your earl's mistress. Did you know about her? When you went missing, she contacted our family, and Mama directed me to go visit her. That was why I was there when you saw me. I learned both you and Miss Findlay have the same goal: to cancel the impending wedding between you and the earl. See, she is a possessive woman and wants him all to herself and I assured her you want nothing to do with the man. This pleased her greatly. He is ugly inside and out, so I assume he pours money and jewels on her, which would be cut back if he married, lest his new bride discover there was another woman.

While we talked, I mentioned I was to head back home to Paris soon but was having difficulty finding last-minute tickets for an ocean liner (I prefer that over noisy, jerky trains). Miss Findlay informed me that she had planned to run off to Paris after your marriage to the earl with the hopes that he would chase after her. But since you ran from the altar, she didn't have a need for them anymore. I was able to pay for a portion of the tickets there with the coin I had on my person but still owed the remainder, which I've since sent.

Miss Findlay is changing her ticket and her housekeeper's ticket to be in our names, and the ship leaves in two days at the noon hour. Don't fret. Both tickets are first class.

Come back to Paris with me. You once had a life there. You have friends, you have familiarity. I know how fond you were of Henri de Toulouse-Lautrec. Suzanne is out of the picture now. Did you know he challenged Henri de Groux to a duel? De Groux insulted Van Gogh, and your Henri wouldn't have it. De Groux of course, backed out like a coward. Henri is a brave and honorable man. He mentioned you recently, too. He painted a picture of the Moulin Rouge, aptly called At the Moulin Rouge, *and commented he thought you would have liked it if you were there.*

Paris awaits you, my dear.

Far more important though: I was not the one who divulged your location, and in fact had no idea where you were until the newspapers reported on it. I must say, however, the gentleman you have been hiding with is exceptionally delicious. After you ran away from me, he accused me of an unkindness. "How could you turn your sister in?" *is what he said. I denied it, of course, but he didn't believe me. What kind of trouble have you gotten yourself into? He looks like the perfect scoundrel to get into trouble with, and I hope his trouble has been endless for you.*

Your loving sister,
Cordelia

Evelyn folded the piece of paper and set it upon the top of her trunk. Her bottom lip quivered, and she fought back the tears of relief she felt knowing Cordelia hadn't betrayed her. As usual, her sister had somehow made everything better. Evelyn's clothes had been returned to her, she'd offered another solution to Evelyn's conundrum of what to do with her life after leaving Ollie's, and Cordelia had even had a kind word to say about him—in her own way, of course.

Paris.

Could she return there? Did she want to? Or would she rather stay here in London? Or even go back to New York, if she was considering locations to which she had old ties?

Evelyn wasn't sure, but she only had two days to decide.

"Can I help you dress in your new clothes, Miss Sparrow—er, Mrs. McNab?" Mrs. Chapman asked.

Evelyn startled, realizing that *she* was Mrs. McNab. "Thank you, but I prefer to dress myself," Evelyn replied, feeling more like herself than she had in a long while.

Chapter Twenty

HAMBONE'S GRAY, FLUFFY tail flicked back and forth as she lay curled up on Ollie's lap in the chair by the fireplace. She stared up at him with those big, round eyes as if waiting for him to do something.

It was impossible to resist petting her—she was too cute to ignore, even in this cloud of melancholy. Not that she would let him ignore her if she wanted his attention, anyway. As he ran his hand over her fur, she began to purr loudly. Hambone really was a beautiful cat and he sometimes wondered how she'd ended up in a rubbish bin with a Christmas ham. Someone somewhere had to have paid a pretty coin to a breeder for her. But she also had to have been on her own for a long while because she'd been absolutely filthy when he'd found her.

"Do you remember that time I had to give you a bath? When I brought you home?" he mused with a chuckle. "I'm surprised you let me survive that."

Hambone replied with a tiny mew.

"Mrs. Chapman was not happy I had brought home a dirty feline and she refused to go near you, told me to do it myself if I wanted to keep you. And I did, didn't I?"

Hambone batted a soft paw at his cheek.

"Do you remember your old owners? Your old humans? Were they good to you?"

The fluffy cat yawned, exposing her sharp teeth. She then began to groom her front paws.

"I suppose if you were treated well, you wouldn't have left. Or, maybe, you were a lady cat scoundrel and wanted to do whatever you pleased." He watched as she licked her paw. "I bet you got the attention of all the tomcats. And I bet you bit any that came near you. Am I right?" He rubbed the top of her head and she glared at him.

Ollie chuckled and watched the fire dance. "Funny how we both came from the gutter. Now look at us, in this nice townhome. You have your collection of bows; I have the best suits a man could buy. And yet we don't really have much, do we? Oh, sure, a house and food. We have survival and comfort. But what's my purpose? Do I really live to work at a pub? Is that truly going to be the rest of my life? Wake up to an empty house, go to work, come back home to an empty house? Aside from you and the house staff, of course."

Ollie looked down at Hambone again and found she had fallen asleep.

He let out a sigh and now that he didn't have a distraction, the guilt gnawed at him like a hungry rat. He felt awful for turning his back on Evelyn and storming out of the room earlier. He was hardly one to do that, and usually, it was she who had the heightened emotions, but he was a jumble of the most bizarre feelings ever since they'd gotten married.

It was to be expected, of course.

What hadn't been expected, however, was how he'd felt after the ceremony.

Happy.

Which was absurd.

They'd been backed into a corner, almost literally, and it made sense to go through with the wedding at the time. They had agreed on rules and expectations. Neither of them wanted to get married to the other, especially for life, but it was the best way to protect Evelyn.

And he wanted to protect her at all costs.

But now, he couldn't stop thinking about the fact that he had a wife. Even though he didn't, not really. His "wife" was itching to leave and go on with her life. She was already planning out their separation. Evelyn was running away already.

Of course, he would agree to it, there was no question about that. He had no business being responsible for a wife. And all she wanted out of life was her career and she seemed to think she could return to her job. He wasn't so sure, in all honesty, but what did he know? She was brilliant at it, so he didn't blame her for loving it, but she didn't have room for him in her hopes and dreams. And she had made sure that was clear to him.

Not that he wanted that, anyway. A husband should love his wife, and he didn't love her. Yes, he cared about her wellbeing. He definitely lusted after her—that would be idiotic to deny at this point. But he didn't *love* her.

But why could he not stop thinking about her? Why couldn't he stop thinking about the ceremony? The way she'd smiled up at him, the feel of her small hand in his, the moment he'd slid the ring onto her perfect finger. A family, none of them related by blood, but who had kept him safe and alive during his most vulnerable years, had witnessed the moment. They'd congratulated him, shared tips for a happy marriage, offered best wishes, hugged him, and shook his hand. For the first time in his life, it had felt like he had a purpose, other than being Victor's scapegoat.

Ollie still couldn't understand why the thief hadn't been there, though. Maybe he was also from their old Whitechapel street gang and thought Ollie might somehow recognize him and turn him in? It was also possible the thief just happened to know some of those men. But Ollie's most pressing question was why the thief made the wedding happen to help Evelyn. That, to Ollie, made the least sense out of everything. He didn't trust the thief for a moment. So, what was his goal? Did he truly want to help Evelyn in some roundabout way, or was he cooking up something to destroy them?

And when would they get the blasted painting back?!

Ollie closed his eyes to level out the irritation the thief always seemed to lift. It helped—marginally.

Tomorrow, they would have her family over for dinner, tell them the news, and then start figuring out the separation aspect. The sooner they began, the better.

Hambone shifted and when Ollie opened his eyes, he found she had woken up. He gave her a little kiss on her forehead. "Did you dream about ham?" he asked while scratching under her chin.

Hambone mewed before getting a spooky, wild-eyed look she sometimes got. The unsettling one where, in the middle of the night, she would stare wide-eyed at one specific corner of the parlor, making him wonder if ghosts might be real. Though she had never done this before in his bedroom, which made him a bit uneasy.

She jumped off his lap and ran to his door, where she began to scratch at it.

"Hang on, hang on," Ollie said while trying to catch up to the fur ball. As soon as he opened his bedroom door, she bolted out and ran down the hallway.

And stopped at Evelyn's closed door.

Ollie swore under his breath. "Do you really need to get into her bedroom right this second?" The last thing he wanted right now was to see Evelyn. But, of course, Hambone insisted. She began pawing at Evelyn's door and meowing loudly.

The door opened and Evelyn's eyes widened at seeing Ollie. But then she looked down and saw Hambone. He noted she had a new dress on. It was a dark-green woolen dress with a yellow panel on the front and yellow piping around the bodice, sleeve openings, and skirt hem. It was one he had seen her wear many times. It fit her form perfectly. Beautifully, really, as if she were a new spring daffodil.

Ollie shoved the thought away. When a man began thinking like a poet, he was already deep in trouble.

Evelyn made a cooing noise to Hambone and said, "Aw, have you finally come to *me* for snuggles?" Reaching down, she picked up the cat.

But Hambone had something else in mind, wiggled out of Evelyn's grasp, and rushed into her bedroom. Evelyn and Ollie exchanged a charged but awkward glance before following.

Hambone didn't stop until she'd reached the window. She hopped up onto a small table beside one, stood up on her hindlegs, and pressed her wet nose against the glass.

Ollie and Evelyn hurried over to see what she was looking at. And down below, they saw a black tricorn hat disappear over the back stone wall.

"Finally!" Evelyn exclaimed, and with an eagerness that made Ollie feel even worse, she ran out of her room and down to the servants' back entrance. She flung the door open and there on the ground was a note underneath another stone.

Evelyn eagerly took it up. "I swear if he plays any more games…" but her words trailed off as she peered down at the piece of paper.

Ollie studied the concentration on her face. It was one she often held while deep in thought in the midst of working on a painting. The corners of her mouth turned down ever so slightly, her brows knit together just a little bit. And if you talked to her while she was deep into her work, she wouldn't hear you. Not for several minutes, anyway. It was oddly endearing.

"It's an address again." She finally lifted her eyes to his and shoved the paper at him. "I don't know if this is good, or if he's playing further tricks on us."

"He did promise the painting as a wedding present, and we did get married, didn't we?" Ollie replied, trying to sound casual.

Evelyn's cheeks flushed and she looked away.

Feeling off-balance, Ollie took the piece of paper and looked at the address. He swore out loud.

"What is it?" Evelyn asked. "Do you know that address too?"

He nodded. "I think it's the tenements across from the Bethnal Green Museum. Looks like we have to go back there." As he gave the paper back to her, he admired her green-and-yellow dress again.

"You changed," he said, realizing how close they stood and needing to fill the moment with something innocuous. Evelyn was only half a step away. He felt her pull, as if she were a magnet and he were iron. As she took the paper from him, her hand accidentally brushed against his. She took in a sharp breath, jerked her hand back, and stepped away.

No, this marriage could never be. Ollie loved touch, everything from embraces to heated intimacy, but Evelyn was wishy-washy regarding that. Sometimes she enjoyed it—she admitted it herself—and sometimes she didn't. And it never made sense why she'd been accepting of it in the moments she had been. Was he supposed to guess for the rest of his life if she were open to touch or not?

She cleared her throat and averted her eyes. "Let me go grab my hat. And then we can go see what he has to say this time."

IT TOOK THEM a while to find the specific tenement the thief had indicated, but they eventually found it on the top floor. Considering what had happened previously, Ollie motioned for Evelyn to stay behind him. This time, it was definitely safest for her to follow. They knew where their foe was. "Whatever we find behind that door, we go in, grab the painting, and leave."

Evelyn nodded.

Ollie knocked and a moment later a voice said, "Come in."

The door was unlocked. Ollie led Evelyn inside and was surprised to find it wasn't a small tenement home with threadbare furniture like he'd been expecting. It seemed to be a large storage area.

"What is this place?" Evelyn whispered as they went farther

into the dim room. It reminded Ollie a bit of the conservation center at the Bethnal Green Museum. There was artwork all over the place, though it was far more organized and there was far less.

"Hello?" Ollie called out, receiving no response, while Evelyn began to study the paintings around the room. She approached a wall where several paintings were hung like in a gallery.

"What is that?" Ollie asked as he watched her study it with deep concentration. She didn't respond right away, so he decided to study it next to her. It was the Westminster Bridge.

Evelyn moved onto the next one and Ollie followed. This next painting was a portrait of a beautiful woman. She had a mass of black hair piled atop her head, brown eyes, and a serene smile. It felt like her eyes pierced into his soul, and it seemed familiar. It must have been something the thief had lifted from somewhere, and likely something he had seen in one of Evelyn's art history books.

"I wonder who she is," Evelyn said to herself as she studied it. "The painter's method is interesting. Look closely, Ollie. See how the paintbrush strokes are full of energy, seemingly erratic and random? Almost violent, in a way. But then you stand back..." She grabbed his wrist and pulled him several steps back. His heart raced and his skin heated from her touch. Oh, the effects she had on him! Mere glances, small smiles, the lightest brush of her fingertips and she sent his mind and heart buzzing as if she had wrapped her body around his. Tommy Malone could have been mugging him again and Ollie wouldn't even notice, too lost in Evelyn in the moment.

Now that they were back to hunting down the thief, everything seemed back to normal. The awkwardness that had haunted him throughout the day had disappeared. Now, he was starting to revisit the memory of kissing her. Or her kissing him, as she'd claimed.

"Ollie, are you paying attention?" Evelyn asked.

"Apologies." He scratched an eyebrow. "What did you say?"

She huffed. "What were you thinking about?"

"Honestly?"

"Yes, of course."

Should he tell her? Or lie? He decided to toe the line a bit, test the waters, see how she would react. He still secretly hoped there would be a moment where he could show her what a passionate kiss felt like. Ollie looked around, ensuring they were still alone. Embracing the scoundrel side of him, he leaned down to her ear and in a deep, low voice, said, "I was thinking about kissing you."

Evelyn let out a tiny gasp and when he pulled back—only a bit—she remained in place, staring up at him, her face flushed. Unable to help himself, he grinned. As she held his gaze, her hand reached up to her hat, patting and fussing with it.

"We should... We should keep looking." She turned and nearly bumped into the wall.

Ollie gently placed his hands on her shoulders and turned her in the correct direction. "This way, wife," he said, finding he was enjoying teasing her a little bit.

"Don't call me that," she replied weakly.

"Why not? You are my wife. For now."

Evelyn cleared her throat, didn't argue further, and studied the rest of the paintings for clues. But to his pleasant surprise, she also didn't stray too far from him. In fact, she kept rather close.

The moment would happen soon, he could feel it, and he could hardly wait.

Chapter Twenty-One

"THIS PLACE IS very strange," Evelyn said while looking around. There wasn't enough light. Only a few candles provided a soft, golden glow in the room, but the corners remained dark and shadowed. She quickly walked along the long wall, eyeing each painting. Ollie kept close, which she found comforting rather than irritating, despite his teasing of her. It was easy enough to explain away, though—the last time they'd been around the Signature Swindler, the thief had taken her for a short time. Something she didn't care to relive, even if she didn't think he would hurt her. "I don't recognize *any* of these paintings."

"Really?" Ollie replied, genuinely surprised. "I assumed these were stolen." As they stopped, he became engrossed in one of the deep-green landscapes and Evelyn studied the way shadows played across the sharp angles of his handsome face. Coupled with the top hat and frock coat, it gave him a severe look. Funny how he seemed to transform, becoming almost ominous, when they snuck around like this. As if he were the night, or mischief itself. It fit him, in a strange way.

"I thought they were stolen, too," Evelyn said. She returned to the haunting painting of the woman with black hair. For some reason, this one felt different than the others. Maybe because it was the only portrait. The other paintings were scenes around London or emerald-green, rocky countryside, sometimes with water and distant hills and mountains. It was a place she didn't recognize. "None of them have signatures, either."

"Is it possible you don't know every single painting housed in London museums?" Ollie asked, tipping up his hat to reveal a roguish brush of a grin.

Evelyn frowned back. "Please be serious, Ollie."

Ollie laughed.

"Well, no matter," she continued. "No one seems to be here, or *wants to emerge*." That last bit was said loudly. "Let's find our painting and get out."

Ollie agreed and together, they began looking around the room, scanning the paintings hung up. When they didn't find it there, they moved on to those carefully leaning against the wall.

Some of these, however, she did recognize. A few she had conserved herself. She looked closely, and the invisible repairs only she would have been able to locate were absent. They were copies. It seemed this was all a joke until she came across a door.

"I don't think we should go in there," Ollie said.

"Why not? He told us to come here, didn't he?"

Ollie clearly was not keen on the idea but sighed and opened the door for her. "After you, wife," he said again with that roguish grin that turned her into putty.

Evelyn flushed again at being called that. Every time he called her his "wife," butterflies fluttered in her stomach. A warning. It was of utmost importance she keep away from him. That she didn't become tempted by him, that she didn't give in to the pleasure his gentle touch gave her. The last thing she wanted, needed, was to wonder what passion Ollie could ignite in her. Nor did she want to admit that she was definitely in love with Ollie, like the blasted thief had said. She could easily give in if she didn't keep her wits about her.

Then again, if Evelyn finally accepted and admitted she was in love with Ollie, she could keep her head on straight a lot easier knowing her weakness.

Fine. She was in love with Ollie McNab. Absolutely madly in

love with him. He was gorgeous, he was kind, he was funny, loyal, hard-working, optimistic. His smile destroyed her every time. His touch sent electric jolts through her body.

Ollie seemed to think that once her parents found out she had married him, that would be the end of everything. But she knew it wouldn't be. They wouldn't roll over and give up. Papa would be furious that she'd married a working-class man, even though he was the third grandson of a duke and duchess. And he would be even more furious she had been hiding at his home, even though they had married. But how the earl would react, she still wasn't quite sure, other than knowing he would sue for breach of contract.

"Are you all right?" Ollie was looking at her, worry etched into his frown.

She gave a noncommittal answer and stepped through the door. "Ollie, look," Evelyn said with wonder. "It's a studio!"

As she rushed forward, Ollie made sure no one else was in the room. Evelyn, meanwhile, came upon a large easel with a stool in front of it and two paintings side by side.

One of them was the Fragonard that had been stolen from the Bethnal Green Museum. And the other was an exact copy of it.

But which one was which?

"He's an art forger!" Evelyn exclaimed as she spun around to Ollie. Without thinking, she grabbed his hands, too excited by her discovery, and had to keep herself from jumping up and down. "That's what all this is about! He copies paintings then sells them as the real deal to naïve wealthy people!"

Ollie cocked his head and studied the twin paintings. It took a moment, but he eventually said, "Oh! Well, that does make sense, doesn't it? But didn't he only recently start lifting paintings from museums?"

She waved him off, unconcerned by this inconsistency. "Quick, let's find ours and get out of here."

They separated to hunt down their Gustave Courbet. This

was a bit different from the gallery-type room next door. Here, there was an old, leather sofa and an unmade bed with a lamp next to it, all sitting in the middle of the floor. It was odd but, the thief himself was odd.

Evelyn turned to call Ollie, who had his back to her when a hand clamped over her mouth. Next thing she knew, she was being dragged out the door and back into the gallery room. The door slammed shut and as Evelyn struggled against the thief, the man locked the door with a key just as Ollie began pounding on the other side, shouting her name.

As Ollie slammed into the door trying to break it down, the thief kept his hand over her mouth and said, "Struggle and this will take longer than necessary."

Of course, Evelyn wasn't going to comply. The point of her elbow shoved into his stomach as hard as she could muster, and the thief crumpled to the ground, gasping for breath.

Shocked by the power she'd exhibited, she stared down at the masked man, who clutched his stomach.

"*Póg mo thóin.*" The thief groaned weakly.

Evelyn snarled at him. "What does that mean?!"

"Kiss my arse!" He rolled onto his back. "You are a devil woman, you know that?"

"Better a devil woman than an art thief!" Evelyn shouted over Ollie's knocking. "Ollie, I'm fine. I got an elbow to him!"

"Good girl!" Ollie shouted through the door. "Now unlock the door!"

"Wait," the thief said while clambering back up to his feet.

Evelyn looked between the door and the thief. Unfortunately, but not unexpectedly, curiosity won. She held up a finger. "You have one minute before I let him in."

The man's dark eyes grinned through the holes of the dark-blue mask, the small stars on it mocking her. "Congratulations on the nuptials."

Evelyn frowned and crossed her arms. "Why did you force us into that?"

The thief chuckled through his gasping breaths.

"Fine, I'm letting him in." Evelyn took a step toward the door.

"All right! All right." The thief took a few more deep breaths. "I was curious to see if you'd go through with it."

"We didn't have a choice!"

"You always have a choice."

"You wouldn't have given us back the painting."

"Have I given it back yet?"

Annoyed to be stumped, she crossed her arms again. "No. I presumed that was why we were summoned here."

"So, you two decided getting married was a better choice than losing the painting. Even though its effect on your lives is far greater."

"Evelyn!" Ollie called through the door. "Open the door!"

She ignored him for the moment because she wanted to see what the thief was trying to get at. "I suppose. So what?"

"It means you two wanted to get married, deep down."

She scoffed. "No. It means you gave me an out from getting married to the earl, and we've agreed to separate as soon as possible. And then, I will never be forced to marry anyone else. I'll be free."

A long pause. "What?"

She gave him a mocking grin. "See? You're not the only one who can weasel their way out of things."

The thief didn't move. "You married my—I mean, Ollie to get out of marrying the earl." The thief let out a breath. "Of course."

Her arms fell to the side. Something about this wasn't right. "Isn't that why you got the witnesses together and sent us all to the church?"

The thief studied her for a long, uncomfortable moment. He didn't answer her question. "So, if I understand correctly, you married Ollie so you legally couldn't marry anyone else."

"That's right."

"No one else will want to marry you because now you're famous for being the runaway bride and your reputation will take a huge hit from the quick marriage and divorce."

She nodded.

The thief pinched his mask's chin. "How did your family take the news?"

"They don't know yet."

"Oh?"

"I'll be telling them at dinner tomorrow."

"When is dinner?"

"Why, so you can continue to watch Ollie? Like some miscreant?"

The thief was quiet for a long moment. "I was asked to watch him."

Evelyn was skeptical. "By whom? His brother? Wait, are you a private investigator?"

"No. I won't tell you, but I will tell Ollie. If he wants to know."

Silence settled between them as Ollie called out to Evelyn. She ignored him again. Something was happening, but she didn't know what just yet.

"Lass…" The thief finally broke the silence. And spoke in an oddly gentle voice. "Have you finally admitted that you love Ollie?"

She shifted. "That's none of your business."

"Aye, but it is," he replied, his eyes glinting with mischief. "I can't watch him forever, you know. It's becoming harder and harder for me to leave this place." He looked around the room. So, he did live here. "I need to pass the responsibility on to someone else."

"I'm not responsible for a man," she said, irritation flaring.

"You are responsible for each other." He held up a finger. "Key difference."

"It's not what I want."

"Really?"

Did this man not know when to quit? "I'm done with this. You had no business poking your nose into my business."

"Yet I don't care. You'll find I was right, in the end."

"Unlikely," she replied dryly. And she began walking back toward the door standing between her and Ollie.

"Wait." He sounded desperate. But surely, that was wrong.

Evelyn clenched her teeth and spun around. "What now?"

The thief hesitated briefly, but then he took off his hat. And then, slowly, he reached up to the mask and lifted it off, finally revealing the face beneath it.

It took a moment for her mind to comprehend what she was seeing. Evelyn gasped and her hand flew to her mouth.

OLLIE SWORE OUT loud. What in the blazes were they doing in there? He could hear low, murmured talking, but not what they were saying. Evelyn was annoyed, and the thief was amused by it. That was all he could figure out. He banged on the door again, but it was no use.

At least she wasn't in distress.

Finally, after what felt like ages, the door clicked, and he straightened. Evelyn appeared in the door opening, as white as a ghost.

Immediately, the world around Ollie disappeared and he cradled her face in his hands. "What's the matter? Did he hurt you?"

She only shook her head.

"Did he say something to upset you?"

But she shook her head again, still silent.

"I'll kill him," Ollie growled out in a dangerous voice. The thief had done something to her, and he would murder the man for it. With long, heavy strides, Ollie crossed the room to the man standing before the portrait of the black-haired woman, his back to Ollie.

Funny, the thief had black hair too.

Wait.

His hat was off. Ollie looked around. The tricorn hat lay on the floor.

And so did the mask.

"What the blazes did you do to her?" Ollie demanded to the thief's back. "If you laid a finger on her, kiss your life goodbye because you're a dead man."

"I didn't do anything to her."

"Then why is she so terrified?"

"Because she saw my face."

Ollie immediately thought about Dantes. The way his brother had often hid his face because of the deep scar. The pain it had caused him all these years later. Too many times, Ollie had heard people snicker at Dantes. People thought the man didn't care about his scar because the rest of him was big and powerful. He was a famous pugilist, after all. But Ollie had seen the pain it had put in his brother's heart. He had seen the pain it had also caused Victor, who, like Ollie, couldn't help his suffering brother. They could only watch from the side.

In thinking about them, Ollie found he missed his family.

A little.

"What is it about your face?" Ollie decided that was the gentlest way to ask.

The thief ignored the question. "May I ask you something?"

Ollie glanced over his shoulder at Evelyn, who stood off to the side watching them, her eyebrows pulled together severely, her lips pursed. He put his attention back on the thief. He could force the man to turn around, if he wanted to. But as much as he hated to admit it, he was a bit afraid of what he would find.

When Ollie didn't respond, the thief continued. "Are you happy you married Evelyn?"

Ollie looked back at Evelyn again and she looked away.

He swallowed hard. "What does that have to do with anything?"

"Answer the question, please."

"Oh, well, since you said *please*," Ollie replied, buying time. Why would he admit anything out loud for everyone to hear? What purpose would that serve? They had already made a decision. He wanted to give Evelyn what would make her happy, and a separation was what she wanted. "No, I'm not happy I married Evelyn."

It felt as if a deep crack had divided his heart in two.

The thief was quiet a long time, as if contemplating Ollie's response. "Do you know who this woman is, in the painting?"

"No, nor do I care. Why did you get that wedding set up? Why did you put together a ceremony for us and have us show up there not realizing what we were walking into?"

"I thought it was what you needed."

Ollie scoffed. "Is that any of your business to decide that?"

"Actually, yes, it is." The thief, in his dramatic nature, chose this moment to turn around and reveal himself.

Ollie stared with his mouth open, his brain stilling along with his heart. But once he was able to recover from the shock, he pointed at the thief and shouted, "You!"

Because Ollie was staring at…well…himself.

A shorter, slightly older version of himself, that is. The man's hair was a few shades darker, like Victor's hair, and his eyes were brown and not green. But otherwise? They were twins. It was like looking in a mirror.

"You were in my pub!" Ollie continued, now furious. But why was he furious? Why was anger burning through him as if he were dried kindling? He rushed forward and grabbed the man's shirt with a death grip. He wanted to hit the thief, he wanted to scream at him, shake him, do all kinds of ghastly things to the man. Evelyn shrieked and ran forward, trying to pull Ollie away.

But the thief didn't react. He took it all, as if he'd expected this reaction.

"Ollie, stop it!" Evelyn choked out as she pulled at his sleeve.

"Let go of him!"

Ollie immediately let go and felt his throat go tight. "Who are you?" he asked. *"Who are you?"*

The thief held a guarded, blank expression. "I'm your uncle, Eamon Lydon. I like to tell the police I'm Bollocks, though." He grinned a sickeningly familiar grin.

Ollie, however, did not find this funny in the least, and his attention went to the painting of the woman.

In the moment, looking upon her helped calm him a bit. "My brothers—they know about you, don't they?"

Eamon's humor fell away. "Aye."

"They never told me about you. They said we had no Irish family in London."

Eamon didn't respond.

Realization hit him. "They kept you away from us."

"No, they kept me away from *you*."

All this time, Ollie had had more family. Family that looked like him. Throughout his life, he had commented on the way he didn't resemble Victor or Dantes, both of whom strongly took after their father. And they'd never once said anything about it, knowing they had an uncle who looked almost identical to Ollie. This was far worse than Victor banishing him from his own business. Ollie's insides felt like they were being shredded apart. "Why?"

Eamon let out a sigh. "When we were children, you always followed me around."

Ollie shook his head, confused.

"I was in the same street gang as you, boyo. I was the baby of my family, and your mum was the oldest. There were seven siblings between us. Our parents—your grandparents—and many of our siblings died from cholera not long after your dad died. The rest, who were all adults like Honora, went back to Galway, where we're from." He nodded over to one of the green, painted landscapes. "She took me in and I lived with you and your brothers. Then she died, and the four of us—you, me, your brothers—joined that street gang, as we had no one else to look out for us." Eamon paused. "You and I went everywhere together. We had a grand time." Eamon grinned widely again. "Wee baby Oliver toddling after me. Even when I didn't want you to. You'd wail if I went anywhere without you. But I mostly enjoyed it."

Ollie frowned. It bothered him that his uncle had been such a big part of his early years, yet Victor and Dantes had hidden his existence from him.

"That still doesn't explain why no one told me about you," Ollie added.

Eamon shrugged. "If I had to assume anything, that was all Victor's decision. Jealousy, maybe? Concern?"

"Why would he be concerned?"

Eamon gave him a sad smile. "I often went into the rich neighborhoods with you, and we would lift whatever we needed from their homes. Food, clothes, money. Jewelry."

Ollie rubbed his forehead. "I have a few very hazy memories of going into those types of houses and taking things. I thought that was with Victor."

Eamon shook his head. "That was with me. I even taught you how to pick locks. You followed me everywhere and it drove Victor mad. And then I guess a few times, he took you to places that he'd lift from, and it distressed him seeing his baby brother's wee hand taking things without a thought. Not long after that, he tracked down your dad's family."

Ollie stilled. That wasn't the story he knew. "They always told me my grandparents found us."

"No. But Victor lied about that to Edmond—sorry, Dantes— too. Victor wanted to get you especially out of Whitechapel. He saw how it had turned your brothers into street rats and he saw you were becoming one, too. Victor told me he contacted your grandparents, and that you all would be gone for good and I couldn't go with. Then he pushed me and told me to stay away from you forever."

Ollie clenched his jaw.

"Of course…" Eamon's face became filled with mischief. "My sister, when she started spiraling not long before she died, told me to keep an eye on you if something happened to her. And so I did both. I watched you grow up, watched you make a fool of yourself at Oxford with the ladies."

Ollie shook his head at himself and hoped Evelyn hadn't heard that part.

"I watched you all the time from a distance because Victor threatened my hide more than once. But I didn't want you to become like me, either. I'm not a good man, Ollie. In fact I'm pretty terrible."

Ollie didn't respond.

"But I still enjoyed watching you grow up, even if you didn't know about me."

Ollie cleared his throat. He put his attention on the painting of the woman, and hot tears began to form in his eyes as he realized who she was. He was able to blink them back. "That's her?" Ollie asked. "My mother?"

"'Tis."

Ollie had of course seen the one photograph of his mother with his father. But this painting looked different. It somehow seemed realer than the photograph.

"She was a tortured woman," Eamon said. "Emotional, angry, sad, yet always quite funny." Eamon looked upon it, his dark eyes misty, tormented. "I wish I could have helped her."

"Did you ever know my father?" Ollie asked.

Eamon scoffed. "Bastard," was all he said.

Ollie almost asked what that meant but decided he would rather remember his father as Dantes had described him: madly in love with their mother. If that wasn't the truth, he didn't want to know.

"Just a second." Eamon clapped Ollie on the shoulder and disappeared back into the studio.

Evelyn approached Ollie but stopped a good distance away.

"Are you all right, Ollie?" she asked gently.

He swallowed hard. "Yes. Just trying to comprehend every-thing he told me. I think it will take a while."

Evelyn gave him a small smile. "Are you glad to know about it?"

"I am," Ollie decided. "But I can't believe Victor kept family away from me. I don't know how I'll be able to look at him the same. A lifelong con like that. He knows how important family is to me. It wasn't his decision to make."

"I know."

Realization dawned on Ollie. "Nor should it have been his decision to kick me out of my own business."

Evelyn looked up at him with a smile and then, to his great surprise, hugged him. She stepped up to him and wrapped her arms around him tightly. For a second, Ollie froze, stunned by her show of affection. But then he wrapped his arms around her and oh, how wonderful it felt to have her so close. He bowed his head down, burying his face in her neck. He was bigger than her, stronger than her, but right now, she was holding him up.

Letting her go would be the most difficult thing he would ever do in his life.

Eamon cleared his throat and Evelyn immediately pulled away from him, leaving Ollie feeling melancholy and empty once again.

The thief, his uncle, had reappeared from his studio carrying something. He walked over to Evelyn, though he raised his eyebrows at Ollie briefly. "You're sure you want to separate?" Eamon asked as he handed over the Gustave Courbet to Evelyn. But it wasn't clear whom the question was for.

Evelyn flushed again and gave a fleeting glance to Ollie. "Thank you for returning this—not that you should have taken it in the first place," she said, unamused. "Is this the real one?"

"Why do you say that?" Eamon asked with a grin.

"I saw your copies of the Fragonard."

"Ah…" Eamon looped his hands behind his back.

"You steal them then sell them to people who don't know any better. Awful of you."

Eamon laughed. "That's not what I do."

"Then what *do* you do with them?" Ollie replied.

"I study them," Eamon said with a shrug. "As I get older, I find it harder for me to be around people. I don't like it much. I used to go into the museums themselves and copy them there. Now, I steal the paintings at night when no one is around, bring them home, and study them on my own time."

"See." Ollie turned to Evelyn. "I told you it couldn't be art forgery. He only just started stealing paintings."

Evelyn smiled and bowed her head. "That was a very intelligent conclusion, Ollie." She gave him a brush of a smile before turning to his uncle. "However, it still doesn't make sense to me," Evelyn said, crossing her arms. "Steal paintings to study them?"

"Sure, it does. See those." Eamon nodded out to the gallery wall. "Those are mine. I'm self-taught. Too poor to take classes or buy supplies. So I taught myself by reading about the masters and copying them."

"But you don't sign your work."

Eamon grinned. "Oh, but I sign my heists. No one wants my paintings. Why sign them when they're for myself? Seems a bit egoistical." As if he didn't have a giant ego.

"Why doesn't anyone want your paintings?" Ollie asked.

"The moment they hear my name, they make a decision about me without seeing my work. No one wants a poor Irish artist. The want bohemian French, English, and American artists."

"Why not use a fake name, like you do with heists?"

Eamon shrugged. "Tried that, worked until they met me. They always want to meet the painter and watch them work. Can't really change my appearance or voice, can I? Don't really want to be around people anymore, either."

"If you don't sell your work, how do you support all of this, then?" Evelyn asked, looking around.

"Jewelry." Eamon grinned again. "While people are starving in the streets, nobs are throwing thousands of pounds at shiny rocks instead of helping others. I, frankly, don't care about them at all, so I take their things to support myself. And I don't feel the least bit bad about it."

Ollie looked at Evelyn. She frowned at this, being an aristocrat herself, but he also knew she wouldn't exactly disagree with the sentiment, either.

"All right, well..." Eamon clapped his hands together. "You can leave now."

"But—" Evelyn began.

However, Eamon wasn't having it. "You got your painting back, and I don't like visitors. Goodbye." He practically shoved them out into the hallway, slamming the door shut behind them.

Ollie knocked on the door. "Will I ever see you again?"

Eamon shouted back. "You know where I live!"

Ollie laughed at the absurdity before turning to Evelyn. "Can you believe I'm related to that man?"

"Am I supposed to say *no* to that?" Evelyn replied with her own laughter. She was teasing him, and he didn't mind it one bit.

Chapter Twenty-Two

THERE WAS SOMETHING exceptionally dreadful about the middle of the night. Where all of one's worries and anxieties came together at once and pressed down upon you as you tried hour upon hour to succumb to slumber. It felt as if you were the only life in the entire world, as if daylight would never reach you again, and the worries would eat you alive, inch by inch, savoring every hair upon your head until the world ended.

Outside, it was raining hard, which had finally chased away the crowd earlier, leaving Ollie's home peaceful once again.

But the rain also reminded Evelyn of the day she had become the runaway bride. As she stared up at the intricate plaster ceiling of the bedroom, she couldn't help but replay that day over and over in her mind. The dread that sickened her, the heaviness of her legs, of her heart. Her sister's pointed stares in the carriage. The sheer relief exuded by her father that he'd done his best to hide. But she'd seen it, she'd seen through his mask. He'd been upholding his end of the contract with the earl and all would be well for him.

Evelyn recalled the freedom she'd felt when she'd run. The way her legs and lungs had burned, yet she had never felt so alive knowing that her future prison had been left behind.

It was the most pleasurable rush she had ever experienced. As if she had been drugged with happiness, positivity. Everything had seemed bright and hopeful as she'd sprinted block after block through the rain-drenched streets of London.

The way she'd felt then was opposite to how she felt at this exact moment.

This time tomorrow, her family would know about her marriage to Ollie. Evelyn would be dealing with the effects of that horrid conversation. But the day after that was the ship to Paris. And she still had yet to tell Ollie about her departure.

Evelyn still had not decided if she would go back to France or not. It made sense to. She did once have a life there, and she did have friends there. The Louvre might even take her back, but if not, there was endless opportunity there.

And yet.

Maybe she was mad, but Paris had been fun for the time she'd been there. But London was home.

A home in which she seemed to be burning down, but home nonetheless.

What if she didn't go to Paris and stayed in London? She didn't know the status of her job, if it would still be there for her when she returned. She knew they would give her a hard time for being absent and for what happened. It would be deserved. But until they said *no*, hope would remain that she could return to her old life, that they would eventually come around. She was an asset there. She knew them well, and knew that if Mr. Burlington had done what she had, he would be forgiven and allowed to return. But would she?

Regardless, that was not going to be an enjoyable visit. But it would also put her in the next step of the rest of her life.

Where she would leave Ollie behind.

They had agreed to separate. He'd helped her by marrying her, knowing that a separation was in the future. But the thought still weighed heavily on her heart. She liked Ollie very much.

Silly girl, you love him, and you already admitted this.

Evelyn stilled. What was that voice? She sat up and looked around. But all she could see was darkness and the low, glowing fire.

Evelyn lay back down, her brow furrowed.

You can really leave him behind that easily?

Oh. Now Evelyn recognized that voice—it was her own internal voice. How tired was she? *There's more to life than love,* she responded to herself. *And if love's so important, what about my love for art? For myself?*

What about it?

Do I only exist for men's purpose? To be someone's wife? Daughter? And mother someday? Can I not exist for myself? Can I not be selfish the way men can be, where it is instead called courage or moxie? Can I not have my own purpose in life?

Do you think Ollie would prevent all of that?

Evelyn's thoughts went quiet, and outside, a crack of thunder shook the house. Wind picked up. The heavy rain was now a roaring storm.

Evelyn continued thinking to herself. *None of it matters, anyway. Even if Ollie changed his mind and decided against a separation, there's going to be quite a mess to clean up after our marriage is announced. I can legally protect myself from marrying others, but once the marriage is announced, the earl will start slinging mud and igniting legal issues. It could become far, far uglier than it already has been if the earl wants it to. The separation will keep Ollie out of it as best as I can.*

But he's your husband, the voice reminded her.

Evelyn let out a chuckle. *Yes, he is. But he married me to help get me out of a bad situation, not because he loves me.*

Have you asked him?

Evelyn frowned. *Have I asked him if he loves me?*

Aye.

Why the blazes would I do that? And anyway, he already told his uncle he isn't happy to have married me. With me standing right there.

But have you asked him?

Evelyn sat up again and looked around again. This wasn't how she would have a conversation with herself. She narrowed her eyes into the darkness. *No, and I won't. I've already heard everything I need to hear.*

The voice didn't respond.

Blaming it on extreme exhaustion, Evelyn fell back to her pillow and continued staring up at the ceiling. Thunder cracked again, and wind rattled the windows.

Somewhere out in the hallway, a door opened and closed.

And then, there was a knock at her door.

Evelyn bolted upright and pulled the blanket up to her chin as she remembered it was her wedding night. Evelyn and Ollie had made an agreement of intimacy—or lack thereof. But had he changed his mind?

After rolling out of bed, Evelyn walked quietly to the door. An unexpected vivid flash of memory struck her. When she'd kissed Ollie. Fire would have consumed them if they had let it.

She rubbed her hands over her face, shaking the memory away. And when she uncovered her face, she realized her heart was racing and warmth burned inside of her. "Insipid body," she grumbled to herself as she cracked the door open.

Ollie stood there in a navy nightshirt with a pinched face. "Excellent. You can't sleep, either. May I come in?" And he helped himself into her bedroom.

Her heart began to race, which seriously annoyed her. Again, insipid body.

Evelyn huffed. "Excuse me, but I didn't invite you in."

But Ollie didn't respond. He hurriedly crossed the room toward her bed, then to her utter surprise passed it without even a glance. Instead, he came to a stop at a window. The wind whistled beyond it. "Bad storm tonight," he said, parting the curtains a bit to watch the water stream down the glass.

Evelyn tilted her head. "Ollie, what are you doing?"

Another crack of thunder shook the house. Ollie let the curtains fall together again and rubbed the back of his neck. "Nothing. I couldn't sleep and since you're awake too, perhaps we could, I don't know. Be sleepless together."

Evelyn raised her eyebrows. "What are you insinuating?"

Ollie grinned that handsome smile of his, which didn't help

her situation. "See, I thought about it being our wedding night and all and while I wouldn't mind passing the entire night in bed with you, I am a man of my word." He placed his hand over his heart and proceeded to plop down into a chair near her fireplace, where tension took over him and he stared into the fire, unblinking, as his shoulders and face turned to stone.

Did Ollie even realize what he had just said? What in the blazes was going on with him?

Ask him if he loves you.

No, she replied to herself.

At another boom of thunder, Ollie flew out of his seat and began poking at the fireplace, his jaw clenched tightly. And then when he was done with that, he rubbed the back of his neck again.

Another crack of thunder, and he returned to the window to peek through the gap. "How long is this going to last?" he asked with dismay.

Evelyn crossed the room and stopped a few steps away from him for her own sanity. It was clear that in her lack of sleep, she was vulnerable to her attraction to him.

A particularly loud crash of thunder caused Ollie to jump. He turned to face her, running his hand through his hair. "Evelyn, I'm being forced to admit something most humiliating and I'm not happy about it, either."

Dread snaked through her. Evelyn tried to imagine what it could be. A secret child or secret family, perhaps. She swallowed, imagining him tossing a toddler into the air while Miss Findlay giggled and clung to his arm. It was ridiculous—Miss Findlay had the earl—but the intrusive thought did its job: It horrified her. Not that she would admit this. "All right."

"I am terrified—I mean, absolutely, bone-chillingly terrified—of thunderstorms."

Her arms fell to her side. "Sorry?"

He closed the gap between them. "It's true. It's humiliating, but it's true."

Evelyn hid the relief she felt even from herself. "I thought you were going to tell me you had a secret child."

Ollie gave her that handsome grin. "No, it was merely about me being a grown man afraid of noisy nature." He paused. "I would prefer you don't tell anyone."

"Of course not. But why are you so afraid of storms?"

"To be honest, I don't know. All I know is when there's a storm, I become completely consumed by fear, especially if it's dark out." His grin fell away, replaced with tension. "Do you mind if I hover around in here for a bit?"

"You don't want to be alone," she concluded out loud, now understanding. "What about Hambone?"

"I thought about that and tried pulling her out from under the bed, when she proceeded to attack me." He held up one hand and there were deep, bloody claw marks on them.

"Oh!" Evelyn shouted. "That needs to be cleaned out. Come over here." She directed him to the washbowl in the corner. She poured the pitcher of water into the bowl, wet a clean cloth, and proceeded to rub a bit of soap onto the cloth. She then turned to Ollie, took his hand without a thought, and gently began dabbing at the cuts.

Neither of them spoke. As she lightly pressed the soapy cloth against his skin, Evelyn realized how intimate the moment was and glanced up at Ollie from beneath her lashes. With not an ounce of shame, he stared back at her, eyes dark and eyelids heavy. The moment crackled like the lightning outside, and her gaze fell to his lips, remembering how lovely they'd felt. Forcing her attention back to her task, she became quite aware of the feel of his rough hand in hers, and her stomach twisted and turned.

Once the cuts were properly cleaned, she wet the towel again and patted away the soap. "There," she whispered. She looked back up at Ollie and allowed herself a study of him, even though he would see what she was doing. Tomorrow, everything would change, and she only had this moment left. His dark hair was slightly mussed from tossing and turning in bed. The beginning of a beard was showing through. And his bright-green eyes focused intently on her, reflecting emotion and desire roiling together like waves crashing against rocky cliffs. Evelyn held on to the image of Ollie at night for too long, losing herself in him, in this beautiful and kind man. But with concerted effort, she forced herself to let go.

Ollie watched wordlessly as she put everything away, rankled from the charged moment that had passed between them. Uncharacteristically nervous, she dropped the used cloth and they both reached down for it.

"Evelyn," Ollie said in a deep voice as she yanked the cloth from him. They both stood back up. "About tomorrow."

"I don't want to talk about tomorrow," she replied quietly, her voice cracking with emotion. "I don't want to think about it, either." Her eyes lifted to his and she could feel the threat of tears. Blasted emotions! Why did she always get this way at the most inopportune time?

"We don't have to talk about tomorrow," Ollie murmured back.

Tears started to slide down her face, but before she could say or do anything, Ollie lifted both hands to her cheeks to cradle her face and wiped the twin stream of tears away with his thumbs.

Seeming to realize too late what he had done, he immediately looked her in the eye with a bit of panic. But he made her weak, and she was overcome by his nearness, by his touch, by the way her body softened and melted. She held his gaze and when she didn't pull away, the panic in his eyes replaced with a tenderness no one had ever looked at her with before.

Ollie angled his face down and kissed her hairline gently. When she didn't move away, he lightly kissed her forehead. Her heart raced and her stomach dropped, realizing what was happening. Still cradling her face in his hands, he tilted her head back so their eyes met.

Ollie's voice was dark and raspy. "I would like to kiss you good and proper now."

"All right," was all she managed to get out.

There was a flash of a crooked smile on his gorgeous face. Time seemed to slow as it happened; all she could hear was their breathing, her pounding heart throbbing in her ears. Nothing else seemed to exist around them.

Still cradling her face in his hands, Ollie pressed his mouth hard to hers the same moment lightning filled the room with bright light. It almost felt as if the electric bolt had gone through her, through him, the way every nerve in her body exploded and crackled. Ollie turned his head to fit their mouths better and she eagerly opened hers for him, wrapping her arms around his neck as his hands fell to her hips.

She imagined those rough, warm hands sliding gently over her bare hips to grip them tightly.

Real fire could ignite inside of her, and she wouldn't have been surprised.

Next thing Evelyn knew, her back was pressed against the wall, her fingers gripping the front of his nightshirt to pull him flush against her. His hands were planted against the wall on either side of her. Tongues danced, hearts raced, heat and passion devoured them and when Evelyn let out a faint moan into his mouth, one she hadn't even meant to release, Ollie moved down to her neck, gently sucking at a tender spot.

It was the most exquisite sensation, and the rush his touch gave her was the same rush she got when she'd broken free and run as fast as she could. She closed her eyes and smiled to herself, lost in whatever this was burning between them.

Ollie's rough fingers brushed against the soft skin of her neck to pull her nightgown aside and placed kisses along her collarbone.

Then his tongue lightly, slowly, slid back up over the line of kisses he had placed, to end with a nibble at her ear.

She gasped. Her body screamed and cried, desperate. Without thinking, she pressed her hips forward against his, and he let out the most wonderful masculine sound of desire.

But it also plunged her back down to Earth.

She stilled as she realized what was happening. "Ollie, stop."

Ollie did, but neither of them moved away from the other. They stood in place panting hard as she reeled from the moment. Oh my. That was nothing like she would have expected.

He swore.

"I-I'm sorry." Evelyn forced out the words. But she couldn't look at him.

"No. Evelyn—"

"No." She shook her head and her throat became tight. "I should have known it would have become too heated." She then dipped under his arms and took a few steps away. "I must insist you leave. I don't know what just happened, but I should have known better. That you came in here for…" Her words trailed off with the guilt that rose. She was just as involved in that as he was.

Ollie rushed his hands through his hair as pain settled into his face. "I do possess self-control, Evelyn. What, you thought I made up a ruse to come in here to bed you, use you? Is that what you think? Is that the kind of man you think I am?"

Evelyn hugged herself and didn't respond.

His hands fell to his side with exasperation. "I came in here making a spectacle of myself, because I really am embarrassingly terrified of thunder. Yes, I've also wanted to kiss you again. I've wanted to show you what…what could be between us. You kissed me first initially, remember?"

Evelyn swallowed and nodded.

"So yes, of course I wanted to kiss you again." His voice climbed with emotion. "And, yes, I would be happy if you went to bed with me because I—" He suddenly stopped and went completely still.

Evelyn lifted a quizzical eyebrow. For some reason, he had paled, but a boom of thunder reminded her the storm continued its roar.

"Never mind." Ollie, suddenly stricken, crossed the room and paused at the door. "Goodnight, Evelyn." And he disappeared into the dark hallway, shutting her door, his own door following a moment later.

Evelyn huffed and returned to bed. Ollie's touch continued to smolder on her skin, and she wondered if the trail his lips and tongue had created on her chest and neck would remain there forever.

Had she done the right thing by stopping?

Of course she had. Yes, it would have been nice to succumb to him. It probably would have been an incredible experience.

But it would have been an absolute disaster.

Her mind was already made up about their separation. Experiencing passion with him would only make leaving that much harder.

Yet a part of her would always wonder, what would it have been like?

The clock ticked. Tossing and turning followed.

She heard the unmistakable sound of Ollie's door opening and closing again.

Hope jolted in her. He was coming back. And against her better judgement, it made her happy.

Evelyn hurried across the room as quietly as she could. She didn't want him to hear her footfalls and realize how eager she was for his return. What would happen after, she couldn't say. But they would figure it out, right?

She stood at the door, hand hovering over the handle, waiting for his knock.

But it didn't come.

Curiosity getting the best of her, she opened the door and looked up and down the dim hallway before realizing it was empty.

Where had he gone?

Maybe he still couldn't sleep, either, and had gone downstairs to get out of his room.

Evelyn quietly hurried to the stairway and looked down it just as Ollie reach the main floor. He was no longer in his nightshirt, but dressed in day clothes.

Confused, Evelyn watched as he stood in place for a moment, as if trying to talk himself into what to do next.

And then, without looking back, he went out the front door.

Evelyn stood frozen in place, stunned to her core.

Ollie had quietly left the house in the middle of the night. And there was only one reason a man would do such a thing.

He was seeking out a cure for his frustration. A frustration that Evelyn had put there.

Evelyn had seen American paintings of the yawning, red canyons they had out west. The impossible size and depth. It felt as if her world had cracked around her just like the canyons. Endless, limitless.

Betrayal and anger cemented together. She stared at the door he had disappeared through. Ollie had promised most convincingly that he would never find comfort in another woman as long as they were married. And she had stupidly believed him.

But here he was, doing just that at the slightest inconvenience. He was a scoundrel, and she should never have let herself trust him for that reason alone.

Because his stepping out in the middle of the night to go to someone else destroyed her more than she ever would have expected.

Chapter Twenty-Three

A FEW TRAMS in London ran this late at night, and Ollie made the short trip he'd made more times than he could count.

Though it felt like ages since he'd made this trip, he still went through the motions by memory. Thankfully, the storm had diminished significantly, though for the first time in his life, he hardly noticed it.

It was a one-block walk from his home, a tram ride, and then another block until his destination came into view. A few deep puddles had to be dodged, and soon enough, familiar lights spilled out of their windows and onto the damp sidewalk and street just ahead.

Ollie stopped and shoved his hands into his pockets. He could feel the tension pulling his shoulders and back. It felt like he had been submerged into a chamber of misery, the way he not only felt it inside of him, but the air that surrounded him as well.

Who knew Evelyn would have such an effect on him?

He had been with more women than he would like to admit, but not one of them had ever turned him into an inferno the way she had. His skin burned from her touch, but his heart was white hot for her.

That… That was new.

As he took a few more steps, his ears echoed with the sharp breaths she'd taken when he'd kissed her neck. The taste of her sweet kisses, the softness of her skin, the memory of her sighing and pulling him to the wall, gripping him with a desperate desire he felt himself. The way she'd pressed herself against him. Her large eyes dark with want, red hair wild and free. She was absolutely, stunningly beautiful.

Against every rule and plan they'd put in place, against knowing better, Ollie had wanted Evelyn Sparrow—or was it Evelyn McNab—in the most animalistic, carnal way. It consumed him as if he were dry kindling, ignited from an impassioned kiss.

She was his wife. And he was her husband.

Shaking away the thoughts and feelings haunting him, he tried to force himself to close the distance between him and the building just ahead.

But what would he do when he got there?

What in the blazes would he even say?

Ollie put his attention across the street, recalling the alleyway there. He angled in that direction, turned into the alley and, once covered by the misty shadows of night, leaned against the old, brick building to watch the building across the street from beneath the brim of his top hat.

He wanted to go there, to that building.

But he couldn't bring himself to do it.

"Rough night?" a voice echoed from the depth of the dark alley somewhere behind Ollie.

Ollie nearly shouted but held it back. He spun around and found his uncle wearing his terrifying costume.

"Would you take that blasted mask off? You're going to give me a heart attack," Ollie hissed through clenched teeth.

Eamon removed the hat and mask, and Ollie watched his own face grin back at him. Having a newly discovered family member who resembled him this closely was going to take a while to get used to. "Where the blazes did you come from? You weren't there two seconds ago."

Eamon shrugged as he set his costume down on a stack of crates nearby.

"What *is* that costume, anyway? Why do you wear it?"

Eamon stepped over to Ollie to lean against the wall beside him. "It depends. Nowadays, I mostly wear it when I leave my place because I don't like people seeing me anymore."

Ollie made a face. "That doesn't make sense. You stand out more with it on."

"Yes, but they can't see me underneath. I could be anyone. And I feel better wearing it. More secure, I guess, with a mask on."

"Right. And what are the other purposes for your costume?"

"I used to wear it to get into the nobs' costume parties. I spent a pretty coin on it. If you look closely"—Eamon pinched his black cape and lifted it so Ollie could see it better—"there're hundreds of hours of embroidery on here."

"Are those stars?" Ollie squinted, trying to see better. It was all done in midnight blue thread against the black fabric.

"It's the night sky. With full accuracy. You can see it better in light, like at the costume balls. Anyway, once the entire party was drunk, I'd break in or climb into a window or balcony, take their jewelry, and then go eat their food, drink their alcohol, and dance with their women. Their staff never questioned someone in a costume like mine." Eamon grinned widely. "Plus, costume balls let you get away with all sorts of debauchery, which I know you are well aware of."

Ollie frowned deeply at this, but he couldn't deny it, either. He put his attention back on the building across the street.

"So, what are we doing here?" Eamon asked.

"I'm here because I had to get out of my house and had nowhere else to go. Why you're here, I couldn't say. Aren't you ever going to get sick of following me around?"

"I made a promise, remember?"

Ollie let out a sigh.

"And I haven't passed the responsibility off. Yet, anyway."

Ollie looked back at his uncle. "And what does that mean?"

"It means you and your wife haven't figured out how dense

you both are, so my shift isn't over."

Ollie narrowed his eyes. "What?"

Eamon laughed but didn't answer the question, a truly annoying habit of his. "I presume you and your wife got into some kind of fight, you stormed out, and since you had nowhere else to go, you came here?"

"I didn't *storm out*. I waited until she was asleep."

Eamon let out a low, long whistle. "You snuck out. That's the worst thing you could do."

"I didn't sneak out," Ollie bit back.

"Did you announce your departure? Did you knock on her door and say, *'Sweetums, I shall return soon. I need to go cool my head'?*"

Ollie glared at him. "No."

"Did you check to make sure she was actually asleep?"

"Of course not. What if I woke her?"

Eamon lifted one dark eyebrow. "If you couldn't sleep, then why do you think she could? Women *always* know what their men are up to. I guarantee she knows you snuck out."

"I didn't sneak out!"

"Of course not, of course not. Then why are you hiding here, instead of going over there?" Eamon pointed across the street to The Harp & Thistle.

Ollie bit his lip. "All right. Evelyn and I did get into…something. I don't know what you would even call it. No voices were raised, but it still wasn't pleasant. Anyway, I came here because I'm in a mood and I feel like I could face Victor right now and argue my way back into work. Evelyn's going to be gone soon and then what? I mope around, pitiful? No. Life needs to go back to normal once she's gone."

Eamon rubbed his chin in thought. "That easy?"

"That easy."

Eamon slapped Ollie on the back. "Well, then get on with it! Go on over there, give Victor a piece of your mind, boyo."

Ollie put his attention back on his pub. Through the windows, he could see lots of movement. It was crowded, so they were doing well enough without him. He couldn't pick out individuals, however. He did know Victor and Dantes were both in there, and maybe even Vivian and Lady Litchfield, though by this time, they were usually gone.

"Well?" Eamon said after a prolonged time.

"I'm not going over there. Not yet, anyway."

"You know, you could always come work for me."

Ollie turned around and furrowed his brow deeply. "Doing what?"

"Like old times. Break into homes, steal their jewelry. You were a very talented thief when you were younger."

"No," Ollie replied immediately. "If you like doing that, fine. But I won't."

"You're sure? We could make some good money. Far better pay than honest work."

"I have money already, thanks. And you live in a tenement."

Eamon shrugged. "I've lived there for twenty years. Don't like to change things up. Happy to stay where I am, where people mind their own business." Eamon studied Ollie. "You're *sure*?"

"Yes. End of discussion." It was absurd, and he wouldn't even humor his uncle by pretending to think about it.

"All right. If you insist. Then what are you going to do?"

"I don't know."

"Convince your wife to not leave?"

"No. She's set on leaving. I can't stop her. Won't."

"But you care for her."

Ollie's heart skipped a beat. "Which is why I'm not going to stop her." He turned to face his uncle. "Her mind is made up. What am I going to do, beg? No."

"You could try it."

"No one should be begged to stay. If she wanted to stay, she would. I have *some* pride."

"But—"

"Why won't you drop it, Christ," Ollie said, now irritated.

Why did the cad keep going on about it? It only made Ollie feel worse.

Eamon pressed his lips together tight and began kicking small pebbles. "All right. Good luck, then."

"Yeah. Thanks."

Eamon glanced up. "What time is her family going to be there for the dinner?"

Ollie narrowed his eyes. So, Evelyn had told him about it. "Why?"

"I want to see the outcome. From a distance, obviously. You can't deny your dear Uncle Eamon that, can you?"

"Are you serious?"

"Am I ever not serious?"

Ollie frowned. Eamon laughed.

He knew his uncle would watch from a distance, as it was pretty clear the man did not like to interact with other people more than necessary. What harm could come from telling him? "Dinner is going to be at eight o'clock sharp. Evelyn sent them a note." Ollie thought back to earlier, the pair sitting together and penning the note to her family.

They had decided to keep it informative but short.

"*Please have dinner with us,*" he recalled her writing across the paper. "*There is something I need to discuss with you and I request you do not bring the earl. It would not be in anyone's best interest, and you'll understand why soon enough.*"

They hadn't responded, not that he or Evelyn had expected them to.

Ollie and Eamon watched The Harp & Thistle in silence for a bit. But Ollie didn't muster up the courage to confront Victor. He would do it another day.

⫸⫷

AT BREAKFAST, OLLIE hoped a new day meant they could move past whatever had happened the previous night. However, when

Ollie entered his dining room, Evelyn ignored him, instead daintily eating toast as if he weren't there. He greeted her, but he may as well have been invisible.

It was the worst breakfast he'd ever had. The food was splendid, of course, but the air was tense. And he could feel Evelyn's anger boiling across the table.

Funny thing was, he couldn't quite pinpoint why she was so furious with him.

When Evelyn had finished her meal, she rose from her seat and hurried out of the room.

Ollie ran after her, as he always did. And for the first time, he felt annoyed with himself. Why *did* he keep running after her? He had pride.

He found Evelyn in the parlor reading a book. He approached and stopped before her, but, like in the dining room, she didn't look up.

Observing the book she had, he had to resist the urge to grin. "You're reading it upside down," he tried to say as seriously as possible.

Evelyn's nose flared as she turned bright red and corrected the book. But still, she remained quiet.

"Look, I get you are furious with me. But can you at least tell me why?"

Evelyn closed her eyes as she flipped the page. "If you don't know, then I can't help you."

Ollie resisted the urge to pull his hair out. "How is that helpful to us at all?"

"I don't feel like talking to you, Ollie."

"Because I kissed you? You can't be serious."

She flipped to the next page.

He swore under his breath. "Look, you were willing, too, by the way. It's not like I made you do something you didn't want to. Actually, if I recall, you were *quite* willing. And you, if I may be so bold, wanted a bit more from me than a kiss. I mean, not that I didn't want that, too."

She turned a page hard. No way she was actually reading it.

Stating the obvious wasn't working. "I'm sorry, Evelyn, all right? You were right. You kissed me that one time and I couldn't stop thinking about it. Day, night, it didn't matter. It followed me everywhere. Forgetting about it was an impossibility. How could a kiss be so memorable? I asked myself that a hundred times. But you hypnotized me. A mere kiss, a pretty tame one at that, and you had me enraptured."

"Stop trying to charm me," Evelyn replied drily.

"I'm not—it's the truth! Charming someone involves embellishment to achieve a specific desired effect."

At this, Evelyn looked up at him with one skeptical eyebrow lifted.

"I do have moments where I have a semi-intelligent thought."

Evelyn sighed and set the book to the side. "Please let me be, Ollie. I'm already in a mood as it is."

"Because of me? Or because of your family?"

She didn't respond and instead stood up and crossed the room to watch the fire crackle in the fireplace.

He took the hint and left.

The rest of the day, they kept away from each other. It hurt. His heart ached. And he hated the feeling. He wanted to repair whatever had ripped between them. But then again, there wasn't a point. Maybe this was for the best.

He spent the day feeling awful. Replaying their building passion in his mind, replaying the shock that had emanated from her. He knew she felt the fire that burned between them. But whereas he wanted to explore what it could lead to, she wanted to snuff it out.

Soon enough, it was evening, and Ollie was as ready as he could be. Mrs. Chapman was a bundle of nerves, but the cook was in excellent spirits having to cook for guests.

Ollie worried the baron, baroness, and dowager *contessa* wouldn't come. That they would have to delay breaking this news further. What if Evelyn was forced to stay?

In theory, he liked the idea. Of her always being there, of them sharing a bed together. They could pass their time together with her reading art history books to him, chatting happily about a subject she had immersed herself in. He adored when that happened, when she discovered something and spoke rapidly and excitedly about it for hours. And he hung on to every word she uttered.

Hopefully, her family would arrive soon and put him out of his misery.

Sure enough, Evelyn's family arrived right on time.

The knock came and Ollie hurried out of the parlor to greet them, right as Evelyn sprinted down the stairway.

Evelyn hesitated but then began moving forward, briefly glancing at him as she rushed by. She was wearing a stunning, low-cut, perfectly fit dinner dress. It was moss-green velvet, with gold, glass bead fringe and metallic embroidery, and it all looked beautiful with her red hair that had been done up with a gold hair comb. He drank in her beauty, trying to capture every little detail so he could hold on to it forever.

Without thinking, he reached his hand out to grab hers.

She looked at him with wide eyes but stopped.

"I'm here," was all he could think to say. "All right?"

Fear shone in her eyes and she nodded, followed by a tiny flicker of relief in her face.

He didn't really appreciate how terrified she would be. Maybe he should have given her a little more grace than he had. This all would be life-changing for her, far more than it would be for him.

"I'm sorry," he said. "And I will expand on how sorry, in intricate detail with bullet points, if you could specify what has made you so furious, you couldn't stand being around me all day."

Someone knocked on the door again. She stared at it down the hallway as Mrs. Chapman hurried past her to answer it. "You snuck out," she said with a whisper. Ollie felt the color drain from his face. "And went to another woman."

"*Went to another woman?*" What in the blazes was she talking about?

"You were so furious at me for not going to bed with you that you found your release elsewhere. Didn't you?"

"Of course not! How did you concoct such a ridiculous idea?"

But she didn't seem to believe him and had no interest in continuing this conversation. She pulled away and hurried forward as Mrs. Chapman opened the door, revealing Evelyn's family.

No one said anything as they entered, bringing in somber air fit for a funeral. The willowy, red-haired baron was first and immediately looked around, inspecting the house his daughter had been hiding in. He set his eyes on Ollie and recognition flashed in his face. But the baron didn't say anything. He stared Ollie down his nose before turning his back to him and removing his hat.

Evelyn's mother came up next, and her study nearly mirrored her husband's. Though she added a little "Hmph."

And then, Signora Orsini. The dowager *contessa*'s attention went straight to her sister. Their greeting was guarded and Signora Orsini quickly whispered something in Evelyn's ear Ollie couldn't hear. Evelyn quietly replied, "I don't know yet."

The *contessa* put her attention on Ollie. There was no animosity there, but as she looked Ollie over, there was a strange look on her face—satisfaction—like she had solved a riddle and understood the solution no one else did. She gave him a mischievous smile before joining her parents. Evelyn introduced everyone. It was quite possibly the most uncomfortable introduction he had ever experienced.

"As requested, we're here for the explanation," the baron said, handing his top hat over to Mrs. Chapman without acknowledging the woman.

"We'll talk over dinner." Evelyn led her family to the dining room.

Mrs. Chapman mouthed "Now?" to Ollie and he nodded. As

they took their seats at the table, which was already set, Mrs. Chapman left the room to gather the food.

"What is it that you wish to discuss with us, Evelyn, that can't be discussed at home?" the baron asked. His eyes narrowed on Ollie. "And do we need an audience?"

Evelyn was seated beside him and shifted in her chair. "Yes, Papa. Ollie needs to be here for this."

"'Ollie'?" The baroness's lips pressed thin.

Silence settled over the room again, and Ollie did the only thing he knew to do. He jumped up. "Would anyone like a drink?"

Thankfully, this seemed to—very slightly—ease the tension in the room and everyone at once confirmed yes, they would like one. Even Evelyn, whom Ollie didn't know to drink much.

Ollie went over to the sideboard where wine bottles and wineglasses had been set up to serve and he began to pour, taking his time. Normally, one served at the table, but this allowed the family a moment together while he could remain in the room.

The baron cleared his throat. "The earl is very cross with you, Evelyn."

"I'm sure he is," she replied weakly.

"We can only imagine what you have been up to living under another man's roof," her father said. Ollie could feel the baron's eyes digging into his back. "He's willing to forgive you for this entire ridiculous situation, including whatever trouble you got yourself into here."

"*With* an inferior man," the baroness mumbled just loud enough for everyone to hear.

"But—"

"One that, I should add, has completely ridiculed the family! I can hardly leave the house now. Every time I go to the gentlemen's club, I'm the butt of everyone's jokes. And I am not a funny man!"

Ollie had to bite his cheek and keep his eyes glued to his task to keep from laughing from nerves, but all of his other senses remained on Evelyn. She didn't respond to her father, and he wished he could see her reaction.

The baron grumbled. "Regardless, we signed a legal document, a contract, and there's no avoiding the marriage. I understand you don't want it, I do. But what's done is done. There's no way out."

Ollie turned and began placing the wineglasses in front of everyone. Evelyn avoided his gaze. The poor woman was terrified, and he wished he could do something to help. But he couldn't, other than being present.

"Yes, about that—" But before Evelyn could continue, Mrs. Chapman and the cook appeared.

The room went quiet for a few minutes as Ollie returned to his seat and the food was served. Everyone kept their eyes on their plate. Ollie wondered if he should reach over to squeeze Evelyn's hand but decided it would be best not to.

Once everyone was served, Mrs. Chapman went over to collect the empty serving trays when there was a knock at the front door again.

Ollie tore a look in Evelyn's direction. She tore a look in his. Both of them stared at each other with widening eyes.

"Are we expecting anyone?" Ollie asked Mrs. Chapman.

But his housekeeper stared in the direction of the door, biting her lip. "No. Give me one moment. I'll send away whoever it is."

Ollie tried to imagine who could be at his door. Eamon knew about the dinner—would he try to insert himself into it? Ollie didn't think so, but who else would it have been?

A deep, booming voice filled the house. "What do you mean I can't come in? Blast it all, Mrs. Chapman. Get out of the way!"

Ollie closed his eyes and dropped his forehead into his hand. It was Fergus. And, Ollie assumed, Marjory as well.

Seconds later, his enormous grandfather stormed into the dining room, rattling the dishes on the table. He stilled upon seeing the baron, and the baron looked equally startled.

Did they know each other?

"What in the blazes is going on here?" Fergus looked over the room. Marjory went around the table and helped herself to a glass of wine while she hummed.

Ollie stood up from his chair but didn't move from the table. "You need to leave. Right now. This is quite possibly the worst time for you to invite yourselves into my house."

Fergus gave him a funny look. "Invite ourselves? *You* invited *us*, you daft fool!"

But before Ollie could respond to such a ludicrous claim, there was another knock at the door.

"Ollie," Evelyn said in a strained voice. "Please tell me I didn't hear that."

But he had heard it, too. Happy to get away and leaving Mrs. Chapman to gather two more place settings, Ollie stormed over to the front door. He couldn't imagine who was here now.

Flustered, he flung the door open and was utterly stunned to find Victor, Dantes, Vivian, and Lady Litchfield huddled together in his doorway.

"What are *you* doing here?" Ollie hissed the words low, but he was looking at Victor.

Victor didn't respond. Instead, he stared back at Ollie with a dark expression and held up a piece of paper.

Ollie ripped it out of his hand and read it over. It was an invitation to dinner, written in overly flourished script.

"You're the one who invited us," Dantes replied. And the entire group filed past him.

But the ever-perceptive Lady Litchfield paused at the end. "Is everything all right, Ollie?"

Ollie glanced over his shoulder. Everyone was now in the dining room. Victor and his grandparents hadn't spoken to each other in twenty years. It appeared his uncle the art forger had forged the invitations and planned for mischief tonight. What in the blazes was Eamon trying to do to him?

"Actually, no, it's not," Ollie replied. "In fact, this is going to be a horrific disaster."

Chapter Twenty-Four

EVELYN TRIED TO stay calm when the rest of Ollie's family, as well as the Marchioness of Litchfield, appeared in the now-full dining room. Their appearance was unexpected, and she didn't understand why they were there.

Mr. Victor McNab was the first one in and his attention immediately went to his grandparents. The duke choked on his wine upon setting eyes on his eldest grandson. Evelyn knew they were estranged. Was this the first time they had crossed paths in all that time?

Neither said a word to the other, and Mr. McNab slid into the first open chair he could find, which happened to be on the same side of the table as Evelyn's family.

The duchess did greet Mr. Dantes McNab and Lady Vivian, though, and was introduced to Lady Litchfield. It appeared Ollie's other brother had had some contact with their grandparents.

The room filled with hesitant conversation, but no one looked happy.

Ollie reappeared and Evelyn felt a bit of pity seeing the raw distress on his face. It was clear he hadn't expected any of them to show up, either. As Ollie lowered into his seat beside her, he wordlessly handed over a piece of paper.

"What is this?" Evelyn asked, taking it.

"An invitation," Ollie replied, holding her gaze with meaning.

"To dinner. Here. Right now."

"What?"

"Eamon."

She looked over the apparent invitation, one neither of them had written, and it dawned on her. Ollie's uncle had invited Ollie's family and friend to the dinner where she would be telling *her* family they had married. By forging invitations!

Evelyn angrily balled up the paper but resisted throwing it across the room and causing a scene. She lowered her voice to a dangerous level. "How does Mr. Lydon know about this dinner, Ollie?" Though she had mentioned it to the thief, she hadn't provided any details of when it would occur. And the invitation gave the right time.

Ollie scratched the side of his nose. "I, uh, might have told him about it."

"During your disappearance?"

"You refused to talk to me earlier. If you had, I would have told you I went to my pub to confront Victor. Eamon followed me there."

She quickly glanced at the elder Mr. McNab, who was now watching Lady Litchfield come around the table to the sit on the other side of Ollie. Her attention went back on Ollie. "You confronted your brother finally?"

Ollie shifted. "No. Anyway, *that's* what I did last night, *not* what you accused me of. I stood in the rain, pitiful, staring down my pub and not doing anything about it."

Unfortunately, the relief this gave her only distressed her further. She was a ball of nerves, and feeling anything positive toward Ollie, when they had already begun to start severing their ties, made everything more confusing.

"Why did your uncle invite them?" she asked, trying to ignore her nerves stringing tight.

"Now, that is the big question, isn't it?" Ollie replied. "To be a pain in the arse? I don't know."

Everyone settled into their seats and Mrs. Chapman, whose

normally impeccable hair was beginning to frizz and loosen, began placing new table settings while mumbling she hoped there was enough food. Silence settled over the room.

Everyone eyed each other. Mr. Victor McNab sunk further into his chair and glared at Ollie. Ollie glared at the duke. Papa glared at Evelyn, and Evelyn looked to Cordelia for some kind of groundedness.

Lady Litchfield leaned behind Ollie's chair and whispered to Evelyn, "A bit uncomfortable in here." She had *no* idea.

Everyone began to eat in the awkward silence. Evelyn had hardly eaten all day yet couldn't stomach the idea of food right now.

But she forced herself to eat because it gave her an excuse to not interact with anyone.

Papa was the first to speak. "So, Evelyn, the man you've been staying with is from this buffoon's family?"

Evelyn closed her eyes at this, fighting back the rising bile.

"Buffoon?" His Grace slammed heavy, giant fists onto the table, rattling everything. "How dare you speak to a duke in such a way! And a man for the Tories on top of that. Ha!"

Papa and the duke started arguing over the heads between them. And when Papa made a dramatic hand gesture, he knocked over his red wine, spilling it straight onto Mama's lap. Mama, in turn, let out a scream.

Lady Vivian and Cordelia rushed to aid Mama, calming her and dabbing at the stain.

"Your senseless daughter"—the duke pointed a meaty finger in Evelyn's direction, his face crimson with anger—"has dragged my family's name through the mud, thanks to your mess!"

As he said this, Evelyn caught the duchess glancing at Evelyn's hair. Was she remembering the horrid words she had uttered? Evelyn felt a brief pang of triumph knowing the duchess was likely quite embarrassed now that she realized Evelyn was not, in fact, a low-class pub woman.

"That's asinine!" Papa shouted back. "Everyone knows your

family is made up of a bunch of brutes! At least my daughter didn't go running off like your son did to basically join a circus! *Her* mistake will be rectified once she becomes countess!" Papa wiped his mouth with his napkin then shook his head with a laugh. "The first and only son of some highlander duke running off to play with trains. What does that say about you? And how dare you judge my family? I may be a lowly baron to you, but at least I'm not a Scotsman!"

The McNabs all gasped. Lady Litchfield let out a groaning noise. The duke sputtered, but in his ire could only get out, "You-You Englishman!"

The two men leapt from their chairs, the furniture flying down to the floor with loud crashes. They continued to hurl insults at each other while everyone else looked on with horror.

"I guess they do know each other," Ollie said to Evelyn with a hint of humor.

She whipped her head in his direction, her eyes wide with anger. "Do you find this funny?"

He cleared his throat. "Of course not." He shifted in his chair while the two men faced off with threatening stances and booming voices.

It was too much for Evelyn. She covered her ears and curled into herself as her heart raced faster and faster. Lady Litchfield leaned behind Ollie's chair again and placed a light hand on Evelyn's shoulder, but Evelyn was too overwhelmed to react. Through the muffled sound, shouting increased. What they were shouting to each other, she didn't know. She didn't care. Additional voices were added. Men's voices, women's voices. Evelyn, with elbows sticking straight out, looked over to Ollie. He was watching her with a clenched jaw.

This had to end now, or her nerves would literally shred and her body would simply explode.

"Stop it!" Evelyn unfurled herself and jumped up to her feet. "Stop it this instant!" she cried out.

Everyone froze in place.

His Grace held the front of Papa's shirt while Mr. Dantes held the duke back. The duchess had scooted her chair back and held a wineglass to her mouth. Mr. Victor McNab, Lady Vivian, and even Lady Litchfield had moved to one end of the table to get as far away from everything as they could.

Evelyn's side of the family did the same, but on the opposite end of the table.

The McNabs and the Sparrows were as divided, as at odds as two families in the modern era could be.

"Look at all of you!" Evelyn was still shouting. She dug her fingers into her scalp. "Is this really how you behave?"

The duke released Papa, who shrugged his shoulders to adjust his jacket. Everyone else seemed to ease just a bit. Maybe the worst of it was over.

Papa put his focus back on Evelyn and planted both palms on the tabletop. "Evelyn, you summoned us here. You cannot be surprised, after the shame and humiliation you brought upon our family, that we are a bit on edge."

"That's right." The duke crossed his arms and gave a single nod as Papa looked at him with narrowed eyes. "You think we want to be tied to your insipid, embarrassing family? Och."

Papa was angry again. "Why, you—"

Papa prepared to lunge at the duke again. This was going to turn into an actual fist fight if she didn't intervene right this second. Desperate, Evelyn shouted the only thing she could think of in the moment. "Ollie and I got married!"

Numerous gasps rang out in the room. Every single pair of eyes and every single mouth gaped in her direction. Only Cordelia held a different expression from everyone, in that she covered her mouth with both hands, partially hiding her reaction.

"What. Did you. Just say." Papa's voice was calm. Too calm. It had been a long time since this particular brand of ire of his had been directed at her. Evelyn had often experienced it as a child, too wild and energetic for her own good, getting into mischief without realizing it. Running in places she shouldn't have been running, talking in places she shouldn't have been talking, crying or causing any sort of fuss. The forced calm in Papa's voice would strike fear into her because she'd known once no one was around, she would get in so much trouble and would be sent to her room for the entire day, banned from talking to anyone.

"It's true." Ollie jumped into the middle of the chaos she had created. "Not the best delivery, Evelyn." He looked at her with a *what are you doing* expression. "But yes, it's true. We got married."

As the news sunk in, the air in the room began to charge, that static before lightning struck.

Papa's eyes became crazed, and without realizing it, Evelyn took a step back. Never had she seen that look on him before. Without breaking eye contact, he drained the rest of his wineglass then threw it against the wall, the glass shattering upon impact. "You ruined the family," Papa said with hatred. "You ruined me! You have to marry the earl, Evelyn. It's in a contract! It's a legal obligation!"

"I can't, Papa. I'm sorry. And the law would be on my side here. I would be a bigamist, if I did. That is illegal." Even though she knew she'd said the words, they sounded funny to her, like they were coming from someone else.

This seemed to be the moment the duke unfroze himself because he started to come around the table. The duchess howled after him to calm down. Mr. McNab and Mr. Dantes followed, probably to ensure the duke didn't pound Ollie into the ground like a railroad spike.

But, surprisingly, the brothers stood behind Ollie instead.

"You married an English harlot?" the duke shouted in Ollie's face.

Ollie jerked forward, his face flushed, and his hands seemed to be shaking. But his brothers grabbed him before he could reach their grandfather. Ollie flailed, trying to get out of their grasp. It took the two enormous men to keep him barely contained.

"How dare you speak that way about the woman I love!" Ollie shouted back, probably not realizing what he'd said, and he nearly fell backward as his brothers continued to pull him back.

Mr. Dantes laughed as his eyebrows lifted high, and he stopped Ollie from collapsing fully. "Did you truly just say that?"

And that was it. The powder-keg room finally ignited. People began running circles around the table. Chairs flew, bread rolls arched overhead. The noise and energy and emotion were so charged, Evelyn couldn't handle it anymore.

Her wall cracked.

Her breathing quickened as if she were running.

Lady Litchfield appeared in front of her, worry set on her brow. She said something, but Evelyn didn't hear it.

Ollie had called her the woman he loved.

In front of *everyone*.

She gripped the closest chair as she tried to catch her labored breath.

Ollie pulled away from his brothers and rushed over to her, alarmed. "I'm so sorry. I didn't mean to—"

But she didn't hear the rest of what he said. She didn't want to. She had to run. It was the only remedy. She couldn't stay any longer.

Her legs, her muscles, screamed to move. And Evelyn happily met their demand. With haste, she ran out of the room, down the hall, flinging the front door open when she'd reached it. Outside, Mr. Eamon Lydon—sans mask—leaned against a gas lamppost and was in the midst of drinking from a flask when she burst out of the house. Evidently surprised by her sudden appearance, he choked and coughed as he swallowed too much of the liquor.

Cordelia's voice shouted after her. And then Ollie's.

Ollie gripped her shoulders and spun her around. His face was fraught with regret, with pain, his hair distressed and his tie askew.

Evelyn's fear was quickly replaced by boiling anger. She wailed, "Why did you say that?"

But Ollie wasn't having it. "Why did you tell them we were married the way you did? Christ, Evelyn, could you have brought it up in a worse manner?"

"Are you two actually married? That wasn't a story you concocted?" Cordelia looked between them.

Mr. Lydon decided to join in and gave Cordelia a long look over as he took another swig. "In the eyes of God, aye. I set it up."

Cordelia glared at him. "Who the blazes are you?"

Mr. Lydon grinned and stuck out his flask-free hand. "I'm Ollie's uncle. Eamon Lydon."

But Cordelia turned her back to him and pulled Evelyn away from Ollie. "All right, well, this was unexpected and I regret to agree your delivery wasn't great, but everything will be fine."

"Will it?" Evelyn's voice cracked and she let out a crazed laugh. "Will everything be fine, Cordelia? Because as far as I can tell, no, it won't be fine."

Cordelia pressed her lips together tight—because Evelyn was right.

"What is Papa going to do about the contract?" Evelyn asked. "He's going to have to pay back the earl. And I know he doesn't have that kind of money."

Mr. Lydon cleared his throat. "Actually, erm—"

"No, he doesn't."

"But I couldn't marry him, Cordelia. I couldn't do it!"

Cordelia pulled Evelyn close and began to shush her.

But it didn't help. Evelyn's legs began to scream again. Running was all that could bring her the smallest bit of happiness right now.

"Funny thing." Mr. Lydon waited until he had the full attention of all three of them. He smiled wide and chuckled. "About your marriage license."

Everyone waited, but he didn't continue. "What about it?" Evelyn asked.

"Well. See. The thing is… It was fake." He grinned again.

There was a long pause in which no one moved. No one said *anything*.

Evelyn was the first to find her voice. "Fake?" she squeaked.

"That it is."

"What do you mean, it's fake?" Ollie's voice ground with suppressed anger. "I saw it with my own eyes, held it with my own hands. Our names were on there. It was signed!"

"Ollie, boy, look who you are talking to." Mr. Lydon spread his hands wide.

"Are you saying we aren't really married?" Evelyn asked. What this meant, she couldn't comprehend quite yet. All she knew was that it felt like she was going to vomit.

"Legally? No."

"You couldn't forge something like that in a day or two. I don't care how talented you may or may not be. The decorative imagery on it would take weeks, even for you!"

"Oh, the paper itself was real, lass. Stole it myself."

"You stole from the Archbishop of Canterbury?" Evelyn nearly shouted.

Mr. Lydon's eyes went wide. "Of course not! I stole it from the people who make them. The paper factory is right in London, you know. Broke in overnight, took what I wanted. Then I wrote your names, the date, and then of course forged the signature."

Evelyn spun her head in Ollie's direction. He stared back at her, pale, and rubbed a hand over his jaw.

This was too much for Evelyn now. They weren't married. She was still at risk from the earl. How foolish she was to have taken something from a thief as truth! It had never occurred to her to question the legitimacy of the license.

"Why?" Ollie nearly whispered. But his voice rose louder as he continued. "Why would you do that to us?!"

Mr. Lydon looked at all of them. "To help you, obviously. And it worked, didn't it?"

Evelyn went to deny it but found she couldn't. She wasn't protected anymore. She wasn't Ollie's wife.

She wasn't Ollie's wife.

"You can, of course, still get married if you…" Mr. Lydon said helpfully.

"No," Evelyn replied immediately. She began shaking her head and walking backward. "No." She needed to leave. Now.

Ollie hurried over to her. "Evelyn." He tried to sound stern, but Ollie couldn't be convincingly stern to save his life. "I know what you're about to do."

She didn't respond—only stared back as her breathing became erratic again.

"Don't run away from me." Ollie's eyes pleaded with her. "Please, Evelyn. Don't run away. Let's figure this out without anyone running. I won't run after you this time. I'm not doing that anymore."

Her heart knocked against her ribs.

Ollie continued. "This is a horrific mess, yes. But I don't want you to run." He stammered. "I don't want you to leave."

"I have to go," she choked out, and the backs of her eyes began to burn. Her breathing became more erratic.

"Please," Ollie whispered, a hint of a plea in his voice.

"I'm sorry," Evelyn replied. With that, she turned and ran.

As promised, Ollie did not follow.

Chapter Twenty-Five

ALL OLLIE COULD do was watch her disappear into the night. He knew he would never see her again. He knew this was final. Evelyn was gone from his life. She had run away, and it had been her choice to do so. And it was his choice to refuse to run after her.

But too many times he had done it. Too many times he had made a fool of himself running after a woman who didn't want him to follow. And now, come to discover, they weren't actually married. It had all been a farce. Intellect may not have been one of his strengths, but he should have known better than to trust a thief for anything.

He also should have been relieved. He was now free to go about his life as he pleased. Free to go back to the way things had been. He could go back to his pub, go back to being a scoundrel, go back to normal. This also made it possible for him to marry someone else and have a family. Yet despite this revelation, everything felt gray and watery.

There was no light, there was no hope. Evelyn had taken it all with her.

"Ollie, lad." A hand patted at Ollie's cheek. "You still in there?"

Ollie blinked and focused on the person standing in front of him.

His uncle.

And next to Eamon was Evelyn's sister, Signora Orsini, frowning up at him.

"She's gone." Ollie stated the obvious.

"Aye," Eamon responded and held out the flask to Ollie. Though angry with his uncle, Ollie took a swig, relished the burn of the liquid, and handed it back.

"Do you often run around nursing a flask?" Signora Orsini directed the question to Eamon.

Eamon twisted the cap back on. "Have to keep warm somehow."

The dowager *contessa* wrinkled her nose, evidently disgusted. But Ollie understood. This was how Eamon had watched him during cold days and nights.

"All right. Mr. McNab." Signora Orsini put her full attention on him. "Please explain everything to me, as I'm not fully understanding."

Ollie glanced back at the house and realized their families were still somewhere inside, probably having a similar discussion to the one they were having outside. He shut the front door, glad to be away from them for the moment.

And then, he told the *contessa* everything.

It began when he met Evelyn upon her assignment to the art restoration, to the Gustave Courbet painting being stolen, to the surprise wedding they'd thought until now had been real. All the way up to the current moment.

It took a good while and she listened patiently, though a few times, she shot some unamused looks in Eamon's direction.

Finally, once the story was over, Signora Orsini knit her hands behind her back. "Well. That is quite the adventure. Thank you for telling me."

Ollie waited for her to say more. But she didn't.

"All right, so…?" He trailed off.

"So…what?" she replied.

"I don't know. Do you have any kind of response at all?"

Signora Orsini considered this. "There's not much to say, Mr. McNab. You didn't really get married. She's still at risk. The earl is going to make her life hell, actually, once he hears about this. You heard our father in there. There was a contract. And soon, he will learn it remains active. And he will be quite pleased with that turn."

Ollie looked at the ground.

"Let me ask you this. Do you love my sister?"

A bit of a personal question. One he didn't care to answer. "Does that matter?"

"Of course it does."

Ollie glanced at his uncle, who watched the scene unfold with evident mild amusement, before letting out a lovesick sigh. "As much as it pains me to admit how pitiful I am, yes. I suppose I do love her." Then he turned to his uncle and mumbled, "Happy now?" to which his uncle grinned.

"That's rather unfortunate for you, isn't it?" Signora Orsini said. "You're truly set on not running after her? You can still get married, if that's what you both want."

"Now there's a brilliant idea!" Eamon replied, his voice full of glee.

Ollie ignored him. "Of course I'm set on it. Why should I chase after a woman who always runs from me? I do have some self-respect."

"And she always will run, Mr. McNab." The *contessa* gave him a small, regretful smile. "She's been doing that her whole life."

"Why?"

"Why does she run away? I don't know."

Ollie shook his head. "I suppose it doesn't matter."

Faint voices carried through the closed front door.

"I need to get out of here," Ollie said to no one in particular. He couldn't face the family and tell them what had happened. Not right now.

"Come on, then." Eamon dropped a heavy arm around Ollie's shoulders. "There's somewhere I'd like to show you."

"Why should I go anywhere with you?" Ollie tried to bite back, but he was too grief-stricken to put any weight behind it.

"Because you're going to want to see it."

Ollie hesitated but nodded, too distraught to wonder too deeply about their destination.

Signora Orsini took a few steps toward the front door before pausing. "Mr. McNab, one last thing." She turned back around. "I'm returning home tomorrow. Paris. I've told Evelyn she's welcome to come with me if she wants."

Ollie felt the blood drain from his face. "She's leaving," he said. The finality of everything was beginning to press down hard on him. And it was the most horrible feeling.

The *contessa* hesitated. "I don't know for certain, as she hasn't told me definitively." She then shared the time and place the ship would depart. "I thought I'd let you know, just in case." And she turned and went through the door before he could reply.

"Just in case of what?" Ollie asked as she disappeared. But she didn't provide a response.

SOMETIME LATER, OLLIE found himself on another late-night tram sitting beside Eamon. Eamon didn't say a word about their destination and Ollie didn't much care, either. He was numb and seemed to simply exist as a bag of bones with the ability to move itself around. Because surely, he wasn't the one making himself move. His brain was in too much of a fog. It felt automatic, as if he were simply existing, not living.

The realization he loved Evelyn had come too late. Though, the strange part was, he couldn't pinpoint when it had happened.

Surely, it had only occurred over the past few days.

No, silly.

Ollie cursed inwardly to himself. *Go away. I'm not in the mood right now.* That was it, he was mad. He was telling himself to go away! *I don't need any self-reflection.*

But naturally, the voice ignored him. *You've loved her much longer than that.*

Even if I did, it doesn't matter anymore, now does it?

Maybe, maybe not.

The voice seemed to be gone, to Ollie's abject relief.

But as the tram stopped to let one of the two other riders off, the voice started up again. *Are you sad she's gone?*

He scowled to himself and Eamon gave him a funny look before returning his attention out the window. *What in the blazes is that question?* Ollie asked himself.

Can you answer it to yourself, though?

Of course I'm sad she's gone! I'm sad, furious, regretful—all kinds of awful things. And to make it all worse, we were never really married, so thanks for bringing it up.

The voice seemed to be amused by this response, which was strange. *Why didn't you run after her tonight?*

Because she wouldn't run away from me if she didn't want to. I've run after her plenty of times and it's embarrassing now. Anyway, she wants her own life, separate from me.

And you know that for sure?

Why was he arguing with himself? *She's said it as much.*

The voice volleyed back. *She's never said she wanted to be away from you, specifically.*

Ollie furrowed his brow. Was this true?

The voice continued. *Your wife knows what she wants. What do you want?*

She's not my wife. And I want to go back to the pub. But that response didn't feel quite right.

The voice was silent a long moment. And then, *You hesitated.*

If I chased after Evelyn tonight, what would it accomplish? Our wedding was a farce. She only agreed to it to get out of marrying the earl. And now, her sister has given her a chance to go back to Paris. She can still escape the earl that way.

But her parents won't be able to escape the earl and the courts.

Ollie had nothing to say to that.

So you want to go back to the pub? That's what you want most of all? the voice asked.

Annoyance sparked inside him. He wanted to argue back—but he had no argument.

I don't know what I want, he finally admitted to himself.

But the voice offered no further comment.

The tram came to a stop again and his uncle stood, Ollie followed, and they climbed out onto a desolate, smelly street.

Horse dung was everywhere. It looked like it had been weeks since it had been cleaned. The street The Harp & Thistle was on was far from opulent, and it looked weary and worn in its own right, but this street was downright derelict.

"Where are we?" Ollie asked after they'd passed a man asleep in the gutter.

"I'll tell you in a minute," Eamon responded.

As they continued walking, Ollie said, "Do you ever hear voices?"

Eamon was so thrown off by this question that he stopped walking. "You hear voices?"

Ollie shrugged.

"Don't be going around telling people that, Ollie boy." Eamon clapped him on the shoulder.

They continued walking again until Eamon stopped and angled his head back to peer up at a building. A woman in filthy, ragged clothing was leaning against it and watched them while smoking a cigarette.

"You looking to throw up some skirts?" she asked. It was said so casually, Ollie was sure he'd misheard her.

Ollie half-expected Eamon to laugh, but the man just shook his head. "No, lass."

The woman took another drag from her cigarette before snuffing it out against the wall and going inside. Ollie almost expected it to collapse. It looked like it was rotting out from the inside, and as if the woman had been holding it up.

Ollie watched his uncle, still confused as to what they were doing here or where they even were. Eamon's face had become hard, and that cocky easiness that usually emanated from him was all but abandoned right now. Ollie's curiosity was piqued, but he kept quiet to let Eamon talk when he was ready.

"See that window there?" Eamon pointed to a second-floor window that was dark, its curtains drawn.

Ollie confirmed he did.

"That was your mother's bedroom."

Ollie was taken aback. "Are you sure about that?"

"Of course I'm sure about it. I lived here too," Eamon replied with a bit of anger.

"Sorry, I just…I've never been here before. They wouldn't tell me where we lived. Where I was born. I didn't know." *That it was this bad*, he didn't add on.

But they both knew what he meant.

"Aye." Eamon nodded solemnly. "Victor never wanted you to see this place. And then of course, your grandparents didn't, either."

"This is where I'm from," Ollie said, almost with wonder. He became fraught with emotion. Not because it was such an impoverished home, but because it was his history. His roots. They had followed him, haunted him his whole life. But he had never set eyes on the place he'd been born, or where they'd lived once their mother had passed and they'd had no home.

Ollie looked around. "It looks a bit familiar now," he admitted. "But I couldn't point anything out to you."

"Allow me, then." Eamon grinned. He led Ollie a few buildings down and then crossed the street. He pointed toward a terrifying alley. "After your mum died, this was where we all slept."

Without hesitating, Ollie took several steps into the alley. There were putrid rubbish bins everywhere, as well as more horse dung, and he swore he saw a few rats scurrying about.

He stared down the expanse of darkness and tried to imagine a baby, a toddler, here. He tried to imagine Victor, much younger, forced to take on the role of parent and watch out not just for Ollie, but Dantes too.

The gang of boys made a whole lot of sense. Protection in numbers.

"How old were you?" Ollie asked, still staring down the alley. "When we were all here?"

Eamon stepped forward to join Ollie's side. "Victor and I are the same age. So, whatever that was."

"I was four when my grandparents found us." Ollie tried counting in his mind. "I mean, when Victor told them where we were, to get me away from you. That means Victor was fourteen."

"There you go, then," Eamon replied.

Strange noises caught his attention, and he noticed some shadows moving in the dark. Immediately, he felt embarrassed, realizing it was two adults grunting against each other. "Come on, lad." Eamon pulled him away. "You ready to return home?"

The thought distressed him. "No."

"I want to show you one more place, then."

A bit later, Eamon led Ollie off another tram, but this time, they had to walk several blocks. Now, they were in a rather affluent area of the city. It wasn't where the titled aristocrats lived, like where Ollie had grown up after leaving Whitechapel, but it was very nice. There was no rot, and none of the buildings sagged or leaned. The streets were clean. The gas lamps gleamed. Nothing painted was chipped.

Eamon paused at a house and Ollie studied it. Again, he didn't recognize it. But he did notice on the sidewalk a toy had been left outside by accident by whatever child slept comfortably inside. It was a small, wooden horse on wheels with a string to pull it around.

Ollie swallowed, beginning to suspect where they were.

"You know where we are, don't you?" Eamon asked gently.

Ollie clenched his teeth and could only nod. Guilt, of all things, rendered him silent.

"This is where your brothers grew up."

"Until I came about," Ollie added with bitterness.

This was the house where his family had been happy. His father had been alive. His mother had been, too, and not yet addicted to laudanum. His brothers had had all the food, all the clothes, all the warmth they could ever want. They had been safe and loved here.

And then his father had died, spiraling their mother into grief, out of this neighborhood, and into Whitechapel. In the midst of this grief, Ollie had been born. The delivery had been difficult and she'd been given laudanum.

Their lives had proceeded to fall apart, and the rest was history.

Of course, he had never seen this house before, either, but this time, he understood why. Victor and Dantes wouldn't have wanted him to see it—they were bitter toward him. It was because of him that their mother had been given the laudanum that would kill her. He also knew they would deny this if he asked. And maybe, they truly believed they didn't hold her addiction and death against him.

But how could they not?

His existence had killed her.

And Victor had been left in charge while mourning the loss of everything in his life.

Ollie had always known this had had a profound, lasting effect on Victor especially. But until now, he had never been able to truly appreciate the stark difference between the two lives Victor had lived. The happy first life Victor had had here, and the darkness that followed him forever after their mother's death.

"What was it like then? For my family?" Ollie hazarded the question.

Eamon was quiet a bit longer. "I don't know."

Ollie looked over at Eamon and frowned. "What do you mean?"

Eamon chuckled with bitterness. "We Lydons weren't allowed here. Once your mother and father married, she was whisked away and there was always some excuse why we couldn't come see her." There was another pause. "Then of course, she needed us once your dad died. She lost this house, and she was about to have…" Eamon hesitated and rubbed the back of his neck. "Well. She suddenly wanted family. But most were gone. And then soon, I was the only one left."

"The men at my wedding, the boys from Whitechapel. They spoke Irish." Ollie tilted his head. "Do you, too?"

"Aye."

"Do my brothers?"

Eamon looked away. "Nah. Your parents didn't want you all to learn it. They wanted you to fit in. Though after living in Whitechapel, I'm sure your brothers could understand a conversation, or partly understand it, if they overheard one. But they can't speak it or write it."

Ollie was overcome by the strangest feeling. As if he had realized there'd been an emptiness within him for his whole life, but he was only finding it in his soul right now.

"Why did you agree to start seeing my mother again? After she ignored you for so long?" Ollie asked. There was a thought beginning to form in his mind, but it wasn't clear yet. But this question seemed to be going in the right direction.

"Because she's family," Eamon said with a shrug. "Lots of families have shite people in them. But to me, family is important. She needed help. I couldn't do much, as I was a wee lad myself, but I did what I could. And I wanted to be around her again. She was all I had left after our parents had died and everyone else had moved away. See, Ollie?" Eamon gave him a sad smile. "You and I aren't so different, once you look beyond the surface."

"Family," Ollie replied, the thought sharpening. "But we don't have much of that, do we?"

Eamon let out a heavy sigh, shoved his hands into his pockets, and looked up at the nice house. "No, we don't. And I hardly had you boys, either. I'm a criminal, Ollie, don't forget. Your brothers rightfully kept you away from me."

A surge of emotion punched through Ollie's heart. "It wasn't their decision to make."

"Maybe, maybe not. I don't blame them for it. But also, they seem to forget you're not a child anymore. You're more than old enough to decide that for yourself. Granted, being an adult is more than age. But, within the last year, I've seen myself how much you've grown. Maybe they couldn't see it. Maybe they didn't want to." He paused a long while. "Anyway, once you three left, I had no one. Or so I thought. But I discovered I did still have family in Whitechapel. You met them at your wedding. Well, the fake one I guess, unless you count…" He pointed up toward the sky. "And can I admit to something? I knew you'd find out eventually that I forged the license. I didn't plan on keeping that from you forever. But I kind of hoped it would make you two see reason."

"See reason?" Ollie asked in an unamused voice.

Eamon grinned. "That you *do* want to be married to each other!"

Ollie frowned at his uncle but thought back to the men who'd witnessed the wedding. He'd thought they had been there simply to be witnesses. But now, he realized that to Eamon, the wedding had meant something. He couldn't actually get Ollie and Evelyn to marry each other, but he'd done everything he could to nudge them in that direction, believing they loved each other and it would be right for them. Though it had been done in the man's own utterly mad way.

Ollie had to admit he was incredibly touched.

"Thanks," was all Ollie could say. "Maybe, in a way, I wish it had worked."

Eamon seemed to understand and clapped Ollie on the shoulder, trying not to let his mouth quiver.

Though Ollie did feel bad his uncle had put forth all that effort and it wouldn't end up the way he had hoped.

What do you want? That question repeated over and over in

his mind. And he stared up at the house Victor and Dantes had grown up in, the one they should have stayed in.

He finally understood there would always be an otherness about him. A wall between him and his brothers. Yes, they were family, but despite spending his life following them around, they would never be Victor, Dantes, and Ollie. It would always be Victor and Dantes, and then Ollie.

All Ollie had ever wanted was to be accepted, loved, not seen as the baby brother born during a devastating time. But he would never get what he wanted, what he needed, from his own family.

But like Eamon had said, family didn't have to be blood.

Evelyn could be his family. After all, he did love her. He loved her brilliant mind. He loved her passion about art. He loved her beauty, her smile, her thick red hair, her troublesome curiosity.

Ollie swore out loud when a rare, brilliant thought pounded like a headache. He knew exactly what to do to keep Evelyn in his life forever. Or at least, what gave him the best chance.

"What is it?" Eamon asked, but he grinned ear to ear as if he already knew.

Letting out a loud, heavy sigh, Ollie replied, "I need to go speak to Victor. Right now."

Chapter Twenty-Six

WHATEVER THE TIME was, Evelyn didn't want to know. All she knew was hours had passed. Several torturous hours before she had been able to knock on the glossy door before her. She was beginning to wonder if it was too late for the butler to hear when the door opened.

The butler stood there with a long face as he hastily shrugged on his coat, his thin hair messy from sleep. As he smoothed it out, he looked her over quickly. It was clear he recognized her from the newspapers, but he didn't say anything about her identity. "Young lady, do you realize what hour it is?"

"Yes," Evelyn lied. "I apologize. But it's an emergency. A familial predicament." That part could be argued to be truth.

The butler took a moment to consider this and let her in. The door shut behind her. "I cannot make any promises," he said as he led her to a room with plush furniture and no light. While she waited for him to rouse the lady of the house, she found matches and lit a lantern, emitting a dim glow in the large room.

Minutes ticked by and Evelyn began to question if coming here had been wise.

But what else could she do?

"Miss Spar—Mrs. McNab?" A surprised voice caused Evelyn to turn around to find Lady Litchfield in the doorway wearing a nightgown and holding a candle. She had done her best to quickly tie up her blonde hair. "Forgive me, but what are you doing here?"

Evelyn took a hesitant step forward and began to wring her hands together. Hearing herself being referred to as "Mrs. McNab" after learning the truth about the marriage hurt more than she ever would have expected. But as she didn't know what, exactly, her next move would be, she decided to keep the fake marriage to herself for the time being. "I'm so sorry, but I quite literally had nowhere else to go."

The marchioness set the candle down on a nearby side table and led Evelyn over to a sofa.

"We were so worried about you when we found out you had left," Lady Litchfield said as they sat on the sofa beside each other. The marchioness looked around the room. "You and Mr. Oliver. He's not with you, is he?"

Evelyn swallowed the lump forming in her throat. "No."

After she'd run enough for the upset to subside, she'd tried to figure out where to go. She couldn't walk around London all night. She couldn't go to her parents' house. She definitely couldn't go back to Ollie's.

Lady Vivian would have been with Ollie's brother, so that wasn't an option.

Lady Litchfield was the only person she knew who, hopefully, wouldn't kick her to the curb. She had been kind to her before. Maybe she would take pity on Evelyn one final time.

Recently, there had been hushed gossip spreading through the parlors of London that Lady Litchfield and her husband had separated. Lord Litchfield's father, the Duke of Chalworth, vehemently denied these allegations. Most accepted this, but some people, like Evelyn's mama, remained suspicious. More than once, Mama had had the driver pass by Lord and Lady Litchfield's townhouse to see if Lord Litchfield could be spotted as they passed by, pointing out the townhouse each time so Evelyn's younger eyes could remain sharp.

Quite embarrassing, really. And Evelyn hoped Lady Litchfield wouldn't ask about this. After all, it wasn't unusual to know which titled peer lived at which house.

Thus, she'd gone to the marchioness's, realized the woman hadn't returned home yet, and begun circling around the block until she had arrived.

And then she'd taken a few more circles around the block before mustering up enough courage to knock.

As she'd done all of that circling, she'd mulled over everything.

Perhaps this was obvious to others, but it had never fully occurred to Evelyn how upsetting it would be to people to run away from them. Her family knew how she was and mostly accepted it. Plus, she didn't give much of a fig what they thought of her, either.

But she cared what Ollie thought. Oh, she cared very much, she was unfortunately realizing too late.

And she had taken advantage of his kindness. Of the fact that he'd always gone after her.

Except tonight. He'd even taken the effort to warn her he was done chasing her, which was humiliating in its own right.

But something about that felt different than the other times her emotions had sent her running. Far more final.

Ollie would never run after her again. He was tired of her. Admittedly, she would probably have been tired of her too in his position.

If only she could control that part of her better! That obsessive physical need to run, run, run.

"What do you need, Mrs. McNab? Can I help you with something?"

Evelyn put her focus back on the marchioness and tried to hide the wince she felt at hearing that name again. "My sister is going back home to Paris tomorrow and I might go with her."

Lady Litchfield's eyes went big. "You are? Does Ollie know?"

She shook her head. "It doesn't matter." Evelyn had been steadfast on keeping the fact the marriage was fake to herself.

Unfortunately, she was a bit of mess right now and started to fall apart. "He was kind enough to marry me to protect me legally, so I wouldn't have to marry the earl. Neither of us intended for it to last and we were going to separate once I was clear of the earl. Unfortunately, we learned right after we both went outside tonight that the marriage didn't really happen."

Lady Litchfield frowned. "What do you mean, it didn't happen?"

"The license was forged."

"Forged? By whom?"

Evelyn stammered. It would probably be best to leave out the Signature Swindler bit. "It doesn't matter. All I know is now we know aren't legally married. And I remain at risk of the earl. Which is why I may go to Paris tomorrow. To keep away from him."

Lady Litchfield seemed lost in thought. "I see. And you're totally, completely sure that is what you want?"

Evelyn hesitated, then cleared her throat. "Of course."

"May I say something?"

Evelyn gave her a nod to go ahead.

"I've known Mr. Oliver for a little bit now, and I've long suspected he felt something deeply for you."

Evelyn's heart skipped a beat. She ignored it. "Why do you say that?"

"He would talk endlessly of you to me. Apparently, Vivian had told him to temper it a bit because of your involvement with the art restoration. But to me, he talked about you all the time. Anytime I saw him, he would say something like, 'You won't believe what Miss Sparrow told me today!' And then he would tell me some interesting art history tidbit, or something about color theory, or the difference between twelfth-century pigments and modern pigments."

Evelyn's brow furrowed. "He did? He always says he never remembers what I say."

Lady Litchfield opened her mouth to respond, then hesitated

before finally speaking. "It was always not long after he had seen you. I don't think he often retained the information long-term. A few times, I had mentioned something he had told me at a later time and he looked at me like I were mad. I'm sure he would have liked to remember it, though."

Charmed, Evelyn smiled a bit despite herself.

"He admires you greatly. And thinks very highly of you."

The smile fell away, and Evelyn looked down at her hands. "For that, I am glad. But he wasn't happy to have been married to me. He's said so himself. He's probably quite pleased by the unexpected turn of events."

To Evelyn's surprise, Lady Litchfield placed a hand over hers. And it provided the same calm she would have gotten from Cordelia. "I'm very sorry to hear that. But at dinner, he did pronounce to the entire room that you were the woman he loved."

Evelyn looked away. She couldn't bear to think about that moment. He had said that to everyone and she'd run away from him. Even after he'd begged her not to. "What happened after I left? Was he relieved I had gone?"

"I'm unsure. He never came back inside the house. I suspect he left to collect himself. The dining room had turned into a madhouse. I would almost be amused by it if I didn't know half the people involved."

Dread pulled at her belly. "What happened?"

Lady Litchfield chewed her lip. "Your father got into a scuffle with His Grace. There was a lot of shouting and yelling. I don't know if you know this, but Mr. Oliver's eldest brother hasn't spoken to their grandparents since he was sixteen years old. After their scuffle, His Grace stormed up to Mr. McNab and instead of saying something like he was glad to see him again, he reminded Mr. McNab he was the heir and one day would have to take up his responsibility, whether he wanted to or not." The marchioness paused. "I think the duke was upset about the scuffle and wanted to take his ire out on someone else. And also knew his little reminder would not go over well. As it was absolutely none of my business, I snuck out at that point."

"Oh, my." Evelyn had never considered the fact that Mr. Victor McNab would the next in line to his grandfather's title. She had an excellent imagination and could not imagine him as a duke.

She hadn't known much about the Duke of Invermark before all of this. It appeared her father and the duke were at odds over politics, so it made sense they ran in different circles.

"I did overhear your sister tell the housekeeper she was going to take your trunk. It didn't make sense then, but now I understand why."

"Oh," Evelyn replied, feeling a sense of dread. She should be glad of Cordelia's quick thinking, but it only made everything seem more final. That her trunk was with Cordelia put Paris more in favor.

"Where are you staying tonight?" Lady Litchfield asked gently. "If you need a place, you're welcome to stay here."

Hot tears stung Evelyn's eyes. "Thank you," she said with a shaky voice. "I feel so lost right now."

The marchioness tried to give her a reassuring smile. "Just think. This time tomorrow, all of this will be behind you."

"Yes." Evelyn forced a smile. "You're right." But it didn't bring her an ounce of comfort.

OLLIE PACED BACK and forth in front of The Harp & Thistle. It was now late enough that the crowd inside was winding down. This would be a good time to go in and confront Victor, since he wouldn't be so distracted by a demanding crowd but also wouldn't knock Ollie out in front of people. But Ollie still couldn't bring himself to do it.

With endless patience, Eamon leaned against the brick wall of the building and watched Ollie pacing.

"You can carry two barrels of beer on your shoulders," Ollie mumbled to himself. "You have never failed at befriending even the most unlikable person." He reached the end of his pace and turned back around. "You've never met a dull evening you couldn't lift. You've never failed to make even the most unattainably beautiful woman giggle and blush." He stopped and turned to Eamon. "Don't repeat that one to Evelyn."

Eamon nodded with a twinkle in his eye.

"You are loyal to a fault," Ollie added.

Eamon interrupted. "No insults."

Ollie sighed. "You are loyal."

"Aye." Eamon gave him a nod of approval.

"You are… What else am I?"

Eamon pushed off the wall. "You are a handsome fella, though admittedly, I'm biased. You have the ability to be wide awake when everyone else is asleep. You were an excellent thief when you were wee and with the proper training could join me again in the family business."

"No."

Eamon circled his hand in the air. "Etcetera, etcetera, etcetera, then. Are you ready?" He gently nudged Ollie in the direction of the door.

But Ollie didn't protest. He had come to realize his uncle was very good at nudging Ollie when he needed an extra push.

Ollie took a few deep breaths, clenched and unclenched his hands, then went into the pub.

No one was at the piano this late because the atmosphere needed to wind down to get people to leave at close.

Dantes, Victor, and Ollie's replacement, a younger man Ollie didn't recognize, were behind the bar and didn't notice his entrance. Not far from where Dantes was putting away clean glasses for the night was their regular Billy. Billy had a half-full pint in from of him. Ollie went over to the empty space beside Billy and could sense his uncle following.

Billy looked up at him and grinned widely, evidently happy to see Ollie again. But just as he was about to say something, he saw Eamon.

Ollie had to force back the amusement caused by Billy squinting between the two men. Billy then said with slurred wonder, "I can see into the future," before looking down at his pint. "I think that's enough for the night," he added while carefully rising to his feet. "Ollie." He gave a goodbye nod to Ollie. And then he said to Eamon, "And Ollie again" before stumbling his way to and out the door.

The amusement didn't last. Dantes noticed Ollie first and put his full attention to him.

"Hello," Dantes said, guarded. His attention went to Eamon, where his eyes briefly widened. But he immediately looked back to Ollie and proceeded to ignore their uncle.

"Hello," replied Ollie, also guarded.

"Some dinner, eh?" Dantes was trying to lighten the mood, but something felt off. Ollie wondered what had happened after he'd left.

"Yeah. Some dinner." Glancing down the bar, Ollie watched Victor fill up a pint before telling another one of their regulars, "That's it. You're cut off after this one." Ollie shook his head, knowing that extra coin was too tempting to Victor to deny one last sale. Victor then caught Ollie's gaze, and something exchanged between Victor and Dantes. Victor came over, his expression giving nothing away. Victor eyed Eamon for a long moment but didn't acknowledge him. Eamon seemed happy keeping back as support to Ollie, not interference.

Ollie had never felt support like that before. He of course knew, no matter what, his brothers would always be there for him when it mattered most. They had shown that briefly at the dinner tonight. But Eamon almost seemed proud of Ollie. Something he had never felt from his family before.

No. He had to remember family didn't require blood. Evelyn supported him, too. Even if she wasn't with him in person as

Eamon was now, he knew Evelyn would always support him.

Victor was strung as tight as a piano string. "If you've come to inquire about your job, one more week should suffice to cover up your errors."

Ollie wanted to argue back. Stick up for himself. But all he could say was "All right," because Ollie had to resist the urge to run away.

Upon this, he stilled.

Was this what Evelyn felt when she got so upset, she had to run? He still didn't like the thought of running after her, but if this was even close to what she felt, he couldn't really blame her for it. Not fully, at least.

It felt awful. Fear and self-loathing rolled into one.

Ollie swallowed and pushed the thought away for now. Because he had to take care of something else first. And for some reason, connecting with Evelyn in this odd way boosted his confidence.

"Actually, no, it's not all right." Ollie forced the words out. "I'm not coming back."

Both Victor and Dantes stilled.

His heart began to race because this was a major decision. But he pressed on, the confidence mounting further. "I'm going on strike. For the foreseeable future."

Victor's jaw tensed to an alarming level. Dantes looked between the two of them and seemed to realize he was going to have to be mediator, as he had been so many times before.

Ollie took a confident step forward. "You had no right throwing me out of my own business, Victor. And Dantes…" It pained him to have to confront Dantes. "You should have stood up for me. You knew it was wrong."

Dantes, with his terrifying size and scarred face, bowed his head. "You're right. I'm sorry, Ollie."

It was, really, all he'd wanted. "Thank you," Ollie replied. He put his attention back on Victor. "I still own a third of the business. I still get a third of the profits."

Victor didn't respond.

"Victor," Dantes warned.

Victor ground his teeth hard. "You think you're better than us, do you, Ollie? That you don't have to work here?"

"No," Ollie immediately cut in. "I love this place. But life has changed in a way where I must decide between family and my business. And for now, family is winning out."

"Family?" Victor scoffed. "We are your family."

"No. I mean *my* family. I mean my wife." He wasn't going to tell them that the marriage was a farce because he was going to convince Evelyn to really marry him. It didn't matter if it took hours, days, or years. How he would convince her, he wasn't sure just yet, but he would find a way. "I have to figure out what family is, first and foremost. That is my priority right now and I don't want anything to take me away from that."

Victor inhaled sharply through his nose. "This is your doing, isn't it?" Victor directed the question to Eamon.

"The lad's nearly thirty years old, Victor, Christ," was all Eamon replied with.

"He doesn't know any better."

"Bollocks!" Ollie exclaimed, trying to hold back his anger. "I'm a lot more capable than you give me credit for. Maybe I'm shite at maths, but I'm brilliant at interacting with other humans, which you are horrifically terrible at by the way."

Victor could only scowl because he knew Ollie was right. "So, you're quitting your job to be with your wife? Isn't that grand for you." And he turned and walked away.

Ollie was proud of himself, and he felt that pride pumping in his veins. It felt shiny and bright, like he could conquer the world. But he could also see Victor was hurt. A surprising outcome. But *why* the somewhat-terrifying man was hurt, Ollie couldn't say.

"He'll be fine," Dantes said, evidently understanding. "You know how he is."

Ollie nodded tightly.

"I'm glad you're back." He paused. "I mean, not here, but in general. You're really not coming back?"

"Not for a while yet. Maybe, down the road, I'll figure out a time that works. Earlier hours, you know? But I need to talk to Evelyn about all of it first."

Dantes rubbed a hand over his jaw. "You really got married?"

Ollie hesitated again. Maybe someday he would tell his brothers about the fake license. But for now? "Yes. I really got married."

"Congratulations, then." Dantes poured out three shots of whiskey, handing one to Eamon.

Eamon seemed taken aback by this, but then appeared happy to be included. Dantes said a few kind words, wished Ollie luck, and they threw back their drinks.

"I don't even want to know what you've been up to all these years," Dantes said to their uncle with genuine amusement as they set their glasses down.

Eamon laughed heartily and the two began to catch up. It was clear they enjoyed seeing each other.

But still, Ollie felt a draw to Victor. Something wasn't quite right there. He looked down the bar to where Victor was, and he seemed oddly sad. An emotion he would never pin on the man.

Leaving behind Eamon and Dantes, Ollie began walking toward his brother, then when Victor left the bar area for their office, followed him back there. In the office, Victor was standing in the middle of the floor staring at the fireplace.

Ollie noted the tintype of their parents had been brought down from upstairs and now sat atop the mantel. The business-man who was set to use the upstairs flat must have moved in.

"You can take that," Victor said, noticing Ollie's gaze. "If you want."

"Shouldn't it be in here?"

"The blasted thing has been an unending source of argument for Dantes and me. He wanted it down here, where we all can see it, but I can't stomach looking it and want it gone."

"That seems a bit unfair to Dantes."

"He had it for a number of years. Now you can have it. And anyway, he won't argue with me about giving it to you."

Ollie hesitated but crossed the room to grab it. He already knew where on the parlor mantel he would put it. "Thanks," Ollie said to Victor, cradling the tintype carefully.

Victor didn't respond.

"Look, I'm really sorry—"

But Victor suddenly turned, his face tense with emotion. "Don't you think I would have wanted to be there?"

Ollie blinked. "Sorry?"

"Don't you think I would have wanted to be at your blasted wedding?"

Swallowing hard, Ollie tried to think of how to respond. That was why Victor was upset? The hardest, coldest man he knew felt this strongly about his wedding?

"To be honest," Ollie slowly responded, "I never would have expected you would want to."

Victor turned back to the fire, and the light threw odd shadows over his face. "I know we have always been at odds with each other. And that probably won't ever change. But I've always tried my best, Ollie. I really did."

"I know," Ollie replied quietly.

"We were only in Whitechapel for four years. I know you don't remember it. But for me, those four years may have been four decades. Too many times your life, Dantes's life, were in peril. I was never at ease, I was always worried and looking over my shoulder."

Ollie didn't respond. Victor had never shown this vulnerable side to him before. And Ollie was afraid if he moved or said something, Victor would retreat like a startled bird.

"I just—I would have liked to have been there."

Maybe, once he convinced Evelyn to really marry him, he would invite his brothers to their real wedding, though he wasn't sure he had the patience to wait weeks or months to plan one. But for now, he had tread lightly and bringing up the fake marriage would only add fuel to the fire. "I would have liked you to have been there, too. It was kind of unexpected."

Victor gave him a tight nod, sniffed, then straightened his back. He seemed to transform back to his usual self. "Fergus spoke to me tonight. First time in twenty years."

"And how did that go?"

Victor chuckled—though it was not one of amusement—and shook his head. "All he did was remind me I'm next in line to the title."

For some reason, Ollie never really thought much about what would happen after Fergus passed. It seemed impossible his giant, terrifying grandfather would one day be gone. "Right. Forgot about that," Ollie said.

Victor glared at him.

Ollie laughed nervously. "Well, I wouldn't be surprised if he lived another thirty years. I doubt death wants anything to do with him."

"You jest, but the man's in his eighties."

Ollie's face twisted in thought. "Seriously?"

"Seriously."

"Oh." A long pause. "I don't think you need to worry about it for a while yet." But Ollie could tell Victor wasn't so sure. And he wondered if maybe Fergus had confided something to him.

Not that he would dare ask.

"Some family you married into." Victor changed the subject.

Letting out a long breath, Ollie agreed.

"Your father-in-law approached me as well," Victor said with bitterness. All his oldest brother cared about was running the pub, yet he always seemed to get dragged into Ollie's and Dantes's messes.

"Oh?"

"He is, understandably, quite furious. And exceptionally frantic as well. Did you know there was a contract signed? For your wife's hand in marriage, the earl loaned the baron a disgusting amount of money, the debt to be forgiven upon marriage."

"I, uh, did know a bit about that, in fact." Ollie rubbed the back of his neck. This was another part of really getting married that he had to figure out. He knew what the reward amount was to turn Evelyn in, and he also knew the loan was much larger than that. He wasn't poor by any means, but he didn't have that kind of money, either.

Victor looked him square in the eye. "And are you going to cover the amount? Because the earl is threatening to take away their home and drag them through court and the newspapers."

"Actually, I don't have that kind of money."

Victor nodded and returned his attention to the fireplace, his usual tension still in place. "I covered it."

Ollie pulled back but was too stunned to say anything. Christ, now he was really going to have to convince Evelyn to marry him.

Victor scowled at him. "The least you can do is thank me."

It took a moment for the shock to subside. Victor was not a kind person. He was hard, unyielding, and as approachable as a rabid dog.

Or maybe, that was all a mask. Like the one Eamon wore.

Ollie hurried over to Victor and gave him the hardest hug he had ever given in his life. Victor, who was larger than Ollie, still let out a pained noise.

"Get off of me!" Victor growled.

"No." Ollie hugged him even tighter before giving him a quick peck on the cheek. He knew it would enrage his brother.

And it did. Victor swore, shoved him off, and wiped the wetness off his cheek while Ollie howled with amusement. "Do that again and I'll punch your teeth out," Victor warned.

"Seriously, though, Victor. I don't know how to repay you."

"You can't. And you won't." He rubbed at his cheek again.

"That wasn't…all of your money, was it?"

Victor laughed, a very rare occurrence. "No."

Where had he even gotten that kind of money? Victor could

be such a mystery that, really, it wasn't surprising at all he was secretly incredibly wealthy.

"Don't ever bring it up again. I'm serious, Ollie," Victor said when Ollie started grinning. "It's a gift. Because I can't help myself. As much as I hate to admit it, I'll always look out for you."

Ollie's eyes were becoming misty. "Thanks. I know I drive you to madness, and you irritate me, but I do appreciate everything you do for me. Truly."

Victor ignored him, not one to like emotionally charged moments. "Don't tell *anyone* what I did for you. In fact, let's just forget about it."

"Promise." Ollie made a crossing motion over his heart. "Obviously, I have to tell Evelyn." Assuming she would agree to marry him.

Victor nodded. "You're going to have some interesting moments with that one."

"Yes," Ollie agreed, feeling nervous about tomorrow. It was his best chance to convince her to come home, to be his wife both legally and in the eyes of God, to live her life with him. If she went to Paris and he had to convince her to come home from such an amazing city, he would have his work cut out for him more than he already did. "But I'll take the hardest moments in life as long as she's with me."

Chapter Twenty-Seven

EVELYN HURRIED DOWN the employee hallway of the National Gallery Museum. She only had a short window of time. She knew she likely wouldn't get her old position back—their wealthy donors would not accept that—but that wasn't why she was here.

She had once been an asset to the museum. A celebrated art conservator. At the very least, the museum director could provide a reference for her next job in Paris. Whatever that may be.

As she reached the doors that led into their studio, she paused to take a few deep, calming breaths. Immediately, her mind switched over to Ollie. It had been happening more and more as the day had progressed. Evelyn found herself feeling rather unbalanced by it and she didn't like that. The sooner she could leave for Paris, the better. There would be a contract dispute with the earl and after the kindness Ollie had shown her, she did not want Ollie to get wrapped up in that mess. And what a mess it would be.

Shaking her hands out and stretching her neck, Evelyn found the courage to push the distressing thoughts away and open the studio door.

She smiled at the feeling of normalcy. At Mr. James Burlington and Mr. David Currow focused deeply on their work. The same exact morning she used to walk into.

"Good morning," Evelyn said brightly as she crossed the room to her desk. She wanted to take an inventory of the work accomplished during her absence and would then go find the museum director. And apologize profusely.

Both colleagues looked up, and their mouths fell open upon seeing her. Mr. Currow nearly dropped the thin paintbrush he was holding. Mr. Burlington was holding a pencil and it snapped in his hand.

"What in the blazes do you think you're doing here?" Mr. Burlington asked with disdain.

That was odd. Evelyn began eyeing the collection of paintings near her desk. "I came by to speak to the director." She hadn't been absent long, and she was pleased to find one of Dantes's paintings had finished its restoration during her absence. "Oh, brilliant work! Look how lovely this is again." She turned around to face the men, smiling brightly. But there was a coldness around them that caused her smile to melt away.

"What's the matter?" she asked, frowning. Mr. Currow didn't respond. He only looked at Mr. Burlington once before huddling back down to his work.

So she turned to Mr. Burlington for an answer.

"You've been gone for days," he finally said.

"Yes. I know, I apologize. I'm sure you understand the circumstances were a bit unique."

He leaned back in his chair and studied her. Something about his demeanor wasn't sitting well with her, so she turned back around and distracted herself by deeply studying the paintings by her desk.

"Well, Miss Sparrow, or whatever your name is now, I don't know who you think you are prancing in here like that." He laughed, but it didn't sound friendly. "I'm sorry, do you think you still have your job?"

Evelyn felt a slap of heat on her face and she swallowed. "I'm here to speak to the director." She was about to tell him about her plan to get a reference for Paris but snapped her mouth shut.

Something told her not to trust Mr. Burlington, and she was going to listen to that feeling. She forced her attention onto her task at hand, and as she looked through the collection of paintings, she came across one and stilled.

It was the Gustave Courbet the Signature Swindler had taken. The woman in the painting continued her saucy bathing as if she hadn't been on an adventure all over London. A rush of emotion hit Evelyn. Ollie may not have been the one to return it. But Evelyn knew he'd asked his uncle to.

And the fact that it was concealed told her there had been great care in making sure no one had ever known it had been missing.

Her colleagues had never found out.

Her client had never found out.

Relief washed over her.

"Miss Sparrow, are you listening?"

Evelyn turned to face Mr. Burlington. "Apologies. I was distracted."

Mr. Burlington, face reddening, stood up and grabbed something off his desk. He went over to Evelyn and handed over the morning edition of the newspaper.

The headline was *Runaway Bride Runs to Another Altar!*

"Oh, dear." She skimmed the article. It announced to all of England she and Ollie had married in secret and theorized the reason for the secret wedding. The journalist concluded it was either the most romantic story of the century, or the most dramatic pregnancy coverup. Of course, both the earl and her father had refused to comment.

But the journalist had failed to uncover the most important point—they weren't actually married.

This did, however, nearly guarantee that the director would give her a job reference. This should have lightened the weight on her shoulders. But it didn't.

She swallowed and gave it back. "What about it?" The words shook.

"I was almost a rich man." Mr. Burlington ripped the newspaper out of her hand. With a quick movement, he tore off the front page and scowled down at it. "I wouldn't have had to work another day in my life! You blasted fool—you ruined everything!"

"What are you talking about?" she nearly shouted back.

"Are you daft? I'm the one who turned you in. It was so obvious that you were staying with the idiot McNab."

Anger began to boil in her veins. "Watch what you say, Mr. Burlington," she warned. Out of the corner of her eye, she saw Mr. Currow spin around to watch.

"I can't believe you married him. *Him*! The man has air for brains. You two will create some of the most mind-numbingly daft children in existence."

Mr. Burlington may as well have hit her with his fists, the words stung that hard.

But before she could even begin to think how to retort, the director walked in. He looked quite surprised to see her. "Miss Sparrow! That is… Mrs. McNab. What are you doing here?"

Her heart was pounding hard in her chest. This was what she'd wanted—to get that job reference from the director.

Right?

"I came to…" She checked the clock. She had come here already with hardly any time to spare. All this conversation, unexpected conversation at that, was delaying her more than she was expecting.

If she didn't leave within minutes, she would miss her ship to Paris.

She thought back over her treatment here. Not by the director, not by the others in the museum. But Mr. Burlington and Mr. Currow, the people she spent day in and day out with. They'd belittled her, they'd bullied her, they saw her as a stupid woman and not an equal. No, not an equal—she was better than them. They knew it. And it made them furious to be beneath a woman.

She cleared her throat. "I came to say goodbye."

The director gave her a knowing smile. "I understand completely. Once a woman marries, she must not work."

Annoyance hit Evelyn. Why did men expect women to give up everything in their life for them?

"No, I'm moving to Paris," she said definitively. "Farewell, then!" She walked past the stunned men, glad to never have to work with them again, shoved the doors open hard, and left her dream behind.

Though she didn't have the reference she would like to have, it wasn't the end of the world. Once settled in to her new life, she could always write the director requesting one.

Despite this, she did begin running across Trafalgar Square as fast as she could. People gasped and shouted, but she didn't care. As she reached the other side, she collapsed onto a park bench, feeling almost elated.

Loud giggling caught her attention and she looked to her left. There was a couple walking together. But wait a minute. Evelyn's back straightened. They weren't walking together—they were roller skating.

"Darling, you'll catch me if I fall?" the woman asked her beau, biting her lip with nervous anticipation.

"Of course. It's rather simple. You'll see. Here, let go of me. You can do it." The man let go of her and she pressed forward slowly, wobbling a bit, but managed to stay on her feet. She made a wide circle around her beau, scaring away a few pigeons in the process, and he watched with a proud grin.

She squealed with glee. "Look at me! Look how fast I can move. It's like I'm flying!" With laughter of pure joy, she then wheeled into his awaiting arms.

Evelyn watched, giggling as the couple began to roller skate together. Evelyn had never learned to roller skate and until now, it had never been something she'd been interested in. But it looked like good fun, and she liked that one could move quite fast. Briefly, she imagined Ollie teaching her to roller skate. Together, they could fly all over London.

But Big Ben began to chime and interrupted the fantasy.

Paris awaited.

⟫⟫⟩✳⟨⟪⟪

THE SHIP ROSE high like a mountain, gleaming in the sunlight like a pretty jewel. Men and women dressed in traveling outfits hurried past her and up the ramp to climb onto the ship's deck.

Evelyn glanced around, seeking her sister. Secretly, she also hoped to find Ollie but immediately scolded herself for something so ridiculous.

He wouldn't have been here. He didn't even know she was here. And he promised to never again chase after her.

It took a few moments, but she eventually spotted her sister looking around fretfully.

"Cordelia!" Evelyn shouted as loud as she could and waved her hand above her head.

Cordelia spun around in her direction and also waved high in response.

Once Evelyn had reached her, they hugged each other tightly. Evelyn looked over her sister's shoulder and spotted something. "My trunk! Oh, you have no idea how happy I am to see it again."

"Yes! I made sure to bring it with me when I left your dinner last night."

Evelyn forced a smile. This was a good thing, she had to remind herself.

"Come. We must get on board now or we'll miss our trip."

Workers lifted their traveling trunks and brought them on board ahead of Cordelia and Evelyn, who followed directly behind.

As Evelyn reached the ramp behind her sister, she turned around one last time. One last hopeful time.

She looked over the crowd again, wishing Ollie were there. Would she run to him if she saw him? Or would she be steadfast in her decision in going to Paris?

It didn't matter. Because Ollie wasn't there.

With a swallow, she took the first step onto the ramp. Then the second.

She was now off of English ground, possibly forever. Step by heavy step, she climbed up the ramp until she reached the deck. As their trunks went left, Cordelia took Evelyn's hand and led her right, along the crowded deck.

"What a crowd!" Cordelia said with awe as she pulled.

"Yes, I suppose," Evelyn replied weakly.

Cordelia glanced back. "Why don't we go to the rail? It will feel less crowded."

"Oh, that's not—"

But Cordelia pulled her again while shouldering her way through the crowd.

"*Excusez-moi.*" Cordelia knocked a man to the side, who exclaimed his offense in French. "*Excusez-moi!*" Cordelia purposely pushed aside another as she said this sweetly.

Finally, they created their own space at the railing. Cordelia looked out at the crowd below. "Papa was in excellent spirits this morning," she said.

"I can't imagine why," Evelyn replied darkly. "Because I'm leaving, perhaps?"

Cordelia shook her head. "I guess the earl came by."

Evelyn remembered how furious her father was about the money they would owe the earl. "I'm going to throw up."

Cordelia laughed. "Silly, the ship isn't even moving yet. No, Papa was whistling as he was reading his newspaper this morning."

Evelyn groaned, remembering the article about her.

"When I inquired about his unexpected good mood, it took some convincing to get it out of him, but he eventually said he no longer owed the earl money."

Evelyn furrowed her brow and tried figuring this out. "How? He doesn't have that kind of money."

Cordelia gave her a one-shoulder shrug.

"Ollie doesn't have that kind of money, either."

"I don't know where it came from, Evelyn, but obviously, it came from somewhere and I'm sure somehow Ollie had something to do with it."

Evelyn scoffed. "That's ridiculous."

"Is it?" Cordelia searched the crowd below. "The man is utterly mad for you and does anything you want him to. Lucky girl, by the way." She sighed dramatically. "And here you are leaving him behind."

Evelyn's heart raced. "Hush up. You don't know what you're talking about."

"I don't?" Cordelia feigned surprise.

"No." She paused. "I'm not leaving him behind. He told me he was done running after me. He's tired of me, obviously."

"Do you love him?"

Evelyn swallowed. She wanted to deny it, but what was the point anymore? "Yes. Unfortunately. But my decision is made and I'm not going to spend another moment thinking about it. As soon as we arrive in Paris, all will be well." She was already on the ship, and her luggage had already been taken away. The news about the earl had come too late. They were all signs that Paris was the right decision.

As she said this, she realized she was twirling the ring on her hand. She hardly ever remembered having it on. She looked down at it and watched it sparkle in the sun. As soon as she got to Paris, she would send it to him to decide what to do with. It was his uncle who'd provided it, after all, and there was no telling where he had acquired it.

"You said he's tired of you?"

"I literally just said that," Evelyn replied, making sure the annoyance was clear in her voice. "Remember? I said he's tired of running after me. And that he won't keep doing it."

Cordelia grabbed Evelyn's arm. "Oh, really? Then why is he down there right now?"

Evelyn's heart stilled. "What?"

"See for yourself." Cordelia pointed. And sure enough, there was Ollie running toward the ship.

Evelyn gasped as Ollie weaved his way through the crowd. "Evelyn!" he shouted out as he searched frantically for her.

"But—how does he know I'm here?"

"I told him," Cordelia said with a grin of mischief. "You two are quite silly. Just need a good shove in the right direction and you'll figure it out together." She looked at Evelyn. "Oh, don't look at me like that. You think I'd let you ruin your life? Of course not."

Evelyn, still not fully grasping what was happening, looked back to Ollie. He kept shouting her name.

She then looked over the railing down and along the side of the ship where the ramp was. On the dock's end of it, workers were preparing to lift it away.

It was already too late.

"Ollie!" she cried out as loud as she could. "Ollie! Up here!"

Ollie stilled and looked up at the ship, but he didn't seem to be able to find her. "Evelyn!" he called back, then he began making his way to the front of the crowd.

Everyone around Evelyn was quiet and watched her with interest as she began to climb up the railing just enough to make her stand above the crowd. She waved her hands about her head. "Over here!" she yelled.

The moment he popped out of the crowd and found her, she felt it. Somehow, she felt that snap between them, like their hearts coming together.

The crowd, both on the ship and on the dock, went completely silent.

Ollie grinned like a fool at finding her and cupped a hand around his mouth. "Where are you going?!" The words traveled easily with everyone quietly invested in what was happening.

"I'm going to Paris! What are you doing here?"

"I came to bring you home!" He paused. "But I'm too late!"

The crowd began to murmur at Ollie's unforeseen barrier.

Evelyn looked down at the ramp. Then over to Cordelia. "What do I do?" she asked.

"Whatever you want to do, Evelyn," Cordelia replied.

"He ran after me."

"Yes, he did."

"Even though he said he wasn't going to."

Cordelia gave her an encouraging smile.

"Ollie!" Evelyn shouted back. "I have to ask you a question." Ollie waited.

"Did you mean it when you called me the woman you love?"

The crowd became agitated now.

But they were so loud and excited that she didn't hear his reply.

She climbed up one more rung and shouted back, "I can't hear you!"

Ollie cupped both hands around his mouth now. "I said, 'Yes, I love you, Evelyn!'" He paused in thought. "I love you madly. I love you from here to every star in the sky, from the beginning of time to the end!"

"Oh my," Evelyn said to herself. Then she shouted back, "I love you too, Ollie!"

The crowd laughed, no doubt charmed by the scene.

"Good, now, I have a very important question, Evelyn. Will you marry me? Make it real this time?"

"What does that mean, 'make it real this time'?" someone near Evelyn mumbled to their traveling companion. But she ignored it.

Ollie continued. "I was thinking, Gretna Green is only a train ride away! We could be married before nightfall!"

Evelyn gasped to herself but immediately shouted back "Yes!" Tears of joy began to fall. "Yes, I'll marry you!"

The crowd began cheering and whistling. Someone tapped her arm, and she climbed back down to the deck. It was a short, elderly woman wearing a large necklace of diamonds. "*Chérie*," she said. "Shouldn't you go to him now?"

"Oh! Right!" Evelyn started to panic. She turned to her sister. "I have to go."

"I know." Cordelia gave her a quick kiss on both cheeks. "Go. Now! And write me when you can!"

Evelyn nodded and began to run through the crowded deck. This time, there was no shoving through because the crowd parted for her, eager to let her through and watch the romantic saga further unfold.

As she reached the exit, though, she found a crewman roping it off and the workers at the bottom untying the ramp from the lower dock.

"I need to get off this ship," she said to the uniformed man.

"Sorry, miss, but you're too late."

"Blast your rules!" She ducked under the velvet rope and began sprinting down the ramp as the uniformed man chased and shouted after her.

The crowd, however, cheered her on.

"Miss!" he shouted from somewhere behind her. "The police won't be too happy!"

"I don't care!" she shouted back, but suddenly, she realized she was approaching a large gap that dropped straight into the Thames.

Determined, Evelyn sped up, leapt, and cleared the nearly six-foot gap, coming to tumble down on the concrete.

The crowd gasped loudly.

But Evelyn was able to get back up to her feet just as Ollie came through the crowd and rushed to her. "Evelyn! Oh, blast it all. Are you all right?"

"I'm fine, I'm fine," she sobbed. She would always be fine as long as Ollie was there. There would be hard days, of that she had no doubt. But he would be there with her for better or for worse. She finally understood that.

Ollie wrapped his arms around her tightly and spun her in a circle. Once he'd set her back down, he wiped away her tears, looked into her eyes with the purest love, and then pressed his mouth down to hers.

As everything around her seemed to still, the crowd absolutely screamed with cheers.

Ollie pulled away, breathless. "I love you, Evelyn. Please be my wife, my family, forever."

She sobbed and nodded.

Ollie looked around as if he was just now realizing hundreds of people were watching them. "Unfortunately, I think we're still going to be in the newspapers after this one."

With a laugh, she buried her face into his neck. It felt like home, where she belonged.

"That's all right." He ran his hand over her back and then leaned down to her ear. "Erm, there is something I should probably mention."

Evelyn pulled back and looked at him with fear. "What?"

"I quit my job. Well, technically, I said I was going on strike."

Evelyn's eyes went huge. "You quit? You told your brother that to his face?"

He pressed a kiss to her forehead. "Yes. I just wanted to focus on us for now, figure out what it is to be married, to be a family. Because you're my family, Evelyn. I've been trying so hard my entire life to make my family fit a specific mold, but it never fit right. I have to create my own family for that. You, any children we have—you're everything to me. And I couldn't go through life not being involved or present. I quit my job so I can focus on us, and you can go back to your job at the National Gallery, like you've wanted to."

"Oh, Ollie." Her voice cracked. "That is… That's the sweetest…" But then a body-shaking sob broke through. She pressed a hand to her mouth. "I quit my job, too. Mr. Burlington was the one who turned me in for the reward money and I—I couldn't work there anymore. The director was perfectly pleasant, but my colleagues were just awful to me. I'm so sorry!"

Ollie rubbed a hand over his jaw. "Well. I was not expecting that."

Evelyn laughed, still not sure she believed this was happening. "What are we going to do?"

He met her laughter with his own. "I have no idea. But we'll figure it out. I'm not worried about it."

She nodded.

"We do need to talk about the running thing, though. I love you, Evelyn. And I understand you run to escape uncomfortable situations. I don't like running after you, but I also know I always will."

Evelyn tilted her head. "That's not why I run, Ollie. Well, not the whole reason."

Ollie blinked. "It's not?"

She shook her head, grinning. "No, silly! It helps elevate bad moods. It gives me such a rush—not unlike when I kiss you, I should mention." She felt her cheeks burn.

"So, then we kiss more."

Evelyn laughed. "Naturally. But also, I saw something today I think will help, too. Roller skates! If running gives me a rush, imagine what kind of mood speeding around London on roller skates would put me in. And we can do it together. And maybe if I move enough each day, I won't want to keep running."

Ollie wrapped his arm around her and held her as close as he could as they began walking. With utter excitement, and as the crowd went back about their business, Evelyn talked through her plan. Perhaps, with the extra time they had now to be together, to strengthen their love, learn what it was to really be married, they would go roller skating together. And perhaps, it would be just the ticket to keeping her restless legs happy.

"I have a good plan. We head straight to Gretna Green. Get married, spend the rest of the day, all night, and all morning in bed. Then, when we come back here, we go get those roller skates," Ollie said with a smile.

Evelyn flushed as her vivid imagination set to work, but she grinned ear to ear. "Yes, let's." But in thinking about traveling up to Gretna Green, she suddenly froze as she remembered something important. She spun around to face the ship and was crestfallen to see it had already started moving down river. "My trunk!"

Epilogue

August 1890

LADY LITCHFIELD SCURRIED about the room, doing her best to sound bright and happy. "Good thing I was back from Vivian's in Brighton. Talk about a bit of good luck." She grabbed a stack of fresh cloths and plopped back on the stool beside Evelyn's bed to dab at the sweat on her brow.

Evelyn's breathing was sharp, hard, and as she felt another wave of the most intense pain of her life, she began screaming again.

"There you go. Scream as loudly as you want."

"I hate this!" Evelyn sobbed desperately. "I'm never letting Ollie touch me ever again!"

"Of course you won't." Lady Litchfield patted Evelyn's hand gently, both of them knowing full well that would never happen.

Getting a break from her labor pains, Evelyn stared up at the ceiling. With neither of them working, Evelyn and Ollie had spent their first days and weeks of marriage—real marriage—in bed at all hours of the day. Intimacy to that degree had taken a bit of getting used to for her, and sometimes she still didn't want to be touched, but as time passed, she'd enjoyed Ollie's touch longer and longer.

He was an incredible lover and brought out a saucy side of her she never would have thought existed.

But right now, she was a bit mad about it.

Another contraction started up and she screamed through it and clamped her eyes closed. Men never joined women during labor, and she had always thought that was atrocious, but honestly, she was rather glad Ollie wouldn't see this side of her. This was definitely a time she didn't want to be touched and Ollie would keep trying to comfort her. Lady Litchfield, meanwhile, had gone through labor twice and understood full well how it was, and that was the kind of support she wanted. Ollie, the dear, would have been absolutely frantic if he were in here and would have made her more anxious.

Though she knew, wherever his uncle had him contained in the house, he was frantic regardless. But she also knew he had the support he needed, too.

"How is she doing?" Lady Litchfield asked the midwife.

"Excellent, you're perfect, Mrs. McNab. Keep pushing. I can see baby's head. A full head of red hair like yours."

Evelyn smiled through her tears—for a second. The contractions were now almost constant.

But before she knew it, there was a babe in her arms wailing almost as loud as she had been.

"It's a boy," the midwife said with pride over the baby's cries. "Congratulations."

"A boy," Evelyn said with wonder as she stared down at his pudgy face.

The midwife then took the baby away to clean him off. It happened quickly, and Evelyn wished he would come back.

Lady Litchfield began cleaning off Evelyn's face. "You did it, Evelyn. How are you feeling?"

Tired, exhausted, and in pain. "It still hurts."

"Well, that's to be expected."

Another wave of pain hit Evelyn. "Ow!"

"That's the afterbirth coming out. Don't you fret," the marchioness said encouragingly. "And for a few hours, you'll still have contractions as your uterus shrinks back down."

"I have to do that too?" Evelyn cried out. "Does it ever end?"

Lady Litchfield laughed. "Yes, it does. I promise."

Another wave of pain hit, and Evelyn screamed. "Are you sure about that?"

But the marchioness's smile had melted away. "Ah, let me go grab the midwife."

Evelyn screamed as another contraction hit her and soon she heard someone running toward her. The midwife was back, and she was looking pale. "Oh my God. All right, Mrs. McNab, keep pushing."

"Is my uterus shrinking?" she sobbed back.

"No. I think there's another baby."

"*What?*" she shouted out, but the word turned into a wail.

For the second time, Evelyn went through labor until, finally, the midwife held up another red-haired baby boy.

"Why are there two of them?" Evelyn was frantic. "Did something happen? Is something wrong?"

The midwife placed the second boy on her chest with her. "Nothing is wrong, Mrs. McNab. You had twins. Unexpected, yes, but it happens often enough."

"Twins," she whispered. But it made everything feel complete.

⋙✦⋘

OLLIE PULLED OUT more and more hair with every scream that echoed in the house.

"You need to calm down," Eamon said from his seat, Hambone asleep on his lap. The infuriating man was so casual, petting the cat as if it were just any other day. "Pacing and worrying won't help your wife."

"I'm never touching her again," Ollie said. He couldn't handle that she was suffering so much. All because of him and his stupid—

"Oh, please," Eamon said with an exasperated sigh. "We both

know that as soon as she's better, you'll resume, uh, normal activities. But perhaps, be a bit careful about it?"

"Yeah," Ollie replied, not knowing what else to say. He felt absolutely crazed. "Yeah, of course. Never again. I'm never letting her go through this again."

A moment later, Lady Litchfield came into the parlor. Ollie immediately rushed over to her. "Is she all right? Is Evelyn all right? Is the baby here?"

The marchioness, who looked utterly exhausted, nodded. "Everyone is just fine. Congratulations."

Ollie looked toward the door and clenched his jaw but couldn't move his feet.

"You can go see her," Lady Litchfield said.

But when he still didn't move, Eamon stood up from his chair while Hambone hopped off, yawned wide, and made a big stretch. Eamon gave Ollie a little nudge. "Off you go, Papa."

Without even a thought, Ollie sprinted upstairs, only tripping over himself three times, and burst into the bedroom.

Evelyn lay there, half-asleep, sweaty, exhausted. But she looked angelic, perfect, and so beautiful.

A tiny, little bundle lay on her chest. Ollie carefully approached as it hit him, finally hit him, that he was a father.

This was everything he had ever wanted in life.

"Evelyn," was all he could say, and he felt himself choke up. As there were no words to describe this moment, he leaned down and kissed her. And then, he kissed the wee red head sleeping on her chest. The baby had round cheeks, a tiny, little mouth, and it was the most amazing sight.

"It's a boy," Evelyn whispered, half-asleep. "And, actually—"

From somewhere behind him, there was a cry.

Ollie stilled. "How did he do that?"

Evelyn, now more alert, furrowed her brow. "How did who do what?"

"Mr. McNab," the midwife said from behind him. Ollie turned around to find the midwife holding another baby.

"Where did that one come from?" Ollie's eyes darted around. Was there another woman in here?

The midwife laughed. "It's twins, Mr. McNab. Twin boys."

Ollie stumbled backward and slapped a hand to his forehead. "No."

"Yes."

He let out a long, low whistle. "Evelyn, we have twins. Two boys. They have red hair like you."

Evelyn chuckled. "Yes, I know."

"We only had two boy names on our list that we agreed to. And we couldn't narrow it down to one."

"All of that, to end up needing to use both." She chuckled again.

"Theodore and Simon." Ollie paused. "Which one's which?"

Evelyn turned her head to the midwife. "How do we tell the difference between them?"

The midwife smiled. "Why don't you rest, Evelyn. I'll get the babies settled in and then I have some tips I can give you."

"All right," Evelyn said as she handed the other baby to the midwife. The midwife then went off to the side of the room to tend to the babies and give the couple a moment together.

Ollie sat on the stool beside his beautiful wife and took her hand in his. He was in awe. Of her, of his life. Nothing could make this moment, their life together, more perfect.

"I love you," Ollie said, kissing the back of her hand.

"I love you, too, Ollie." Evelyn paused. "It will be quite the adventure having twins, won't it?"

"It will, but I can't wait."

"You thought when I start my new job in a few months at the Bethnal Green Museum, it would just be you and one baby. Now, you'll be outnumbered."

"Extra fun," he reassured her, though in truth, it was a bit of a frightening thought.

"You'll be a good papa," Evelyn said, her voice emotional. "That, I know."

"And you'll be a wonderful mama, too," he whispered. She looked so tired. "Go to sleep, my love."

"Stay with me until I do?"

"I will." Ollie held her hand and, still sitting on the stool, laid his head next to hers until she fell asleep. Too full of life and happiness to sleep alongside her, he watched her sleep instead. Yes, an entire lifetime of joy and love awaited his family.

About the Author

Born and raised in Chicago to an artist family, Arden Conroy grew up attending museums and played piano and cello for fifteen years. When she isn't writing or reading, Arden enjoys historical fashion, art history, and historical dramas and comedies. She has lived all over the United States from the Hudson Valley, NY to Tulsa, OK. Currently, she resides between Chicago and Pennsylvania with her husband and two children.

Website – www.ardenconroy.com
Facebook – facebook.com/profile.php?id=100083677291622

9 781967 169245